T0156467

THE SHOW MAYOR

Matthew Williams

BALBOA.PRESS
A DIVISION OF HAY HOUSE

Copyright © 2020 Matthew Williams.

All rights reserved. No part of this book may be used or reproduced by any means, graphic, electronic, or mechanical, including photocopying, recording, taping or by any information storage retrieval system without the written permission of the author except in the case of brief quotations embodied in critical articles and reviews.

Balboa Press books may be ordered through booksellers or by contacting:

Balboa Press
A Division of Hay House
1663 Liberty Drive
Bloomington, IN 47403
www.balboapress.com
844-682-1282

Because of the dynamic nature of the Internet, any web addresses or links contained in this book may have changed since publication and may no longer be valid. The views expressed in this work are solely those of the author and do not necessarily reflect the views of the publisher, and the publisher hereby disclaims any responsibility for them.

The author of this book does not dispense medical advice or prescribe the use of any technique as a form of treatment for physical, emotional, or medical problems without the advice of a physician, either directly or indirectly. The intent of the author is only to offer information of a general nature to help you in your quest for emotional and spiritual well-being. In the event you use any of the information in this book for yourself, which is your constitutional right, the author and the publisher assume no responsibility for your actions.

Any people depicted in stock imagery provided by Getty Images are models, and such images are being used for illustrative purposes only.
Certain stock imagery © Getty Images.

Print information available on the last page.

ISBN: 978-1-9822-4792-8 (sc)
ISBN: 978-1-9822-4793-5 (e)

Balboa Press rev. date: 10/14/2020

CONTENTS

CHAPTER ONE

SEE YA NEXT YEAR

Have you ever had a summer that was so horrible and so boring that it made you question the meaning of summer. I used to, in fact there was a time where I almost gave up on summer. Until one summer changed it all. This is my story, my name is Benny Breezy. Don't ask me what the last name stands for. It will only irritate me. I'm an African American and proud to be one. I'm originally from Iceland, where I stayed with my Grandma Maroochy, who is the best cook you'll ever find. And my close Aunt Antiquity.

My mom is a Fashion Designer who divides her time between New York, Los Angeles and Paris. Her name is Conceicao. She barely comes home. Only on the holidays. But we do stay in touch. Now I'm in Seattle where I attend an incredible school called Glass Art along with my close friends. This is a school where only talented and prodigies can get in. Our story begins in the music gallery. The whole school was watching a play 'The Little Mermaid', starring my best friend and bro Simon Ford, and my wacky and crazy friend Mallory Styles.

They were playing the roles of Ariel and Eric, where was I if you're wondering, I'm playing the piano. That's how I got into this school. I'm a talented Piano Prodigy. However, only my friends and family know this. But I have Stage Fright. I always get nervous in front of people. Plus, I don't embrace change very well. There's a part of me, that has yet to show the world what I'm really made of.

I need to believe in myself. Little did I know that this summer would make me believe again. I was playing the piano. As everybody listened to Mallory sing, 'Part Of Your World'. The scene where Ariel rescues Prince Eric from drowning. Then they were getting to the scene, where Ariel tries to get Prince Eric to kiss her and Simon couldn't wait, until they get to the end. So he can kiss Mallory.

Unfortunately the play got interrupted, by our archenemy, Garrett Silguero. A popular jerk, who thinks he's all that. All he cares about is his looks, body and popularity. He's one of the biggest bullies in Glass Art. Anyway, the doors swung open. And suddenly there was fog everywhere, before we could ask what is going on, Some music was played, and Garrett Silguero and his minions came in. He was singing, Say Something! By Austin Mahone and took over the stage.

After he was done performing, Garrett said, "Listen up my peeps and losers. I'm having a party this summer! Wait, no a mega party. It's going to be awesome, and why is that?"

When I asked him he replied, " Because Mr. Nobody ", it's going to be a pool party in River Pelagia. When he said that, the whole school became quiet . The reason why is because everybody knew River Pelagia is one of the biggest and most richest neighborhoods in Seattle. "Everybody, look underneath your seat." Garrett said. So when they did, to their surprise they found a box. However, not everybody got an invite.

So for the ones who did get invited. They slowly opened up there box and when they did, confetti came out along with a bobble head that looked just like Garrett, this is what the bobble head said, "You are invited to my awesome and out of this world party that starts next week. It'll be a night you'll never forget. The only rules are, no unattractive people, nerds, geeks or losers. Can't wait to see your sexy face there. From the one and only, Garrett Silguero."

After the message stopped, the students clapped their hands. Everybody except for me, Simon, Mallory and Ms. Reba, our favorite Drama Teacher. And the rest of the students, who didn't get invited. "Out of my way losers", Garrett said. As he makes his way over to Mallory. He reaches for her hand, and kiss it. "I hope to see you there beautiful." He walks away after that. Along with his minions. Leaving Mallory there, who was blushing. Much to Simon and me dismayed, she didn't know what to say. That's when Dean Dipper came onto stage. Due to an unexpected interruption, the play is over. Everybody back to class, he said while rubbing his head. He had a headache. I was shocked and disappointed. So was Simon, and Mallory just stood there like a statue.

Ms. Reba was upset that all our hard work, and the play was ruined. After the play Ms. Reba told me and my friends and the rest of our classmates the same thing she says to all of her students. "Every year! On the last day of school, some of you I'm going to miss. Never stop dreaming and always believe in yourself. And remember to be creative, inspirational and unique. As for the rest of you, well hopefully, you won't be in my class next year. She tried her best to hide her aggravation. Especially when Mallory asked her, aren't you going to miss me? Before she could give Mallory an answer, the bell rang. "Oh thank god. I mean enjoy your summer everyone." "Well, I'll see you two in the lunchroom." Mallory said to me and Simon. As Simon was grabbing his things, I could tell something was bothering him. I asked him, "You wanna talk bro?" "Talk about what? There's nothing to talk about man, the play was a disaster and Mallory is going to Garrett's party. So everything is just fine." He said while slamming his locker. He was heading towards the exit. And I was right behind him until I thought about something, that has been bothering me all year long. "Um! I'll catch up with you." "Is everything alright, bro?" "Yeah, I just need to talk to Ms. Reba about something." Okay! Simon said. He could tell though, something was wrong.

So after that, I walked over to Ms. Reba who was just sitting on stage. I sat by her, can I ask you something I said? "Sure kiddo. What's on your mind?" I didn't know how to say it at first. It's a good thing Ms. Reba knew me so well. "Let me guess, does this have something to do with next year?" I shook my head, and my eyes started to get a little watery. "Tell me what's wrong?" "I'm afraid about next year." Why dear? Ms. Reba asked me. "Are you kidding me? It's going to be my senior year. Everything is going to change. Especially Hmm..." "Especially what?" "Never mind." "Oh you think your friends are going to forget about you don't you?" "Wow, you know me so well. Yes, I'm terrified. We have been through good times, bad times, rough times and crazy times. We have learned so much from each other. Our bond is strong.

3

At least, I thought it was." "What makes you think that any of your friends would forget about you" "Because of my cousin Eustace. He told me what happened to him when he graduated from high school. And how he and his friends went their seperate ways. So it worries me that the same thing will happen to me and my friends. And another thing that has me concerned is that none of my friends, especially Simon, have mentioned what's going to happen to us? After school is over with, people grow apart, and I'm afraid that the others plan on leaving me behind and start the next chapter of their life." "I see! Wait right here." Ms. Reba said. She came back with a video camera and handed it to me. "What's this for?" She smiled and told me, "I want you to go out there and have an incredible and once in a lifetime Adventure! With your friends. Cherish each moment, and wherever you go this summer, make a video postcard. So I can see all the fun you're going to have." "But!" " No buts. You need to believe in yourself again, there just might be someone you'll meet this summer who might change your life." "Like who?" "Just remember, let your faith be bigger than your fear."

After my conversation with Ms. Reba, I joined my friends in the lunchroom. It was a pizza buffet day. So, I grabbed 10 slices of pepperoni pizza. When I arrived at the table, only 3 of my friends were there. "Ok, what happened bro?" Simon asked me as I sat down. It's not important bro, I told him. "It's important to us." My friend Nasser said. Before I go on, let me introduce you to all my friends. Simon is my best friend, bro and roommate. We have been through a lot together. There's a lot I can say about Simon. He's cool, laid back, popular and all the girls fall for his charm and looks. Which really annoys me. But he has learned not to let his looks and body get to his head. Simon is an Acting Prodigy, he dreams of becoming a huge movie star or a model. He's from New York. He has a mother, who's a wedding planner and he has a sister named Cinnabar, who has a gigantic crush on Jackson Dockery . And makes out with pictures of him, it's unknown what happened to his father. Simon has at times gotten me in some crazy situations. He also has a peanut allergy.

A lot of people don't know this. But my bud, Simon, has a thing for Mallory since the day these two have met, unfortunately, they're too stubborn to admit that they have feelings for each other. But that doesn't stop them from getting jealous. Anytime Mallory sees Simon talking to a girl. Or even hugging a girl. She goes crazy. And if she ever saw a girl, kissing him, She might destroy the girl or have a heart attack. When it comes to Mallory you never know. As for Simon, when he sees Mallory talking to guys, he comes up with these crazy schemes. That usually, don't end well.

Like one time. The School took us on a camping trip and everything was going fine. Until Simon heard one of Mallory's friends tell some of his classmates that Mallory was going to meet some boy at the lake. So, he came up with some ridiculous plan and dragged me along. Simon and I ended up hiding in a bush, just spying on Mallory. That didn't last too long. Unknown to us, the bush we were hiding in had poison ivy. It caused me and Simon to freak out, Simon ran to the lake and jumped in. For some reason, he thought the water would stop the itching. He learned quickly that water doesn't get rid of poison ivy. Things turned from bad to worse, when Simon came out of the water. His whole body was covered with leeches. So that's a trip I'll never forget. I will tell you this though, Mallory and Simon have kissed before. But that's a story for another day. One more thing, Simon's last name is Ford.

Next, we have somebody who loves to be the center of attention. She's crazy, wacky, self-absorbed and the most popular girl in Glass Art. The one and only, Mallory Styles. Now there's a lot I can say about her. But I'll just tell you what you should know about her. Mallory is fame crazy. She'll do whatever it takes, to be noticed. Anytime there's a school play, she's always in them. No matter how big or small, she just loves to be in the spotlight, Mallory is also vain, competitive, stylist, creative and sometimes she can get a big head. She's tough, she knows martial arts and somewhat protective of her family and friends. She lets her looks get to her head. She thinks everybody, should be just like her. Mallory has 5 sisters. Their names are. Starry, Unity, Neviah, Panna and Azubah. And a brother named Demosthenes. Unlike his sisters, Demosthenes doesn't let his looks or body get to his head. He's the only kindhearted person in the family. Mallory is from Texas. Her mother is a model. Mallory dreams of becoming a star. She also has a talent for designing clothes, she can act and sing. That's how she got into this school, also Mallory is a humongous Boy Band Fan! She always tells us that someday she'll kiss Shawn Mendes and be the future, Mrs. Mendes. She also has a crush on Vinny Balbo, Jonah Marais and James Mcvey.

The next ones. Are two buds of mine, The Stickle Brothers. The first one is Doyle. He's really something. There's never a dull moment when he's around. Doyle is full of life. He's a prankster and always getting into trouble. He's tough, outgoing, a daredevil and funny. He doesn't always make the right choices. He stays in trouble with Dean Dipper. They share a hate / love relationship. He has a short attention span and doesn't like following the rules. He's a Directing Prodigy, he dreams of making a movie that might become Hollywood's next big thing. He always has our back. Next we have my other bud and Doyle's brother. Nasser! Unlike his brother, Mallory and Simon, who get all the attention, Nasser is invisible. No matter how many times he tries to get noticed, it always ends the same. Nasser is smart and loves learning. Nasser has a talent for cooking. That's how he got into this school. He never lets you down, and he's a loyal friend. He dreams of becoming a chef and opening up his own restaurant. Even though his brother doesn't show him the respect or the brotherly love that he deserves, Nasser always has Doyle's back and he's a good influence on his brother. Nasser is kind, a neat freak, a comic book geek and has the cooking touch. One more thing, Nasser and Doyle's parents are detectives.

And last we have Darcassan Moots. He's just some weird and annoying boy, who nobody likes. But to me and my friends, he's more than that. He's an incredible scientist, whose inventions are worth seeing. Darcassan is one of the smartest guys at Glass Art. He gets all A's. If he ever got a B or even an F, it would tear him apart. His family motto is, "A Moots doesn't fail, they succeed", the Moots family are interesting and crazy people. However, he has a hard time getting the ladies. And has never had a real girlfriend before or been kissed. He keeps telling us that someday he'll find the future Mrs. Moots, he wants to have 10 kids. He shares a close bond with me and Nasser. He and Simon are kinda close. As for him and Mallory. They don't see eye to eye, and he definitely doesn't get along with Doyle. Darcassan dreams of going to college. And he's determined to invent things that will make the world a better place.

Anyway, those are my friends. So like I was saying before. I was sitting at the table. Trying to eat my pizza, but Simon and Nasser kept staring at me. "Can I help y'all with something?" I asked them. "Yeah, you can start by telling us what's wrong?" Nasser said. "I told you, I'm fine". Unfortunately! Simon and Nasser weren't so convinced. "Ok, let's change the subject. Has anybody seen Doyle?" When I said that, both Simon and Nasser looked at each other. "Um no we haven't." Nasser said, that's when Mallory came to the table. She could tell we were all concerned about something. "Who died?" She said. Nobody died. Simon told her. "We're worried that nobody has seen Doyle, have you seen him?" Nasser asked her. "No I haven't." She told us. She's been in her room, trying to pick which outfit she wants to wear while eating lunch, yeah that's another thing you need to know about Mallory. She thinks she needs to change her outfit three times a day.

Nasser just rolled his eyes, "Um Benny. There's something me and the others need to tell you", Simon said. But before he could go on, Simon and Nasser noticed that Mallory was on her phone. Simon snapped his fingers to get her attention. Unfortunately! Not caring what he had to say, Mallory just ignored him, then he came up with an idea. "Hey Mallory, Devin Hayes is here and I heard he wants to kiss you on the lips." When he said that, Mallory dropped her phone and started freaking out. All she could say was, "I wanna kiss Devin Hayes " causing our classmates to stare at her. Simon and Nasser calmed her down, "Where is Devin?" Mallory asked Simon, "In your dreams." He told her. "You lied to me? Big mistake. You better have a good reason for lying to me before I drop kick you." "Yes I do. Did you forget that there's something we have to tell Benny." "How can I forget? You have been blabbing about it for weeks." "Okay! I don't know. What's going on. But before you tell me, there's something I want to show you guys."

I took out my iPad and started smiling. "What is this?" Mallory asked me. "This is our summer to do list. I thought since next year will be our final year together, that we could have one last summer adventure together!" Simon, Mallory and Nasser looked at each other and had no idea how they would tell me their news. "Alright! Guys, first we have Universal Studios, after that we are going to The Smithsonian Museum, then we're going to Wild Adventures and then to The Holy Land." Before I could finish. I could tell something was wrong with my friends and I asked them regarding what they had to tell me. Nasser could barely look at me. And Mallory didn't know how to tell me. So, Simon decided to be the one to tell me. "I'm sorry bro, there's no easy way of saying this, but I'm going to magic camp this summer, Nasser and Doyle will be spending their summer working at their aunt's restaurant. And Mallory will be in Paris with her mother and sisters. So we all have plans for this summer." I was shocked, I couldn't believe this was happening. "Why didn't you tell me?" I asked them. Simon told me that he knew this would hurt me, Mallory for once didn't know what to say and Nasser couldn't stop apologizing. "So this is really. Happening? All of my so-called friends are too busy this summer?"

After finding out that I'll be spending my summer all alone, I got up from the table and went to ask my other classmates if they had plans for the summer, and boy did I get more than I bargained for. First I asked Rocky, who's a Soccer Prodigy. He told me he plans on going to Spain, to visit his cousins. Then I asked Kaci, a Debate Prodigy. As always, He was surrounded by his bodyguards. I tried to get through his guards, to talk to him. So when I got to him, I asked him what was he going to do for the summer? He told me he was going to Washington DC, with his parents. After that I went to Chiquite. A girl who is crazy about Alex Aiono and dreams of making out with him. She has a talent for art. That's how she got into this school. She's always talking about Alex Aiono and making portraits and sculptures of him. Anyway, Chiquite plans on meeting her idol this summer and finally getting that kiss. I thought to myself that things can't get any worse.

I went back to the table. Grabbed my things and was about to leave until my friends stopped me. "Bro! I'm really sorry. We didn't tell you, we wanted to tell you. It's just we didn't know how." Simon said. Mallory told me that maybe we could all get together before school reopens. That's when I snapped. "No! that's out of the question. Just forget about it." "What is the big deal?" Simon said. "It's not, the end of the world." Mallory said. "Come on bro," Nasser said. "You guys just don't get it do you?" "Get what?" I looked at Simon, Mallory and Nasser and told them this. This summer is important, more than you know. So much for friendship, I said as I walked away, leaving my friends there to wonder. "Why! I'm so upset?" That's when Doyle popped up. "Hey guys. What have I missed?" "A lot! Bro." Nasser said, "Where have you been bro?" Then they all noticed he was carrying two big bags. "Um! What's in the those bags!" Simon asked. "Oh, you'll see." Doyle said with a smile on his face. Uh – oh, Mallory said. Doyle rubbed his hands together. Making his brother and friends nervous, they knew he was up to something. But what? He decided to show them what was in the bags. Since they were so curious.

When he opened them, Simon, Nasser and Mallory were concerned. What they saw were balloons. Several carts of eggs and a big water gun. "Bro! What is all this stuff?" Nasser inquired as he started to panic. But before he could answer his brother's question, Doyle grabbed a balloon and threw it at Garrett Silguero. However, what was inside the balloon disgusted everybody in the cafeteria, all eyes were on Garrett Silguero. He was covered in macaroni, mashed potatoes and pudding. And boy was Garrett mad. Who threw that? He asked angrily. "Food Fight", Doyle shouted out. Doyle acted like he was in a war or something. He put on a bandana and joined the food fight, Doyle threw 8 more balloons and each one had a nasty surprise in them. Simon, Mallory and Nasser just stood there, trying not to get hit. But when Garrett Silguero threw a peach whip cream pie at Simon, he wiped the pie off his face and joined the food fight. He grabbed several balloons and eggs and started throwing them at his classmates. He and Garrett Silguero were fighting now, as for Mallory, she hid underneath a table. That's where she found me, "I thought you left?" Mallory asked me. I told her I did but I decided to come back. After I ran into Doyle I had a feeling he was up to something and decided to find out what. "Where's Nasser?" I asked her. "To be honest, I don't know." She answered back.

We looked up from underneath the table and saw Nasser. He was trying to make his way to us. However! Doyle and a few other students covered him in spaghetti and mashed potatoes causing me to do something. "Where are you going?" Mallory asked me. "That's my friend out there and he needs our help. You ever heard the saying. 'Never Leave A Man Behind'. Well I'm not leaving a bro behind." "Oh jeez! You guys drive me crazy," "but you still love us." I said with a smile on my face. Before I went out there, Mallory grabbed my arm. "Hey what are you doing?" "You know I'm coming with you." I smiled at her and said thanks. So, there we were, making our way to Nasser while dodging food. When we got there, Nasser was just lying on the floor. We couldn't even see his face. We wiped some of the food off his face. Then we got him up and the three of us ran towards the exit. But unfortunately, something unexpected happened. As we tried to get to the door, Doyle jumped from table to table, blocking the exit. "Where do you think you're going?" He grabbed his water gun and covered us with mud and sardines, and when he did, Mallory started shaking and her eyes turned red. "You better run." Mallory said to Doyle. Before he had a chance to run, Mallory knocked him down. We watched as Mallory beat Doyle up like there was no tomorrow. That's when Dean Dipper finally came to the cafeteria and he was furious. He blew his whistle. "What the heck. Is going on here? And who is responsible for this?" At first, nobody said anything, until he threatened to start calling parents and expelling students. So, "everybody" Including the teachers who joined the food fight, pointed their fingers at Doyle who was still getting beat up by Mallory. "That's enough Miss Styles. I can take it from here. You have really done it this time." "Mr. Stickle, did I do something wrong?" Doyle asked. Dean Dipper, aggravated with him, simply pulled him by the shirt and took him to his office and told the rest of us to clean up the mess or suffer the consequences. While our classmates spent their last day cleaning up, I and Nasser were worried about Doyle. So, we followed Dean Dipper and Doyle. As for Simon, he stayed in the cafeteria to help clean up, and Mallory left to go clean herself up. She was quite angry and told us that Doyle better stay away from her if he knows what's good for him. After that, me and Nasser made our way to the front office. We were eavesdropping on Dean Dipper and Doyle's conversation, and the lady who works in the front office joined us. "You just don't stop." Dean Dipper said, "year after year, I have to put up with your foolishness and misbehavior. It needs to stop, you're the reason why my blood pressure stays so high and why I'm taking aspirins. I can't sleep at night, I have no patience anymore. You little demon." "Isn't that a bit harsh Dip Dip." "How many times do I have to tell you, my name is Dipper, we are not best friends or bros."

"Whatever you say man. Look, if you want me to apologize, just say so. Wait, I'll just do it since I'm that awesome, I'm really sorry. Is that better?" Doyle said. But, Dean Dipper wasn't buying it. He opened a file cabinet. Shaking his head, he couldn't believe how many files were in there. "Whose files are those?" Doyle asked, "You're kidding right? All these files belong to you. Mr. Stickle, each file is a record of every prank you have ever pulled at Glass Art." "All of them, Seriously?" "Yes! It got so bad that we had to build a special room just for you. "It can't be that bad."

"Really?" Dean Dipper said, he took out a few files and started reading them. "Remember the time you filled the teachers' lounge with your dirty laundry." "That's not too bad." "Mr. Stickle you also left some stink bombs that caused the teachers' lounge to smell like a garbage bin. Then, there was a time when you stole some of Darcassan's unstable chemicals and blew up all the teachers' cars. Or the time you filled all the water fountains with soda. You know, we could be here all day. Going on and on talking about the past." "Or, we could move forward. And let the past go. I mean seriously. How many, files could there possibly be?" "Hmm, Let's see. There are about, 10,000 files." "Whoa! That's a lot." Doyle said, "yeah I know Mr. Stickle, This is really bad. So how do we fix this Mr. Stickle?"

Meanwhile listening from outside, me, Nasser, and the office lady didn't realize how many things Doyle has ever done to this school. "Let's change the subject. Who is this guy in the picture with you?" Doyle asked, "if you must know, that's my son Telmo." Me and Nasser looked at each other. "He has a son?" Nasser said. "Tell me more" Doyle said. "You really want to know? Fine! Well, here it is. My son hasn't been in touch with me in years ever since me and my ex-wife got a divorce. I guess he blames me for not getting custody, and not being there for him." "What state does he live in?" "That's none of your business." Dean

Dipper said, Doyle could tell how upset Dean Dipper was and decided to leave. "Where do you think you're going." "Back to my room." Doyle said. "Oh no you're not. We still have some things to go over." "Oh! You mean my other prank." "Yes, your other, wait what?" Doyle smiled. He took out a walkie talkie. "Are you ready?" He asked the person on the walkie talkie. "Yes sir." The person replied, "what is going on?" Dean Dipper said. "You'll see!" Doyle said. All of a sudden, a trash can came crashing into Dean Dipper's office. "Where did that come from?" Dean Dipper asked him. Before Doyle could answer him, a wrecking ball came smashing through, making a gigantic hole. Dean Dipper couldn't believe that half of his office was destroyed. He got even more angry. When he saw who was driving it, it was Branch, one of Doyle's friends.

"Hey! Dean Dipper. I hope you don't mind the mess." Dean Dipper was speechless. Before he could say anything else, a trash truck made a hole on the other side. Now, there were holes on both sides. Dean Dipper thought he would have a heart attack. "Oh no! Not you." Dean Dipper said, it was Doyle's other friend, Jagu. He unleashed the garbage in Dean Dipper's office and Doyle quickly got out of the way. Dean Dipper couldn't believe his eyes, his office was destroyed. Thinking that things can't get any worse. He tried to remain calm. Unfortunately! Something else happened. Jagu used the claw on the trash can and grabbed Dean Dipper and placed him in the trash can. Doyle and Branch closed the lid and pushed the can where he landed on a water slide that Doyle made. That's when me and Nasser plus the office lady came in. We couldn't believe how far Doyle had gone. So, me and the others, plus the rest of the students and the teachers watched as Dean Dipper went down the water slide in that stinky trash can. After going down a water slide, the trash can landed in the school water fountain. So! Me, Nasser and Simon helped him out. After getting out of the trash can, Dean Dipper was about to explode. We couldn't get too close to him because he smelled so bad and he was soaking wet. His anger towards Doyle grew that day as he made his way towards Doyle. Me and the others tried to protect him. Suddenly, we heard a loud noise, and everything started shaking.

This is the moment where everything changes for Glass Art. "Oh man! Now I'm in trouble." "Doyle, what did you do now! Bro," Nasser said. We couldn't believe it, half of the school was gone, scaring all of us. Me, Simon, Doyle, Nasser, Rocky and the others, Dean Dipper and the teachers looked around at the damage of our favorite school. That's when my friend. Darcassan! Came out along with Mallory. She and Darcassan were relieved that we were alright. "Can anybody tell me what has happened to my school?," "Yeah I can." Darcassan said. "Alright, tell us Mr. Moots. Who is responsible for this?" "I'll give you one guess, no surprise there." Dean Dipper said. "Mr. Stickle, what were you thinking?" Darcassan told us that earlier that day, Doyle visited him in the science lab. As usual being a pain, he told Doyle not to touch anything. At first, Doyle was playing with some of Darcassan's inventions. However, Darcassan had to go to the bathroom. That was a huge mistake. He forgot that he left some unstable chemicals in the room with Doyle. So! Darcassan figures that. Doyle mixed the chemicals up with his newest invention.

CHAPTER TWO

POOR MONTY AND THE DAILY MAGLORIX NEWSPAPER FINAL HOURS

ausing this mega problem, Dean Dipper asked Doyle if this was true, and his response was yes. But before he could tell them why, Dean Dipper and the whole school didn't even give him a chance to explain himself. One teacher shouted out, "Rotten Seed ". And another one called him, a devil child and a student told him, He's a sorry excuse for a human being. It was official that the whole school hated him now, to make things even worse, Glass Art was surrounded by Cops, Fireman, several news reporters and the sky was full of helicopters. At that moment I decided to call home. It was a decision I had been thinking about since my friends told me their news. To my surprise though, My Grandma Maroochy and Aunt Antiquity didn't answer. So, I listened to the answering machine. This is what the message on the machine said, "Sorry that we can't come to the phone right now. Me and my sister are spending our summer in New York, visiting my daughter. She needs us right now. Beep." I hung up after that and wondered why my Grandma Maroochy and Aunt Antiquity were visiting my mom all of a sudden. They hate New York.

Me and the others joined the rest of our classmates, and watched Dean Dipper get interviewed by news reporters, it turned out that the explosion was bigger than we thought. And that not only was the Science

Lab destroyed, but Art, Math, Music, The Drama Gallery and Home etc. as well. The good news is nobody got hurt, unfortunately, what happened next, " Shocked " all of us. "Due to a series of unfortunate events, Glass Art is closed until further notice. I'm very sorry, Dean Dipper said. He also told the press, no more questions at this time. As he walked over to us, "as for you Mr. Stickle!" "Dean Dipper, If you would just let me explain." "Time after time you have caused destruction to this school and I have had enough. You are expelled." "Sir?" Nasser said. "Goodbye, Mr. Stickle and good riddance. Oh by the way, I'll be sure to call your parents," he walked away after that, Leaving me and the others shocked.

Doyle just stood there like a statue. "Did that really just happen?" Doyle asked us. "Yes bro, it did." Simon told him. "Mom and Dad are going to kill me." Doyle said, the next thing we know, it was time for me, Nasser and Simon to go to work. We grabbed our things and went to the bus stop. It felt good being off-campus for once. We were happy to see Monty the bus driver. The only thing you need to know about Monty is that he's a grouch, he doesn't talk much, he collects stamps and he doesn't have any friends. Usually, Monty rolls his eyes when he sees us. But today was different. I could tell something was bothering him. So, I asked him what was wrong. At first, he didn't say anything, then all of a sudden, Monty actually spoke back for once. He told us that his roommate has him stressed out. "I didn't even knew you have a roommate." Nasser said. "That's because I don't like y'all." Monty said. Anyway, he told me, Simon, Nasser and Doyle that he's being evicted from his apartment because the police found out that his roommate was running an illegal pharmacy. And scamming people for money. Now his roommate is in jail and Monty is being accused of being an accomplice and facing charges. So! Monty is homeless now. I actually felt sorry for Monty. I was seeing a side of him that I had never seen before.

After we got to our destination, I told Monty before I got off the bus that somehow I'll find a way to help him. Monty couldn't believe I would help him out because of the way he treats me and my friends. He looked at me and said "Thank you". Something he has never said before. So, after that we got off the bus and went inside the building wondering how our boss Mr. Zed was feeling today. At The Daily Maglorix Newspaper, you see me and Nasser are Investigative reporters. And Simon is our Photographer. Little did we know that today would be no ordinary day at The Daily Maglorix Newspaper. As the elevator door opened, me and the gang were shocked to see that nobody was there. So! We went to our supervisor's office to see what was going on. As usual, Mr. Zed was in a bad mood. He has short patience and he's not friendly, but, Ms. Sheatara stopped us from going into his office. Now! Ms. Sheatara is nothing like Mr. Zed. She's kind, caring and has a lot of love in her heart. She's Mr. Zed's Assistant. Simon asked her "How come we can't go in? I'm sorry to tell you fellows this, but The Daily Maglorix Newspaper is facing closure due to poor stories and money situations. "That's right ", Mr. Zed said as he came out of his office. We're done, so clean out your desk, then come to my office to pick up your last checks. But…. Nasser said. Those are my final words, so suck it up and deal with it. Life at The Daily Maglorix Newspaper is over. He walked back into his office and slammed the door.

Don't, take it to heart Guys! Mr. Zed is just hurt that he's losing the one thing he loves the most. The Daily Maglorix Newspaper. Means the world to him. She hugged us and went into. Mr. Zed's office. I remember what happened next. While me and Nasser were cleaning out our desks, Simon just stood there thinking about our first day at The Daily Maglorix Newspaper and how far we had come. As for Doyle he was playing on the computer. "We have to do something," Nasser said. "But what can we do?" Simon said. Then all of a sudden, me, Simon and Nasser received an email.

So we clicked on the email. And discovered that someone had attached a video along with the email. The email said, *Dear Benny Breezy, and his friends. If you're reading this, I have some news that might save The Daily Maglorix Newspaper, if you want to save your job and your summer then you need to fly to Los Angeles immediately! A famous celebrity needs your help. The one and only, AJ Mitchell is in trouble. He's been accused of stealing The Ape Skull from The Diamond Museum Amsterdam. Someone named The Mad Ffraid Brat is the real culprit and is trying to ruin his career. So, he's being called a Jewel Thief. AJ is offering a huge reward to whoever can clear his name. This is the opportunity of a lifetime and a chance to show your boss and the world what you're made of. Sincerely, Mr. Thersander. P.S, AJ Mitchell is staying at a hotel called The Show Mayor.*

After reading the email, me and the others didn't know what to think. The four of us were shocked. Then we watched the video. In the video AJ was in court trying to prove he's innocent. "This is it," Simon said. "What do you mean bro?." I asked him, "this is how we're going to save The Daily Maglorix Newspaper." Simon said. "Are you guys with me?" He asked, at first Nasser was quiet. Then he saw it as an opportunity to get noticed. And Doyle thought of it as an adventure, then they looked at me. "Are you in bro?" Simon asked me. "Come on man we need you." Nasser said. "We can't do this without you." Doyle told me. "Um, I'm not sure guys. Me in the land of stars? I don't think I can do it." "Why now?" Simon asked me, "because Los Angeles is full of shallow people who care about image and fame. It's a place where dreams are supposed to come true." "Unfortunately! Not everybody makes it. Los Angeles is not the place for me. I wouldn't survive one day in Los Angeles, and I seriously doubt that AJ would become friends with me. I'm afraid, I really am." "We'll be by your side." Simon told me. I looked at him and the others and said "How long though?" "What is that supposed to mean?" Simon asked me. Nothing, I told him. We went into Mr. Zed's office after that. "The checks are right there. Take them and go." "Sir we have something to tell you." "Yeah, What is it?" "We just got an anonymous tip about a story" Simon told him. "A story that could save The Daily Maglorix Newspaper. All we need is some money to get there."

"And what story could possibly save us?" Mr. Zed asked. "It's AJ Mitchell. He's in trouble, and he's offering a huge reward." "How much?" Mr. Zed. inquired. "Enough to save The Daily Maglorix Newspaper." When he said that, Mr. Zed and Ms. Sheatara started to get excited. "Well, It's settled. You'll go to Los Angeles. Interview AJ Mitchell, save his career and save The Daily Maglorix Newspaper." He gave us some money. Enough for a plane and told us not to blow this. If we do, Our jobs would be on the line. "Remember guys, we're all counting on you." "No pressure there," I said before we left. Mr. Zed told us that we had 6 days to get the story. Then we left, "do you think they can save us?" Ms. Sheatara asked Mr. Zed. "At this moment, I have no other choice. Those boys are our only hope. The future of The Daily Maglorix Newspaper depends on it." "Well, at least they left us the story of what happened today at their school. We can sell that," Ms. Sheatara, said "we made our way.

Back to Glass Art. Our day has been just awful. I wanted to go home, now more than ever. The cops were still at Glass Art and there was Caution tape on the part of the school that got destroyed. We got back to our rooms and started packing. Plus, we had a few visitors. First, Mallory popped in with four big bags and, eight suitcases. "Alright, I'm ready guys." "Ready, for what?" I asked her. "Well. Nasser told me that y'all are travelling to Los Angeles to interview AJ Mitchell and clear his name." "And what does that have to do with you?" Simon asked her. She closed our room door. Grabbed us by the shirt and told us this. "Look, this could be my only chance of stardom and my chance to kiss Kaden Dayton, Tal Fishman and Logan Shroyer. So, I'm going." But. "End of discussion." She grabbed her things and told us she'll be waiting for us in the student lounge.

"What, do you see in her?" I asked Simon. "Her beauty I guess, we could have ditched her." He told me. I just rolled my eyes. Next, Darcassan walked in. "I just wanted to apologize for ratting out Doyle," Darcassan said. He gave me a number and an address. What's this? I asked him. "Well, since you'll be in Los Angeles, I figure my cousin, Leonel, could help you on your assignment.

After that Chiquite came into our room, crying. "Is everything alright?" Simon asked her. She told us that her parents are going to Jacksonville Florida for the summer. Ruining her chances to meet Alex Aiono. "I guess I'll never get to kiss Alex Aiono now," Chiquite said. She gave us a picture of her future husband and told me and Simon if we run into Alex Aiono, while we're in LA, to make sure we get him to autograph it for her. Meanwhile I still wasn't convinced I was going.

CHAPTER THREE

SURVIVING RUSTY BUSTY

The way our day had been, I just wanted to go home. I thought this day couldn't possibly get any worse, but I was wrong. It all started when we arrived at the airport. I put Nasser in charge of getting the airplane tickets but somehow Doyle took the money without his brother knowing and bought the tickets. Unfortunately thinking that he could save some money, Doyle got tickets for a much cheaper plane. He took us to the plane that we would be riding on and all we saw was a sorry excuse for a plane. "I'm not riding that death trap." Mallory said. "Same here!" I told him, Simon and Nasser agreed as well. "Oh come on guys, what's wrong with Rusty Busty?" Doyle said.

"Hmm let me see, the windows are all cracked." Simon said. "One of the engines has duct tape." I told him. "It's dangerous and unsafe." Nasser said. "There's nothing wrong with this plane guys! Rusty Busty is in perfect condition." Doyle said as he tapped the plane. But when he did, a part of it came off. "They don't call it Rusty for anything," Mallory said in a sarcastic voice. "I can't believe you threw away our money for something like this," I told him. "Bro, that was the only money we had. Now! What are we going to do?" Nasser said. "Okay, this is the new plan," Mallory said. "me, Benny and Simon will go on a real plane that won't fall apart and kill us. While you two fly in this one." "Why do I have to go?" Nasser said. "Because I said so, also, someone has to keep Doyle from getting into trouble, so move it." He didn't say anything after that. He and Doyle got on Rusty Busty while the rest of us found another way to get to Los Angeles. "What are we going to do guys?" Simon asked me and Mallory. "I already have a plan," she said, "wait right here." She came back disguised as a Flight Attendant. "What do you guys think?" "What are you doing?" Simon asked. "This is my plan,"- which is? I asked her. "Oh boy!" Mallory said as she rolled her eyes. "The plan is for me and Simon to disguise ourselves as Flight Attendants. As for you Benny! You will be hiding in this suitcase. We're going to sneak into an airplane that's heading to Los Angeles. Any questions?" "Plenty," I said. "But I have news for you guys, I'm not going." "What are you talking about bro?" Simon asked. "You have three minutes to tell us why before I drop kick you." Mallory said. "Do you always have to be so violent?" Simon asked her. "Talk Benny!" This is what I told them. "I am just simple old Benny Breezy. A Piano Prodigy that nobody wants to talk to. People judge me before they get to know me and you seriously think I want to go to Los Angeles? I don't have what it takes to make it in Hollywood. People like Noah Urrea, Chris Villain, Parker Queenan, and especially Matthieu Lange, Tyler Barnhardt, Luke Korns, Sam Cushing, Anthony Ortiz, Lachlan Buchanan, Britton Buchanan, Anthony De La Torre, Owen Teague, Michael Cimino, Nathan Kehn, Jackson Dockery, Dylan Sloane, Van Hansis, Anton Narinskiy, Joshua Bassett, Erik Altemus, Aaron Hull, Patrick Luwis, Wolfgang Novogratz, Victoria Park, Brandon Butler, Kelly Blatz, Anthony Turpel, Herman Tommeraas, Dominic Brack, Nicholas Galitzine, Christian Collins, Cody Saintgnue, Jeremy Hutchins, Katherine McNamara and Nicholas Podany. Will never give me a chance. I'm better off in New York with my family. I seriously doubt AJ Mitchell would give me a chance."

I also told Simon and Mallory that I'm getting a one-way ticket to New York. After telling them my news, I grabbed my things and started walking away, Simon couldn't believe this and tried to stop me. As for Mallory, she had a special surprise for me. "Wait! Before you go, I wanna show you something," Mallory said. She reached into her bag and pulled out something, It was a whoopee cushion. "Why are you showing me a whoopee cushion?" I asked her. "You'll see," she said. She put the whoopee cushion closer to my face and a blue fog came out of the cushion. At first, I didn't pay any attention to the blue fog, but suddenly

I felt strange. And before I knew it, I was out like a light. "Benny, can you hear me?" Simon said as he tried to wake me up. "Oh relax, he's just sleeping," Mallory said. "What did you do to him?" Simon asked her. Mallory told Simon that before they left, she asked Darcassan for a favor. She promised him if he could help, her get me to go to Los Angeles, she would help him get a girlfriend. "Wow! Darcassan must be really desperate to give you one of his gadgets." Simon said. "You know how I am Simon. Nobody can resist a Styles! Now, put on your flight attendant uniform and help me get Benny in one of these suitcases." Simon didn't want to, but he knows how Mallory is and knew he didn't have any other choice. So he hurried up and helped Mallory put me in a suitcase and the three of us got on the plane, Simon asked Mallory, "What is the name for Darcassan's whoopee cushion gadget?" Mallory told him Darcassan calls it "The Zotique Poppy Goebel." A gadget that can release a sleeping gas. Simon was impressed. After that, we were in the sky. I was dreaming that I was back home with my family and that everything was going to be alright. Suddenly I woke up and when I did, I found myself sitting by three women who were just staring at me. "Um, where am I?" "Hi there, my name is Orangina and these are my sisters, Orangetta and this is Orangia. We're The Delahoussaye Psych Sisters," "HI, my name is…" "No! Don't tell us. Your name is Benny Breezy right?" Orangetta said. "And you and your friends are heading to Los Angeles to interview AJ Mitchell clear his name and save The Daily Maglorix Newspaper." Orangia said. "But you're afraid, afraid of getting close to people and that AJ won't like you, am I right?" Orangina said. "Okay, I have two questions. One, how in the world did you know all of that? And two, where in the heck am I?" "Me and my sisters are psychics, and oh, you're on a plane." When Orangetta said that I started freaking out. "You seem intense." "You think? I mean seriously, first I find out that all my friends have plans for the Summer, then finding out about The Daily Maglorix Newspaper facing closure and now I'm on an airplane." "And what's wrong with that?" Orangia said. "Because, I'm afraid of flying. This day couldn't possibly get any worse." I told them

"Maybe a reading might help?" Orangetta said. "Look! I really don't believe in Psychics." I told her, "Please just give me and my sisters a chance, what's the worst that can happen?" "Trust me you, don't want to know, but I'll take a leap of faith." The Delahoussaye Psych Sisters smiled, "Hands please." they said. So, each sister took a turn and I couldn't believe what they predicted, Orangetta was first. " Hmm, very interesting." "What do you see?" I asked her. This is what she told me. "This summer will be unlike any summer you ever had. Filled with new adventures and new friends, I see you becoming good friends with Shawn Mendes, Logan Shroyer, Devin Hayes, Why Don't We and many more. They will play a big part in this adventure of a lifetime." Orangia was next, "I see a lot of romance for Mallory, and I see you playing as a Cupid who must help bring a few people together. Love and friendship will play big parts in this adventure." And Orangina was last, "Whoever framed AJ is very dangerous and will do whatever it takes to get you and your friends out of the way. Be very cautious of this person, and one more thing, you will discover a secret that will change your life forever." After they were done, I wanted to know more, "Wait! That's it? Seriously, you can't just pile all of that information on me and expect me to believe that." "This will be an adventure of a lifetime." "I'm sorry, I just don't believe and I especially don't believe that Shawn Mendes, Logan Shroyer and Devin Hayes and Why Don't We will become my friends. None of it is real." "Why are you so doubtful?" Orangetta said. "Why can't you just believe?" "Don't you think I want to? I would love to believe that Jonah, Corbyn, Daniel, Zach and Jack would become my friends and give me a chance, but they won't. And I know I don't stand a chance of becoming friends with Devin Hayes. He's popular and so is Logan Shroyer and Shawn Mendes. You and your sisters just don't know what I've been through in my life. I'm afraid of letting new people in my life. These days people care about image and popularity. If you aren't attractive or cool, people don't want anything to do with you. I'm tired of people not giving me a chance. Do you really think Shawn and the others would treat you. Like that?" "I honestly don't know Benny, you just gotta take a 'Leap Of Faith' and take chances. If people aren't willing to get to know you, it's there loss, just don't give up. On making friends, you have a bright future ahead of you." Orangetta said, "I'm more concerned about this case. So can you tell me more about the future?" Unfortunately! The Delahoussaye Psych Sisters started arguing about their crush Trevor Donovan. "Hello? Can you at least tell me who is the Mad Ffraid Brat?" "Sorry Benny, here's our card if you need our help. Just come by our shop in Los Angeles." While I listened to The Delahoussaye Psych Sisters argue, that's when Simon and Mallory came. They were passing out snacks. "Look who's up," Simon said. "Oh! Um hi Benny." Mallory said, all I could do was stare at them. "Look bro. It was Mallory's idea to use the Zotique Poppy Goebel." Simon told me, he tried to offer me a pretzel and I slapped it out of his hand. "Mallory! You should've went to Paris. As for you Simon, I'm already mad at you." I went to another seat away from them. While I looked for an empty seat, I realized that I'm in first class. "Excuse me, is that seat taken?" "No, it's not man." the person replied. When I saw who it was, I couldn't believe it. "Are you…" "Yes I am," he shook my hand and introduced himself. It was the one and only Shawn Mendes, I was really nervous.

However, before I could introduce myself, Mallory fell into Shawn Mendes' lap after the plane got a little bumpy. "Are you alright?" Shawn Mendes asked, realizing who she's talking to, Mallory started freaking out and couldn't stop screaming. She was so excited that she couldn't help herself. Unknowing to me and Shawn, Mallory was imagining herself making out with Shawn Mendes. Meanwhile on Rusty Busty, Nasser and Doyle were terrified. The plane kept shaking, it smelled really bad. There were crows in cages, boxes filled with illegal stuff and the plane is unsanitary. Plus the bathroom stinks. Also, Nasser and Doyle couldn't help but to stare at the gigantic hole that was in the middle of the aisle. And if that wasn't bad enough, the passengers were even more scary. One was a Hobo who wasn't a people person. The next passenger was a depressed mine who played with shrunken heads and the last passenger was a clown with a creepy laugh which kept Nasser from sleeping. For some reason it didn't bother Doyle. He slept like a baby. Nasser was too afraid to go to sleep. Suddenly, a flight attendant named Eamhair appeared next to him. "Is anything wrong sir?" "Yeah, I can't sleep." Nasser said. "Well, would you like something to eat or drink?" Eamhair said. At first, he was nervous to ask because earlier Eamhair gave Nasser and Doyle hot dogs that were covered with some green stuff and worms were crawling out of the dogs. And the lemonade had roaches plus rat droppings. "I can't believe I'm asking this, But do y'all have anything besides those disgusting hot dogs?" Nasser said. "Yes sir," Eamhair replied. "We have meat balls covered with beetles and spaghetti with chocolate. Muffins with liver inside of them and toss salad." "I'll definitely have the toss salad." Nasser said, "excellent choice." Eamhair said. "Please let me know if you need anything else." She walked away. After that, Nasser was nervous. At first, he thought the salad was safe to eat, suddenly he noticed how black the lettuces was. Also, there was a finger nail allong with whipped cream. "Bennyyyyyyyyyy!!!" Nasser said as he watched Rusty Busty fly them into a storm. He got on his knees and prayed for a miracle and looked out the window. He started freaking out after noticing that smoke is coming out of the plane. Back on the good plane, Mallory was just staring at Shawn Mendes while Simon was handling the passengers much to his dismay. As for me, I felt stupid that maybe, just maybe there could be a chance for me to become friends with Shawn Mendes. Mallory grabbed her bag and took out a scrapbook. She made for her and Shawn Mendes' future wedding. She had everything, where the wedding will be, what kind of wedding cake, what song will be played at their wedding. Their vows, her wedding dream, where the honeymoon will be and the name of their future kids. Both me and Shawn Mendes were shook. "Wow Mallory, you sure have put a lot of work into this." "Thanks!" Mallory said. Then she took out another book. "This is my song book. I was hoping I could show you some of my songs I have been working on." After she said that, I got up and went to another seat. Mallory didn't even notice. She just kept running her mouth. However, Shawn did notice. He got up from his seat and sat right by me. "What do you want?" I said. "I just wanted to see if you were alright." "Why do you care?" I asked him. "Because I want to be your friend." When he said that, I thought I was dreaming. "What did you say?" "I want to be your friend." Shawn said with a smile. "I really do, so what's your name?" At first, all I could do was stutter, then the words came out. "My name is Benny Breezy," he shook my hand. "It's nice to meet you, Benny." "You too," I said. For the rest of the flight, me and Shawn

Mendes got to know each other. I told him what happened at Glass Art and about my dreams. We also talked about the case, then I got a call from my mother. She was with her assistant, Yelysaveta, "hey mom." But before my mom could answer, Yelysaveta started freaking out when she saw who was sitting beside me, "OMG are you…" "Hi" Shawn Mendes said, "and yes, it's me." My mom and Yelysaveta couldn't believe that I was hanging out with the one and only Shawn Mendes. Anyway the reason why they were calling was because my mom found out that I was going to Los Angeles to interview AJ Mitchell and that she wasn't happy that I and my friends were going to Los Angeles unsupervised. She decided that since we're going to Los Angeles, she wants me and my friends to stay with my estranged Aunt Fanny who lives at The Show Mayor. I was shocked though because nobody in the family has seen her in years. I tried to tell her that we don't need to be supervised, but she didn't care and Yelysaveta told me to not argue with my mother and to do what she says. "The preparations have already been made. She's expecting you." My mom told me. Then Yelysaveta asked me if I was working for Shawn Mendes now? "No, he's not. He's my friend." Shawn Mendes said, I looked at him And said thanks. I wanted to ask my mom why Grandma Maroochy and Aunt Antiquity are coming to see her, but the video chat ended, leaving me to wonder. "You think your mom is okay?"

Shawn Mendes asked me, "I hope so," I told him. Then Simon and Mallory joined us, I told them what my mom said and they weren't thrilled. Then a real flight attendant came into first class wondering why Mallory and Simon aren't working. After that, the Pilot announced that we're about to land. Mallory and Simon were excited, but I felt bad for the passengers in coach. That's when I came up with an idea with Shawn Mendes' help. "Ladies and Gentleman please put your hands together for the talented and kind and my friend, the one and only, Shawn Mendes." He sung nervous. We got those passengers out of their seats and helped them dance to the music. Then at the end of the song without even paying attention, Mallory kissed Shawn Mendes on the lips and the two started making out. I just stood there smiling and Simon was furious. Then the plane landed. I was sad that I might not see Shawn ever again and he could tell how down I was. He told me to call him if I needed him. He gave me his number and said that we'll always be friends. Then he said his goodbye to Mallory, she started kissing Shawn again. The kiss lasted 90 minutes, then she hugged him and wouldn't let him go. So, I and Simon had to pull her off of him. We grabbed our bags. Little did Mallory know that the bag she grabbed belonged to Ashley Tisdale, who was also at the airport. Me and the others stood there wondering what happened to Doyle and Nasser. I took out my phone to call them. Sadly, things were just getting worse for Nasser and his brother. After taking a short nap, Nasser found a skunk sleeping on his chest. That's it, I've had enough of this plane. Doyle put his hand over Nasser's mouth because he didn't want that skunk to spray them. He called Eamhair for assistance. "Yes?" she said. "Um there's a skunk on my brother's chest." Doyle said, "and your point is?" Eamhair said. They looked at each other and then they looked at her. "Are you crazy? That's a skunk." Doyle said. "Looks more like a cat to me." "Ok, we're getting off this Death trap now." Nasser said. "I agree with you bro." Doyle said, then the hobo came and took the skunk off Nasser's chest. He told them that the skunk is his pet. "Alright passengers! The good news is, we're finally in Los Angeles. The bad news is, Rusty Busty never stops," "then how do we get off?" Nasser said. Eamhair opened the door and smiled, "OMG" Nasser said. The Hobo grabbed a parachute and was the first one to jump out along with his pet skunk. Then the creepy mine and psycho clown who kept laughing. The only ones left were Doyle and Nasser. They were taking their time with Nasser. Going so slow, Doyle gave his brother a push. A few minutes later, me and the others heard screaming. We saw Doyle and Nasser falling. Nasser pulled the string, he ended up landing in a water fountain outside of the airport. So me and the others helped him get out of there, but Doyle landed on Mallory, knocking her and him in the water fountain. "What took y'all so long?" I asked them. "Trust me, you don't want to know." Nasser said. The four of us were wondering how we're supposed to get to The Show Mayor without any money. "Hey, a guy over there is holding a sign with your name on it." Mallory said. So we walked over to him. I couldn't believe how young he is. "Hey, what's up? Are you Ms. Fanny's nephew?" He asked me. "Yes I am. I'm Benny Breezy and these are my friends, Simon, Mallory, Doyle and Nasser." "It's nice to meet all of you, my name is Porfirio. I'm a Limousine Driver who works for your Aunt."

CHAPTER FOUR

MY KINDA WELCOME TO THE SHOW MAYOR

Me, Mallory, Simon, Doyle and Nasser couldn't believe how beautiful Los Angeles is. Then I asked Porfirio why is he working for my Aunt Instead of some celebrity. His response was, "Dude, are you kidding me? I love working for your Aunt. She's a great boss and fun to be around. I know most people don't like her, but once you get to know her, you'll learn she's not so bad. I want you to remember this, never judge a book by its cover." "Are we almost there?" Nasser asked, "I'm starving. You wouldn't believe the food they had on Rusty Busty." Nasser said. Porfirio smiled. "We're here guys," Porfirio said. Me and the others couldn't believe how big and unique The Show Mayor was. As we went inside, we got the surprise of a lifetime. Some music started playing, "what's going on?" I asked Porfirio. "You'll see." he said with a smile. Two people backflipped into the lobby. Then three ropes came down. They were clowns, but they were no ordinary clowns. "What's Happening?" Mallory asked. "Guys! Get ready for a performance of a lifetime. Meet The Ptarmigan Seissylt Clowns." The lead singer started off with the song first. Then the rest of the group joined in. The Ptarmigan Seissylt Clowns were singing a song called. 'My Kinda Welcome To The Show Mayor'. Me and the others couldn't believe how good they were. The lead singer did a magic trick and made a rose appear. Then he gave it to Mallory making her blush. Then an elephant and other circus performers came in. At the end of the song, confetti and balloons came down and then The Ptarmigan Seissylt Clowns disappeared. Mallory was wondering where did they go. Then one of the balloons that Mallory was holding started to grow, It got so big that I and the others were starting to get worried. Then it popped and when it did, The Ptarmigan Seissylt Clowns reappeared. It turns out that they were inside the balloon. Me and the others, plus the rest of the guests applauded them. "Thank you," the lead singer said. Then he came over to Mallory.

"Hi, my name is Seissylt. What's yours?" Mallory couldn't stop staring at him. "Huh? Oh sorry, my name is Mallory Styles and these are my friends, Benny, Simon, Doyle, Nasser, and that's Porfirio." "It's nice to meet all of you." Seissylt said. "Maybe we can hang out?" Seissylt said. "Yes, most definitely," Mallory said. "Cool! and these are my friends, Publio, Placydo, Nazzareno and Tripta. She's a little clumsy. Welcome to The Show Mayor. Guys, you're going to love it here." Seissylt said. "I'll see you around Mallory," he said with a smile. He left after that with his band. "Who, was that?" Mallory asked Porfirio. Those are the performers / Band that work for The Show Mayor. They can perform, sing, act and do magic tricks. "Wow! Mallory said." "Are you okay Mallory?" I asked her. "I think I might be in love." When she said that, Simon's face turned red. He was getting jealous.

Okay guys, I have to go, but don't worry. Stiles, the desk clerk will take you to Ms. Fanny. After that, he left. So me and the others waited patiently for Stiles to get off the phone and when he did, we introduced ourselves. "Hi, my name is Benny Breezy and these are my friends, Simon, Nasser, Mallory and Doyle. We're here to see my Aunt Fanny. When I said that, everybody in the hotel froze. "Are you okay? I asked him." "Huh? Oh yeah. Sorry Benny, it's just none of us have ever met anybody from her family." "Seriously? She has never mentioned any of us?" "I'm afraid not." Stiles said. "Sorry, but it's nice to finally meet another Breezy. Welcome to The Show Mayor, I'll call your Aunt to see if she's ready for y'all." While he calls Aunt Fanny, me and my friends saw some familiar faces and Mallory thought she would pass out. "No way, Why Don't We! Mallory shouted out." Jonah, Corbyn, Daniel, Zach and Jack. came to the front desk. They asked Stiles if he could send more towels to their room. They just came back from the beach. Mallory kept staring at them and asked them if she could have their autograph. Then she introduced herself and us while my friends got to know them. I just walked away thinking that Why Don't We wouldn't care or notice. But Jonah, Corbyn and Daniel did notice while Zach and Jack signed several plain color t-shirts that Doyle had in his bag. For some reason "What's with him?" Jonah asked Mallory. "Huh? Oh Benny doesn't think you'll become friends with him, so he's keeping his distance away from you." "Why would he think that? Corbyn said. "I'd rather not say." Mallory said. "Of course we would be his friend." Daniel said, Nasser and Simon just looked at each other. Meanwhile, Jonah couldn't get me off his mind. He wanted to become my friend. As for Mallory, she tried to get Jonah's attention and came up with an idea. Suddenly she passed out, causing Simon, Nasser, Doyle, Stiles and Why Don't We to see if she's alright. She told Jonah that she needs mouth to mouth resuscitation. So when he did, Mallory started making out with him.

After she was done kissing him, she couldn't stop smiling. As for Jonah, he was smiling too. Then he and the others said goodbye to Mallory and my friends and left the lobby. That's when I came back into the lobby shaking my head. "You just couldn't resist could you?" I asked her. "I am a Styles remember," she said, "I always dreamed of kissing each member of the band" "But you only kissed one." Nasser said. "Don't worry, I plan on getting the rest," Mallory said. I just rolled my eyes when she said that. "And you Mr., should be ashamed of yourself." "What are you talking about?" I asked her. "Hiding from Why Don't We." "Look, you wouldn't understand, everybody loves you and wants to be your friend, but people like Jonah. Corbyn, Daniel and the others wouldn't give me a chance and I'm tired of trying to get people to know me." "Anyway, is my Aunt ready for us?" I asked Stiles. "Um not quite yet." "She told me I should give you and your friends a tour of The Show Mayor. In the meantime I'll get Telmo to take your bags." When he said that, I stopped for a second wondering why that name. Sounds so familiar, then it came to me. "You're Dean Dipper's son," I said, "oh great, are you students or friends of my father" Telmo said.

"LOL, friends? Are you kidding me?" Doyle said. "Um forgive my friend, I'm Benny Breezy, these are my friends, Simon, Mallory, Doyle and Nasser and yes, we're students of your father." "It's nice to meet all of you, but if you came here to make me talk to my father then you came all this way for nothing." "Sorry to burst your bubbles we're here to clear AJ Mitchell's name. Not for you," Mallory, said. "Oh" Telmo said. Me and the others followed Stiles and Telmo. I could tell that getting through to Telmo won't be easy. As we took a tour of The Show Mayor we learned that The Show Mayor has a Mall. A sound Studio. A, Arcade, and a Movie theater, plus a Beach. Then Stiles took us to the Big Top Show Mayor. Inside, there was a Circus Ring and Bubble Hanging Chairs. "What is this place?" I asked Stiles. He told us that this is where the guests watch the performance from." He also told me that my Aunt is part of the show. "Where do the guests sit at?" Mallory said. "The Bubble Hanging Chairs, Duh" Stiles said. "Now go find a seat. The show is about to start." So, Mallory and the others quickly got in a Bubble Hanging Chair and pressed the remote to be closer to each other. As for me, I just wanted to be by myself and kept my distance away from the others. I thought that it was cool that there's a remote that can control the chairs. Just when I thought I would be watching the show by myself, somebody put their chair next to mine and I couldn't believe who it was. "Hi, my name is Grant Knoche. What's yours?" At first, I was shy. I never imagined that one day I would meet Grant Knoche. I also knew that Grant Knoche wouldn't become my friend, but then I remembered what The Delahoussaye Psych Sisters said and I took a chance. "My name is Benny Breezy. It's nice to meet you. What are you, doing here? " I asked him. "Well, I heard about this place and wanted to check it out. So what brings you to The Show Mayor?" He asked me. "Well, me and my friends are here to interview AJ Mitchell, clear his name and get the reward money. I'm an Investigative reporter, I work for The Daily Maglorix Newspaper." "Sounds interesting," Grant said. Thanks! I said. Then me and Grant, my friends and the rest of the audience got ready for the show. A man with a hat came onto the circus ring. "Who's that?" Nasser said. "That's Mr. Stumbo. The Ring Master/Hotel Manager." Stiles said. "He seems like a nice guy," Simon said, "don't let him fool you guys. Mr. Stumbo is a strict and a workaholic. Nobody likes him. He just puts on an act for the guests at the hotel." Stiles said. Mr. Stumbo started introducing the act. "Ladies and Gentlemen, Boys and Girls, welcome to The Show Mayor. Please put your hands together for the amazing and talented, The Ptarmigan Seissylt Clowns." When Seissylt saw Mallory, he blew her a kiss. Making her blush and aggravating Simon. The room got dark and the gang started off with glow juggling, then Seissylt started the song as they continued to glow juggle. The song they were playing was called 'The Show Mayor Madness' and boy was it good. After they were done, Mr. Hildefuns, The Greatest Magician was next. Stiles told the others that Mr. Hildefuns is a little bit crazy.

First, he started the show with some bubbles. At first the audience wasn't impressed. Then the bubbles grew a lot bigger. Me and Grant looked at each other as Mr. Hildefuns walked on the bubbles one by one and started riding them like they were flying carpets. Then he asked for an assistant for his next performance and Mallory happily volunteered, she quickly changed before she went inside the box. Mr. Hildefuns warned her that sometimes his assistants go missing and don't come back causing Mallory to freak out, that's when Seissylt rushed onto the ring and kissed her on the lips to calm her down. When he was done kissing her, Mallory froze. Then she told Mr. Hildefuns that she's ready. Simon was about to explode. He couldn't take anymore of this. Mallory got into the box. Then Mr. Hildefuns closed the box and said the magic words. After that, he opened the door and Mallory was gone. However, instead of bringing her back, he brought back all the assistants he had ever lost, surprising him and the rest of us. "Where is she?" Seissylt asked Mr. Hildefuns, "I'm not quite sure," he said. So he said the magic words again. This time a hundred doves came, out. Then he grabbed his magic cards and shuffled them together, then he released them. There were about a hundred surrounding him. He smiled and created a magic cards twister. Suddenly something came out of the magic cards twister. It was Mallory. "Give it up for the beautiful Mallory." Mr. Hildefuns said. "Now that was amazing," Grant said. "I know right." I told him. Even Mr. Stumbo was impressed.

The other acts were. A human cannonball, trapeze artists, a motorcycle stunt driver, a fire breather, a mine, a human statue, diving, acrobatic gymnastics, puppetry, a knife thrower, a block balancing act. A strong man, stilt walking, some animal acts and a Contortionist. Then Aunt Fanny was the final performer. So the circus ring went away and a stage appeared. "Please put your hands together for Ms. Fanny Breezy." Mr. Stumbo said. It turns out that my aunt is a female vocalist. She sung " You Can't Stop The Beauty Of The Show Mayor". To my surprise, Aunt Fanny can sing. I couldn't wait to tell the rest of the family. After she was done performing, Mr. Stumbo told everybody that the show is over and that he hopes everybody enjoyed the show. "Also please send your reviews to Mr. Accerly Jamison." "Who in the heck is that?" I asked Stiles. "He sounds like a boring person." Doyle said. "I beg your pardon" Mr. Stumbo said. "Guys, this is my boss, Mr. Stumbo. Sir I would like you to meet, Mallory, Simon, Doyle, Nasser and this is Benny Breezy, Ms. Fanny's nephew." "And this is?" "Hey, my name is Grant. I'm Benny's friend." "You mean that?" I asked him. "Yes, we're really friends" Cool, I said. "Well isn't that nice," Mr. Stumbo said in a sarcastic voice. Then he started laughing. "You're joking right?" "No sir, I'm not" "Wow! So the cold hearted dragon does have a family." "Excuse me, that's my aunt you're talking about." "It's okay Benji, I'll take care of this." Aunt Fanny said, "don't you have some divorce papers you should be signing? Hmm" "It was nice meeting you Benny," He walked away after that. "Well, it has been quite some years since I have seen you Benji." "Okay, why does she keep calling you Benji?" Mallory said. "It's a nickname." I told her, I tried to give her a hug but she made it clear to me that she doesn't do any hugging or kissing. "Who are your friends?" She asked me. "This is Simon, Nasser, Doyle and Mallory and you already know Stiles," "yeah who doesn't know him. How are you Stilson?" "My name is Stiles." Sorry, did you say something because I wasn't listening. Well come on Benji. I, need to take you and your friends to my suite. And thanks for watching out for my nephew Stinky" "Once again, my name is Stiles." Before he left, he told me and the others to call him if we need anything. I gave him a twenty dollar tip and said thanks. Grant had to leave too but he told me this wasn't goodbye. I told him thank you for being a friend. Before he left though, Mallory grabbed him and started making out with him.

Me and the others wondered how big Aunt Fanny suite is as we went up in the elevator. To our surprise, Aunt Fanny lives in a penthouse.

"No way" Mallory said. Aunt Fanny showed us around. "This is where the guys will be staying." Aunt Fanny, said. Me, Simon, Doyle and Nasser couldn't believe it. Our room had a flat screen TV, a snack refrigerator and a game room. As for Mallory, she thought she would faint. Her room. Also had a flat screen TV and a closet full of clothes and shoes plus jewelry. After showing us our rooms, Aunt Fanny continued to show us around the penthouse. We found out that she has a nice kitchen with a pizza oven, two hot tubs, an arcade, an even bigger TV. A library, a huge fire place, 5 bathrooms, and her very own elevator. "How come we didn't come in this elevator?" Nasser said. "Because I don't allow anybody to go in my elevator except for me. You got a problem with that? No, that's what I thought." Aunt Fanny said. Then she introduced us to her Chef. "This is Chef Acer, my personal chef." "It's a pleasure to meet all of you," Chef Acer said. "You too." He asked us if we would like something to eat. I told him that me and my friends don't have time to eat, but I quickly changed my mind after seeing the food he made us. Some jumbo burgers with fries and he made some pizza and blueberries muffins. So we washed our hands and dig in. After we were done eating, me and the others got ready to go interview AJ Mitchell. "Can't we take a nap?" Doyle said. No, I told him, Mallory came out of her room dressed as a maid. Aunt Fanny allowed her and only her to go in the elevator. As for me, Simon, Nasser and Doyle, we had to go in the hotel elevator.

I called Stiles to ask him which Suite was AJ staying in. As Doyle and Nasser stepped into the elevator, suddenly my phone rang. It was my editor/boss, before I could answer, a bunch of fans pushed me out of the way and got into the elevator. My friends tried to stop it from closing but they were too late. So I had to wait for the next one. When the elevator came down again, there was only one guy in the elevator. To my surprise, the guy was no other than Jack Maynard, I couldn't believe that I was in an elevator with Jack Maynard. At first, I didn't say anything because I didn't think he would give me a chance, but then he got to know me and we became fast friends. I was happy that he liked me for me. Then I reunited with the others. "Hey guys. I'm here." "Finally, where have you been?" Simon asked me. "Oh, I was hanging with Jack Maynard." "You're joking right?" Doyle said. No, I actually met him and now we're friends. Jack Maynard is a nice person. So what did I miss?" I asked them. "Well, when we got here, there were security guards everywhere, and they took away all those crazy girls." Nasser said. "Where's Mallory? I ask them, "I'm right here Benny." She tried to get the security guards to let her in. Unfortunately, it didn't work. Then Doyle tried, he disguised himself as a Chef which didn't work. Nasser disguised himself as a pizza delivery guy and that didn't work either. Simon pretended to be a security guard. Then Mallory dressed me up like a baby and she and Simon pretended to be a fake couple. Once again, our plan failed. So without any choice, me, Mallory, Simon, Doyle and Nasser went through the heating vent to AJ's Room and our plan was working until Doyle started feeling bad. Before I could ask him what was wrong, he started passing gas. Now when Doyle passes gas, it can either knock you out for weeks or destroy things. But this time his gas caused a big problem. His gas caused the heating vent to fall, thankfully we weren't hurt. Then I saw some awesome shoes and I knew they didn't belong to any of my friends so I looked up and I started getting nervous. So did my friends, it was AJ. "Um hi, who are you guys?" AJ Mitchell said. "I'm your future wife." Mallory said. "Look we can explain ourselves." I told him. "Sure you can. Security!", he said, the security guards came in and grabbed us. "Where are you taking us?" Mallory said. The security guard just smiled making me and the others nervous. "You know what, do whatever you want. This day can't possibly get any worse. Summer is dead, I give up." That's when AJ stopped his guards.

"Let them go." "Are you sure?" "Yes, let them go and leave us." The security guards didn't want to leave him but he told them that he'll be alright. AJ looked at me and asked me what my name is. "My name is Benny Breezy and this is Mallory, Simon, Nasser and Doyle, my friends." "Well, it's nice to meet you. Welcome to California." Thanks, I told him. "So what brings you to Los Angeles?" He asked me. I wanted to tell him but the words wouldn't come out. I was nervous, I didn't think AJ would talk to me because I'm not cool or popular. However, he got to know me and told me that everything will be alright and that I don't have to be nervous to talk to him, that he likes me for me. After hearing that, I told AJ that me and Nasser are investigative Reporters and that Simon is our photographer. I also told him we're here to clear his name and collect the reward money to save our jobs and to prove a point to the world. AJ smiled, then he ordered some pizza and we started the interviews. I took out my tape recorder and Mallory took out a notepad. "So tell us man, how did all of this start?" "It all started on Oct 31st. I was performing at a Halloween concert. I had a good crowd and everybody was enjoying themselves. Then all of a sudden a cloak figure popped up on the screen. I was a little frightened. 'Who are you?' I asked them. The person just laughed and told me to call them The Mad Ffraid Brat and that I'm going to pay, and that I can kiss my career goodbye. Then the screen exploded. After that, fireworks came out of nowhere. They were aimed at me. Some blew up the tour bus. The others blew up some of my fans' cars. Thankfully nobody was hurt. The last fireworks went in the air and spelled, '**You Will Lose Everything,**' I cancelled the concert after that and the world tour. It was just too dangerous. Things didn't stop there. Throughout the months, I continued to get threats and more hate. The Mad Ffraid Brat sent me a box of chocolate filled with worms and a picture of me with an 'X' on it. Then I started getting strange phone calls and a lot of hate mail. That's when I decided to stay at The Show Mayor. I couldn't believe how amazing this place was. Unfortunately my arrival didn't turn out the way that I hoped. The Presidential Suite they had for me was a complete mess. Like someone did it on purpose. Mr. Stumbo assumed that one of the employees did it. Later on, I went to the sound studio. I also ran into Gerwazy Pooser, a famous movie star. We hung out and went to the Big Top Show Mayor. Then later on that night, several cops came storming in The Show Mayor. Me and Gerwazy and Mr. Stumbo didn't know what was going on, so we went to investigate. That's when my life changed forever. For some reason, the cops were checking my room. At first, I didn't know why. Then things got interesting when they found a skull. They told me it's called 'The Ape Skull from The Diamond Museum

Amsterdam'. One of the cops told me The Ape Skull was just stolen last night and they accused me of stealing it. The Mad Ffraid Brat sent me a text that night saying there's more to where that came from. Anyway, I convinced the judge to give me time to clear my name. That's why I'm offering a reward to whoever can clear my name. Can you help me?" AJ asked me and the others. I told him we're going to try our best no matter what it takes. We left after that because it was really late and we were all tired. Before I left, I shook AJ's hand and said goodnight. Me, Simon, Mallory, Doyle and Nasser couldn't wait to get back to Aunt Fanny's penthouse and go to bed.

We had so many questions about who this person is. As we got into the elevator you'll never guess who we saw. It was Luke Korns. They all introduced themselves. Everybody except for me, I knew Luke Korns wouldn't become my friend or even give me a chance, so when the elevator stopped, I couldn't wait to get off. Mallory told Luke. Why we were here. Then she started making out with him, shocking me and the others. Things suddenly got creepy when me, Mallory, Simon, Doyle, Nasser and Luke got back to Aunt Fanny's penthouse. There was a message on the door written in red paint. The message said **'Leave Now Or Suffer The Consequences'** "What does this mean?" Nasser said, "to be honest, I don't know." I told him. Simon took a picture. He was terrified, so were the rest of us. Luke spent the night with us but none of us could sleep. The next day, I woke up and checked my phone. It was 8:30 am. Simon and the others were still asleep and Luke as well, so I decided to get up. Then I sneaked out, Unfortunately that creepy message was still on the door. I got in the elevator and ran into another familiar face. It was Chris Salvatore, another person I didn't think would become my friend. So I didn't say anything to him, but when we reached the lobby, he asked me what's my name. I told him Benny, "it's nice to meet you." He said. Then, I went to the front desk hoping Stiles would be there. To my surprise, Mr. Stumbo was behind the desk. "What do you want?" Mr. Stumbo said. "Good morning to you too." "I was looking for Stiles." I told him, "he doesn't come in until later. Now if you would excuse me, I have some work to do." Mr. Stumbo said. After that, I walked over to a café shop. However, I was concerned about the guy who works there. He kept shaking. I asked him if he was alright. "Yeah, I'm fine." The guy said. "Okay. Well, I'll have a cappuccino." I told him. As he poured the coffee, he accidentally poured some on his hand. Are you okay? I asked him. "Trust me dude, I'm fine. This happens to me on a daily base. I'm accident prone. Anyway, here's your coffee and have a nice day. I could tell this guy needed some kindness. So I decided to leave him a twenty dollar tip and he couldn't believe what I did. Are you feeling okay?" The guy asked me. "Yeah, why?" I asked him. "Because you left me a twenty dollar tip." "What's wrong with that?" "Well, it's just nobody has ever given me a tip before and I have been here six years." "You're not from around here are you?" The guy said. "No I'm not, is it noticeable?" I ask him. "Um pretty much, but that's okay. Welcome to The Show Mayor, my name is Edvardas. It's nice to meet you." "Same to you. My name is Benny Breezy." "I just can't believe this, Edvardas said." "Believe what? I asked him." "That after six years, I'm meeting a nice guest for a change. I have never gotten a thank you or a raise or felt appreciated. You're the first person to ever show me kindness." Edvardas told me that he sees himself as a wimp, timid, shaky and that he's afraid of his own shadow. Before he could go on he froze like he was in a trans or something." "What's wrong?" I asked him. Edvardas just pointed. I turned my head and saw who Edvardas was so afraid of. "Who is that?" I ask him. Edvardas started stuttering . Then the words came out. "That's Deveral Jamison. The son of Mr. Accerly Jamison and Mrs. Bannnerjee." "You know that's the second time I have heard his name. But I still have no idea who he is?" "Mr. Accerly Jamison is the owner of The Show Mayor and he's one of the richest men in the world. His wife is a famous fashion designer, they have two kids. Deveral the one who's coming this way and Sollie." Seriously? I ask him. "Yep, The Jamison family are well known." "You got that right, hello loser," Deveral said. "Give me a cappuccino on the double. Move monkey." Deveral said. I couldn't believe my eyes. Deveral was bullying Edvardas, I knew I had to do something. "Um, excuse me" I said. But Deveral was texting on his phone. So, I poured sugar on his phone. "What's the big idea?" Deveral said. "I need to talk to you." I said. "Um monkey. Who is this person?" Deveral said.

"This is Benny Breezy." Edvardas said, "Oh let me guess, you're new right?" Yeah, I said, "well let me give you a proper welcome and explain how things go around here. I'm attractive and you're not. I'm cool and popular and you're a slop. You're nobody and I'm somebody. Girls love me and my parents are filthy rich, and oh, my father is the owner of this amazing Hotel." Deveral didn't mind making me feel bad about myself. "Do you feel welcome yet?" He said with a devious smile on his face. Then, I notice that he has a pet parrot. "Yeah, this is Kangi. He only listens to me. You are really full of yourself." I told him. "At least I'm somebody. People like being around. You probably don't even have friends." Deveral said. After he said that, I decided to look up any information I could find about Deveral Jamison. I found out that Deveral is a model. That girls love him and he has his own talk show. "Now it's your turn." He said, "well this is pathetic. You're an Investigative Reporter for The Daily Maglorix Newspaper and you're a piano prodigy. Well isn't that nice. Wow, you really have no life, but your friend Mallory looks hot. Make sure you give her my number."

"So that's why you're here. To clear AJ Mitchell's name and be somebody. Well, sorry to burst your bubble, but there are no heroes in this story. You and your friends will fail." Deveral said. "I don't care that your Mr. Accerly Jamison son. You're nothing but a bully and a spoil rich kid. I'm not afraid to stand up to you. I'm not rich or famous, or the best looking guy in this world. But at least I have kindness and know how to treat people. All you do is scare people and make fun of others. You're a self-absorbed person and you use your looks to manipulate people." Deveral was getting a little aggravated with me because nobody has ever stood up to him. Edvardas was impressed. All of a sudden, Deveral told Kangi to grab Edvardas' phone. Then Deveral threw Edvardas' phone down the laundry shoot. He smiled and told me to fetch. I looked at Edvardas. I couldn't believe how scared he was of Deveral. Then, some clowns passed by us. They were pushing a cart full of custard pies. I grabbed two and threw one in his face and one in his hair that he loves so much. After that, I grabbed some coffee and poured it on him. "Oops, I am a tourist you know. Catch you later clown," I said as I went down the laundry shoot. Deveral was angry. He grabbed some towels and told Edvardas you know who is waiting for us. Unknowing to Deveral, Edvardas felt bad for what he did to me. Meanwhile, I landed on some clean sheets Thank God, I started digging for Edvardas' phone. As I dug, suddenly the sheets started moving, freaking me out, I noticed a nearby wrench and grabbed it as the sheets continued to move. I was ready to fight whatever, was underneath the sheets. Something popped up or should I say somebody, it was Reed Horstmann, "Hey, is this your phone?" He asked me. "Um no, it belongs to a guy named Edvardas." "Hi, my name is…" "Oh, I know who you are. But what are you doing here?" "Oh, somehow my room key accidentally got thrown in with the sheets. So, what's your name? "He asked me. At first, I was frozen because I always wanted to meet Reed and become friends with him. But I always doubted that he would talk to me. "My name is Benny Breezy. I'm an investigative Reporter. Me and my friends are here to clear AJ Mitchell's name and catch The Mad Ffraid Brat. This person is dangerous. They left a threatening note on my Aunt Fanny's door. Sounds like you have a lot on your plate." Reed said, "Unfortunately I do." "Well, it was nice meeting you." Before I got to the door, Reed shouted out "Can he join our team?" At first, I didn't think it would be a good idea. But Reed Horstmann wouldn't take no for an answer. "Alright, welcome to the team, thanks friend. "I must be hearing things because it sounds like you called me your friend." "I did" Reed said. "I can cross that off my bucket list," I said with a smile on my face. Then we walked back to Aunt Fanny's penthouse. When we got there, Stiles and some guy were trying to get that creepy message off the door. Stiles told me and Reed that some of the guests have been complaining to Mr. Stumbo. Stiles was shocked to see who was with me. "Wait, how did you two meet?" He asked us. "It's a long story," I told him.

Me and Reed walked in and my friends were shocked to see me with Reed Horstmann. Then Mallory came in the kitchen and started screaming when she saw Reed. She asked Reed if she could hug him and he told her yes. He whispered to me, "I don't know why you were worried about her doing something crazy." I smiled at him and told him to just wait. I told my friends that we have a big day ahead of us. But before we did anything, Chef Acer made us some breakfast. He made

Blueberry waffles, French toast, sausages, eggs, pancakes, breakfast casserole, bacon, croissants, blueberry scones, bagels and biscuits. So we dug in and Mallory was still holding onto Reed. Then, I asked her isn't that Ashley Tisdale's shirt that she's wearing. "Yeah, somehow our suitcases got switched. Well, don't you think you should return her stuff." I asked her, "and when are you going to let me go?" Reed said. "No, I'm not going to return her stuff. At least not right now. This is my chance to meet the sister I always wanted. And no Reed, I'm not letting you go." Mallory said. "I'm not crazy guys," Mallory said. "Who are you trying to convince?" I asked her. That's when Aunt Fanny came into the kitchen in her night robe. Plus she had some curlers in her hair. "Wow, Chef Acer. You wouldn't believe the dream that I had last night. In my dream, my nephew and his friends came to Los Angeles to solve some mystery and clear AJ's name. Anyway, what did you make for breakfast?" Aunt Fanny said. "Um Fanny." Chef Acer said, "yeah what?" He pointed at me and my friends causing her to split out some orange juice that she was drinking. "So that wasn't a dream?' "Oh no, good morning to you too Aunt Fanny." I said. Then AJ came in while Stiles and that guy continued to work on the door. AJ told me and the gang that he wasn't feeling too good and that his stomach was bothering him. And that he has been running to the bathroom all morning. He showed us some basket that somebody had left for him this morning outside of his door. I found that suspicious and decided to investigate. Inside the basket were breakfast cookies. Then I found a hidden note inside the basket and when I opened it, I quickly slapped the cookie out of AJ's hand after he tried to eat another cookie. "Dude, what are you doing?" He asked me. "I'm trying to save your life" I told him. Before I could read the note, Why Don't We and Luke Korns showed up along with Grant and Chris Salvatore. "What are y'all doing here?" I asked them. "We want to help." Corbyn said, "I don't think that's a good idea." I told them. Unfortunately, Mallory told them that they could. I just rolled my eyes and read the note to everybody. The note said '**You Have Been Warned – Signed your biggest fan.**' Me, AJ, Simon, Nasser, Doyle, Mallory, Why Don't We, Grant, Chris Salvatore, Luke Korns, Aunt Fanny and Chef Acer didn't know what to think. "You can't eat these cookies. In fact, we're going to burn them. The Mad Ffraid Brat put laxatives in those breakfast cookies. That's why you have been going to the bathroom so much." I told him. "You think The Mad Ffraid Brat left that basket for me?" AJ asked me. I believe so, I told him, then Stiles told me and the others that he and that guy were done with the door. He also gave me that list that I asked for of all the suspects. "Come on guys, where are we going?" Doyle asked me. "We're going to Darcassan's cousin's house." I told him, Porfirio gave us a lift, to our surprise, Leonel lives in a two story house. Me, Mallory, AJ, Simon, Doyle, Nasser, Reed, Chris Salvatore, Luke Korns, Grant and Why Don't We were just standing at Leonel's front door. We were worried to knock on the door because there was a camera watching us plus other gadgets around the house as well. So, Mallory ringed the doorbell. Nobody came to the door. She did it again and again. The seventh time, a hologram appeared saying "The Moots family aren't available, at the tone leave your message and we'll get back to you in 7 or 9 months. Do not ring the bell the eighth time or suffer the consequences." The hologram, went away after that.

v"Okay, it's time to go." Nasser said. "Where, are you guys going?" Mallory said. "You heard what the hologram said." Jack said, "we came here for help and we're going to get it." Mallory said. "Maybe this isn't a good idea." I told her, "please, what's the worst thing that can happen?" Mallory said. She pressed the doorbell again and when she did, a metal laser came out and shot out a yellow beam at me, AJ, Luke, Simon and Grant. Nasser was freaking out. Then a tube sucked Nasser and Chris, after that several metal tentacles grabbed Why Don't We and Reed. The only ones left were Mallory and Doyle. Suddenly, the rug they were standing on dropped them underneath the house. At first, there was nothing but darkness. Then the lights came on and we found out that we were stuck in a cage. Things continued to get worse. Suddenly, Mallory started screaming. She told us that she was surrounded by spiders and she wasn't the only one seeing things. Doyle was stuck in summer school and couldn't escape. AJ was face to face with The Mad Ffraid Brat. It seemed like everybody was seeing things. As for me, I found myself all alone. Then I realized that none of this was real and that me and the others were facing our worst fears. I grabbed a pen from my pocket and stabbed it into some red orb thing, causing it to mess up and free us from the cage. "Okay, what was that?" Chris said, "well that was my fear simulation. It still needs work but I guess your friend figured it out." "You must be Leonel?" "Yes, I am. Who are you?" "I'm a friend of your cousin, Darcassan." When I told him that, Leonel turned off his lasers and any other weapon he has for Intruders. "My apologies," Leonel said. It's okay I told him. "My name is. Benny Breezy and this is Simon, Mallory, Nasser, Doyle, AJ, Reed, Chris Salvatore, Luke Korns, Grant and Why Don't We. I'm an Investigatie Reporter who works for The Daily Maglorix Newspaper. Me and my friends are here to clear AJ's name and catch The Mad Ffraid Brat." "It's, nice to meet you. Welcome to my lab. Let me show you around." He typed in a password and did an eye scan, opening up a door to his lab. We couldn't believe, how big his lab was. There were so many gadgets. First he showed us an invention called The Trini Nazor. Mints that can give anyone the ability to freeze people. The more you chew, the bigger the ice breath becomes. "Over here is The Procter Pendo, it can turn people into different colors. This right here is the Nimrod Narses Demos. It's a robot that can make pizzas." While Leonel continued to show us his inventions, Jonah asked me why won't I talk to him and the rest of Why Don't We. He wouldn't stop asking until I answered his question. "Okay. You really want to know?" I asked him. "Yes, I do." He told me. "Well, here it is. I have dealt with a lot of mean people in my life. People look down on me and don't give me a chance. People care about image when it comes to friendship. If you aren't attractive or cool, nobody wants to be your friend. They don't even bother to try to get to know you. Guys at Glass Art are like that and everywhere for that matter. I don't want to pretend to be something I'm not in order to be friends with somebody. That's why I keep my distance from you and the others." "Do you honestly think any of us would treat you like that?" Jonah said. "I don't know what to believe." I told him. "You know what, I'm going to prove it to you." "Prove what?" I asked. "That me, Corbyn, Daniel, Jack and Zach want to be your friend."

"Same here," Luke Korns and Chris Salvatore said. I just looked at them and then told Leonel that we are in a hurry and that we need some spy gear. He took us to a vault like room. He told us to line up. Mallory was first. He gave her a spy bag. Inside was a spy suite that fitted her. Laser lipstick and something called The Plasedo Tango. A mind control spray bottle. Simon got an invention called The Anselmi Arrie Speed Flies, shoes that can give anybody the ability to fly and the ability to run really fast. Faster than a cheetah, he gave Doyle an invention called The Audio Nolsen. A pen that can release a powerful spray that can force anyone to tell the truth. It can also shoot out a spray that can knock a person unconscious for 24 hours. Nasser got something called The Dieter Bandos, very powerful stink bombs. One of these can make a person stinky for months. AJ received Aigeos Juppar Jawbreakers, but they aren't like other jawbreakers. They have tiny bombs inside of them and can cause a huge explosion. Grant got a bag of Aigeos Juppar jawbreakers as well along with The Olutosin Noak, a ring that can make whoever wear it shrink things. He gave Luke The Nymphas Onesimus Goggles, that allows the user to zoom in on people even if they are miles away . It also has X-ray vision, can take pictures, see In the dark, and it can tell when a person is lying. Why Don't We got The Aluxio Plaxico, a freeze ray gauntlet. Each member got one. He told them these gauntlets can create ice balls, blizzards, and shoot out a powerful freeze ray. Chris was next, Leonel showed him The Onesimo Purves. A bandana that allows a person to talk to animals. Also, he got an invention called Shock Dust along with some special gloves that must be worn while touching the Shock Dust. He also told Chris that the Shock Dust can electrocute people and as for me and Reed, we both got the Aristotelis Setser Suits, tuxedos that allow the users to disguise themselves. They can become anybody they choose to be and nobody would know that it's them. The suits looked nice. He also gave each of us a communicator called The Cybernetic Falconieri Penzance. Wrist mounted model Watches that can record things, shoot lasers, and, each one has a tracking device and can send out an emergency signal. In case something has happened to the user, If you aren't able to send out the signal, you can hit the watch against something and the signal will go through sending for help. Leonel gave me one more thing, an invention called The Zayenthar Spyder. Very tiny robot spiders that are designed to spy on people. So he gave me a jar full of them. Me and the others thanked him. He asked us how Darcassan is doing. I told Leonel that his cousin is preparing for his senior year and college, "typical Darcassan" Leonel said. Then I ask him where are his parents? Leonel told us that his parents are always travelling and that his older brother and sister never have time for him. We felt sorry for him. "You got anything for me?" Aunt Fanny said. She and Porfirio came into the lab. "Um, what are you doing here Aunt Fanny?" I asked her. "I followed you and your friends. I want to help." "Why?" Mallory said. "Hmm, let me see. Oh, now I remember. Because some psycho wrote a disturbing message on my door and I want to unmask this creep and protect you Benny." Leonel gave Porfirio a jet pack and gave Aunt Fanny a jug of prune juice. "Seriously kid, Prune juice?" Aunt Fanny said, Leonel smiled, "this is no ordinary prune juice. Let me demonstrate. He poured some on a chair and the whole thing melted. Shocking all of us. "Now we're talking." Aunt Fanny said, "I call it The Valvoline Prune Breath. It can melt anything, be careful." "Okay guys, let me tell you who you're going to be interviewing. Mallory you get a woman named Zuly, a maid. Doyle and Grant you will be interviewing Mr. Stumbo, Nasser, Luke Korns and Chris Salvatore are going to interview a handicapped girl named Orssa. Simon and Why Don't We will interview a girl scout named Raysel. Me and AJ along with Reed will interview Gerwazy Pooser. As for you Aunt Fanny and Porfirio, see if you can dig up any information from the employees. And Leonel, see if you can find any information on Deveral Jamison. I have a feeling he's a part of this." "Wait, you want my help?" Leonel said. "Yes I do. We're going to need all the help we can get. Are you in?" I asked him. "Definitely, Leonel said." "Alright guys, let's do this." I told them before we left. Leonel introduced us to Penzance Frisco, A supercomputer that doesn't play.

CHAPTER FIVE

THE INTERVIEWS

Mallory didn't know how she would get Zuly to talk to her. Since Stiles told her that Zuly doesn't talk to anyone around here. Not even her co workers. So she decided to disguise herself as a maid once again. But this time she was wearing a blonde wig. As she walks to Zuly's room, all of a sudden somebody got her attention. At first Mallory thought it was some annoying guest but when she turned around, her world came crashing down. She thought she would have a heart attack. She couldn't believe the one and only Lucy Hale, from Pretty Little Liars was talking to her. The only thing she could say was, 'oh my gosh.' Lucy Hale could tell Mallory is a huge fan and told her to calm down and to take a deep breath. First, Lucy, asked her was she alright. Mallory nodded her head. Then, she asked Mallory her name after she finally settled down. Mallory introduced herself. Lucy could tell she wasn't a real maid because one of the guest came out in the hallway and asked her If she could clean his toilet. Mallory looked at him and said, "Do I look like a Maid?" Lucy reminded her that she's dressed as one. "Oh right, silly me." Mallory said. Lucy just needed some towels, then she asked Mallory would she like to hang out and Mallory couldn't stop screaming. "I'll take that as a yes." Lucy said. She told her to meet her in the lobby at two o clock. Before Lucy left, Mallory gave Lucy her script ideas, thinking this is her chance to get noticed. Lucy left after that. Mallory posted what happened on her blog and her followers went crazy.

Anyway, after cooling down, she finally made it to Zuly's room. However, she was a bit nervous, but she knew me and the others were counting on her so she did what a Styles always does. Act confident and show her beautiful face. She knocked on the door, at first nobody answered. Then, when Mallory knocked a second time, someone opened the door. "Are you Zuly?" Mallory said. "Yeah, who are you?" "I'm Mallory Styles. I was wondering if I could ask you some questions about the day AJ Mitchell was framed." That's when Zuly started snapping. "Are you kidding me? First the police questions me, then I lose my room and now you. Why can't y'all leave me alone." Zuly slammed the door in Mallory's face. She was shocked, she didn't know that Zuly has feelings because Zuly is supposed to be the tough one around here. Mallory leaned against the door to listen, she heard some noise. She went inside and found Zuly crying. She was in her recliner. "Are you okay?" Mallory said. "Why do you care? You don't know me. You're just like every other pretty girl in the world." "What do you mean by that?" Mallory said with a shocked look on her face. "Listen sweetie, no offense but pretty girls are mean. They treat others like they are nothing. They rather date guys who are attractive and have abs. Or rich, the type that usually will break your heart. Pretty girls only care about their looks, body and hair. Some are shallow, stuck up, rotten, spoiled, selfish, hateful, have no respect for themselves or others. Plus they make women like me feel bad about myself. Just look at me." "What are you talking about?" Mallory said. "There's nothing wrong with you." "Yeah right, I'm overweight and unattractive. I just want a guy who will like me for me. Out of all the guys that have ever came to The Show Mayor, none of them have ever showed any interest in me." "Look, it doesn't matter. If you aren't beautiful or hot or even sexy. What's inside and how you treat others is what truly matters. Never let anybody tell you that you aren't beautiful. Sometimes the real beauty comes from inside." Mallory said, "guys are slobs, but there are some good ones. But sometimes it's hard to find them." Mallory said, Zuly couldn't believe how nice Mallory was being to her. She went in her kitchen, made some lemonade and some snicker doodles. Then Mallory took out a tape recorder and asked Zuly how did all of this start. Zuly told her it all started on that terrible day. She did what she always does. She set her alarm for seven and got ready for the day. She told Mallory that being the head Housekeeper isn't easy. Telling the maids where to go and keeping them in line. Zuly told her that there are 150 maids at The Show Mayor and that during the summer, The Show Mayor is always crowded. The hotel gets visitors from all over the world because everybody loves The Show Mayor, especially celebrities. Anyway, Zuly told Mallory that that morning, she and all the maids, including the rest of the hotel staff had a meeting with Mr. Stumbo. He wanted to make sure that they realized how important AJ's stay at The Show Mayor is to them. Mr. Stumbo was also in a bad mood that day for some reason. He gave each employee a task to do and Zuly had to clean the Presidential Suite. Mr. Stumbo told Zuly to make sure The Presidential Suite or should I say The Show Mayor Circus Plaza, which is one of the biggest rooms at The Show Mayor, to make sure it's clean.. So she did. However, something terrible happened. After AJ checked in, Mr. Stumbo took him to his suite. After they opened the door, water came bursting out, leaving AJ and Mr. Stumbo wet, they went in the room and found so many problems like muddy pigs on the bed, the toilet was overflowing, the tub had nothing but roaches crawling everywhere. The curtains were burned. There were worms in a gift basket. The ceiling was falling apart. Garbage in the front room and frozen bugs in the refrigerator. It was a complete disaster. AJ asked Mr. Stumbo what was going on. Then Mr. Stumbo got an unknown phone call who told him that a certain employee was to blame. So that afternoon, Mr. Stumbo gathered all of his employees in his office, questioning each one. Zuly thought she had nothing to worry about. Sadly she was wrong. Mr. Stumbo called her into his office and showed her a video of her destroying the suite. Zuly couldn't believe it. She tried to tell him that she's innocent but Mr. Accerly Jamison came into Mr. Stumbo office without giving her a chance to prove her innocence and fired her. They got rid of her just like that. Stiles ran after her because she was so upset. She couldn't believe that her own boss didn't believe her. Zuly told Mallory that since she can remember, she has been at The Show Mayor. She grew up here. Her mother started out as a maid. Then she became an assistant manager. Zuly and her sister would always explore and watch the shows/performance. They barely saw their mom. Things got even worse after their mother passed away. Teenager Zuly had to take care of her sister. It was rough. They had their good days and bad days without their mom. Great! Great! Great! Dunixi Jamison, Aka Mr. Accerly Jamison's father was really rough on Zuly. He would make her work daily and treat her so bad. Then, when Zuly and her sister got older, her sister decided to leave The Show Mayor once and for all. She couldn't take Dunixi Grand Jamison any longer, she gave Zuly a choice to either come with her. Or stay at The Show Mayor.

Zuly didn't know what to do. She knew how hard their mother worked so Zuly decided to stay and lost her sister. After all these years, Zuly and her sister still don't talk to each other. Zuly told Mallory that The Show Mayor is all that she has. She also mentioned that Mr. Accerly Jamison has decided to kick her out of The Show Mayor. Throwing her out of the only home she has ever known. Mallory had no idea that Zuly was going through so much and wondered why would somebody frame her. Then they both heard a knock on the door. So they opened the door and what they found was frightening. There was a knife in the door with a note saying, "**you deserve it.**" Mallory couldn't believe that The Mad Ffraid Brat thinks Zuly deserves this. Mallory put the knife and note in a plastic bag. Then she put the bag in her purse. Zuly felt threatened and was happy that she's leaving The Show Mayor. She didn't feel safe. Mallory checked her phone and realized it was time for her to go but she knew Zuly needed a friend and asked her if she would like to join her and Lucy. "Doing what?" Zuly said. "Just hanging out," Mallory said. Having nothing else to do, Zuly told her 'Sure,' so they got in the elevator and Mallory ran into one of her biggest crushes. Once again, it was the one and only Ruel. She passed out. when she saw him but she quickly got back up and started digging in her purse. "Um, what are you doing Sweetie?" Zuly said. "I'm looking for my mistletoe." Mallory said, "what are you doing with a mistletoe?" Zuly said. "Just watch." Mallory told her. Ruel noticed that Mallory was getting closer and closer to him until they were both underneath a mistletoe. Ruel smiled and realize that Mallory really wanted to kiss him. So he kissed her on the lips and Mallory couldn't stop blushing. Zuly stood there smiling and watched as Mallory and Ruel make out, Mallory played the song (Kiss Me – By Sixpence None the Richer) as she continued to kiss Ruel. Then, when they reached the lobby, Ruel said goodbye to Mallory and Zuly. Before he left. Mallory kissed him on the lips again. After that, Mallory and Zuly walked over to Lucy Hale who was waiting for Mallory. At first Zuly thought Lucy wouldn't be happy about her joining them. But Lucy thought it was a great idea and the three went shopping. And out to eat.

After Mallory was done, Doyle and Grant were next. They knew talking to Mr. Stumbo wouldn't be easy. So they broke into his office and went through his emails, trying to find any useful information. They learned that Mr. Stumbo gets two hundred emails a day from Mr. Accerly Jamison. Before they could check the rest of the emails, Mr. Stumbo came into his office. He was really mad. "What are y'all doing in my office?" Mr. Stumbo said. "We need to talk to you Stumbo man," Doyle said. "What did you just call me?" "We're sorry Mr. Stumbo, we just need to ask you some questions about the day AJ Mitchell got framed." Grant said. "That's none of your business," Mr. Stumbo said. "Yes, it is our business. Especially when me and my friends are getting threats from some psycho." Doyle said. Then Mr. Stumbo called security and warned them to stay out of his office. "What do we do now?" Grant asked Doyle. "Hmm, let me think." Doyle went through his Cybernetic Falconieri Penzance Communicator and told Grant that the communicators watches also have a voice disguising app. So Doyle called Mr. Stumbo while pretending to be. Mr. Accerly Jamison and told him that after 10 years and for being a loyal manager, that he has decided to give him a raise and a free pass To The Show Mayor Steam Room. for an entire day. When Doyle said that, Mr. Stumbo left his office and told Stiles that he's in charge and to hold all his calls. Doyle and Grant smiled and went to the steam room to wait for the next phase of their plan. So Mr. Stumbo walked into the steam room and felt relaxed. He hasn't felt this relaxed in years, then Doyle and Grant popped up. "What's up?" Doyle said, "oh no, I must be having a nightmare." Mr. Stumbo said. "So how is it going?" Grant said. "Well it was going alright until you two showed up. Ever since you and your friends came to The Show Mayor, life hasn't been the same. Y'all sure know how to shake things up." Mr. Stumbo said. "What can I say, me and my friends rock." "Whatever you say, now what do you want, whatever your name is." "My name is Doyle and this is Grant." "Okay! Well if you don't mind, I'm trying to relax. So bye and good riddance." Mr. Stumbo closed his eyes thinking that Doyle and Grant were gone. Unfortunately, they were still there. "This is insane. Look Mr. Stumbo, we're not going anywhere until you tell me what we need to know. Even if it takes all day." "Mr. Stumbo just tell him." Somebody said. Doyle, Grant and Mr. Stumbo were wondering who said that. Doyle was psyched when he saw who it was, Antoni Porowski. Also, Austin P. McKenzie was there as well. He told Mr. Stumbo that he needs to have more kindness and to be less strict. Antoni told him that there are two sides to every story and that it's time Mr. Stumbo tells his side of the story. With no other choice. Mr. Stumbo gave in and told Doyle and Grant what happened. So Doyle took out a tape recorder and so did Grant. Mr. Stumbo told Doyle and the others that was the hardest and most stressful day he has ever had. He did what he always does in the morning . He got up around five. He brushed his teeth. Then he took a shower. After that, he went for a jog. Later on, he worked out and ate some breakfast. After all of that he got ready for work. Mr. Stumbo told them that he's always dressed up because he's the manager and that running The Show Mayor is a big job. He has to look presentable. Anyway, when he got to The Show Mayor, he gathered up all his employees after receiving a call from Mr. Accerly Jamison telling him that AJ will be staying at The Show Mayor and to make sure he enjoys his stay. Mr. Stumbo told Doyle and the others that he didn't mean to be rough on his staff. Unfortunately, unknowing to his staff, Mr. Stumbo got a phone call that morning from his wife asking for a divorce. She used to be an important person in his life back then. His wife used to work at The Show Mayor as well, her and Mr. Stumbo were a good team. But their marriage started falling apart after Grand Dunixi Jamison could no longer take care of the hotel and decided to put his son in charge. With Mr. Accerly Jamison in charge, The Show Mayor became a depressing place. He did something that caused Mr. Stumbo's wife to give up and leave The Show Mayor for good. A few months later, she found out that she was pregnant and gave birth to a healthy boy. Things continued to get worse. After Mr. Accerly Jamison offered Mr. Stumbo to become the new hotel manager, Mr. Stumbo became a totally different person and spent less time with his family. All he could think about. Was work and money. So she got fed up and left him and didn't look back. Now his son is a teenager and wants nothing to do with his father. "That's all I know. Now you know my story." Mr. Stumbo, said. Doyle and the others felt sorry for Mr. Stumbo. Suddenly, the door shut close and the room got foggy. "What's going on?" Antoni said, things got creepy when the fog went away and a black crate appeared. "What is that?" Austin P. Mckenzie, said. "I don't know." Doyle said. He and Grant walked up to the crate and slowly opened it. What they found wasn't dangerous. Just a bunch of fortune cookies. But only five had their names on them. So Doyle was the first. His fortune cookie said. '**You and your friends – Will lose this battle.**' Mr. Stumbo's cookie said. '**You are nothing but a puppet to Mr. Accerly Jamison. No wonder your wife left you.**' Austin P. Mckenzie's cookie said, '**You better watch your back. Because if you hang out with Doyle and his friends. You will become a target as well.**' Antoni Porowski was next, '**Do you want me to mess up your career next?**' And Grant was last. '**Do you really think you can protect Benny from me?**' Thinking that things couldn't get any worse, Doyle and the others tried to remain calm. Unfortunately, their problems were far from over. Suddenly Grant heard. " ticking ", he and the others dug through the rest of the fortune cookies trying to find the noise and for some reason they couldn't find where the noise was coming from until Doyle found a secret compartment and inside was a bomb, scaring Doyle and his friends. "What are we going to do?" Grant asked Doyle. Without much hesitation Doyle grabbed one of Grant's Aigeos Juppar jawbreakers and threw it at the wall. "duck ", he shouted out and blew up the door. They were happy to be alive. Mr. Stumbo was upset that the steam room was destroyed. He knew Mr. Accerly Jamison won't be happy about this. Doyle quickly sent me a text. Then he and Grant plus Mr. Stumbo, Austin P. Mckenzie and Antoni Porowski went to the hotel security room checking the footage to see if anybody went inside the steam room before they did. At first, there was nothing. Then they saw a cloak figure walk into the steam room and never came out so that meant whoever was behind this was in the steam room with them the whole time and escaped before the bomb went off. This person had there plan figured out. "Who is that?" Doyle wondered.

So, with two suspects down, Nasser and Luke Korns and Chris Salvatore were next. Stiles told them that Orssa spends most of her time in The Show Mayor Library, to their surprise, the library was big. At first, Nasser, Chris and Luke didn't see her. Then she pulled up in a wheelchair. She was asking the librarian a question. However, she could tell somebody was watching her causing Nasser and the others to hide behind the bookshelves. As Orssa searched the library for some books that she was looking for, Nasser, Chris and Luke followed her, as they watched Orssa, Nasser got a text message. "shh ", Luke told Nasser because they were in a library and he did not want Orssa to know that they were watching her. Luke and Chris could tell that Nasser was concerned about something and asked him who was the text message from. Nasser told them that the message is from Doyle and that he and the others got attacked by The Mad Ffraid Brat, or someone who's working for The Mad Ffraid Brat. Well this isn't good. Luke said in an aggravated voice. Things got interesting when someone came into the library to talk to Orssa. Nasser and the others could barely see the person's face. The person was wearing a hoodie. Whoever this mysterious person was, they were having an intense conversation with Orssa. She slammed her hands on the table. Luke grabbed The Nymphas Onesimus Goggles and zoomed in to listen to their conversation. He gave Nasser and Chris ear pieces so that they could listen as well. This is what Orssa said. '**You idiot! If they catch on to us. It will be the end of me and my master plan. Don't mess up again or you'll be sorry.**' "I didn't see that coming." Chris Salvatore said, suddenly someone. tapped Nasser on the shoulder and he couldn't believe who it was, Amarr Wooten, "excuse me, but what are you guys doing?" Nasser was freaking out because he's a huge fan." However, he knew he was on a case and told Amarr what they were doing. So Amarr decided to join him and the others continued to watch Orssa and her friend. Unfortunately, the mysterious person was about to leave. So

Luke used his goggles and found out a shocking surprise. "Guys you won't believe this." "What? Nasser said." The person who's talking to Orssa is Deveral Jamison". "More bad news," Chris said. "Benny was right about him." Chris told the others. Then Deveral left the library. Now more than ever, Nasser and the others wanted answers. Suddenly Orssa disappeared and the lights started flickering on and off. Then some books fell off the shelves and each one spelled out. **'I know who framed AJ Mitchell, and now you're next.'** After that Nasser and the others ran to the door but it wouldn't open. They were the only ones in the library. "Can things get any worse?" Amarr said. "Yes! They can." Somebody said. Nasser, Luke, Chris and Amarr turned around to find Orssa. "Well, what do we have here. You three sure know how to find trouble. Didn't your mothers ever teach you to mind your own business. The same goes to you. Whoever you are. You want me, well here I am. So what do you want?" Nasser took out a tape recorder. "What can you tell us about the day AJ was framed." Orssa smiled. "Your friend deserves that and everything that's coming to him. You and your friends might think that you're heroes, but you're messing with the wrong people. This is my warning and make sure you passed it along to Benny. Stay away from AJ Mitchell and stay out of this. This isn't your fight." "Oh yeah, and if we refuse?" Orssa smiled and rolled her chair closer to them, "hmm let's see. Bad things can happen to people who don't listen." Just when they thought all was lost, Doyle came smashing in. Nasser was relieved to see his brother. "Guys, are you okay?" Doyle said. Orssa was furious. She shouted out that this isn't over. She jumped out of her wheelchair, pushed Doyle out of the way and ran. "OMG she can walk." Nasser said, "so what does this mean?" Amarr said. It means Orssa could be working with The Mad Ffraid Brat as well or she could be The Mad Ffraid Brat." Nasser said in a freak out voice. He ran over to his brother and hugged him, for once they were acting like brothers. "What do we do now?" Luke asked them.

With their friends dealing with their Interviews, Simon and Why Don't We were next. They found Raysel, the girl scout, in the lobby. So, Simon decided to use the old Simon charm on her. He thinks that works on all the girls. Unfortunately! Simon had to wait because Raysel had customers. He, Jonah, Daniel, Corbyn, Jack and Zach noticed that the customers were acting funny. They got even more suspicious when they learned how much Raysel was charging. The Thin mints were sixty nine dollars, The Peanut butter patties were seventy nine dollars. Eighty nine dollars for Thanks – A - Lot and the rest of the cookies were about a hundred dollars. After she was done with her customers, Simon and Why Don't We marched over there. "Hi, my name is Raysel. Would you like some girl scout cookies?" "You can drop the act." Simon told her. "Excuse me?" Raysel said. "You know what I'm talking about." Simon said, "these prices are outrageous." Jonah said. "A good girl scout would never do something like this." Corbyn said. "So who are you?" Daniel said. "We should report you," Jack said. "This little game of yours stops now." Zach said. After they said that, that's when Raysel's smile and her perkiness went away. She started laughing. Then she slammed her fist on the table. "Look Mr. Perfect and my favorite boy Band, you don't know who you're dealing with." Then another customer popped up. He pushed them out of the way and asked Raysel for 8 boxes of Tagalongs that cost two hundred dollars. Simon, Jonah and the others tried to stop him but he wouldn't listen. He gave Raysel the money and ran. Simon and the others watched as Raysel counted the money. Simon asked her why are her customers acting so nutty. Raysel told him she's not telling them anything, so Corbyn came up with an idea and huddled the guys together. Then Jonah walked up to Raysel and started making out with her while the others used The Cybernetic Falconieri Penzance Communicators to analyze the cookies. After getting what they needed, They gave Jonah the signal and Jonah stopped kissing her. He rejoined his friends. Simon asked Raysel about the day AJ was framed. Simon took a picture of her and took out a tape recorder. Raysel told them that she got up early that morning and started packing the cookies up in her wagon and came to The Show Mayor to sell cookies. She made over six hundred dollars. She met AJ in an elevator and asked for his autograph. Plus she sold him some cookies. That's all she remembers. Simon and the others didn't know whether to believe her or not. Simon told her he's going to find all that he can on her. Raysel told him to have fun. Simon and the others left The Show Mayor, leaving a suspicious Raysel to make a phone call. "We have a problem." Raysel said to the person on the other side. "What do we do now?" Jack asked Simon. "We're going to talk to the troop leader." Simon told them. When they got there, several girls started screaming. All of them were huge fans of Why Don't We. Simon and the others calmed them down and asked them if they knew a girl named Raysel. Suddenly things got quiet in the building, "who said that? Everybody knows that Raysel is a rotten girl." The Troop leader said, "who are you?" She asked them. "This is. Why Don't We," all the girls shouted out. "I see, and who is this guy?" The girls told her they didn't know. "Hi, my name is Simon. Me and my friends would like to ask you some questions." "Alright! Follow me into my office." The Troop leader said. She locked her door and told them she thought she knew her but she was wrong. She told Simon and the others that Raysel used to be the sweetest and most caring person she ever met. She would always help out her fellow troopers, plus volunteer. That all changed a month ago, she started acting like a completely different person. She was always late and she bullied the other girl scouts. She also stole. It got so bad that she decided to kick Raysel out of the group. Unfortunately, Raysel started her own business and started charging people for cookies. Somehow her cookies were selling like hot cakes. "Do you know how much money she made." Simon asked her. "Yes, I do. One thousand dollars." Each year, the amount goes up." "Did you talk to her parents?" Daniel said. She told them that she tried but she never got an answer. She even went to Raysel's house, still no answer. It was like Raysel's parents vanished. Simon asked her if they could check out Raysel's locker. The Troop leader said no, and that they should leave now. But Simon wasn't giving up. So they got the girl scouts involved. The girls tied up their Troop leader. With the girls watching her, Simon got the keys. He and Jonah started searching through the locker while Daniel, Jack, Zach and Corbyn went through the troop leader computer. Simon and Jonah found a bunch of stuff in Raysel's locker including her diary. They read through it and found out that Raysel has a crush on a guy named Severeano. They flipped through the pages and discovered that Raysel has been getting this feeling that someone has been watching her. Then they found a printed out email and saw something suspicious.

After that, Simon and Jonah went to see what the others found. Corbyn, Daniel, Zach and Jack learned that someone has been hacking into the troop leader's computer, stealing money from the girl scout foundation. Before they left, Why Don't We sung 'These Girls' to thank the Girl scouts. They came back to the hotel to confront Raysel causing her to run. Simon and the others went after her. She led them into the hall of mirrors, then she disappeared. "Where did she go?" Jack said. All they could hear was Raysel laughing. After that a message popped up on all the mirrors saying, **'You know the truth now. But will you be able to find the real Raysel before time runs out?'** Simon and the others got out of the hall of mirrors and wondered what happened to the real Raysel?

With Mallory, Simon, Nasser and Doyle done with their interviews, elsewhere me, AJ and Reed were on our way to Paramount Pictures to talk to Gerwazy Pooser. Unfortunately, getting in wasn't going to be that easy . When we arrived at Paramount Pictures, me and the others were surrounded by guards. "Can we help you?" I asked them. One of the guards told us that we don't have permission to come in Paramount Pictures. "Why?" Reed said, "because AJ is a jewel thief." "No he's not," I told him. "He's innocent." "Sorry, have a nice day." The guard said. "Well, there goes my career." AJ said. "We're not giving up yet." I told him. "So what's the plan?" Reed asked me. I went through The Cybernetic Falconieri Penzance Communicator and told AJ and Reed to follow me, we walked up to gate once again and I used some knock out gas on all the guards and we went inside. Our troubles were far from over. I came up with another idea after seeing a bunch of understudies getting costumes from a trailer. I pointed out to AJ and Reed how we're going to talk to Gerwazy Pooser a few minutes later, three mysterious guys were walking around seeing how movies and shows are made, the first guy was AJ! dressed as Zorro. He had the gloves, the mask and hat. The only thing that was missing was the horse. Reed used The Aristotelis Setser Suit and disguised himself as Captain America. And as for me, I used, my Aristotelis Setser Suit as well and disguised myself as a Magician. I had the hat, the cape and even a wand. So just call me Benny The Spectacular. AJ got his costume off one of the racks. We couldn't believe how good our costumes were. I couldn't believe how beautiful and amazing Paramount Pictures is. Then, we arrived at the studio where Gerwazy Pooser TV show films at, I thought it was cool that we were on the set of The Black Butterfly. AJ asked me was I a fan of the show. I told him I am, but I'm not a fan of the guy who plays the character. "Why?" Reed, asked me. I told him "You'll see." Anyway, The Black Butterfly is a show about a young boy named Ejiroghene who lives in a city called Sesto Hive City and attends Sesto Hive High. One day, he and his classmates were conducting an experiment. The Plaisance Entriken with their Professor. It was something that was supposed to change the world. Unfortunately, something went wrong and it caused an explosion. That mutated Gerwazy's character and half of his classmates. Ejiroghene became a mutant like bug that gave him different abilities, he can morph into any bug that he chooses, shoot out powerful energy balls, cast spells, enlarge his wings, has the power of antenna protrusion, darkness manipulation, and his costume comes with smoke bombs, explosive discs, and butterfly rangs. His professor was turned as well but he mutated into something dark and became The Black Sting and used his powers for evil. So The Black Butterfly and the others became a team and set out to protect the good citizens of Sesto Hive City over the seasons. The Black Butterfly and his friends fight The Black Sting as he tries to release a serum called The Mad Scent Game Bee that can turn people into Mutant bug monsters which are called The Amisquew Ortegon Physco, me and the others watched as the cast filmed a scene for an upcoming episode where The Black Butterfly and his team deal with The Black Sting, The Starless Bug Queen, Wasp Face, The Windy Bee and Doctor Toxic Tic Tock teaming up to take over the world. Anyway, the names of The Black Butterfly team mates are played by familiar faces. Sean Grandillo is Firefly Jackson, he can create a glow that is so powerful, it could possibly kill his attackers. He can fly, shoot out powerful glow bombs that can lead to powerful explosions depending on how big he makes them and he can shoot out a powerful glow ray from his eyes. Ashley Tisdale, The Pretty Bee, she has the powers to create powerful stings that can knock her foes out. Create honeycomb explosions and make powerful stingers that can do different things like paralysis. Make people fall asleep, turn people into stone and shoot out acid stingers. The Pretty Bee can also trap her foes in wax cocoons and make acid honey plus lava honey that can melt anything. Colton Haynes, The Skull Ant can duplicate himself. Body shedding, infestation, where he can take control of his enemies' bodies and minds, super strength, bring dead bugs back to life and used them as his minions to fight his foes. Callan Potter, The Heat Checked Beetle can produce manipulation fire, create portals, teleport, has dermal armor, can use his colors to attack his foes . Thermal resistance, meaning he can survive in extreme temperatures. Alex Whitehouse, Bee Bop has the power of invisible speed, electrical, can shoot out missiles, lasers, bombs, Bee Bop has the ability to turn into a swarm of bees and has the power of bulletproof durability and a poison generation. Can create a variety of poisons. Brandon Rowland, Blood Bite can absorb people's energy and blood, draining them. Create ticks called Blood Bite Mines where he can paralyze his foes and control them. And Bloodlessness, the power to have no Blood or other circulatory fluid and Enhanced Agility. Next, Zayne Emory, The Gethin Jacket. He's a yellow jacket who has the power of shapeshifting, telekinesis, burrowing. Which is the power to tunnel through the earth and Stinger Protrusion, the power to possess stingers. Plus The Gethin Jacket, has hypnotic vision. Thomas Kuc, Sand Tucker has the powers of high speed flight. Meaning he can fly at incredible speeds, wall crawling, enhanced agility, sandstorm creation, sand mimicry, enhanced reflexes, bone spike protrusion, force field generation and Golem Physiology. Austin Rhodes, The Cold Bee has the power of Molecular Deceleration, meaning he can slow down molecules of an organism and object and he has freeze Vision, Ice breath, Ice transmutation, Ice Magic, Ice Mimicry, Ice wall Generation, Cryoportation, meaning teleport via ice and Air Bomb Generation. Sebastian Croft, Bone Mantis powers Bone Bullet Projection, Bone Weaponry, Bone Manipulation and Osteokinetic Blade Construction, Sam Cushing! Fleeting Bite, powers Mouth Manifestation and Mouth Removal. Peter Bundic, The Shotgun Bug powers Gun Mimicry, Bulletproof Durability and Gun Destruction. Chandler Massey, The Hypnotic Mantid Storm Hopper powers

Hypnotic Pollen, Hypnotic Vision, Storm Embodiment, Storm Negation and Storm Manipulation. And last is. Matt Cornett, Hornet's Ploy, he can spit out stingers, has the power of Retractable Stinger, Molecular Immobilization, and the power of Stun attack, the power of Contaminant immunity, and Plasma Generation. As for Matt Bomer, The Black Sting, he has the power of Insect breath, meaning he can generate from within oneself insects. Insect like creatures and release them from his mouth. And he has the power of poison generation. And more anyway. They started filming the scene where Syrin. Peter Bundic, character crush finds The Rancho Sting, the lair and he tries to keep her from finding out his identity. And his friend's identity. However, me and the others couldn't believe who was playing Syrin, It was Mallory. The directors noticed that Syrin was being played by a different girl, but they went on ahead. and allowed it. Syrin tried to unmask The Shotgun Bug, but he stopped her by kissing on the lips. The two made out and Mallory was enjoying every moment of it. After they were done with the scene, the girl that usually plays Syrin was furious and told the directors that Mallory tied her up, causing them to call security. Mallory ran up to Callan, kissed him on the lips, then she quickly got out of there. Me and AJ and Reed just shook our heads, we walked over to Gerwazy who was flirting with the girl that plays Syrin. He told her no girl can resist a kiss from him. The girl fainted and I just rolled my eyes. We tried to ask him some questions but he was too busy texting on his phone, So I just took his phone out of his hands. "Hey, what's the big idea?" "Oh hey, AJ and Reed. Who is this guy? Some intern or assistant?" Gerwazy said. "What did you just call me." "Um Reed, why don't you take Benny over to the table where they serve food for the cast and crew while I talk to Gerwazy." AJ said. So, Reed and me went to the table and I put some germ x on my hands. Then, I ate some grapes. I knew Matt Cornett, Austin Rhodes, Peter Bundic, Zayne Emory, Matt Bomer, Brandon, Chandler, Sam Cushing, Callan Potter plus the others would never become friends with me. So, I kept my distance from them. But Sean Grandillo, Matt Bomer, Colton Haynes, Peter and Thomas Kuc came up to me and introduced themselves. I was really nervous to talk to them. However, Reed encouraged me to get to know them and he didn't leave my side. I became fast friends with Colton, Sean, Peter and Thomas. I couldn't believe that they liked me for me. Meanwhile, AJ was dealing with Gerwazy. "Geez, I think your friend hates me," Gerwazy said. "He doesn't hate you. He just doesn't care for your ways. Sometimes you can be a jerk." AJ said. "You can say that again." I told him. "Seriously, who is this guy?" "My name is Benny Breezy. I'm an Investigative Reporter. I'm here to interview you." "For what? Gerwazy said. He's here to clear my name." AJ said. "So please tell us what we need to know." "Okay, follow me into my trailer." Gerwazy said. Seeing how he didn't make a good first impression, he tried to make things right by signing some of his merchandise and he gave me some VIP passages to a private screening of The Black Butterfly. I just looked at him and started asking him questions about the day AJ was framed. Before we started, he wanted to know why I was dressed up like a magician. Why Reed was wearing a Captain America costume and why in the world AJ is dressed as Zorro. I told him first he tells us what we want to know, then we might explain why we're dressed like this. Gerwazy told us it was like any other morning. He got up early because he had a meeting. He brushed his teeth, took a shower, worked out and ate some breakfast. Later on, he had lunch with his parents. His parents are billionaires. His mother is a model and his father is one of the biggest movie directors in Hollywood. Unfortunately, his parents had some upsetting news that caused him to spend the rest of his day at The Show Mayor. AJ asked him did he see anything, unsunsal or suspicious. Gerwazy remembered seeing a creepy girl scout snooping through Stiles, the desk clerk's computer. When he said that, me, AJ and Reed looked at each other. "How come you didn't tell any of this to the police?" I asked him. "Why? It's not like she has anything to do with this." Gerwazy said. "Dude, she could be The Mad Ffraid Brat." Reed said. "Is that it?" I asked him. "Yeah! Pretty much. Also, I have nothing to do with this, I'm innocent." Gerwazy said. "Yeah, we'll see. Anyway, thank you for your time and bye," me and the others left the trailer. We were about to go find Mallory until Gerwazy stopped us. He told me there was something he wanted to ask me so I told him to go ahead. He asked me what do I know about my father. "This conversation is over.

Come on guys, let's go find Mallory." Gerwazy got in my way, "please this is important," Gerwazy told me, "why do you even care? Just leave me alone." Then he shouted out, "I think I'm your half brother." When he said that, I couldn't move, neither could AJ and Reed. They both looked at me, I turned around slowly, "what did you say?" "I'm your brother! Isn't your mother's name Conceicao?" "Yeah," "and your birthday is on Christmas." "Correct!" I told him. "And you have a twin sister." "Yeah I have, wait what? I don't have a twin sister." "Of course you do. Here's a picture of our dad holding you both." When he showed me that, I passed out. A few minutes later, I woke up. to find AJ, Gerwazy, Reed, Sean,, Brandon, Colton, Alex, Austin Rhodes, Zayne Emory, Peter, Matt, Thomas and Callan over me. They helped me up. I was shocked and I couldn't stop staring at my half brother. Our brotherly moment got interrupted after one of the security guards recognized me, AJ and Reed causing us to run, leaving Gerwazy and the others. He told Colton and the others to find me as they all split up. Me, AJ and Reed split up as well. Reed found himself on a Christmas set starring in a Christmas music video. As for AJ, he was rescuing a girl. Then the two made out. As for me, I was hiding on a set for a movie about a murder mystery weekend. Thankfully nobody was around. Then, I heard something. Whatever it was came closer and closer, I tried to make a run for it. "It's just me Benny! Take it easy." I looked and realized who it was. "Zayne! You nearly gave me a heart attack." "I'm sorry man. Are you okay?" Zayne, asked me. "I'm sure you wouldn't care." I told him. "You're wrong, of course I care. We're friends." "Yeah right, I doubt one of the coolest dude would be my friend. So excuse me, I have to go find my friend." "Can I ask you something?" Zayne asked me. "Sure, why not," I told him. "Why do you think me, Brandon, Matt, Austin Rhodes, Ashley, Alex and the others wouldn't want to be your friend?" "Why do you care?" I asked him. "Because that's the kind of person I am, I care about you, so please tell me." Zayne said . "Alright, I'll tell you," I said. "Celebrities only hang out with attractive people. Just like regular people they only care about looks and image, if you aren't good looking or cool, people want nothing to do with you. You either got it or you don't. Kindness is dead. It's so hard to believe that there are some good and genuine and kind people in this world. People just don't give me a chance. There were three people who I wanted to be friends with. The first one is a guy named Logan, Somebody I tried to become friends with, but he never gave me a chance. When he wasn't around his friends, he would speak to me. But when he's around them, he acts like a totally different person. I guess I wasn't cool enough or popular to be his friend so I gave up. Same goes to a jerk named Mack. I thought he was a nice person but I was wrong about him. People are mean but I don't care what him or his friends think about me because I am somebody . And the last one is Kyler, another jerk who never got to know me. I was wrong about him too, I feel like I have to be something I'm not in order to make friends and I'm just not okay with that. I want people to like me for me and show that they care about me. I don't know what I'm going to do without my friends. After we graduate, It's hard to make friends. I don't want to be someone else, that's why I think people like you, Luke and the others, also Pearce Joza, Luke Eich, Shaun Sipos, Austin North, Austin Butler, Raven Symone, Ty Wood, Nyle DiMarco, Keegan Allen, Grant Jordan, Myylo, Boman Martinez Reid, Ted Sutherland, Vinny Balbo, Timothy Granaderos, Tristin Mays, Danielle Panabaker, Tiera Skovbye, Elizabeth Lail and Miles Heizer will never give me a chance. So there you go." After telling Zayne why I don't believe, Zayne told me that I don't have to pretend to be something I'm not in order to be his friend and that I shouldn't worry or care what Logan, Kyler or Mack think. It's their loss. "I'm your friend Benny, whether you believe it or not. I want to be in your life." When he said that, I knew at that moment I made another friend. Then we left the set and started looking for Mallory. Unfortunately! Our search got a detour when some security guards found me. So I and Zayne gave them a chase they would never forget. First, we ran through a jungle set where Zayne was dressed as Tarzan and I was dressed as a Gorilla. Then we ran through a space set driving a moon rove. Next, was a cowboy set where me and Zayne were fighting security guards on top of a moving train. After that, we passed through a ninja set and a pirate set. Somehow we lost them when we ran through an army base set. Then we resumed our search for Mallory. We finally found her in the one place that could get all of us into some serious trouble, a celebrity trailer. So me and Zayne quickly went inside. "Oh hey Benny. Where have you been?" She asked me, then she started screaming when she saw who I was with. She also asked me why I was dressed up as a magician. I told her I'll explain it to her later and that we have to get out of here. No! She told me. "Have you completely lost your mind?" I asked her. "Do you guys know where we are at? We're in Ashley Tisdale's trailer." "Yeah we know, the same person whose luggage you haven't turned in yet." I told her. "Seriously?" Zayne said, "I shook my head." Suddenly Ashley Tisdale walked in causing me and Zayne Emory to join Mallory's scheme. Mallory disguised herself as a Hair Stylist and me and my bro were her assistants. Just when we thought everything was going to be fine, Mallory accidentally used pink and green hair dye, making Ashley's hair look crazy. She couldn't believe her hair stylist would do this to her. Then she realized that the hair stylist was Mallory. "You're the girl that has my suitcase and the same girl that's always tweeting me, Mallory Styles." After she said that, Mallory started panicking. She tried to explain but then she decided to jump through a glass window, shocking me. Zayne and Ashley. Thankfully Mallory was alright. "You could've used the door." I told her. Me and Zayne apologized, then we ran out of the trailer. Once again Mallory was missing, Finally AJ, Reed, Sean, Colton and the others caught up with us, and Gerwazy. I still couldn't believe that I'm related to one of the most famous stars in the world. I decided to give Gerwazy a chance. Things got ugly though when a few fans wanted some autographs from the cast of The Black Butterfly. While signing a autograph, a fan of Gerwazy asked him who I was. His response shocked me, AJ, Reed, Colton, Sean, Zayne, and the others. His response was "This is my assistant, Benny Breezy, he means nothing to me." When he said that, I pulled him to the side. "What was that?" I asked him . "Why didn't you tell them the truth?" "Look bro, I'm sorry. But I have a reputation. If the world found out that I have a long lost half brother who's not famous, it could destroy my career. No offense." "Why should I be offended just because my half brother is ashamed to be around me." "Wait, that's not what I meant" Gerwazy said. "Can't we talk about this?" No. I, walked over to Sean, Zayne,

Colton, and the others and gave them each A Cybernetic Falconieri Penzance Communicator. Then, I told AJ and Reed to find Mallory, but they were more concerned about me. Gerwazy tried to stop me but I told him he's a jerk and that he only cares about his looks, body, fame and following the crowd. I grabbed a smoke ball that comes with my magician costume and disappeared without a trace. After the smoke led up, Gerwazy found AJ and the others looking at him. "Do y'all have a problem?" Gerwazy asked them. "Yeah! It's you." AJ said. "How could you treat Benny like that." "You don't understand," Gerwazy said. "Actually I do understand. Benny was right about you." AJ said. "Stay away from Benny," Reed told Gerwazy. Then he and AJ left Paramount Pictures along with Zayne, Sean, Colton, Austin Rhodes, Brandon, Peter, Matt, Chandler, Thomas, Sam, Sebastian, and Alex. They couldn't believe what Gerwazy did.

Meanwhile, after a long day, I just wanted to go to bed. I just couldn't believe that I have a twin and a half brother who's self absorbed. I wonder why my family kept this secret from me. Before I got in the elevator, Stiles got my attention. He told me that someone sent me a fax. So when I checked who the fax was from, I got a little aggravated. It was from Mr. Zed. He wanted to know if we had cleared AJ's name yet. "Are you okay man?" Stiles asked me. I told him that it's been a long and rough day. He also told me that Chef Acer wanted me to pick up a bag from Poppa Xathieur. "Who is that?" I asked him. He told me Poppa Xathieur, is the hotel chef and that I can find him in The Show Mayor Restaurant. So as I made my way to the restaurant, I called Shawn, asking him can he meet me at The Big Top Show Mayor. He told me he'll be there in five minutes. After I was done talking to him, I went into the restaurant and it was nice. Unfortunately, there weren't any customers. Shocking me because The Show Mayor is a wonderful place and you would think the restaurant would be crowded with people. Then I met a waitress named Kimbriella. I told her that I'm here to pick up a package. So she went in the back to get it, then a familiar face came into the restaurant and I couldn't believe who it was. The one and only Mitchell Hoog. I just kept my distance away from him because I doubted Mitchell would become my friend. But to my surprise, he tried to get to know me so I told him a little about myself and that I'm an Investigative Reporter who's trying to clear AJ's name. But after the texts I got from my friends, I started to wonder can we defeat this person. I showed Mitchell the text messages that my friends sent me. Then Kimbriella came out of the kitchen and when she saw who I was with, she fainted, a few minutes later she woke up and found me and Mitchell standing over her. She ran back into the kitchen and didn't look bad. I told Mitchell that I'll be right back and went in the kitchen to check on Kimbriella. I found her eating some cookie dough, crying her eyes out while she looked at a picture of Mitchell. "If you only knew how I feel about you." Kimbriella said. "You're in love with him, aren't you?" I asked her, "yes Benny." "Then why are you hiding from him? Just tell him how you feel," "look I know you're new to LA, but you don't know anything about celebrity boys. Just look at me, do you think a guy like that would fall for a waitress? Don't get me wrong, I love my job and my father. But sometimes I wonder how my life would be if I was rich and famous. Then maybe guys like Mitchell Hoog might like me," Kimbriella said. I grabbed her hand and told her that being honest and true to yourself is more important than pretending to be something you're not. After that, we went back to the front. "Is everything okay?" Mitchell asked us. I told him yeah, and that Kimbriella has something important to tell him. "Alright," Mitchell said with a smile. However, Kimbriella had a hard time bringing the words out. "Remember to let it come from your heart. You got this." I told her, Kimbriella was so nervous that she decided to lie. "I'm in a play. Wait what?" I asked her, "a play?" Mitchell said. "Yes, it's called *Agent Styles*. It was written by a girl named Mallory Styles," she told Mitchell she was hoping that he would help her. Rehearse, after she said that, I grabbed the package and left. Kimbriella tried to talk to me but I didn't want to hear it. I was so mad, Mitchell stopped me and asked me why I was so upset. I just ignored him and left the restaurant. Then I got in an elevator. Just when I thought this day couldn't get any worse, the elevator suddenly stopped and I heard some noise. Someone was on top of the elevator. I tried to push the emergency button but for some reason it wasn't working. Then I sent out an emergency signal to Shawn, hoping he got it. Whoever was on top of the elevator was cutting the cable causing me to panic. I was so scared that I started shooting lasers using The Cybernetic Falconieri Penzance Communicator and I managed to hit the person that was trying to kill me. Unfortunately, the person didn't give up and continued to cut the cable. Just when I thought all was lost, Shawn came to the rescue, using The Anselmi Arrie Speed Flies, he knocked out the masked person. Then he came into the elevator. I was so happy to see my bud and he was relieved that I was alright. Suddenly a message popped up from The Mad Ffraid Brat saying, '**Mind your own business**.' Me and Shawn got out of there and watched as the elevator dropped. I was still trying to catch my breath and couldn't believe that The Mad Ffraid Brat almost killed me. Shawn told me that I'm safe now and we started walking. Then, I got a text message from Simon telling me that he and the others can't find Mallory. So me and Shawn asked some of the guests if they had seen her. Just when we were about to give up, we saw a young girl wearing a wedding dress and went over to her to see if she has seen our wacky friend. We both got concerned when we saw who the bride was. It was Mallory. "What are you doing?" I asked her. "And why are you wearing that?" Shawn said. "Well guys, you know how we keep meeting celebrities in this elevator." Mallory said. "Yeah! I told her." "Well, I think this elevator is magical." When she said that, me and Shawn looked at each other. "Are you kidding me?" We're in Los Angeles at an amazing hotel that's run by a snobby family. This isn't Disney world." I told her. "Think about it though, we met Luke Korns. You met Jack Maynard and Chris Salvatore, and I made out with Ruel," Mallory said. "Wait! You what?" I asked her. "Oh nothing." Mallory said, "well can you at least tell us why you're dressed as a Bride?" Shawn said. "Mallory looked into her bag and gave me and Shawn a script that she wrote." I asked her did she give one of these to a girl named Kimbriella. She shook her head no and told me that she had. Stiles pass them out hoping that she'll get noticed by some famous Hollywood Director. She told us that in her script, she marries her crush. "And who exactly are you supposed to marry?" I asked her. Mallory started searching through her bag again and gave us some book, and boy it was heavy. "What is this?" I asked her. "I call it my 6 years plan, it's a scrapbook of all my future husbands. The tops name are Devin Hayes, Luke Korns, Owen Teague, Sebastian Croft, Tal Fishman, Harris Dickinson, David Mazouz, Drake Bell, Mark Thomas, Josh Beauchamp, Noah Urrea, Timothy Granaderos, Logan Shroyer, Ruel, Cameron Dallas, Jack Johnson, Jack Gilinsky, Collins Key, Devan Key, Milo Manheim, Gavin Leatherwood, Cody Linley and Jonah Marais." "You have really thought this through." I told her. "Of course, I am a Styles remember." I just couldn't believe Mallory. As for Shawn, he was shocked. Then she asked me, "Are there any celebrities I want to meet and become friends with." I looked at her and Shawn and told them.

"Tom Holland, Adam Hagenbuch, Kat Graham, Alex Neustaedter, Shane Coffey, Levi Miller, Brandon Routh, Adam DiMarco, Austin P. McKenzie, Luke Mullen, Houston Stevenson, Greg Hovanessian, Steven Strait and Rhys Kosakowski would never in this lifetime give me a chance. People take one look at me and instantly judge me so why should I pretend that any of these celebrities would want to be friends with me. I'm just a loser," when I said that, Shawn hit me in the back of my head. "What was that for?" I asked him. "For calling yourself a loser. You are an amazing person and if people can't see that then it's their loss. You are my friend and brother for life and I never want to hear you say that again." Shawn told me, I was shocked and told him thanks. Then, Mallory gave me a hug and told me I'm one of a kind. Then she walked over to the elevator. "Um what are you doing?" I asked her. "Just watch." So, me and Shawn watched as Mallory tapped her feet and started making a wish. "Um, Mallory, we're not from Kansas and this isn't Oz." "Shh, just trust me." She said. After Mallory was done making her wish, the elevator came up. A different elevator since the other one got destroyed thanks to The Mad Ffraid Brat, inside was another familiar face. Mallory grabbed me and Shawn and we got in the elevator with the one and only Logan Shroyer who was wearing a tuxedo. He told us that someone left him a tuxedo along with one of Mallory's scripts. At first I was going to ask her how in the world did she find out that he's staying at The Show Mayor. Then I changed my mind because I didn't want a headache. Logan tried to get to know me

71

but I knew he wouldn't become my friend so I just kept to myself. Then Mallory gave me a bible and gave Shawn some wedding rings. She also told Logan to read his line. She wanted all of us to act out her play. I was the minister. Shawn was the best man and Mallory and Logan were the couple. To our surprise though, the rings looked real. Anyway, Mallory told me to hurry up so she can finally kiss Logan, "I announce you husband and wife. You may kiss your bride." I told them after I said that. Mallory grabbed Logan and started kissing him. Me and Shawn played kiss on my list.

Unfortunately, Mallory made out with Logan for ten hours. Then, when she was done kissing him, I saw Mallory pull out some list. So after we finally got out of the elevator, I asked Mallory what is that list for. She told me and Shawn and Logan that's her Kiss Printes List. A list of some of the celebrities guys she always dreamed of kissing. Me and the others read the list and boy it was long. I just rolled my eyes. Okay then, well, me and Shawn have to go help Aunt Fanny interview the staff of The Show Mayor. "Can we come?" I looked at Logan and told Mallory fine, then before we left, Mallory tapped her feet again, making me and Shawn worried, we watched as the elevator came up and this time two famous people were in the elevator, Mark Thomas and Hunter Rowland. Mallory started screaming because she's a huge fan. She got to know them, while I kept my distance. Once again because I knew Mark Thomas, and especially Hunter Rowland would never become my friend. Anyway, Mallory asked me could they come too. I looked at Shawn and told her sure. I stormed off and Shawn caught up with me trying to calm me down. While Hunter tries to catch up with me and Shawn, Mallory couldn't stop staring at Mark and then she made out with him. Anyway, Shawn could tell that I was really upset and knew something else was on my mind. I almost told him about the discovery of my twin sister until we got to The Big Top Show Mayor, when we got there, Aunt Fanny was furious. "I have five questions to ask you, number one, why are you dressed like a magician? Number 2, is that Shawn Mendes? Number 3, why is Mallory wearing a wedding dress? Number 4 who are those other guys? And number 5, what took y'all so long?" Aunt Fanny asked me. "Sorry, we ran into some problems and we had to wait until Mallory's wedding was over. She decided to make out with Logan Shroyer for ten hours. Anyway! We're here now. So where are the suspects?" I asked her, she blew a whistle and told them to come out here. " Everybody, I would like you to meet my nephew Benny Breezy. An Investigative Reporter and his friends Mallory, Shawn, Logan, Hunter and Mark. They would like to ask you a few questions about the day AJ was framed. So let's get this over with."

Before we got started interviewing the staff, AJ showed up. He asked me was I alright, but I didn't answer him. I was just mad and Shawn could tell I was upset. So, me, AJ, Mallory, Shawn, Logan, Mark, Hunter and Aunt Fanny interviewed the first suspect, a guy named Hesed, a Human cannonball. He told us that all he can remember is going to the hospital. After he crashed into a few of The Stilt Walkers, thinking this is his chance to redeem himself, Hesed decided to put on a show for me and the others. "I don't think this is a good idea." AJ said. "Of course it's a good idea" Hesed said. I got this, Hesed told him. Anyway, here I go. Me and the others had a bad feeling about this. So when Hesed got into the cannonball, he thought he would land on the horizontal net. Unfortunately he went straight through the roof and landed in a garbage can. The good news is that he was unharmed. Next was Knollys, a Human Statue who didn't notice anything unusual going on that day. We also met Andorra whose act is hand walking. Sewek a Martial arts specialist, Xever does a Block Balancing Act, Orenthal a Strong man, Urjasz an Acrobatic Gymnasic and Kelila, a Contortionist. Then we met Husayn and Jelica, a married couple and Trapeze Artists. Heroot, a Motorcycle Stunt Artist who rides in the globe of death. So far we had nothing. There were sixteen suspects left and we tried to speed the process up because I was tired, and so was Mallory, AJ, Aunt Fanny, Shawn Mendes, Logan, Hunter and Mark. The next suspect was Ouray, whose act was Trick Riding. Then a Mime named Tullio. We can skip him. Mimes don't talk. Mallory said Tullio tried to act out what he wanted to tell us but we still couldn't understand him. So, he made a map out of balloons and wrote a message on it saying Deveral was here that day and that he wasn't alone. "Now we're getting somewhere." I said, "who was he with?" Hunter asked him. Tullio looked at the security cameras and started getting nervous. "Are you okay?" Mark asked him, He shook his head and started shaking. Then, he made a paper airplane and threw it to us. Me and Shawn and the others opened it up and read the message. This is what the message said. **Beware, the cameras.** After reading the message, Tullio ran. "What, does this mean?" AJ asked me. "It means that The Mad Ffraid Brat could be watching us." I told him. Next on the list was Edvardas. Unfortunately, he didn't show up, making me suspicious. Xidorn, one of The Stilt Walkers was the next one to be interviewed and Mallory started flirting with him. I think she has a crush on him. Anyway, he told us that day Deveral came to The Show Mayor. But before he could go on, he noticed two guys in the back watching him, he told us he had to go now and quickly got off the stage. "Who are those guys?" AJ asked me. I told him I don't know. Then, Mr. Hildefuns was next. He made a grand entrance. We asked him what does he remember about that day. Mr. Hildefuns knew that someone was watching so he put handkerchiefs on all the cameras, then he took some of the curtains from the stage and tied the guys up and threw them out of The Big Top Show Mayor. After that, he started levitation and put on a show for us using his hands to make Shadow Puppets and he turned the lights off. This is what he told us while planning for the show. He heard Deveral talking to someone. Whoever it was didn't sound too happy. He assumes it was one of his co workers but he doesn't know who. So that means one of The Show Mayor staff members is working with Deveral. The question is who. Mr. Hildefuns disappeared after that. Stiles and Telmo were next but they weren't happy being accused of being suspects and I wasn't comfortable asking them questions. So AJ and the others did it for me. Stiles told us that day Mr. Stumbo was really demanding and treated everybody like they were nothing. Also, Stiles went into Deveral's room. He told me and the others that Deveral and his brother both have rooms at The Show Mayor and that Stiles found a suspicious bag in Deveral's room. But before he had a chance to see what was inside, Deveral came into the room and threatened him. When he said that, me, AJ, Shawn, Mallory, Hunter, Mark, Logan, Aunt Fanny and Telmo could see the fear in Stile's eyes. "Are you okay?" I asked him, Stiles shook his head.

Then it was Telmo's turn. He also had a confrontation with Deveral after accidentally running into him while carrying some bags for a guest. Telmo threw us a key that Deveral dropped. The initial on the key was 'N J.' The next suspect was a maid named Vigdess. Realizing that this is getting dangerous, Vigdess walked up to us and gave us a bag. Then she left. So we opened it up and found a blue glove, inside the glove was a receipt from a store called Iron Brave, Mark looked it up and told us that Iron Brave is a costume store not far from The Show Mayor. Badaidra, a Puppetry was next, we thought we had nothing to worry about, but we were wrong. When she came onto the stage, she had a chest with her, and decided to put on a show. Unfortunately, the puppets looked like me, AJ, Mallory, Simon, Nasser, Doyle, Aunt Fanny and Leonel. But we weren't the only ones. She also had puppets of Shawn, Zayne, Colton and the others, creeping us out a little. So after introducing the puppets, she started the show. Once upon a time there was. An investigative Reporter who didn't mind his own business and before she could go on I stopped her, "that's enough, you are definitely a suspect. Stay away from me and my friends." I told her. After that, I used The Cybernetic Falconieri Penzance Communicator and destroyed those creepy puppets and she was furious. "You haven't seen the last of me and you better watch your back". Badaidra shouted out. Me and the others quickly wrote her name down. We wondered could she be The Mad Ffraid Brat or a minion. So a guy named Panini and his co-star Andi, who are Physical Actors came onto the stage. Panini said nothing interesting happened that day. Just another day of acting. As for Andi, she had some information for us but wouldn't tell us unless Shawn performs a few songs for her. Seeing how she's a big fan and knowing how important this is, he went on stage and started performing. First he sung Stitches. Then he sung Treat You Better, Mercy, Nervous, In My Blood, There's Nothing Holding Me Back and Believe. After he was done, Andi couldn't stop staring at Shawn until Mallory snapped her fingers. " hey". Mallory, shouted out. "What?" Andi said. "You told me and my friends you know something. So tell us." Mallory said. "Oh, I just told you that in order to get Shawn to sing a few songs for me." "That's all, are you kidding me?" I asked her. "Sorry." Andi said. Then she quickly kissed Hunter on the lips and ran towards the exit. Me, Shawn, AJ and the others couldn't believe this. Mallory was furious. She grabbed a custard pie from one of the clowns and threw it at Andi before she could reach the exit. "Thank you," Panini said. He also apologized for his co star's behavior. "I didn't know Mallory could throw that hard." AJ told me. I told him Mallory can do almost anything.

Our next suspect was an Animal Trainer named Jumoke. She introduced herself. Then she introduced us to the animals of the show. The first animal was an elephant named Diot. He gave me, AJ, Shawn, Logan, and Mallory a ride while Hunter, Mark and Aunt Fanny rode an elephant named Nazy, Diot's sister. after that we met six Chimpanzees, Matita, Koppel, Emi, Anju, Chip and Tripp. And we also met Julka, A female Capuchin Monkey, Lazer, a black and white capuchin Monkey. So while Jumoke tells us what she remembers about that day, me, AJ, Shawn, Logan, Mark and Hunter were holding the monkeys and Mallory was on Diot. Jumoke told us that usually nothing goes wrong at The Big Top Show Mayor, but that day Tiriro, a tiger, started acting aggressively. So, Mr. Stumbo had to use a tranquilizer. Tiriro's eyes were black. The animal doctor couldn't figure out why this was happening. Unfortunately it got worse because the same thing happened to her other animals. Brio a bear, Burly a lion and Caisi a seal, who are missing and the rest of her animals started acting aggressive and became very dangerous. Mr. Accerly Jamison decided to take them out of the show until further notice. Jumoke made it clear to us that she loves her animals and that she didn't frame AJ. Tears started coming from her eyes. I told her we're going to find out what happened to her animals and get them back in the show. Before she left, she introduced us to Serio, a parrot who took a disliking to Mallory. Chef Xathieur was next. He told me and the others that Deveral came to the restaurant drunk and started bothering his customers. Then he took money out of the register and when Chef Xathieur tried to stop him, Deveral threatened to tell his father on him and promised to ruined his career. He knew he couldn't do anything because Mr. Accerly Jamison would believe his own devil son over his employees. Nobody ever stands up for us. It's a sad life, Chef Xathieur said. We felt sorry for how Chef Xathieur and the rest of the employees are treated. He apologized for his daughter for not being here. Then we met Terentilo, a Knife Thrower, Contant a Fire Breather and Montagew, A snake charmer. These three were creeping us out. The first one said he doesn't know anything and started laughing. As for the fire breather, he started breathing fire and escaped with Terentilo, leaving Montagew who told us that we're wasting our time and left. Now we had some new suspects. The only ones left were The Ptarmigan Seissylt Clowns. For some reason they were missing, so Stiles left and went to go find them. Then Mallory told us we have one more suspect. "Who?" Hunter said. "Aunt Fanny," when Mallory said that, Aunt Fanny cut her eyes at her and couldn't believe this. "The only thing I did that day was perform as usual, nothing else. Sorry to burst your bubble." I couldn't stop apologizing but Aunt Fanny told me that it wasn't my fault.

Then Stiles came back. He was out of breath. He told us some shocking news. The Ptarmigan Seissylt Clowns have been arrested, but he didn't know why. So, me, AJ, Shawn, Logan and Mallory went to investigate while Mark, Hunter and Aunt Fanny used the balloon map that Tullio made and see where it leads. Aunt Fanny made sure the coast was clear and told Mark and Hunter to come on. Her, Hunter and Mark followed the map and discovered that the map leads to The Show Mayor safe where they protect valuable possessions of the guests and some have a safe deposit box. But the vault was locked and they had no idea how they would get in there. Meanwhile, me, AJ, Shawn, Mallory and Logan were in a waiting room waiting for Seissylt, Publio, Placydo, Nazzareno and Tripta. However, when they came into the waiting room, Seissylt wasn't with them and Tripta couldn't stop crying. She was so scared I asked her what happened. Tripta told me, Mallory, AJ, Logan and Shawn that they have been accused of helping AJ steal the Katana sword that's covered with diamonds and rubies. "And where is it from?" AJ asked her. "The Diamond Museum Amsterdam," Tripta said . "I never stole The Katana Sword." AJ said. "Well, they think we're accomplices" Nazzareno said. "How did this happen?" I asked them. Placydo told us the cops got a call from an anonymous person and found the Katana sword in our dressing room. "What happened to

Seissylt?" Mallory said. The Ptarmigan Seissylt Clowns looked at each other and told me and the others that Seissylt started acting strange and got into a fight with one of the cops. Now he's in the hospital. Mallory couldn't believe this. Suddenly, a mysterious guard came into the room. He handed me a box and then he left. I took my time and opened the box. Inside was a burner phone shocking me and the others. After I took it out, the phone started ringing. "Hello?" I said. I couldn't believe who it was, Mr. Thersander, he warned me that Seissylt is in terrible danger. So, me, AJ and the others got in the car and rushed to the hospital. Meanwhile, Aunt Fanny and the others were still trying to find a way to get inside. Aggravated that they can't get in because they don't know the password, Aunt Fanny decided to use the Valvoline Prune Breath and melted the door down, shocking Mark and Hunter. Then they went inside. They had no idea what they were looking for until Hunter found a deposit box with Grand Dunixi Jamison's name on it. So he, Mark, and Aunt Fanny opened it up and found a key inside of it along with a picture of some guy named Fuji. Written on the back of the card was a room number, Room 5 B 12. After that, they went looking for the room. Unfortunately they couldn't find the room, just a book shelf, or so they thought. Mark was curious about the book shelf. and grabbed one of the books. When he did, it opened up. Behind it was a room. Aunt Fanny used the key and they went inside and couldn't believe what was inside. Aunt Fanny, Hunter and Mark learned whoever Fuji is, he is a hoarder, there were newspapers stacked on top of each other along with plastic bottles and more. Aunt Fanny, Hunter and Mark started searching. They found several pictures of Fuji and wondered what happened to him and why somebody would hide his room. As they searched, Mark, found what they were looking for. An old reel to reel tape recorder along with an audio reel.

Elsewhere, Me, AJ, Mallory, Shawn and Logan were arriving at the hospital. Shawn stayed in the car. He was our look out while me and the others went inside. The nurse told us we couldn't see him because we're not family and she wouldn't tell us how he was doing, causing me to take action. I used the Falconieri Penzance Communicator and used knock out gas on her. After I did, AJ and Mallory went to check on him while me and Logan checked Seissylt's file. I was the look out and Logan searched through the nurse's computer and found some shocking news. I told him somebody was coming so he printed out a copy of Seissylt's file. Then we hid in an empty room. "You're never going to believe this." Logan told me. "What?" I asked him. He showed me the file and told me that Seissylt was drugged with Scopolamine, one of the most dangerous drugs in the world. It's a drug that turns people into complete zombies and blocks memories from forming. It's also known as Devil's Breath. "It sounds awful." "It is." Logan told me. After the coast was clear, we joined the others. Unfortunately Seissylt wasn't his self. He couldn't remember anything. "What's wrong with him?" AJ asked us. We told him and Mallory that somebody drugged Seissylt. Logan also told me and the others that even when the drug wears off, victims have no memory as to what happened and that not only can it wipe a person's memory, it also eliminates free will and that it's made from A Borrachero Tree which blooms with deceptively beautiful white and yellow flowers. Mallory couldn't believe that someone would do this to Seissylt. We wondered did he see something that he wasn't supposed to see. Things continued to get worse after Shawn warned us that four guys with guns were coming in the hospital. "What are we going to do?" Mallory asked me. I looked at Seissylt and could tell how afraid he was. With so little time, I called Leonel using the Falconieri Penzance Communicator and asked him is there any way he can teleport us to Aunt Fanny's penthouse. He told us that he can but he can only teleport three people due to the power of his machine. With Seissylt's life in danger, I told Logan and Mallory to go with Seissylt and keep him safe. Logan didn't want to leave me behind and called me his friend, shocking me, he told AJ he could go instead. But AJ didn't want to leave me behind either. With time running out, I told Leonel to start the machine and to hurry. So he quickly started the machine and Logan told me and the others to be careful. Then, he, Mallory and Seissylt teleported out of there. When they did, me and AJ hid. Whoever those guys were, stormed in and started shooting. Unfortunately, when they discovered that Seissylt got away, they were furious. I was quite scared but AJ told me that everything will be okay. He used his Cybernetic Falconieri Penzance

Communicator to create a distraction so we could get out of there. But one of the guys noticed me, causing me to use my Cybernetic Falconieri Penzance Communicator, creating a wall made out of spider web, giving me and AJ time to escape. However we discovered those guys weren't alone. AJ broke one of the windows and told me to jump. I asked him is he crazy. We were up way too high. He told me to trust him. I closed my eyes and we both jumped. Then, he shot out an industrial stunt mat out of his Cybernetic Falconieri Penzance Communicator and we landed safely. We couldn't stop laughing. Shawn was happy to see us and he mashed the pedal.

While we drove back to The Show Mayor, Mark called me telling me that he, Aunt Fanny and Hunter have found something. I told him we're on our way back. Then I sent out an emergency text message to everybody, telling them to come to Aunt Fanny's penthouse.

CHAPTER SIX

INVESTIGATING THE JAMISON MANSION

After getting back to The Show Mayor, Chris Salvatore and the others were waiting for us. Aunt Fanny made sure I was alright shocking me and my friends. So we all gathered around and listened to The reel to reel tape recorder on the video. We learned That Grand Dunixi Jamison has a brother named Esdras and he kept saying," I killed my brother " and that was the end of the tape. "Wait, Grand Dunixi Jamison has a brother?" Aunt Fanny said. Wondering why the Jamison Family would keep this a secret from the world, Chris decided to go online and found out that Grand Dunixi Jamison was accused of killing someone but they never mentioned a name and kept the details classified. After discovering the existence of another Jamison, we went over everything that we have found out. So far we knew that Raysel and Orssa are definitely suspects. And Badaidra, Conant, Terentilo, Edvardas, Mr. Accerly Jamison and Montagew, especially Deveral. Also someone is pretending to be Raysel and the real Raysel need our help. "But how are we supposed to find her." Simon asked me. We couldn't believe how crazy things were getting dealing with The Mad Ffraid Brat who has a lot of helpers. Now there's a kidnapping involved. AJ has been accused of another crime and The Ptarmigan Seissylt Clowns have been arrested and accused of being accomplices to the second crime. Seissylt was drugged and almost killed, Grand Dunixi Jamison has a brother who he might have killed and The Mad Ffraid Brat attacked us today. One by one I told the others what happened in the elevator and they couldn't believe how dangerous this person is. Anyway, Leonel couldn't find anything about Deveral making us more suspicious about Deveral. After the day we all had, I told everybody we're going to The Jamison Mansion to find any evidence that could clear AJ's name. Seissylt wanted to come too but he still wasn't feeling good and I knew he couldn't be left alone. Not with The Mad Ffraid Brat around. So I asked Leonel to stay with him and told him to keep Seissylt safe. I also asked him did he have any vehicles that we could all fit in. He called Penzance Frisco and she sent over a bus called The Simplicius Transito. He told me and the others to go to the window. So when we did, we were all impressed. Leonel told us that The Simplicius Transito has 18 seats, rockets, can shoot torpedoes, shoot miniature bombs, fly, it has a force field, fire launchers, seat ejectors, auto pilot, thrusters, laser turret, can shoot out a sticky foam that can trap people. It also comes with a grappling hook, escape pods and The Simplicius Transito can morph into a train, a boat, a air balloon, a house, a blimp and a spaceship. Leonel also introduced us to his spaceship, Stranger Red! And it has a Plasma cannon, it has the ability to turn invisible, shrink, has a freeze ray, seat ejectors, auto pilot, torpedoes, escape pods and it can regenerate itself. After showing us The Simplicius Transito and Stranger Red, we changed into some black clothes and grabbed some skully hats. Before we left, worried what The Mad Ffraid Brat might do next, Mallory grabbed Amarr by the shirt and started making out with him. Knowing how long it took her to make out with Logan, I told the others to come on.

Then Gerwazy popped up, he wanted to talk but I didn't want anything to do with him. I told him if he wants to come with us, then put on these black clothes and a skully hat. After he did, he followed the others while they got on The Simplicius Transito and some got on Stranger Red, AJ wanted to talk to me. He asked me if I was okay and he asked me did I tell the others. I told him not yet. He told me the others should know. "Know what?" Shawn said, "I'll let you tell him." AJ said as he joined the others. "Tell me what?" Shawn asked me. "It's not important." I told him. "Yes it is, something happened today and it really upset you. So tell me bro. I'm not leaving this spot until you tell me." Shawn said. "Alright bro, today I found out that Gerwazy Pooser is my half brother." "That's great news, isn't it?" Shawn asked me. "At first,

I had mixed feelings about it. But then, I decided to give him a chance which was a huge mistake. Gerwazy doesn't want his fans or the world to know that he has a half brother who's not famous. He's afraid it might kill his career." "I'm sorry bro. I didn't know." "Oh, there's more. I have a twin sister." "Wait what?" "That's right bro." "What's her name?" I don't know. "Where is she?" "I don't even know that. I just feel lost bro, I'm sorry I didn't tell you." "It's just you thought I wouldn't care right? What would give you that idea?" "I don't know, I guess because of all the people who have ever hurt me and everything I have been through, I'm just afraid to let people in." "Bro, I will always be there for you. And you can talk to me about anything and trust me. Remember, bro's for life." "Thanks bro," "anytime, and don't let Gerwazy bring you down. Never let somebody make you feel like you have to change in order to be in their life. Always stay true to yourself and you will find your twin sister." After talking to Shawn, I felt better and we got on the bus. Shawn was in the driver seat, I sat next to AJ, Mallory and Logan sat together. So did Grant & Luke, Amarr & Nasser, Doyle & Mitchell, Zayne & Simon, Lucy & Ashley, Ruel & Reed, Colton & Antoni, Mark & Hunter, Matt & Callan, Alex & Sean, Jack Maynard, Gerwazy & Brandon and Aunt Fanny and Porfirio. As for Why Don't We, Chris, Matt Bomer, Sebastian, Austin Rhodes, Peter, Chandler and Thomas Kuc, they were in Stranger Red. As we drove to The Jamison Mansion and the others flew, Brandon kept staring at Gerwazy. "Do you have a problem?" Gerwazy said. "Yes I do, I want to know when are you going to apologize to Benny?" "Why should I?" Gerwazy said. "You know what, I have known you for a long time and I can honestly say you are a selfish person who will never change. All you care about are your looks, fame and wealth. You will never get far in life if you continue to act like you're better than everybody else. Remember, the world doesn't revolved around you." "What, do you want me to do? Benny doesn't want to be around me. He rather talk to AJ, Shawn, Zayne and the others." "That's because Shawn and the others are like big brothers to him. And they didn't judge him when they first met him. Unlike you telling your half brother your career would be finished if the world found out that you have a long lost half brother who's not famous. You made him feel like you're ashamed to call him your brother. You need to make this right." Brandon said. "Remember. never be too busy to meet someone new. You made a lousy first impression," "so what should I do?" Gerwazy said. "Get to know him, let him know you want to be in his life. You just found him and if you aren't careful enough, you're going to lose him forever." Brandon said.

An hour later, we arrived at The Jamison Mansion. Aunt Fanny and Porfirio stayed on the bus. They were our look out. Aunt Fanny grabbed my hand and told me to be careful. Then we walked up to the gate. At first we thought we could go over the gate, but when Doyle tried, he was executed, scaring all of us. Me and the others ran to his side wondering if he was okay. Suddenly he jumped up, "woo, that was awesome." Doyle said. Me and Nasser looked at each other and told the others he's fine, "so we can't get over the fence because it's electric, rich people." Mallory, said. "What do we do now?" Callan asked me. I thought to myself, and then I looked at AJ and Doyle's shoes. "That's how were getting in. Okay new plan, instead of going over the fence, we're going over the brick wall. AJ and Doyle will fly us over one by one." So AJ flew Mallory over first, and Doyle flew over Nasser. AJ took me over next. Unfortunately thinking that this is taking too long, Doyle did something stupid and grabbed ten of AJ's Aigeos Juppar jawbreakers and threw them at the wall. "duck ", Doyle shouted out. The explosion was big, half of the wall was gone. "Have you lost your mind?" Simon asked him. "What? That was more easier." Doyle said. "Bro do you have any idea what could happen to all of us if someone heard that explosion." Nasser said. "Wait, what do you mean?" Doyle said. Suddenly, several security guards surrounded us. "Now do you get it?" Mallory said. Me and the others waited in the front room while one of the security guards went to get somebody. I was so worried that it could be Mr. Accerly Jamison or Deveral. The guard came back with someone, however, it wasn't who we thought it was going to be. The guy walked over to us and offered us some soda, shocking me and the others. The guy introduced himself. "Hi, my name is Sollie Jamison." To our surprise, he wasn't mean or nasty. In fact he seemed like a decent and nice guy. He just wanted to know why we were trying to break in.

We told him everything that we have been through and that his brother could be working with The Mad Ffraid Brat. When we told him that, Sollie knew that he could trust us. Sollie told us when he and Deveral were kids, Deveral always had it out for him and that he always has something up his sleeve. Our conversation got cut short when the door bell rang. So Docherty, The Jamison Family Butler opened the door. But nobody was there, just a package. Docherty told me the package was for me because it had my name on it. So I opened it up and found 30 small maps of The Jamison Family mansion. The maps revealed all their hiding places. Sollie couldn't believe this and wanted to join our gang. I told him welcome to the team.

We all split up. Ruel, Gerwazy and Austin Rhodes went to search Deveral's room. Simon and Doyle went to the attic, Nasser the Conservatory. Why Don't We the Library, Mitchell the Courtyard. Alex the guest house. Amarr the Home Theatre. Sollie the study. Reed the basement. Sean will check the horse stable and the infinity pool. Matt the tree house. Callan the Jamison Family maze. Sebastian will check. Mr. and Mrs. Jamison's bedroom. Zayne the garage. Chandler the trophy room. Lucy and Ashley the Spa. Antoni Porowski the allroom, AJ the wine cellar. Grant the indoor swimming pool. Mark the bunker. Hunter the game room. Austin P. McKenzie the Sound Studio. Peter the 1st bathroom in the mansion. Logan the north wing. Colton the carriage House. Shawn the zoo. Jack Maynard the Larder, Thomas will check out the storm cellar. Matt Bomer the lap pool. Me and Luke will check out the Root Cellar. And as for Mallory, she'll be checking out the panic room. Little did we know that we aren't alone. Before me, AJ, Luke and Mallory left, we helped Gerwazy and the others get inside Deveral's room. However something told me not to go in there, so I told Gerwazy and the others to not go in yet. Then I threw a quarter, activating the lasers. "How are we supposed to get in there?" Gerwazy asked me. Mallory told us to step back and that this is a job for a woman. She was wearing her spy suit. She was acting like a real spy dodging lasers and darts. After dodging all of that, she reached the button to turn them off. All we could do was stare at her. Then we clapped our hands and left Gerwazy, Ruel and the others. Deveral's room was big and a little creepy. While snooping the room, Gerwazy, Ruel and the others met Kangi. That annoying parrot. Ruel and the others tried their best to ignore Kangi. They quickly got on Deveral's computer and called Leonel for help. Leonel helped Gerwazy hack into the computer by using the Cybernetic Falconieri Penzance Communicator and downloaded Deveral's files, sending them to Leonel's computer while Ruel and the others Snooped through Deveral's journals. Meanwhile, Simon and Doyle were searching through the attic trying to find anything that could help. They were using flash lights. So far the only things they found was junk, Doyle was looking through Mr. Accerly Jamison's old records and high school stuff. He found an old yearbook and couldn't believe that back then Mr. Accerly Jamison was a normal boy who wasn't the most hated man in the world. Doyle found some old bead and put it on, annoying Simon. However, it didn't take him too long to take it off after Simon made a joke about the bead having spiders causing Doyle to freak out. Simon smiled and continued to search for clues. He then found a tape inside the floor. It said private. He got Doyle's attention and the two found an old TV that still worked. They played the tape and were shocked. Sollie was in the study, searching through his father's stuff. Sollie found out that his father is running a Ponzi scheme and has been blackmailing a lot of people. Also his father is planning a new investment plan, one that could ruin the family and their name. Reed went down in the basement. Then suddenly the door shut close. He ran back upstairs trying to open the door but it wouldn't budge.

Elsewhere, Mitchell was in the courtyard. He grabbed a shovel and started digging. As he dug and dug, he finally found something. It was a chest. So when he opened it, he found an old movie projector along with some film and wondered what could be on here. Alex checked the Guest House. Unfortunately it was locked. It had several booby-traps all around, shocking him. So he used the Cybernetic Falconieri Penzance Communicator, dodging the booby-traps and got inside the Guest House. He soon learned quickly why the guest house is so heavily guarded. He found a lot of illegal candy. First he found Candy Cigarettes, Lollipipe, Road Kill Gummis, Kinder Surprise, Valentine's

Candy – candy hearts, Maoam Candy, Chinese Candy Medicine, Mexican Candy – that has lead, Hippy Sippy and Smarties. Matt was in Deveral's old treehouse and started searching for any secrets that Deveral could be hiding. He then realized that the floor is squeaky and found a money eating coin bank. Underneath the floorboard, the only thing he found inside was a US Mint ½ Dollar Micro SD Card Covert Coin. And he found a secret compartment and discover a Micro SD card. As for Brandon, he searched through the Jamison graveyard and started digging. After he was done digging, he found a buried trick Secret Haunted House Jewelry Box and opened it. Inside, he finds a map that reveals where Grand Dunixi Jamison kept his fortune, Callan went into the Jamison Family maze and found a Da Vinci Code Mini Cryptex and he tried to get in it. Sebastian tried to find anything useful in Mr. Accerly Jamison and Mrs. Jamison's bedroom. At first he didn't find anything, then when he opened the closet door, he found a metal tube in the top of the door. And inside the metal tube was a flash drive. Zayne was next, he was searching the garage. He decided to check Deveral's second car since he has like 10 cars. He found a spare tire and discovered something unusual. He found a cell phone that belongs to Raysel and continued to search the car and found Raysel's wallet underneath one of the mats. Chandler was in the Trophy Room and couldn't believe how many trophies The Jamison Family have. Especially, Mr. Accerly Jamison who used to be a track runner. Then he found something in one of the trophies and discovered a dumbbell that had blood on it. He wondered could this be a murder weapon. Ashley and Lucy checked the spa and started searching through the mud and found a key. So they tried to see which door it would open. After trying 52 doors, they finally found the right door. Inside the room, Lucy and Ashley found a room where Mrs. Jamison keeps illegal coats. Including Leopard fur, Tiger Fur, Ocelot Fur, Cheetah Fur, Bear Fur, Gorilla Fur, Monkey Fur, Seal Fur and Sea Otter Fur, they couldn't believe it. In the Ball Room, Antoni tried to find anything that could clear AJ's name. It took him some time but he found a hidden outlet Safe, inside it were old promissory notes that belonged to Sollie's Great! Great! Great! Grandfather, Novelo Jamison. In the wine cellar, AJ went through all the bottles trying to find any clues. Then he spotted something. Inside one of the bottles was a small wooden box, so he grabbed the bottle and smashed it. Then he picked up the wooden box and opened it. Inside he found a syringe needle. He put on some gloves and wondered what was inside the syringe needle. He decided to use The Cybernetic Falconieri Penzance Communicator and started scanning the needle. When he got the results, he found out that the syringe needle has opiates inside of it. Grant went in the indoor swimming pool and found a secret compartment. Inside was a journal that belonged to Grand Dunixi Jamison. After he got out of the pool, he started reading the journal and found out some important information.

In the Bunker, Mark found out that Deveral has several pirated movies and a list of the people he's been selling them to. He also found out that Deveral has been selling illegal diet pills. Like Fen – phen, Meridia, Star Caps and Rimonabant. Hunter was in the virtual reality game room and discovered that in each game case, Deveral has every member in his family's Social Security number. Austin P. Mckenzie was in the hall of mirrors and he felt like someone was watching him. So he quickly got to his destination, A Sound Studio and started searching for clues. He looked at the map again and found a wall clock safe. Inside was a journal that belonged to Esdras and discovered that some of the pages were missing. Meanwhile, Colton was checking the carriage house and found a great hollow keyboard. Inside was a tape. He learned that the table belonged to Raysel. After finding her name on it, Peter was in the bathroom trying to find anything that could help solve this mystery and discovered a bathroom tile storage. Inside was a key, one that belonged to Grandma Bregusuid, and he found a hair brush diversion safe that belonged to Mrs. Jamison. Inside was a flash drive. On the North Wing, Logan was looking around, making sure nobody was following him. He couldn't believe how big this place is. Then he got to the water park. He was shocked that The Jamison Family have their own water park. He learned what he was looking for was under the water. So he got in and started swimming. He found a lair underneath the water park and found out that Deveral has a lot of illegal explosive devices, M -100 Silver Salute, M – 250, M – 1000 Quarter Stick and wondered why Deveral had these. Shawn was walking into the Jamison Zoo and couldn't believe they have there own zoo. He passed by Elephants, Giraffes, Zebras, Lions, Tigers, Snakes and more. Then he reached a dead end and wondered where the hiding spot was. He found a wireless light switch in a bust. So when he pushed it, he activated a hidden door that led to a secret lab where he found several animals . Shawn wondered why they were here and discovered how black their eyes were. He then found a serum called The Princella Khione Of Aurex and put it in his backpack. He also found tapes of Deveral testing on the animals. Before he left, he took pictures of all the animals using the Cybernetic Falconieri Penzance Communicator. As for Jack Maynard, he was in the larder and wondered why The Jamison would have a Larder. As he checked the larder, all he could find was food. Then he found a floating shelf with a secret compartment and discovered a hollow deck of cards filled with pictures. He learned that these are pictures of girls that Deveral has gotten pregnant. The first girl named is Prideaux. Thomas was in the storm cellar searching the cellar for clues. He found a stuffed dead owl and discovered a blue print inside the owl. He learned that Deveral has made a powerful bomb called Doom Fault, and wondered where the bomb is at. Matt jumped into the lap pool and found a secret compartment underneath the water where he found a hidden yearbook. When he came back up to the surface, he found a maid standing over him. "Hi", Matt said. "Um, hello. What are you doing?" "Um, I really can't tell you that." "OMG. You're Matt Bomer." "Yes I am." "What are you doing here?" "I'll answer all your questions after me and my friends are done with our investigation." The maid walked away and Matt quickly opened the yearbook and learned that a guy named Tielyr went to school with Grand Dunixi Jamison, Esdras and Grandma Bregusuid. He also found some numbers that were really tiny and used The Cybernetic Falconieri Penzance Communicator and a magnifying glass, and discovered that those numbers opened up something, but what. Sean was on his way to the infinity pool, he realized whatever he was looking for was underneath water. So he got in and started looking. Then he found a package. He grabbed it and discovered that someone named Shaviv might have been murdered by one of the Jamison. After finding a fire poker that has blood on it and a note wrapped around it that said, 'I thought I could trust you.' He also found Shaviv's journal.

Mallory tried to get into the panic room but she needed a password. So she used her laser lipstick and made a hole to get inside. When she got in, she found something called Hade Wild and wondered what was this stuff. She took a jar and got out of there. Meanwhile, me and Luke were in the root cellar. I was scared to go inside. but Luke made me feel better and to my surprise we became friends. We took our time going inside. As we went inside, we found vegetables, Fruits and Nuts. We didn't know what we were looking for but we didn't give up hope. Then Luke found a small Safe lettuce storage that looked like a head of lettuce. Underneath the bottom was a flash drive. Me and Luke wondered what could be on this flash drive. Then, we got a call from Reed who told us he was trapped in the basement. We ran out of the root cellar to go help Reed. When we got there, we noticed that someone melted the door knob off. Me and Luke used The Cybernetic Falconieri Penzance Communicators and melted the door down. We asked Reed how come he didn't use The Cybernetic Falconieri Penzance Communicator. He told us it was acting funny and that he could barely get a signal out. And he was right, my Communicator was acting up as well and so was Luke's communicator, it was like someone was jamming the signal. Anyway, Reed showed us some letters that Mr. Accerly Jamison wrote to several women and told us that for years, Mr. Accerly Jamison has been cheating on his wife. Having affairs with different women. While we read the letters, Chris was in the Jamison pool and found a box inside the pool. When he came back up to the surface, he was laying low because someone in a cloak was going into the Jamison Mansion. He used The Cybernetic Falconieri Penzance Communicator and alerted me and the others. Then he opened up the box and discovered it was a music box. So as the song played, he found a blue locket inside and a note. He read the note and was confused. After reading the note, he opened up the locket and found a picture of Raysel and Deveral. Elsewhere, outside of the horse stable, Sean was being careful after me and the others warned him that we aren't alone. Then there was a flash of lighting. Sean remained calm and used his flash light trying to find clues. He quickly hid in one of the horse stalls after hearing footsteps. Whoever the person was didn't stay too long. But they did make a mess meaning they was looking for something, something that could help us. The question is though what. Sean thought to himself and pretended that he's a Jamison and wondered where would he hide his biggest secret. He smiled after figuring it out. He went to a horse named Bucky, picked up his hove and found a flash drive. He grabbed it and ran back into The Jamison Mansion. Meanwhile, Why Don't We were searching through the library. While looking through the books, Corbyn pulled one that opened a secret passage, surprising him and his friends. They each grabbed a torch and started walking. They found a lair. At first they thought it was Mr. Accerly Jamison's lair. But they soon discovered that it belonged to Deveral. Jonah found a huge white board that had every member of The Jamison Family. It seemed like Deveral had a plan to destroy his family one by one. Zach and Jack found some videos and decided to play them. In one of the videos, Deveral and his buddy who didn't show his face were in a room with other cloak figures having a secret meeting about AJ. Suddenly, someone came in the room and joined them. Whoever the person was had a mask on and gave each cloak figure their next assignment. Jack and Zach looked at each other and realized Deveral isn't The Mad Ffraid Brat. He's just working for The Mad Ffraid Brat. They have proof now that Deveral is involved in this mystery, but wondered who is The Mad Ffraid Brat and made a copy of the tape. Corbyn found a huge portrait of Deveral and discovered a secret room behind it. He went inside and found several fake IDs, money scams, but what he found next blew his mind. Corbyn found pictures of Raysel everywhere. As for Daniel, he turned on Deveral's big computer and found out Deveral has cameras. One at The Show Mayor, one at Jamison industries and he has one in Raysel's room. And he has cameras in every member of the Jamison Family Mansion. Nasser was walking into the Conservatory, a green house.

Nasser didn't think he would find anything and was a little scared. Then, he found a fly trap and discovered a key with the number 5666 and discovered it's from a storage called the Storm Gorilla. Nasser wondered what could be in that storage. He grabbed the key and was about to leave until someone wearing a clown mask with American colors stood in his way. Nasser tried to call for help but the signal was being jammed. He picked up a few plants and started throwing them at the mask person. The masked person smiled and threw some chattering teeth at Nasser. But these weren't no ordinary chattering teeth, they started attacking Nasser. He managed to use The Cybernetic Falconieri Penzance Communicator and his lasers to destroy each one. Amarr was in the Jamison home theatre. He was impressed how big it was. He searched through the seats and saw something that looked like a CD. So he grabbed a pair of scissor and cut it out. After finding the mysterious CD, he got a surprise from The Mad Ffraid Brat. Before he left, the screen started acting funny and then a cloak figure popped up on the screen. It was The Mad Ffraid Brat. The Mad Ffraid Brat told Amarr that me and the others are wasting our time and that we will fail. "Tell Benny to go back home before things get ugly." Amarr showed The Mad Ffraid Brat that he's not afraid of them. The Mad Ffraid Brat started laughing and said Tick tock. Then they vanished. Amarr found me and the others and told us what happened. Before we got out of the basement, me, Reed, Luke and Amarr found a letter that revealed some new information. We discovered that Mr. Accerly Jamison has another son while we looked at the birth certificate. That's when Chris showed up and showed us the locket and note. I knew for a fact now that Deveral is responsible for the disappearance of Raysel. Later on, Sean and Matt joined AJ and the others. We all tried to regroup but whoever was with Nasser wasn't alone. Aunt Fanny called me and the others and told us we have company. I told everybody it was time to leave. Without us knowing, Kangi had a button on his collar where he can alert his master. So, he used his beak and pressed the button. Somewhere in California, Deveral was on a date. He cut his date short after getting an alert from Kangi. He smiled and activated some plan called ZxZ. He got in his car and mashed the pedal. Meanwhile back at The Jamison Mansion, Nasser was fighting for his life. He still couldn't reach us and to make matters worse, the masked person was shooting arrows at Nasser. He tried to find some service. The unknown person continued to shoot arrows. They weren't giving up. Nasser set The Cybernetic Falconieri Penzance Communicator power to the max and shot out an electric ray at the masked person to electrocute them, which damaged the device that they was using to jam the signal. Nasser quickly made a call and tried to get out of the conservatory. Unfortunately, there was another masked person. This one had a flame thrower.

As for me and the others, we found Sollie inside the Jamison vault and we couldn't believe our eyes. There were stacks and stacks of cash everywhere and blocks of gold. Without any of us looking, Mallory stashed some of the cash inside her purse while we waited for the rest of the gang. Suddenly Plan ZXZ went into action. The whole mansion went crazy. Each door and window was locked shut. I realize that Mitchell, Alex, Lucy, Mallory, Matt Cornett, Callan and Mark were closer to the door. So I pushed them before the vault closed. Just like that, me, AJ, Gerwazy, Luke, Reed, Sollie, Austin P. Mckenzie, Colton, Ruel, Peter, Sebastian, Chandler, Logan, Simon, Matt, Austin Rhodes, Amarr and Grant were trapped inside. Then, Why Don't We, Antoni, Hunter, Brandon, Thomas, Jack Maynard, Shawn, Zayne and Sean showed up and they couldn't believe this. "Okay, what just happened?" Doyle asked Sollie from outside of the vault. Sollie told us that someone, maybe his brother activated plan ZXZ. "And what is plan ZxZ." Colton said. Sollie told me and the others that when someone activates plan ZXZ, the Jamison Mansion goes on lockdown and that whoever is in the vault will get overheated and pass out until someone comes to let them out. "Well it's a good thing you know the password." Matt Bomer said. "Well." Sollie said. "You got to be kidding me." Simon said. Before we knew it, it started getting hot.

Things got even worse when I got a call from Nasser. He told us that he was in danger and needed our help. Then the signal was lost. Doyle told us he'll be back and went to help his brother. Unfortunately, he forgot that we are trapped but that didn't stop him from trying to find a way out. Fed up with The Mad Ffraid Brat, Aunt Fanny came crashing in, making a way for Doyle to get out. He walked over to The Simplicius Transito and found out where Leonel kept his weapons. However, all he found was a weapon called The Purple Bust. He grabbed two of them and ran to the conservatory. As for the rest of us, we were in trouble. It was getting hotter. Mallory and the others were trying their best to get us out. Why Don't We even used The Aluxio Plaxico but it didn't work. Meanwhile, Doyle finally got to the conservatory and saw five cloak figures with masks attacking his brother. Doyle turned The Purple Bust on high blast. Even though he had no idea of how to used this gadget, he took a chance and aimed both of the gadgets at the cloak figures. Both of those purple balls caused a huge explosion that took out most of the cloak figures. Nasser was impressed, but before the brothers could celebrate, one of the cloak figures shot a few tranquilizers at Nasser. Doyle was furious and tried to save his brother but another cloak figure showed up and took Nasser away. But before he fell unconscious, Nasser threw the storage key at Doyle and then he called Leonel and told him to teleport Doyle back to The Show Mayor. Doyle tried to get Nasser back but it was too late. He was back at The Show Mayor in Aunt Fanny's penthouse. Back inside, me, and the others were burning up and started to lose consciousness. Shawn and the others were trying to guess the password to get us out. But it seemed hopeless. Before I passed out, I told Mallory and the others to save themselves and to solve this mystery. When I said that, tears started coming from Mallory's eyes and she shouted aloud, 'True friends don't quit.' She told the others to move aside while she cracks the code. First she used Greedy. Then she used Deveral is the devil's child and she typed in Rich, but none of them worked. Then an idea popped up in her head. She pressed in Pie, which is. 3.14159265. When she pressed in the last number, the vault opened up and we all had a group hug. We were so proud of Mallory. Aunt Fanny was so happy that I was alright. I whispered to her you do care about me. She told me, don't flatter yourself. Then Lysistrata showed up wondering what's going on. Grant simply kissed her on the lips. After that, we got out of there and left Sollie. He had no idea how he would explain the hole and everything else to his parents.

CHAPTER SEVEN

TIME TO CHAT WITH MALLORY

We made it back to The Show Mayor and Aunt Fanny and the others quickly ran to the elevator while me, AJ, Simon, Mallory, Shawn, Why Don't We, Logan, Chris, Amarr, Luke and Grant stayed behind after who we saw. We watched as the fake Raysel sold Bobble Heads that looked like AJ for ninety dollars shocking me and the others. AJ wasn't happy about it. He walked over to her with me and the others behind him to see what her problem is. " Well, look who's back. Mr. Perfect, and I see you brought some company this time as well. The jewel thief, who stole The Ape Skull from The Diamond Museum Amsterdam and finally, I get to meet the famous Benny Breezy." "First of all, I'm not famous, and second of all AJ is Innocent and we're going to prove it." I told her. "Also, one more thing. We know you're not the real Raysel and it's only a matter of time before we expose you." "You have no idea how dangerous I can be. I think it's time for y'all to leave Los Angeles while you still can." The fake Raysel said. I looked at her and told her we're not going anywhere. She smiled and started laughing. "You and your friends better watch your back. And here, take a Bobble Head," the fake Raysel said. We left after that and joined the others in Aunt Fanny's penthouse. Unfortunately, things just got worse when we got back to the penthouse. Doyle was breaking things. Chandler and the others tried to calm him down but he pushed them out of his way. I've never seen Doyle so upset. Me and Simon grabbed him and didn't let him go until he told us why he's so angry. Then I noticed Nasser was missing and asked Doyle what happened. Tears started falling

95

from Doyle's eyes. "The Mad Ffraid Brat and there minions, that's what happened. I tried to save him. But ...." Doyle said. "It's going to be okay bro, we're going to get Nasser back. No matter what it takes." I told him. "We're in this together," AJ said to Doyle. Always, Mallory said as she patted Doyle on the back. I couldn't believe this, the Mad Ffraid Brat took one of my best friends. Suddenly things got worse when a Detective named Plaxido showed up in Aunt Fanny's elevator with a few cops. "Can we help you?" Simon asked them. "Yes, me and my colleagues are here to arrest AJ." "Under what charges?" I asked him. "He stole The Severed Head presented as Henri Landru's." from The Museum Of Death. "Are you kidding me? I've never even heard of that place. I'm innocent." AJ said. "Unless you have proof, I'm not going anywhere." AJ said. Detective Plaxido smiled. "Actually we do." He showed us the video and me and the others couldn't believe it. "I didn't steal anything. That's not me." AJ told Detective Plaxido. "We already charged you for stealing The Ape Skull and The Katana and now this. It's time to go to jail. We can either do this the easy way or the hard way. It's your move," Detective Plaxido said. AJ had no idea what to do. Then I stepped in, "he's not going anywhere." I told Detective Plaxido. "I think it's time for you gentleman to leave or else this isn't over." Detective Plaxido said. "I'm so scared" Aunt Fanny said. Before they left, Detective Plaxido asked us how come we were dressed like we were about to break into a bank or something and wearing skully hats. Mallory told him we're all in a play.

After that, Detective Plaxido and the cops left. "Okay, Detective Plaxido is definitely a suspect." I told the gang. Then, Chef Acer made us some ice cream. Mallory tired and scared, grabbed Alex by the shirt and started making out with him. Me and the others told them goodnight as we all got ready for bed. I checked on Seissylt and he was upset because Mallory was making out with another guy. Mallory and Alex made out for twenty four hours. Anyway, I was so happy to finally get some sleep. The next morning started out crazy. I heard somebody call my name and woke up to find Logan standing over me. I asked him what time is it. He told me it was eight in the morning and that he wanted me to go investigate the Museum Of Death with him. I told him wouldn't he prefer Mallory or Simon since they are cool and popular. But he told me he would rather do some investigating with me, his friend. When he said that, I looked at him and got up. Then we ate some breakfast. We made our way to The Museum Of Death and we were wearing The Aristotelis Setser Suits and disguised ourselves as security guards. As we walked through the museum, we couldn't believe some of the exhibitions. They were kinda freaking us out. Logan noticed that I kept checking my phone and asked me is everything alright. I told him yeah but he didn't believe me. So I told him I can't stop thinking about my twin sister. And not only that, I'm also worried about Nasser and hoping he's alright. I was actually afraid and started to wonder do we stand a chance against The Mad Ffraid Brat or is this the end. Logan realized how scared I was and told me no matter what The Mad Ffraid Brat or Deveral does! He'll always be there for me and watch out for his bro, he promised. I never imagined that me and Logan would become such great friends and brothers since nobody ever gives me a chance. I told Logan thanks for being a friend and for liking me for me.

Then, we went into the security room and tried to find any footage from yesterday that could help us. At first, there was nothing. Then suddenly we found footage of someone putting on a mask that looks like AJ. But we couldn't see who the person was. As we tried to zoom in, the footage was being erased. After it was gone, a message popped up saying, 'I'm watching you.' Me and Logan looked at each other and quickly left. After The Mad Ffraid Brat alerting the real security guards with The Mad Ffraid Brat watching our every move, me and Hunter went to Iron Brave to see who bought the blue glove. We went up to the cashier and asked her did anybody buy a blue glove. Unfortunately, the cashier looked in her computer and told us 'No'. But I didn't believe her and neither did Hunter. We wondered why she would hide information from us. Me and Hunter pretended to look at some costumes while trying to come up with another idea. I was dressed as Santa Claus and Hunter was dressed as Tarzan. Suddenly, someone in a Gorilla suit bumped into me and placed a phone in my hand. "Who was that?" Hunter asked me. I told him I don't know. We tried to catch up with the mysterious person but they were gone. Then me and Hunter realized that this is a burner phone. Before I could say anything else, the phone started ringing. Me and Hunter answered the phone and the person started talking. It was Mr. Thersander. He told us that what we are looking for is in the back of the store and that we must find a way to check the computer without the cashier knowing. After that, he hung up. "Who is Mr. Thersander?" Hunter asked me. I told him he's the one that told us about the mystery. I placed the burner phone in my pocket. Then, me and Hunter quickly came up with an idea. I used the Cybernetic Falconieri Penzance Communicators and caused the costume store to get really foggy. The cashier and the rest of the customers couldn't see anything. We used special goggles and started snooping. Hunter was checking through the computer to find out who bought that glove and any other useful information. As for me, I was in the back surrounded by several costumes. I didn't know what I was looking for. Then I got a text from Mr. Thersander who told me to look in the Iron Brave Safe. So when I did, I found something shocking. Two plaster masks, one of AJ and the other one was Raysel. I couldn't believe it. Then I found three bracelets, however, they weren't any ordinary bracelets. They were Morse code bracelets.

Meanwhile, Hunter found something as well and quickly printed out a copy of what he found. Then, he joined me in the back. I showed him the masks and the Morse code bracelets. We both used The Cybernetic Falconieri Penzance Communicators and translated The Morse code bracelets. The first message said 'Help me,' the second one said 'Deveral Jamison has this crazy plan to kill every member of his family with a bomb called Doom Fault to collect his family inheritance. I have to warn his parents before it's too late.' And the last one said, 'If anyone finds this bracelet, please warn Mr. Accerly Jamison about his assistant Gewnsnay, she can't be trusted.' Me and Hunter looked at each other and wondered why this stuff is in here. Then Hunter showed me what he found. He told me Deveral bought the American clown mask and costume and someone under the name of Karitas bought the blue glove . Me and him wondered who is Karitas and why is she working with Deveral. Then the cashier came in the back. After the smoke went away, me and Hunter hid and watched the cashier go to the safe.

She started to panic after finding out that the masks and Morse code bracelets are gone. She grabbed her phone and called someone. Whoever she was talking to was furious and couldn't stop yelling. The person told her to put Iron Brave on lockdown and make sure nobody gets in or out. Hunter told me we better get out of there, but I figured there could be footage of Deveral with Karitas shopping in Iron Brave. I told Hunter I have to get that footage of the day Deveral and Karitas got the costume and gloves. And I wondered who put those masks and Morse code bracelets in the safe, and why hide it at Iron Brave. I told Hunter he has to get out of here and that I'd be alright. But he wouldn't leave. He said I'm not leaving my friend behind. When he called me his friend, I couldn't believe it. However, I knew we were on a case and I tried to remain focused. We sneaked into the security room, trying to find the footage. After we found what we need, we made a copy and wondered how are we supposed to get out with the store being on lockdown.

Things got even worse when Deveral and some cloak figures showed up. "What are we going to do?" Hunter asked me. That's when I called Leonel and asked him if he could teleport us back to The Show Mayor. Leonel told us the machine is low on power making me and Hunter worried. We had no idea how we were going to get out now. Then I saw an air vent. So, me and Hunter used The Cybernetic Falconieri Penzance Communicators once again and shot out two grappling hooks and we quickly got in . We found ourselves outside on top of Iron Brave wondering how are we supposed to get down before Deveral and the others find us. We searched through The Cybernetic Falconieri Penzance Communicators and pressed some button that gave me and Hunter grappling hook gauntlets. After that we got off the building and got into a taxi. "Where too?" The Taxi driver asked us. "The Show Mayor." Hunter told him. As we made our way back to The Show Mayor, I asked Hunter are we really friends? He smiled and told me he really wanted to be my friend. And that our friendship is real. I was happy that I made another friend. I called AJ and told him what I and Hunter found. Later on, At The Show Mayor, I was looking at a board of all the information me and my friends have! I was trying to figure out who The Mad Ffraid Brat is. Then I heard singing and went to investigate. It was Vigdess, the maid. She was cleaning. She got a little nervous when she saw me, "Oh sorry. I didn't think anybody was in here. I hope I'm not bothering you." "You're not bothering me, so stop assuming that you are. I'm not Mr. Stumbo." "Anyway, Aunt Fanny and Seissylt are down at the police station trying to bail out the rest of The Ptarmigan Seissylt Clowns. And my friends are out taking a break. How come you aren't taking a break?" Vigdess asked me. "Because I only have a few days left before The Daily Maglorix Newspaper is closed down and save AJ. I just have a lot on my mind." "Well if you would like, we could talk about it, I'm a good listener." Vigdess said. So we sat down and I told Vigdess about everything that's been going on. Especially the part about my half brother and my twin sister. I also thanked her for telling me and the others about the blue glove. That information really came in handy. Vigdess was happy that she could help and started humming some song. I told her she has a beautiful voice and has she ever considered becoming a singer. Vigdess looked down and said dreams don't come true. At least not for a maid. Vigdess told me she doesn't feel like she has what it takes to make it in the music world. And figures nobody will listen to her. Vigdess also revealed to me a secret that she has never told anybody. She's in love with Sollie Jamison. When she said that, I was shocked and asked her what's stopping her from admitting her feelings to Sollie. "Wow, you're definitely not from around here." Vigdess said. "Is that a problem?" I asked her. "No, but everybody knows that a Jamison doesn't date waitresses, maids or girls like her." She started crying and told me her life will always be the same.

Then I noticed that she's wearing a Mulan Necklace and I asked her is she a Mulan fan. Vigdess stopped crying and said, "Mulan is inspiring, brave, she didn't give up, she proved that girls are powerful and can be heroes. Mulan was trying to find herself, trying to find her worth, the meaning of honor and bravery. She showed that a woman doesn't have to be graceful or beautiful. Mulan is a model to all girls and her movie didn't get the credit that it deserved. It should've done better at the box office just like every other Disney movie. But you know how critics are." Vigdess said. After explaining to me how much Mulan means to her and the powerful message, Vigdess had to go back to work. Before she left, I told her to always follow her dreams and her heart. And to not give up on Sollie. Vigdess thanked me and left. Then I got a phone call from Mr. Zed. He was yelling at me and told me that the mayor was about to cut off the power . But before he could say anything else, the connection was lost. That's when Aunt Fanny came in. "Are you okay Benji?" She asked me. "I told her no, I'm not." I also asked her where is Seissylt. She told me that Seissylt is with Porfirio and that he's safe. Unfortunately they couldn't bail out the rest of the band. I couldn't believe this, more bad news. Aunt Fanny could tell that I was down and told me to sit down. At first I didn't want to. I just want to solve this mystery. But Aunt Fanny didn't care. "Alright Benji, start talking." "There's nothing to talk about." I told her. "What did I just tell you." Aunt Fanny said, "I'm afraid that me and my friends will lose. Whoever this person is doesn't want this mystery solved and they're willing to do whatever it takes to make sure we fail. Like taking one of my best friends. I'm worried about Nasser and I just feel like we're all in danger. Not only that, I feel like after we do solve this mystery, AJ, Shawn, Zayne, Hunter, Luke, Logan and the others will forget about me and go on with their lives like nothing ever happened." And I told her my friends will do the same when we graduate. That's why I don't get close to anybody. "Because you're afraid that they won't give you a chance right?" Aunt Fanny said. "Sometimes you have to realize that you don't stand a chance of becoming friends with people who are from a different world. I don't stand a chance of becoming friends with Parker Queenan, Tyler Young, Owen Joyner, Charles Gillespie, Evan Feeley, Charles Vandervaart and Pierson Fode. The sooner I solve this mystery, the sooner I can leave and never see AJ and the others ever again." After I said that, I heard a voice. "Is that how you really feel?" AJ said as he came in. "Uh oh, um hey bro. How long have you been there?" I asked him. "Long enough," AJ told me. Aunt Fanny told me she'll see me later. Before she left, she told me two things. First, she told me you were given this life because you're strong enough to live it. So never have any regrets. Because at some point everything you did was exactly what you wanted. The second thing was That Grandma Maroochy and Aunt Antiquity called and left me an important message.

I told her thanks. After that, Aunt Fanny left. AJ wasn't happy with me and wanted to talk but I told him we have better things to do. However AJ didn't care at the moment. He told me to take a break and asked me do I really think he, Luke, Shawn, Hunter, Reed, Colton and the others will forget about me like I was nothing to them. I told him maybe. It's just hard for me to believe that he and the others want to be my friend. I also told him these last two days have really been something, dealing with my friends, worrying about them, especially Nasser. Then I told AJ that I'm trying to save his career and The Daily Maglorix Newspaper. "Being in the land of stars where people judge you. Based on your looks, people not giving you a chance and being questioned by some people about whether or not me and the others can actually save your career, I just don't belong here, or have what it takes." "That's enough bro. I believe in you, but you have to believe in yourself as well. Our friendship is real and if people don't like the real you then who cares. No matter what, I'll always have your back. In fact, I want you to play one of your songs for me." AJ said. "Who told you I write songs?" I asked him, AJ smiled and told me that Mallory told him that I have lost my voice for music and she wants him to help me rediscover my voice for music. She even downloaded some of the songs I have sung on an iPad and showed them to AJ. AJ played the first song and asked me do I remember that one. I shook my head and I told him it was the time I sung at the Christmas talent show at Glass Art. I was wearing my red jacket and Santa hat singing I'll be home for Christmas. AJ was impressed and asked me what happened? I told him I guess I lost my confidence. AJ asked me could he see my song book. So I went in my backpack and introduced him to Konstanty . He went through the pages and found three he actually liked. He asked me could I sing this one. I told AJ I have stage fright. But he encouraged me. The song was called, Nobody Ever Gives Me a Chance. As I played the song, AJ was secretly recording me, while Aunt Fanny was in her room listening to me sing. Unfortunately the song got interrupted when Kimbriella showed up in Aunt Fanny's penthouse. I wasn't happy at all to see her. She had a basket full of banana and blueberry muffins and they were big. She asked me could we talk. AJ grabbed the basket and told me he'll be in the game room. He also shook Kimbriella's hand which caused her to faint. "Is she going to be alright?" AJ asked me. "Trust me, she'll be fine bro. She does that a lot." I told him.

Twenty minutes later, Kimbriella woke up wondering what happened. I told her she passed out after meeting AJ Mitchell. "Oh no, not again." Kimbriella said. "Why does this keep happening to me?" Kimbriella asked me. I told her, I don't know and asked her why was she here. Kimbriella told me she wanted to apologize to me and wanted to know can we be friends. To be honest, I didn't want to be friends with a liar. So Kimbriella tried to explain why she lied to Mitchell. Kimbriella said guys don't care for her. And when they find out she's just a waitress and that her father is a Chef, she would always get stood up and picked on just because of her job title. She also told me that she has never been kissed before and was hoping that Mitchell would be her first kiss and her first relationship. But she doesn't think a guy like him would fall for her. Kimbriella dreams of a life outside of The Show Mayor and to be somebody. Kimbriella told me last night she had a dream that she and Mitchell were dancing and that the song, The Heart Never Forgets came on. Anyway, just when she and Mitchell were about to kiss, Kimbriella's dress disappeared and she was suddenly back in her waitress outfit. She was so upset, and even more upset after Mitchell turned his back. Then she woke up. "Maybe I'm not meant for true love or happiness." Kimbriella said. That's when I hugged her and told her she's beautiful and that everybody deserves happiness and that her job doesn't define her. How she treat others and herself is more important. "Just tell Mitchell how you feel," I told her. After that, she left and went back to work. AJ came back out and told me good job and that he hopes everything works out for Kimbriella and Mitchell. After talking to Kimbriella, I decided it's time to check the message machine. But before I had a chance to check it, the elevator came up and me and AJ met some guy. "Um, hi. Can we help you?" I asked him. "Yes, I'm here to talk to you Benny." The guy said. "How do you know my name?" I asked him. "Because I work for Mr. Thersander. I'm his assistant. My name is Klazinaveen. It's nice to meet you. And you too AJ." Klazinaveen gave me a package and told me to pay close attention to the details. Before I could ask him any questions, Klazinaveen was gone. Me and AJ opened up the package and found a diary with a note. The note said, '**Not Everything is What it Seems.**' Unfortunately, when we opened the diary up, the pages were blank, confusing AJ and me. Then I checked the message machine. Finally the message was from my grandma and Aunt. This is what the message said. **You're probably wondering why we never told you about your twin sister or your half brother. I'm sorry we kept these secrets from you. Give us a call so we can explain, I hope you can forgive us. Also there's something we have to tell you but you have to be here in order for us to tell you. It's about your mother. Anyway, we love you and we believe in you and your friends.**

After listening to that message, I wanted to leave and join my family in New York. AJ told me that everything is going to be fine. After the day was over with, that night me and Mallory, AJ and Doyle, and Shawn, Jack Maynard, Why Don't We, Logan Shroyer, Austin Rhodes, Grant, Zayne Emory, Amarr Wooten, Chris Salvatore, Luke Korns, Ashley Tisdale, Lucy Hale, Ruel, Reed, Colton Haynes, Mark Thomas, Hunter, Austin P. McKenzie, Brandon, Thomas Kuc, Matt Cornett, Callan Potter, Alex, Sean Grandillo, Chandler Massey, Peter Bundic, Sebastian Croft, Antoni Porowski and Matt plus Aunt Fanny, Porfirio, Sollie and Leonel went over all the clues that we had found and were trying our best to figure out who is The Mad Ffraid Brat. Everybody had their own theory. Simon and Doyle found out that Mrs. Jamison is pregnant with decuplets. Gerwazy, Ruel and Austin Rhodes discovered that Deveral hates his family. Especially his father and brother. Mitchell showed us the old projector and played the footage. It was a video about Grand Dunixi Jamison, and this is what he said in the video. **I had a dream. To build something that was unusual. Something that would blow a lot of people's minds. A place where people from different worlds could come together. A place of magic and performance. A place unlike any other. I call it The Show Mayor. A place where anybody is somebody. Where you could be yourself. The Show Mayor is a wondrous place where anybody can fit in. I want to make a place that would have people talking for years and**

years. These people aren't just employees to me. They're my family and that's what The Show Mayor is all about. Family and love and friendship.

That was the end of the video. Me and the others looked at each other. We couldn't believe that Grand Dunixi Jamison used to be a nice person. The next video was an argument between Grand Dunixi Jamison and his son Mr. Accerly Jamison who wanted to sell The Show Mayor. But Grand Dunixi Jamison wanted to turn The Show Mayor into a travelling circus to see the world and meet new people. Alex found out that Deveral had several boxes of illegal candy. Callan told us he unlocked the Da Vinci Code Mini Cryptex and discovered a secret letter. He read the letter and said Grandma Bregusuid wrote a letter to Grand Dunixi Jamison. Trying to warn him about Tielyr after finding out that Tielyr stole Grand Dunixi Jamison's secret projects. We wondered why that letter never got delivered. "That explains why some of the pages in Esdras' journal are missing." Austin P. Mckenzie said. He showed us the journal and told us that Esdras used to invent things, including a cotton candy freeze ray. "Some of these gadgets are incredible," Austin P. Mckenzie said. Hunter was next. He discovered that Deveral has every member of his family's social Security numbers. Mark told us that Deveral has been selling pirated movies and selling illegal and dangerous diet pills. Logan showed us the pictures he took. He told us that Deveral has a secret laboratory underneath his family water park. Inside the laboratory, he found illegal explosives. Colton showed us the tape he found in the carriage house, so he played the tape in a tape recorder. And we all listened on the tape, we found out that Raysel was spying on Deveral and saw something she wasn't supposed to see. And that was it on the tape. Jack Maynard showed me and the others pictures of girls that Deveral had got pregnant. There were ten pictures. We couldn't believe that Deveral was a dad. Then, Thomas told us about the blue print. And Leonel was worried how dangerous this bomb is. We all wondered what was Deveral planning. Sean discovered a flash drive. Brandon found a map that leads to Grand Dunixi Jamison's hidden treasure. Sebastian found a flash drive as well. He uploaded it to a laptop and what we saw shocked all of us. In the video, we watched as

Esdras is murdered and discovered that the dumbbell is the weapon that was used to kill Esdras. Unfortunately we couldn't see the killer's face. Sollie was hurt. He couldn't believe that somebody killed the grandpa he never knew he had. As for the others, Antoni found old promissory notes that could be worth a lot of money. Ashley and Lucy discovered that Mrs. Jamison had illegal fur coats. Chandler couldn't believe that he found the weapon that killed Esdras Jamison. Zayne told me and the gang that he found Raysel's cellphone and discovered that Deveral was the last person she talked to before she went missing. Also he found a mysterious key in her wallet. Chris uncovered a secret and believed that Raysel and Deveral might have been in a relationship after discovering a picture of Raysel and Deveral in the locket. Doyle showed us the storage key. Mallory discovered something called Hade Wild, a serum in a jar. Grant revealed to us what's in Grand Dunixi Jamison's journal. It turns out that Grand Dunixi Jamison had sensitive information about every member of his family.

Sean discovered a fire poker and believed that this could also be a murder weapon. Leonel analysed the fire poker and told us the blood belonged to a guy named Shaviv. "Who is that?" Sollie said. "Your family's first Butler." Sean said as he showed us Shaviv's journal and read some of the pages. It turns out that Shaviv used to work for the Witness Protection program but the question is though why as Sean continued to read. Matt was next. He showed us a yearbook and discovered that Grand Dunixi Jamison's Grandma Bregusuid, Tielyr and Esdras used to be great friends. He also found a code. He thinks that it will unlock something. AJ showed us a syringe needle that has opiates. He believes that this could also be a murder weapon. Sollie found out that his father is running a Ponzi scheme. He has been blackmailing people and is planning an investment plan that could ruin his family name forever. Peter found a key that belongs to Grandma Bregusuid that opens up a locker at Los Angeles Union station and he found a flash drive. So once again we watched another video. On this video we discovered that a woman named Quintonette was secretly working with Tielyr. "Who is Tielyr?" Simon said. "My father's archenemy." Sollie said in a down voice. "Smalley is his last name and he owns a circus theme hotel as well. However, his theme is darker and scary. It's called The Horror Herculano." Sollie said. Matt uploaded the Micro SD card and discovered sensitive information on every enemy of The Jamison Family. Information that could get Mr. Accerly Jamison's enemies arrested. Reed revealed to Sollie about his father's secret affairs and the existence of Mr. Accerly Jamison's other child. "I have a half brother?" Sollie said. "Yes, you do." Reed told him. Why Don't We told us that Deveral has a secret lair. A lot of fake IDs. A devious plan to kill every member of his family. A mysterious buddy that could be helping Deveral. Several pictures of Raysel and that he's spying on people. Plus the really big news was Deveral isn't The Mad Ffraid Brat. When Jonah and the others told us that, everybody became quiet. "Then who is The Mad Ffraid Brat?" Mark said. Shawn found out that Deveral has created a serum called The Princella Khione of Aurex and using it to make animals aggressive and very dangerous. He also told us how black their eyes were. "That would explain why Jumoke's animals aren't acting like themselves." I told them. Shawn gave the serum to Leonel so he could run some tests.

Shawn also told us that he found Jumoke's missing animals. Then Luke got my attention. He was on his laptop and showed me what he found on the flash drive. The one that was inside the Safe lettuce storage. We looked at each other and knew we have to keep this information a secret for now. Anyway, me and the gang decided not to check out what's on the flash drive that Sean found and the CD that Amarr found. We were too concerned about what we could find next. After that Chef Acer made us some jumbo burgers with cheese and barbecue sauce along with some fries. While we were eating, Mallory was nervous about this mystery and thought making out with Zayne would ease her mind. Me and the others just ate our food as the two made out. Sollie told us that his birthday is next Wednesday. However he wasn't happy about it. Before I could ask him why, my phone started ringing. It was Chiquite. She told me to turn the TV on. So when I did, me and the others were shocked. It turned out that AJ's fans all around the world are tired of their favorite star being accused of something he didn't do and have decided to take matters into their own hands. They're going on strike.

They call it The Stand For AJ Mitchell. With his fans getting themselves into trouble, AJ decided to host a meeting to talk to his fans. That night. AJ, me, Simon, Mallory, Doyle, Aunt Fanny, Leonel, Sollie, Luke, Jack Maynard, Hunter, Grant, Shawn, Why Don't We, Amarr, Zayne, Lucy, Colton, Antoni, Mark, Thomas, Mitchell Hoog, Chandler, Matt, Sebastian, Peter, Sam, Logan and Chris went to the meeting and the room was packed. Also, Colton Shires, Chris McNally, Case Walker, Collins Key, Devan Key, Nick Mayorga and Rudy Pankow were there as well. Mallory fainted when she saw Rudy . Anyway, when the meeting started. AJ couldn't get a word in because his fans were talking among themselves and arguing with one another. Just when AJ thought this was a bad idea, Mallory stood up and told everybody to shut up and listen. After she said that, they settled down and drew their attention to AJ. First he told them how much he appreciated them and what they mean to him. "But protesting is not the answer." He said. When he said that, his fans started asking questions. They each had something to say. However, some of there questions were a bit annoying. Especially, when some of them were trying to ask out Rudy and the others. Then one girl raised her hand making AJ nervous. He whispered to us that's Seini, a crazy fan who's always trying to kiss him. Before she got a chance to ask any questions, another girl knocked her out of the way and asked AJ how could he let his fan base down. After that the mysterious girl shouted out you're "Guilty". Then she showed all the fans a video. In this video, AJ was stealing The Ape Skull from The Diamond Museum Amsterdam shocking me and the others which could make his case even harder. I knew with this evidence, it could ruin everything. I asked Grant for one of his Aigeos Juppar jawbreakers and destroyed that video before it got out. The mysterious girl angry at AJ decided to start a riot making AJ sad while all the fans fought one another. Me and Chris Salvatore watched as the creepy girl disappeared in the riot. We wondered how did she get that video.

Meanwhile, thinking that this is their chance to make their move, Seini and her friends, The Hinkley Youga Shirk used this opportunity to kiss their crushes. Hinkley Youga Shirk 1 went up to Sebastian, grabbed him by the shirt and started making out with him. Hinkley

Youga Shirk 2 made out with Mark. Hinkley Youga Shirk 3 made out with Jacob. Hinkley Youga Shirk 4 made out with Zayne. Hinkley Youga Shirk 5 made out with Nick Mayorga. Hinkley Youga Shirk 6 made out with Grant. Hinkley Youga Shirk 7 made out with Callan. Hinkley Youga Shirk 8 made out with Chris McNally. And the others made out with Jack Maynard, Collins Key, Devan Key, Ruel, Thomas, Hunter, Logan, Case, Jonah, Luke, Zach, Daniel, Alex, and Amarr. Then Mallory joined in. She grabbed Rudy and started making out with him. Seini tried to kiss AJ and ended up falling . "Not today," AJ said. He was upset and couldn't believe how bad things have gotten. Me and the others went to comfort him while we dealt with his fans and The Hinkley Youga Shirk. Meanwhile the mysterious girl got in a car and took off her disguise. She smiled and told the driver that phase 4 is complete. The cloak person said well done and handed her an envelope full of cash and gave her. Her next assignment, they drove away after that. Just when I wanted to go back to The Show Mayor, Mallory announced that me, AJ and Shawn will be guest starring on The Late Late Show With James Corden. So after we left the meeting, me, AJ, Simon, Mallory, Doyle, Aunt Fanny, Sollie, Jack Maynard, Why Don't We, Luke, Jacob, Logan, Lucy, Callan, Ruel, Zayne, Hunter, Grant, Colton Shires, Reed Horstmann, Colton, Shawn, Chandler, Alex Whitehouse, Sebastian, Case and Chris Salvatore went to the show. I felt like I was going to puke. I was so nervous, as for Mallory, she was so excited. However, when James Corden told her that she won't be guest starring on his show, she reached in her purse and sprayed The Plasedo Tango on him and Reggie Watts .

A few minutes later, Mallory introduced the guest stars. Tonight we have AJ and Benny Breezy. Me and AJ were shocked to see Mallory introducing the show. But before we could ask her what was she doing, she introduced the other guest stars. "Please put your hands together for my future husbands, Devin Hayes and Darren Barnet and the one and only Shawn Mendes. As for our musical performance, we have Bruce Wiegner, Grant Knoche and Will Jay." Mallory said. But even Shawn wanted to know what was Mallory up to. Mallory told them to start the show. After the introductions, Mallory introduced herself to the world.

"Welcome to The Late Late Show With Mallory Styles." When she said that, the sign changed. "Okay! Come on out AJ, Benny, Shawn, Devin and Darren." Mallory said. AJ and the others sat down but I couldn't, knowing that Devin and especially Darren will never give me a chance . I walked off the show, "Where are you going?" Mallory said. I told her that I'm not the type of friend. Devin Hayes, Wyatt Nash, Andrew Dunbar, Matthew Andrew Welch, Antonio Marziale, Jeremy Pope, Matthieu Lange, Alex Saxon, Aidan Alexander, Kaden Dayton, Patrick Luwis, Laurence Coke, Finn Wittrock, Josh Green and Tom Glynn Carney or The Stokes Twins and especially Dominic Brack would ever hangout with. Before I left The Late Late Show With James Corden, I told Aunt Fanny to keep Mallory out of trouble. Shawn wanted to join me but Mallory wouldn't let him leave. Simon wanted to come with me too but I told him to take my place on the show. Then I left. I started walking back to The Show Mayor, to my surprise, Chris caught up with me. He wanted to make sure that I was alright. I asked him "Why do you care?" "Because you're my friend," Chris said "whether you believe it or not." I looked at him and couldn't believe that Chris Salvatore would want to be friends with me since people never give me a chance . Then we got a call from Leonel who found out that Fuji has an ex wife. He sent us her address. "We should go talk to her." Chris said. "This time of night?" I ask him, "why not?" Chris said. Since I had nothing else to do, I decided that Fuji's ex wife might know something. So me and Chris left to go find Fuji's ex wife. Meanwhile, AJ and the others were dealing with Mallory. She asked her fans to send her some questions or dares. She picked out the best dare and couldn't stop smiling. Before she answered it, she told the world that someday she and Dominic Brack lips will touch and that it will be the best kiss ever. "Alright, somebody dare me to break the world record for the longest make out with Devin Hayes and he has to wear a spider Man mask" she said. So Mallory asked for a mask and Devin put it on. Mallory lift the mask up only showing his lips and started kissing him. As they kiss, Bruce Wiegner performed. He sung Everybody Dies. After he was done, Shawn used this opportunity to grab The Plasedo Tango and called Leonel to see if there's a way to reverse the mind control on James and Reggie. After

Leonel told him what to do, Shawn broke the mind control freeing James and Reggie. Shawn went to go find me, AJ and Simon. And James Corden came along with him while Mallory and Devin continued to make out. Doyle came up with an idea, he whispered something to Sollie and the two went on the show. "Hey everybody, Sollie's birthday is coming up and he has a surprise for you." Doyle said. "That's right, usually I just have a pool party but this year I'm having a Masquerade party. One you don't want to miss. Everybody is invited." Sollie said. After announcing his big news, Will Jay performed I Can Only Write My Name. Grant Knoche sung Unfair. After that a girl made out with Peter and her best friend grabbed Grant and made out with him. Then some other girls decided to do the same. The first one made out with Jack Maynard. Another one made out with Ruel. One girl made out with AJ Mitchell before he had the chance to leave. Her friend grabbed Darren Barnet and made out with him. And the last six made out with Case Walker, Zayne, Bruce, Alex, Jacob and Sebastian.

CHAPTER EIGHT

SIGNS

Elsewhere, me and Chris were arriving to Fuji's ex wife house. We knocked on the door and waited for somebody to come. "What do you want?" The person behind the door said. "Are you Neaira Cienfuegos?" Chris said, "yeah I am. Who are you?" "My name is Chris Salvatore and this is my friend Benny Breezy, he's an Investigative Reporter. We're here to ask you about your ex husband." "I don't know what you're talking about. Go away," Neaira said. "Please, you have no idea what me and my friends have been through. We're dealing with somebody who's trying to frame AJ and won't stop at anything until they succeed. We think something might have happened to Fuji and we need your help." I said. Neaira opened the door and told us that Fuji is at The Rasalas Retro of Words Worth, A Mental institution. Me and Chris looked at each other. "He's alive?" I asked her. "Of course he's alive, why?" Neaira asked us. "Um no reason." She gave us the address and we left. When we arrived at The Rasalas Retro of Words Worth, we couldn't believe how creepy it looked. "I'm not going in there, I can't." I told Chris. He could tell how afraid I was and told me he won't let anything happen to me. So we went inside and asked the nurse what room Fuji was in and we found Fuji talking to himself. He was completely out of it. "Hi, my name is Benny Breezy. I'm an Investigative Reporter and this is my friend Chris Salvatore, we would like to talk to you. What do you know about The Show Mayor and The Jamison Family? Why did somebody try to hide your room and how did you get that old reel tape recorder and the audio reel? Please, we need something. If you can help us we would really appreciate it." I told him. Fuji looked at me and Chris. He grabbed some paper and drew a picture. Then he whispered to us that none of us are safe. Whoever Fuji was afraid of had him worried. Me and Chris looked at the picture and went to the front desk. "Who is this man?" I asked the nurse. "That's Dr. Silouanus Prater. He's a therapist that works here." The nurse told us. "I see, and where is his office?" I asked her, "it's down that hallway, but you aren't allowed to go in there and visiting hours are over with. Have a nice night," the nurse said. "Are we really leaving?" Chris asked me. "Heck no." I told him.

A few minutes later, the nurse watched me and Chris leave the building or so she thought. Unknowing to her, those were holograms that we created using The Cybernetic Falconieri Penzance Communicators. "Man I love these Communicators." I told Chris. We used a picklock and we went inside Dr. Silouanus Prater's office where we discovered pictures of every employee at The Show Mayor and pictures of Mr. Stumbo with darts in them. "Why does he have all this stuff?" Chris asked me. "I don't know bro," I told him. We discovered that Dr. Silouanus Prater is obsessive with The Show Mayor. Question is though why. So we searched through his office for any clues. I searched his files on every patient that he had and discovered that Fuji Mendonca's file is missing. Chris was on his computer and found out that Fuji was dosed with some mysterious drug that made him go insane for over thirty years. We knew that we had to get Fuji out of this place and fast because Dr. Silouanus Prater and the nurse were talking. "It's time to go." Chris said. Me and he went back in Fuji room, grabbed him, and the three of us started running after Dr. Silouanus Prater saw us and alerted security. He and a few of the workers started chasing us. Just when we thought we were trapped, Shawn and the others came busting in. " Get in ". AJ said. After we got in, Shawn mashed the pedal and we got away. Much to Dr. Silouanus Prater dismay, he grabbed his phone and told somebody we have a problem. I asked AJ and the others what were they doing there. "I told you. I'll always be there for you." Shawn said. "Same here." AJ told me. "And you know I always will be too." Simon told me. "Me too." James Corden said. I smiled and told them thanks. As we drove back to The Show Mayor, me and Chris introduced Fuji to the others. When we got back to The Show Mayor, me, AJ, Chris,

Shawn and Simon went to talk to Mr. Stumbo while James Corden took Fuji to Aunt Fanny's penthouse. "What do y'all want now?" Mr. Stumbo said. "It's nice to see you too Mr. Stumbo. We need to ask you something." I told him, "well spit it out, I don't have all day." "Alright, what all do you know about Dr. Silouanus?" When Simon said that name, Mr. Stumbo got up from his desk and closed the door. "What has he done now?" Mr. Stumbo said. "So you do know him?" Shawn said. "Unfortunately I do. You see, Silouanus Prater used to work here at The Show Mayor. He was The Show Mayor Hypnotist, one of the best." "What happened?" Chris asked him. "Well Silouanus started misusing his abilities and caused The Show Mayor to get into some serious trouble." "What kind of trouble?" AJ said.

"Where do I begin?" Mr. Stumbo said. "Hmm let's see, one time Silouanus hypnotized the guests at The Show Mayor into giving him all their money, another time he hypnotized some policemen and had them rob from a bank. He even used hypnosis on the clowns and turned them into criminals and had them attack the guests. Then there was a time when he hypnotized Mr. Accerly Jamison and had him sign a check for ten million dollars. I was the one that convinced Mr. Accerly Jamison to finally get rid of Silouanus. Especially after the check thing." "That would explain why he hates you so much." I told him. "Is there anything else you can tell us about him?" Chris said. "Yes! Be very careful. Silouanus is dangerous." Mr. Stumbo said, "he loves to play with people's minds. Why are you asking about him anyway?" Mr. Stumbo asked us. "Because he's a therapist at The Rasalas Retro of Words Worth, a mental institution and I believe he's the reason why Fuji Mendonca is in a mental institution." I told him. "Who is that?" Mr. Stumbo said. "He's a hoarder who used to live at The Show Mayor." "You can't be serious. We have never had a Hoarder at The Show Mayor." Mr. Stumbo told us. Me and the others looked at each other. The next morning I woke up and noticed that Simon and Doyle were missing so I got up and found them in the kitchen with Mallory, Luke, Shawn, Lucy, Chris, Logan, Why Don't We, Callan, Brandon, Rudy, Reed Horstmann, Zayne, Thomas and Devin. "Good morning sleepy head." Mallory said, "come join us. Devin made us breakfast." I grabbed my breakfast and went out on the balcony. I wanted to be by myself. I couldn't believe the breakfast Devin made. I had Jumbo waffles with blueberries and a scoop of vanilla ice cream, french toast, bacon, yeast biscuits and pancakes. Then Mallory came out on the balcony. "What's wrong with you?" She asked me, "what do you mean?" I said. "How come you don't want to be around Devin?" "It's not important," I told her. "Yes it is. He really wants to be your friend." "Please don't lie to me, Devin Hayes did not say that." "Yes he did. Why is it so hard for you to believe that Devin wants to be your friend," "I don't want to talk about it." I told her. "Benny Michigan Breezy you better tell me this instance or I'm going to drop kick you. So start talking." "Alright, geez you can be a pain sometimes. Some people love to judge you before they get to know you. Me and Devin are from two different worlds and I just feel like I don't stand a chance of becoming his friend. It's just hard for me to believe that people like Noah Urrea, Christopher Sean, Lachlan Buchanan, The Dobre Brothers and especially Kaden Dayton would want to be my friend. I'm sure none of them would ever want to be seen in public with me. Are you happy now?" I asked her. Mallory got up from her seat and hugged me. Then she told me this. "There will always be a reason why you meet people. Either you need them to change your life or you're the one that will change theirs," after she said that, Gerwazy showed up. "Oh great." I said, me and she went back inside. "What do you want?" I asked Gerwazy. "I came to talk to you. Well, grabbed a number." "In case you forgot, I'm trying to solve a mystery and I don't have any time for a jerk like you." "I know I messed up and you probably hate my guts, but I'm still your half brother." Gerwazy said. When he said that, everybody drew their attention to me, especially Mallory. "He's your half brother? How long have you known?" Mallory asked me. "For a few days now, I'm sorry I didn't tell you guys. I just didn't know how." "We're supposed to be honest with each other, remember bro?" Simon told me. "Trust me you don't want an answer." I said, "what is that supposed to mean?" Simon asked me. "Nothing bro. Alright Gerwazy, you have my attention. So what do you want?" "I would like you to join me at a celebration that our father is throwing for me. It's on a yacht." Gerwazy said. "Are you kidding me,

I have better things to do than to be around a bunch of snobs. I am not going and that's final." "Come on bro, this could be an opportunity for us to get to know each other better. So are you with me?" Gerwazy said,

I was about to say no until Mallory told me to take a leap of faith. "What about Sollie's party? We're supposed to help him decorate." I told her. "We got it, go spend some time with your brother." Mallory said. "Let me go find AJ first, he's in the sound studio. I'll be back." So when I got to the sound studio, I noticed how upset AJ was. "What's wrong bro?" I asked him. AJ showed me a song book and when I opened it up, I was creeped out. AJ sung the first song. The song was called Hush Little Pop Star. I quickly closed the book and asked AJ where did he find this. He told me he found the song book on his pillow along with an AJ Bobblehead. "Okay, this is getting out of hand." I told him. "I know bro, I don't know how much more I can take." AJ told me. I looked at him and said we're in this together no matter what and that giving up is not an option. After that, we joined the others in the lobby. While in the lobby, we met Anima, Porfirio's Girlfriend, A Roving Performer. Unfortunately she wasn't in the mood for talking. She started yelling at Porfirio. She was so upset and told Porfirio she can't wait any longer. Then she started crying and left. "What's wrong with her?" I asked Porfirio. He told me and the others that he and Anima have been dating for 23 years and that Anima is upset because he hasn't proposed. "How come?" Doyle said. "I'd rather not talk about it. I'll see you guys later," Porfirio said. After that, Sollie pulled up and told the others to come on. Before she joined the others, I stopped Mallory and congratulated her for making the front page and breaking the world record for the longest make out. "Thank you, wait what?" Mallory said. "Oh, you didn't know that there's a picture of you kissing Devin Hayes while he wears a Spider Man mask. This picture is on today's Newspaper, Magazines, every social media account and more." Mallory started blushing. "Let me guess, you're still thinking about that kiss aren't you?" I asked her. "I don't know what you're talking about." "Uh huh, well it's time for me to go. If y'all need me, just call or text." I told her.

Before Mallory caught up with the others, she told me that I'm an amazing person and that anyone who gets to know me will learn that.

"Your point?" I asked her. "You feel like Jonah, Corbyn, Daniel, Jeremy Kost, James Mcvey, Pierson Fode, Taron Egerton, Shannon Kook, Gus Kenworthy, Eva Gutowski, Chace Crawford, Christian Collins, Ben Lewis and especially Devin Hayes won't be your friend and become part of your life because of all you have been through in your life. Benny there are good people in this world. You have to believe me." "Really? Because, I'm having a hard time believing that. I don't know what I believe in anymore so please stop talking about James Mcvey, Michael Provost, Jonah, Pierson and the others. We have better things to worry about. Now go and please be careful. We can't lose anyone else." Mallory shook her head and walked away. AJ told me to be careful and that he's proud of me for telling the others about Gerwazy. Then he joined the others. The only ones left were Shawn and Chris Salvatore. "Are you sure you want to go with Gerwazy?" Shawn asked me. "Because you don't have too go." Chris said. "Guys, I'll be fine." "Yeah don't worry dudes. I'll take care of my brother." Gerwazy said as he pulled up in an Apollo Arrow. I got in and we drove away. "That's what I'm afraid of." Shawn said. He and Chris looked at each other. Meanwhile, at The Jamison Mansion, the others were helping Sollie come up with ideas for his birthday party and decorating. AJ was in the hot tub, Doyle was feeding his face, Simon was in the tanning booth, Mitchell Hoog was swimming in the pool and so was Reed. Thomas, Rudy and Zayne. Devin and Logan were at The Jamison Water Park. Brandon, Lucy and Callan Potter were the only ones helping Sollie. Jonah, Corbyn, Zach and Jack were in a snow room and started snowboarding. As for Mallory, she decided to cross off another name on her Kiss Printes List and set up a kissing booth in The Jamison Mansion. She called Zayne over and had him wear a Spider Man mask.

Then she pulled up the mask and started making out with him. While Luke investigated The Jamison Mansion some more, suddenly a fog appeared and it knocked everybody out. However Simon who was conscious a little bit saw a cloak figure come out from the wall. The person started laughing. Without them knowing, Simon saw his face a little bit. But when Docherty tried to save the others, he actually saw who the person was and ran to get help. Elsewhere, me and Gerwazy were on our way to the celebration. As we drove, Gerwazy thought this was a great time for us to get to know each other better. "So tell me about yourself bro?" Gerwazy said. "Why" I ask him. "Because I want to get to know the real you." "Yeah right," I told him. "How about I start with you. First I want to know how much this car cost." He told me it cost one million dollars. "Alright next question, if you're dating a girl, what kind of girl would you date? Nerdy girls and overweight girls, or would you date hot and sexy girls?" "The second one of course, Gerwazy said, I mean look at me." When he said that, I told him to stop the car. "Why are we stopping?" Gerwazy asked me. "Because I'm walking back to The Show Mayor so I can join my friends." "What, why? Did I say something wrong?" "You always say the wrong things. All you care about are your looks, hair, body and wealth. I just can't stand to be around you. You are just like every other jerk in this world. Unless you can tell me something good about yourself or show me that you have a heart, I'm walking away and never coming back." I told him. Gerwazy didn't know want to do. "It was nice meeting you, goodbye bro." I said. "Wait! I love The Black Butterfly." "What?" I asked him, "The Black Butterfly means a lot to me. You know how my character says Awana. The spell he uses to make his costume appear. And the same spell he uses to control and enhance his darkness manipulation and to cast spells." Yeah, I told him. "Well, I love doing that. Playing this character is an honor. The show helps me escape from all my problems. Especially at home." "What's going on at home?" I asked him. "Remember when I told you and your friends that my parents had some upsetting news ." Yeah, I told him, "well my parents are getting a divorce." "Oh, I'm sorry to hear that. That must be hard." I told him. "Not really bro. My parents have never had a happy marriage. They always fight and never have time for me. They don't even care who gets custody of me. All my parents care about is money and looking good. So The Black Butterfly is all that I have. But now I have something else . A brother." I looked at Gerwazy and told him let's go.

Before we went to the celebration, Gerwazy decided to take me shopping. He wanted me to look presentable. We actually had a good time. Then we finally made it to the yacht . I was so nervous but

Gerwazy didn't leave my side. He told me to just be myself, shocking me. We got on the yacht and Gerwazy told me to stay close. The yacht started moving and the celebration began. Gerwazy introduced me to his friend Fisk. To my surprise, he was actually a nice and decent guy. He got to know me. Meanwhile, Gerwazy went looking for our father and found him drinking with his director. "Hey son, where have you been?" "Um I need to talk to you dad okay?" So they went inside the yacht and Gerwazy told him about me and boy was he furious. "Why would you bring him here?" "Because I thought you would like to meet him. I don't care about him. He's nothing, but a mistake and you're my second mistake, when are you going to learn that?" "Are you joking?" Gerwazy said . "Do I look like I'm joking? Get rid of him." "He's your son." Gerwazy said, "I don't care." "No! I won't. He's my brother and I need him in my life. In fact, I plan on announcing this news to the world tonight." "Oh really? I don't think so. You see, not only will this kill your career. It will kill my career as well and our family name. Remember! Fame, looks and wealth are the only things that matter in life. If you go through with this, I'll make sure The Black Butterfly is cancelled and make sure nobody ever remembers your name. It'll be like you never existed. You'll never star in another movie or TV show ever again. It's your move son." Gerwazy couldn't believe this.

While Gerwazy dealt with our dad, I met his assistant. "Hi I'm…." But before she could tell me her name, she fell. "Are you okay?" I asked her. "Oh yeah, this happens all the time, I'm a bit accident prone. Anyway, my name is Mohogony. It's nice to meet you," she told me. "Are you a friend of my boss?" "Um" I said. I didn't know whether or not to tell Mohogony and Fisk the truth. Then I met Gerwazy's other friends. Unfortunately, they were nothing like Fisk. "Who is this loser?" One of the guys said. "He has no right to be here." "Wow, I was wondering when I was going to meet some spoil brats." I said. "Enough," Gerwazy said . "Leave him alone. Come on Benny." I followed him inside and asked him how can he hang out with people like that. He told me they were just playing. I looked at him and asked him do you see me laughing. Gerwazy apologized. Then he told me what our father said. I stood there like I was frozen or something. I was upset and couldn't believe that this man is my father. Gerwazy started to tell me something but he was interrupted when our father came looking for him. "There you are, I've been looking for you. It's time for your announcement. Who is this?" "The first mistake you ever made in your life." "Well isn't this interesting. I'm meeting my first son for the very first time, too bad I don't have any tissues or care. So this is Benny, wow you sure aren't anything to look at. Nothing but a huge disappointment. How is your ungrateful mother doing?" "Dad! He's your son and you're treating him like he's nothing." Gerwazy said. "Don't tell me how to talk boy. Remember what I told you." After meeting the father I never knew and seeing his true colors, I walked away. Gerwazy went after me. "Bro wait," he said. Before we could talk, Gerwazy's Director and our father, whose name is Demetric told his guests that Gerwazy is about to make his announcement. "Come on son, everybody is waiting." Demetric said, "don't go anywhere." Gerwazy told me. He went up in the front and told everybody he has something important to tell them. I was wondering does his news involve me. Gerwazy looked at me and our father. He had a hard choosing. So he finally made up his mind and told everybody his news. This is what he said. "I have signed a contract with Maine Kin and will become their next top Model, I can't wait. That's all. Please, enjoy the party." After he was done, I started walking away. "Wait Benny, let me explain." We went on the other side of the yacht to talk. "I know you're mad at me and probably hate me now but I had no other choice. I was planning on telling the world about you but dad threatened my career and I just panicked." Gerwazy said. All I did was look at him. "Say something." Gerwazy said, this is what I told him. "What's your favorite boy Band or male singer? Do you think men should cry?" "Are you kidding me, I don't have any and real men don't cry." Gerwazy said. "Typical stereotype. My favorite boy bands are Why Don't We and The Vamps. My favorite male singer is Shawn Mendes, Charlie Puth, Ruel, Cody Simpson, Aj Mitchell, Nick Jonas, Troyve Sivan, Jack and Jack and Alex Aiono . I'm not ashamed and neither should you. And men can cry. There's nothing wrong with that. It's part of being human. That's your problem, you like following the crowd. You're close minded and judgemental. You're just like everyone else. I thought you were different but I was wrong. You're one of those type of guys, the one that only cares about having good hair, looks, muscles, leading girls on, making fun of guys like me who have nothing. Taking shirtless pictures and walking around shirtless. Also hanging around the wrong crowd. Have you ever dealt with a racist or been bullied or ever felt like you have to be something you're not in order to fit in. Life isn't about having a six pack. Having good hair. Muscles, arm muscles, popularity, fame, wealth or being perfect and snooty. Life is about the meaning of family. Real and true friendship. Compassion, loyalty, love, hope, faith, helping others, having good morals and being a good person. Somebody people look up too. When was the last time you helped someone besides yourself like visiting sick children in the hospital. Getting to know your fans. Answering fan letters and showing your fans that you love them and appreciate them. I don't care that our father is a drunk and a sorry excuse for a dad. I have a loving mother and grandma. And an aunt who love me and raised me right. You on the other hand should always remember being yourself is more important than pretending to be something you're not, all you do is hang around a bad influence and make people believe that you have a perfect life. Where is the love, the morals." I asked him, "not all of us had a happy childhood. I know I didn't, I had nobody to love me. I have always been alone. For the first time you could've but now you don't. Goodbye bro," I told him. "Benny please, I need my brother in my life."

I used The Anselmi Arrie Speed Flies and didn't look back. When I got back on land, I called AJ but he didn't answer. None of my friends did, that's when I knew something was wrong. Suddenly I got a phone call from Shawn asking me do I need a ride. Before I could answer, he and Chris pulled up asking me am I alright. I asked them how did they even find me. Shawn told me they followed me. At that moment I realize that Shawn and Chris were becoming my best friends and I couldn't believe it. I told them what happened, then we heard a noise. I thought it was my phone but it turned out that it was Edvardas' phone. I forgot I had it and it's a good thing I didn't give it back to Edvardas. When I opened it up, me, Shawn and Chris found text messages from The Mad Ffraid Brat. I couldn't believe this. "Does this mean that

Edvardas is working for The Mad Ffraid Brat." Shawn asked me. "I think so," I told him. Chris read the new text message and the three of us got worried. Whoever sent the message wanted me to come alone to a skating rink to talk. "You're not going alone." Shawn told me. A few minutes later, I arrived at the skating rink alone. I had a hard time not falling on the rink, a cloak figure appeared and was surprised I was alone. "He's never alone." Shawn said. "You and your friends should know that about now." Chris said. The cloak figure was getting nervous. and tried to escape but Shawn started skating and threw a hockey puck at the mysterious person knocking him down. "Who are you?" I asked the cloak figure. Whoever it was, hid his face and handed me a bag. The person told us this should help us unmask The Mad Ffraid Brat and finally put an end to this mystery. Then they ran. Me and the others looked inside and found a laptop inside the bag. After that we went to The Jamison Mansion to check on the others. When we arrived, all the security guards were unconscious and the door was open. Me, Chris and Shawn ran inside and found all our friends unconscious. I used smelling salt to wake everybody up. However when they came to their senses, they couldn't believe what happened. Simon had a nasty sunburn due to sun tan oil, AJ was green. He looked like the incredible hulk. Doyle was covered with syrup. Mitchell Hoog's whole body was blue. Thomas was yellow, Reed was silver, Rudy was red . Zayne was purple. As for Callan, he was covered in chocolate. Brandon was gold. Lucy was wearing a gorilla outfit. Logan was covered in custard pie. Devin was dressed as Hercules. Sollie was taped to the wall. Why Don't We were glued together. But when we saw Mallory, she was dressed as a clown. She had the clown makeup on. Red nose and everything. She couldn't stop screaming. She ran into the bathroom and locked the door. However, I noticed that Luke was missing and I went to find him. I found a secret passage that led to a secret laboratory that belonged to Esdras. I found Luke. He was frozen in a cotton candy ice cocoon.

I called Shawn and we used The Cybernetic Falconieri Penzance Communicators and we defrosted him. He was shaking. After we got him some towels and found everybody, me, Shawn and Chris wanted to know what happened. Mallory told us that all she remembers is making out with Zayne. Aggravated that someone interfered, Mallory went over to Zayne and started making out with him once again. We all just rolled our eyes. Then we checked the security footage. Unknowing to the others, someone was in the mansion the whole time and they had help as well. Simon told us he saw one of the cloak figure's face a little bit but Luke saw their whole face when someone used the cotton candy freeze ray on him. He told me it was Edvardas. However, things got even more crazy when we saw footage of Docherty seeing The Mad Ffraid Brat's identity and getting electrocuted. We tried to zoom in but all of a sudden the footage was being erased. Sollie was upset that someone kidnapped his butler. Then, AJ got an email from The Mad Ffraid Brat who told him to look up. So, we all looked up and found a creepy message written on the ceiling. It said this. **The more you help AJ, The more I'll kidnap someone very close to you. P. S. You might want to check the horse stable.**

We went outside and found some guy in one of the stalls. We didn't know who this guy was but Sollie did. He told us that this is his best friend Severeano. We took him inside and got to know Severeano. He told us that earlier today, he got a message from Raysel, his admirer asking him to come to The Jamison Mansion so they can finally meet face to face. It turns out that not only has Raysel been getting emails, but Severeano as well. Or so they thought. When Severeano arrived at The Jamison Mansion, he told us that Raysel wanted to meet him at the horse stable. Unfortunately someone knocked him out. I told him that someone has been impersonating Raysel and him as well. Severeano couldn't believe this. Me and the others told Severeano about The Mad Ffraid Brat and there minions. Suddenly, I got a phone call from Grant .Then I sent an SOS text to the others. Me, AJ, Mallory and all the others arrived at our destination. Grant told us an anonymous person sent him a message telling him that there's something he should see. We couldn't believe what we were watching. On a billboard, we watched a video of AJ stealing from The Federal Reserve Bank of New York. Stealing gold bullions and a video of him stealing The Katana Sword. Then the fake AJ was waving at the camera. AJ couldn't believe this. Grant threw 20 Aigeos Juppar jawbreakers and told all of us to get out of the way, blowing the billboard up. We all knew with this evidence and another crime, AJ's career could be over. With his parents never around when he needs them and his butler's capture, me, AJ, Mallory, Simon, Doyle, Rudy, Shawn, Luke, Nick Mayorga, Lucy, Chris McNally, Devin, Logan, Grant, Colton, Why Don't We, Jacob, Matt, Hunter, Alex, Jack Maynard, Sean, Callan, Chris Salvatore and Mark spent the night with Sollie. It was stormy outside and I couldn't sleep. Neither could Grant. We went downstairs after hearing some noise and found Doyle and Alex Whitehouse. We asked them what were they doing up. Alex told us they couldn't sleep and decided to watch some TV. Then, AJ and the others joined us since none of us could sleep. We thought this was a good time to check out the laptop. Unfortunately, we couldn't see anything because it needs a password. So we decided to see what's on the flash drive that Sean found and we couldn't believe our eyes, especially Sollie. On the video, we saw Deveral visiting his grandpa in the hospital, the one and only Grand Dunixi Jamison. Deveral was arguing with his grandpa. He wanted to know where his grandpa's fortune was and the deed to The Show Mayor. But Grand Dunixi Jamison told him he'd rather die. Deveral walked up to him and whispered, 'That can be arranged.' He took out a syringe needle that had opiates and placed in his grandpa's chest. Me and Sean looked at each other. Mallory started panicking and thought making out with Jacob would ease her mind. As for Sollie, he was furious. He couldn't believe this. AJ just wanted this to be over while Mallory and Jacob made out. Me and the others were getting concerned about our safety while the storm continued. Unknowing to us, Detective Plaxido was outside of The Jamison Mansion just watching us.

CHAPTER NINE

THE STORAGE TRAP & TRAPPED ON A WINDOW WASHER'S PLATFORM

The next morning, Jonah woke me. He told me that he, Corbyn, Daniel, Jack and Zach are going to investigate The Jamison Museum. The one and only The Akoobjee Saliym Kulture, I asked him why? He said . "Great Grand father Novelo's journal is in that museum, and that there might be something there to help us," I told him to let me know what they find. Jonah looked at me and told me they want me to come along. "Wouldn't y'all prefer Simon or Mallory?" "No, we want you. Come on bro, we need you. Jonah said." I didn't know what to do until Grant told me to think of it as a adventure and to take a leap of faith. "Alright, let's go to a museum." I said. When we arrived at The Akoobjee Saliym Kulture, we couldn't believe how big the museum was and the amazing and very expensive exhibits. I kept my distance from Jonah and the others. I just didn't think they would become my friend due to people never giving me a chance. Then, I got a phone call and sat on a bench while Corbyn and the others explored the museum. But Jonah didn't leave my side. After I was done talking, I hung up and Jonah noticed that I was upset and asked me was I alright. I told him that was my mom. "What did she say?" He asked me. "Well, I told her about my sorry of an excuse dad and what's been going on with this case. She told me she's sorry that happened and that she wished she was here. My mom also told me I had a hard time saying it and Jonah told me it's okay and that he's here for me. I looked at him and told Jonah my mom told me the name of my twin sister. "It's Beneve." "That's amazing news bro and she has a beautiful name." Jonah said. "Yeah she does." I told him. Jonah could tell I was still upset and asked me how come I'm not smiling. I asked Jonah what if I never find her and what if she doesn't like me. Jonah smiled, "you are an incredible and amazing dude, who wouldn't like you? I'm glad to have met you and the others. We all like you but you keep assuming that we don't want to be your friend and I want to know why." Jonah said. "I don't think you would care." "Yes I do bro. So please tell me."

Jonah could tell how shy I was and decided to use this opportunity to get to know me better. He started by asking me questions like where am I from, my family, my favorite food, movies, TV shows and what my dreams are. I could tell Jonah really does care. He had my full attention so this is what I told him. "I'm from Iceland. It's one of the most beautiful places in the world and I miss it so much. I never thought I would attend a school so far from home." "Okay, tell us about your family next." Corbyn said as he joined us. "Well my mother's name is Conceicao. She's beautiful and very talented. She's a fashion designer. She can make anybody laugh. I hardly get to see her though. My Grandma Maroochy is wise, caring, has a lot of love in her heart, kind, strong, tough, smart, dependable, loyal, she uses tough love on those she cares about. And she has the cooking touch. As for my Aunt Antiquity, she's tough, strong and she makes me laugh. We look out for each other. I can always depend on these incredible three women in my life." "Go on," Zach said. "My favorite food is Cheese Burgers, Pepperoni pizza, homemade Macaroni, fry chicken, pork chop, ribs, bacon, sloppy joes, lima beans, squash, fry okra with onions and bacon, greens, cabbage, black eyed peas, string beans, corn, peas, smoke neck bone and blue berry muffins." "Keep going bro." Daniel said. "Okay, I have a lot of favorite movies. But these movies that I'm about to name are movies that never got the credit they deserve. Nothing but criticism. The first one is around The World in 80 Days, the one with Jackie Chan and Steve Coogan. Now I can watch this movie over and over again. This movie was epic . It taught you to never give up on something you believe in. Everything about this movie was awesome. In my opinion it should've gotten an award. I really love this movie. My second favorite is Newsies." I was a little nervous to tell them that I'm a huge fan but Jonah encouraged me and I went on ahead. "Like I was saying, Newsies is one of the best movies they ever made. It's a movie about the New York City. Newsboys strike of 1899 where a courageous and brave group of newsboys come together to fight a newspaper tycoon and set out to make a stand against Child labor and learn how powerful a voice can be and that there are strengths in numbers. One of my favorite things about this movie is the friendship between Jack and David. At first, they didn't get along but then they got to know each other and form an important friendship and I think that's incredible. I wish I had a friendship like theirs. These two were definitely Friendship goals. My favorite characters are Jack, David, Skittery, Crutchy, Spot Conlon and Kid Blink. As for the songs, Carrying The Banner. Santa Fe, The World Will Know, Seize The Day, King of New York, High Times and Once and For All. This movie has an important message, Always believe in yourself and that anything is possible if we all come together and stand up for what we believe in. My third favorite is Miss Congeniality 2 Armed and Fabulous. This movie should've got some credit. Sandra Bullock and Regina King did an amazing job on this movie and it would've been cool to see these two work together again. Not every movie has to be about romance or killing. What's wrong with a buddy film? Titan A.E was epic, it was one of the best animation movies they ever made. I just wish it got the credit that it deserved. So was Kronk's New Groove. There was nothing wrong with this movie. It was awesome. And Home on The Range. I cannot believe that this movie didn't win an award. This movie has excitement, adventure, the meaning of friendship, love, family and most of all believing in yourself. These three cows, Kick butt, The Rugrats Go Wild. I really enjoyed this crossover. No matter what people say, these two families make a great team and I love the friendship between Angelica and Debbie. Christmas With The Kranks was hilarious and way too funny. It's one of my favorite Christmas movies with two of my favorite stars. Fred's Clause was another Christmas movie that didn't get any credit. It was too funny and had a meaningful message. Mom's Night Out was good and funny. It taught us that moms aren't perfect and that they will have their good days and bad days and that being a mom is the best thing in the world. I love the song at the end. Alvin and The Chipmunks The Road Trip was amazing. It has an important message about family. I like how Alvin, Simon and Theodore were bonding with Josh and the part when Dave officially adopts The Chipmunks. Mar Needs Mom, this movie deserves a lot of love. It was incredible. It teaches you to appreciate your mom and to always show your mom how much you love her. It should've won an award. Judy Moody and The Not Bummer Summer should've got something as well. This movie was hilarious and teaches you what summer is all about even when your plans don't go the way that you hope. Hey Arnold The Movie, Treasure Planet, Jungle 2 Jungle, Ella Enchanted – Ella Hathaway did an amazing job in this movie. Happily N ' After, Fat Albert, You Again – Kirsten Bell is hilarious and too amazing, When In Rome, Madea Big Happy Family, Scooby Doo The Movie, Scooby Doo 2 – Monster Unleashed, College Road Trip, Mirror Mirror, The Haunted Mansion, Ace Ventura Jr. Pet Detective, Mighty Joe Young, Legally Blondes, Digimon The Movie, The Adventures Of Rocky and Bull Winkle, Atlantis The Lost Empire, Max Keeble's Big Move, Wild Wild West – was good too. But you know how critics are, Big Fat Liar, Pocahontas 2 – Journey To a New World was good too. The only problem with this movie was Pocahontas' new love interest and how different John Smith was in this movie. Lilo and Stitch 2 – Stitch Has a Glitch, Batman & Robin, Raise Your Voice, The Country Bears, Fantastic Four 2, Honey I Blew Up The Kid, Honey We Shrunk Ourselves, Doctor Dolittle 3, Charlotte's Web 2 : Wilbur Great Adventure, Valiant, Mighty Morphin Power Rangers. Now this movie was good. Ivan Ooze was incredible and hilarious and the ending was too funny when Zedd and Rita return causing Goldar and Mordant to panic. These are some good movies that never got the credit that they deserve. Disney's Kid, some people don't like this movie but I love it. This movie teaches you that sometimes we need to look inside ourselves and bring out our inner child. It's one of the best movies in the world.

Eight Legged Freaks should definitely got some credit. It's one of the best spider movies. Into the Storm is one of my favorite storm movies. Clue The Movie is definitely an amazing movie. It's hilarious and full of suspense. I could watch it over and over again. The Green Lantern is another great movie. Too bad they never made a sequel. Muppets From Space, I'm a huge Muppet Fan and I can't believe people didn't like Muppets From Space, in this movie. We learned what Gonzo is and where he comes from. The same thing with Kermit Swamp Years. In this movie people learned where Kermit came from. House Arrest with Jamie Lee Curtis and Kevin Pollak. This movie was good too. In this movie, the parents and their kids work out their differences with each other and come together. The Giver was amazing and The Gods of Egypt. They should've gotten more credit. Brenton did a great job. It would be cool to meet him. Home Alone 3 deserves an award. It didn't get any credit which wasn't right. It was hilarious and an awesome movie. And the last movie that deserves an award and credit is Unaccompanied Minors. This is one of the best Christmas movies ever. People shouldn't say bad things or criticize movies. Not every movie has to be number one. Just appreciate the magic of movies and the stories behind them. These writers, Producers, Directors, actors, actresses and others work so hard to make these movies and bring them to life. People just don't care. They rather have movies that have cussing instead of meaningful messages and movies that are family friendly. "Keep going bro." Daniel said with a smile. I told him and the others that Raven's Home, Andi Mack, 7th Heaven, Arthur, Charmed, Supernatural, Touched by an Angel, The Good Doctor and SpongeBob SquarePants are my favorite shows. Also, I told them about three of my favorite shows that got cancelled. Number one, Ghost Whisperer. I really miss this show. It was one of the best shows. I always hope Professor Payne would return to Grand View, him and Melinda were good friends and had good chemistry. My second favorite is George Lopez. George's mother cracks me up every time she opened up her mouth. Angie was another favorite character of mine. My Wife and Kids was too funny and it's sad they left the show on a cliffhanger. After finding out that Jay was pregnant, I was upset when Resurrection, Living with Fran and The

Crossing got cancelled. My other favorite shows are Pretty Little Liars. I love how the girls always have each others back and their unbreakable friendship and bond. Once Upon A Time taught me about hope and belief and how they always find each other. You gotta love these characters. Hetty Feather, there's never a dull moment. At The Foundling Hospital, Hetty and Mathias are my favorite characters. Wind At My Back is a touching show. Honey is one of my favorite characters. Her mother in law was a horrible person who treated her so badly. She forced Honey to give up her kids. Honey was a good and loving mother. One of the things that I admire about her is that she never gave up even when all seemed lost. I was sad that the actress who played Honey in Seasons 1 – 3 left the show. She will always be one of my favorite characters. The original Honey, Honey went through a lot. Honey is an incredible and strong character and my second favorite is Grace. She was the only one who showed sympathy and kindness to Honey and the boys. The only decent and kind Bailey who wasn't against Honey. I like how Grace and Honey became so close and how Honey and her kids taught Grace how to stand up for herself. Especially against her controlling and manipulative mother. Season 1 is the only season that I like because it seemed to have more love and the power of hope than the other seasons.

"And what about your dreams?" Jack asked me. I told him "I have two dreams, my first dream is to become the next big thing and share my music with the world and to become an Author. But it will never happen." I said in a down voice. "Why would you say that?" Jack asked me. "Because all my life, I have kept my head down. Too afraid to talk to people. I'm a piano Prodigy who has stage fright and I'm afraid to show people the real me. So there, sorry if I bore you." After telling Why Don't We a little about me, I started walking away until Jonah got in my way. "Stop bro, you didn't." Jonah said. "It was interesting getting to know the real you." Corbyn said. "And you my bro are one of a kind." Daniel said. "You are incredible." Zach said, "and I would love to hear some of your music and read some of your manuscripts." Jack said. I looked at them and asked them why would you want to be friends with me. "Why not make new friends?" Jonah said with smile. "There will always be a reason why you meet people. Either you need them to change your life or you're the one that will change theirs." Corbyn said, "we want to be your friend. I know you have been hurt in the past and feel like nobody wants to be your friend. But we do." Daniel said. "We like you for you." Zach said. "We're part of your life now, whether you believe it or not." Jack said . "And you don't have to pretend to be something you're not. In order to be in our lives, just be yourself." Jonah said.

I looked at him and the others and couldn't believe I made some more friends, especially with people I didn't think I stood a chance of becoming friends with. "Have we finally convinced you?" Jonah asked me. I smiled and shook my head. After that, me and Why Don't We took a tour of The Akoobjee Saliym Kulture Museum. As we walked through the museum, we realized that every exhibit in this museum is made with real diamonds and other jewels. Some are made with real gold and others are made out of real money. Then we got to Great Great Great Great Great Novelo Jamison's exhibit and found the journal. We created a distraction while Corbyn looked through the journal. Meanwhile, Sean was taking the laptop to Leonel. When he walked into the lab, he found Seissylt and Fuji. He asked Leonel what were they doing there. Leonel told him that I thought it would be more safer for Seissylt and Fuji to be in the lab. Sean showed the laptop to Leonel and told him whatever is on the laptop could help them unmask The Mad Ffraid Brat. Leonel told Sean that he'll try his best. After that, Sean was about to leave but Leonel asked him if he could stay. Sean told him sure and watched as Leonel tried to hack into the computer. Back at The Akoobjee Saliym Kulture Museum, Corbyn was still looking through the journal. So far he hadn't found a thing. Then he found a hollow page and used The Cybernetic Falconieri Penzance Communicator to cut it open. Inside was a secret document. Unfortunately it was written in Invisible ink. Corbyn used The Cybernetic Falconieri Penzance Communicator and started reading. He was shocked while he read. I had a bad feeling that something bad was about to happen and I whisper something to Daniel. He told the others he'll be right back. Suddenly the roof shattered into pieces and five black ropes came down. "What's going on?" Jonah said, "something bad." I told him. We watched as five thieves came down. One of the thieves took off there mask. When they did, everybody in the museum was shocked except for me and Why Don't We. It was AJ or should I say a fake AJ. The tourists started running. I walked up to the fake AJ and told them this. 'I don't know who you are. But me and my friends will stop you no matter what it takes.' The fake AJ smiled and told me to bring it on. Then they took out a cannon – net and trapped me and the others in a net. "You won't get away with this." I told them. "I just did," the fake AJ said. The fake AJ and their minions were about to steal Mr. Accerly Jamison's most prized and valuable Diamond, The Nation Diamond which is worth a lot of money, more than anyone could ever imagine. Just as they were about to break in, Daniel appeared and tried to stop them but the thieves to his surprise had acrobat skills and used the cannon – net on him. The thieves broke the glass and a metal claw came down and grabbed The Nation Diamond. The thieves used their Acrobat skills and jumped out. "Sorry, I would love to stay but I have things to do. See you guys next time." The fake AJ said as he laughed. He and the others escaped on the helicopter. "Now what do we do?" Zach said. "Don't worry guys. I have a plan." I told them. "Okay Daniel, it's clear." Daniel took off camflouage mode and used The Cybernetic Falconieri Penzance Communicator to get us out of the net, shocking Jonah, Corbyn, Zach and Jack. "If you're Daniel then who's that?" Jack said. Me and Daniel smiled and told them that was a hologram. I had a feeling that The Mad Ffraid Brat would place yet another crime on AJ so I had a backup plan in case anything went wrong.

Unfortunately they got away with The Nation Diamond and a lot of people noticed the heist. Now we have another problem on our hands and we're no closer to unmasking The Mad Ffraid Brat. "Don't worry bro, we will save AJ and catch whoever is framing him." Jonah said. Corbyn showed us what he found and told us that Great – Great Grand Father Novelo was the first ever rich Jamison but there's something his family and the world doesn't know. He was a fraud. Great – Great Grandfather Novelo stole money from banks and he even killed people. "He was no role model." Corbyn said, "this news can ruin The Jamison Family's name." Jonah said. Me and the others destroyed the footage

134

before the cops came and left the museum. A few hours later, me and Mark Thomas went to The Jamison Adonijah Industries and broke into Mr. Accerly Jamison's office. While we searched his office, Mark noticed how quiet I was and tried to get to know me. "What's your favorite animation shows?" Mark said. "It's not important." I told him in a down voice. "Yes it is bro. Just name two." Mark said, I told him that I'm a fan of the old Pokemon. Back when the show had charm, love and the meaning of friendship. No matter what, I'll always be upset that they took Misty off the show. Misty leaving the show was the hardest thing for me. She was important to the show. She and Ash belonged together. Misty will always be his one true love. I just miss the old days of Pokemon. Pokemon taught us the importance of friendship and how powerful it can be. I also liked Tracey, May, Max and Dawn. It would've been nice if they were all together travelling around the world discovering new Pokemon, saving the day and defeating Team Rock. Things were never the same when Misty left. Misty's Goodbye Song makes me sad. Anyway, I'm also a huge fan of The Simpsons. I love this show and Springfield. The Simpsons is one of the longest running shows and I hope it continues. They also have some of the best songs as well. I love how no matter what Homer does, Marge still loves him. They really are a great couple. I also like some of the crossovers like when they met the Futurama gang. It was really cool how Homer and Bender became such great friends. And the crossover they had with Family Guy, now that was interesting. I like how the music plays as The Griffins Family head into Springfield and when Lady Gaga came to Springfield. No matter how old I get, I will always be a fan of The Simpsons. "Why do you want to know anyway?" I asked him. "Because I want to get to know my friend." Mark said. "And who's that?" I asked him. Mark smiled, "It's you bro." He said. "Really, I'm your friend?" I asked him. "Yes you are. So stop doubting." Mark said. After that, we continued our search. I went through Mr. Accerly Jamison's files while Mark checked Mr. Accerly Jamison's computer.

I didn't find anything useful but Mark did. He showed me an email and told me that Mr. Accerly Jamison is preparing for his annual Flame Feast at The Zvezda Three Ples. A mansion that belongs to

Grand Dunixi Jamison. When I saw the name of the mansion, I quickly called Brandon and asked him where the treasure map leads to and he told us The Zvezda Three Ples. "So that means the fortune and maybe more important things of Grand Dunixi are somewhere inside his old mansion." I told him and Mark we are going to crash a Jamison ball. Mark checked the guest list and told us The Flame Feast,is booked so I called Sollie and he told me that he'll make sure our names are on the list. Me and Mark wondered what is a Flame Feast. Suddenly we heard someone coming into Mr. Accerly Jamison's office and hid. It was Gewnsnay, Mr. Accerly Jamison's assistant. She placed some papers on Mr. Accerly Jamison's desk and left. Me and Mark looked through the papers but realized it wasn't anything interesting. We saw Gewnsnay's desk and left Mr. Accerly Jamison's office to snoop through her desk. Mark tried to get into her computer and I went through her drawers and discovered some of the gold from The Federal Reserve Bank of New York. Me and Mark couldn't believe it, and Mark found out that Gewnsnay has been stealing money from Mr. Accerly Jamison for years. "What are you doing?" Me and Mark looked and found Gewnsnay behind us. "I have been dying to meet you, Benny Breezy. My sources tell me you and your friends have been a real problem. So you found my stash of gold." Gewnsnay said. "Yeah, my boss is not going to like that. In fact, I may have to hurt Nasser." Gewnsnay said with a smile. When she said that, I almost lost my temper. Mark had to calm me down. "Why are you doing this?" Mark asked her. "Doing what? Oh, you mean working with The Mad Ffraid Brat. Well I have my reasons but I won't tell you. Anyway, I can't let y'all leave." "Catch us if you can. Run," Mark told me. As we tried to escape, Gewnsnay put The Jamison Adonijah Industries on a major lock down. The doors and windows were shut and there was no way out. Me and Mark were trapped. There were security guards everywhere. Realizing how dangerous things have gotten, I told Mark I'm going to turn myself in to save him, but Mark grabbed me. "What are you thinking?" Mark asked me. "I'm trying to save my friend. This isn't your fight, so just go and save yourself." I told him. "I am part of this too and I'm not going to let you give The Mad Ffraid Brat what they wants. They already have Nasser. Can you imagine what they will do to you. You can't give up now. Not when we're so close. Remember bro, we're in this together." Mark said. Thanks I told him. Mark smiled and we continued our search for a way out of The Jamison Adonijah Industries. Then we stumbled upon a conversation between Gewnsnay and The Mad Ffraid Brat. The Mad Ffraid Brat was furious that I found some of the stolen gold from The Federal Reserve Bank of New York. They started threatening Gewnsnay and told her to make sure I don't escape.

After that, The Mad Ffraid Brat sent Gewnsnay a list of names and told her to make sure she takes care of that. Me and Mark wondered who are those people. Mark used The Cybernetic Falconieri Penzance Communicator and took pictures of all those names. After that, we called Leonel and asked if he could teleport us. Unfortunately the machine was still acting up. So I used The Cybernetic Falconieri Penzance Communicator and we looked at a hologram map of The Jamison Adonijah Industries and saw how many security guards were in the building. They were everywhere including the roof. Mark realized the only way to escape was to go down the sewer line and boy did it stink. I saw the water and started panicking a little. Mark asked me what's wrong, I told him I can't swim and that I'm afraid that I might drown. He told me to trust him and that everything will be okay. So, I closed my eyes and we both jumped in and got away from Gewnsnay and the guards. Mark told me that he was proud of me. After that, we climbed out and were back on the surface. Me and Mark went back to The Show Mayor and were drawing a lot of attention. We ran into Mr. Stumbo who covered his nose. "What happened to y'all? And what's that smell?" Mr. Stumbo said. "Trust us, you don't want to know." Mark said. "Anyway, we need to talk to you." I told Mr. Stumbo. "Let's go to my office," he said. We followed him into his office, Mr. Stumbo grabbed several cans of air fresheners and started spraying. "Speak fast," Mr. Stumbo said. "Okay then, what can you tell us about Flame Feast?" I asked him. "Well the annual Flame Feast is something Mr. Accerly Jamison does every summer. It's an auction / ball where Mr. Accerly Jamison sells some of his most valuable jewels. It's one of the biggest events in Hollywood. Each year gets better and better and the food is to die for." Mr. Stumbo said, but he decided not to go on. He wanted us to see everything that Flame Feast has to offer. Then I got a phone call from Callan telling me to meet him at the hospital. I told him I'll be there after I take a shower. A few hours later, I made it to the hospital and asked him what was going on. He told me there's something I should see, so I followed him in the back and couldn't believe who was in the hospital. It was Stiles but he didn't look like himself. He was constantly sweating and shaking. I asked Callan what happened to him. Callan told me that a few days ago Stiles started to feel really bad and only told him. I noticed a rash on Stiles' arm. Me and Callan talk to the doctor. She told us that they don't know why this is happening and that Stiles isn't the only one dealing with this mysterious illness. "What do you mean?" I asked her. The doctor told us to follow her. She took me and Callan to a room that was being quarantined. We put on some Contaminant Suits and discovered 30 patients that had the same illness that Stiles had. However, these patients symptoms were far worse than Stiles. Me and Callan couldn't believe this. The doctor said most of these patients ate some girl scout cookies and for some reason, they became ill. Me and Callan looked at each other and asked the doctor. "Did Stiles eat some of those cookies?" She told us no and said Stiles ate some Mccanna Bomboons. "What is that?" I asked her. She told me and Callan that Mccanna Bomboons is a candy but they can't figure out why the candy would make him ill. But the doctor said if we don't find out what's causing this, Stiles and the others will die. When she said that, I walked out of the room and wondered why is this happening. Callan told me that we will find a way to save Stiles and the other patients. Before we left the hospital, I told Stiles to hold on.

Then me and Callan used The Cybernetic Falconieri Penzance Communicators to find out who sells Mccanna Bomboons and when we found out we weren't shocked at all and discovered that Tielyr sells them and runs a candy store called The Pythias Olyver Swirls. So we went to check it out and bought one of the biggest bars they had. We unwrapped the paper. Then me and Callan opened up the Mccanna Bomboons and found some icky and slimy green stuff. I quickly called Leonel and asked him to analyze Hade Wild and to check the results,

Simon and Why Don't We sent him after they analyzed those girl scout cookies . So Leonel checked both results and told us that Hade Wild is some kind of virus. Then he checked The Mccanna Bomboons and told me and Callan that Hade Wild is in the girl scout cookies and The Mccanna Bomboons. That's why Stiles and the others aren't feeling good. "Somebody is making people sick. Question is though, is there a cure?" Callan said. "I really hope so," I told him. We got back to The Show Mayor and told AJ, Mallory, Simon, Doyle and Aunt Fanny what we found out. Aunt Fanny was actually showing sympathy. She was worried about Stiles. I told her and the others that I'm going to break into Silouanus Prater's house to find Fuji files. AJ turned the TV on and told me that everybody thinks he stole The Nation Diamond and that he can't take anymore of this. I told him we're getting closer and that we will unmask The Mad Ffraid Brat and to hold on. Suddenly, Devin showed up and I tried to hurry up and get out of the penthouse, but Mallory stopped me. "Why are you blocking the door?" I asked her. Mallory smiled and handcuffed me to Devin. "Um Mallory, what are you doing?" I said. "I want my future husband and my best friend to bond and to become friends." Mallory said. "Yeah? Well I want to be friends with Jackson Dockery but that won't happen either. So why don't you uncuff us now before things get out of hand." I told her. "No, I won't." Mallory said. "How many times do I have to tell you, me and Devin come from two different worlds. I'm not his type of friend. To think Devin would ever become my friend is something that will never happen. People just don't give me a chance okay. I know the kind of people he hangs out with and I'm nothing like that. I wouldn't fit in. I'm not good looking or popular, I'm just me. These days, people rather hang out with attractive people. So get these things off now." "Sorry, I can't do that." Mallory said. "Alright then," I told her as I walked away. "Where are you going?" Mallory asked me. "Nowhere, I'm just trying to find something that will break these cuffs." I told her. "Well have fun with that because those aren't any ordinary handcuffs." Mallory said with a smile. "What do you mean?" I asked her. Mallory told me these are The Inderpal Venanzio Indeeo Handcuffs. "Another gadget that Leonel made." Mallory said. "Getting out of these handcuffs will be impossible and that the only way to unlock them is the key." "What key?" I asked her, "this one." Mallory told me as she twirled the key around. I tried to grab it but Mallory stopped me. "You'll get this key when you and Devin finally become friends." Mallory said. "Hmm, we'll see about that." I told her, I started looking for anything that could break these cuffs. I used a hammer, then a pickaxe. I also used pincers, a drill, and a hacksaw. I even used a sledgehammer. But nothing worked. Every time I tried something, The Inderpal Venanzio Indeeo Handcuffs would electrocute me. "Seriously Mallory, get these things off of us." "Have fun," Mallory said.

I grabbed my stuff and me and Devin left the penthouse. I found out where Silouanus Prater lives and made sure the coast was clear. I used a picklock and we went inside. To our surprise, Silouanus had a nice house. We started searching through his stuff. While we looked for Fuji's files, Devin tried to talk to me but I completely ignored him. Then we found a hidden safe behind a book shelf. So after we guessed the combination, we found Fuji Files. Me and Devin read Silouanus' notes and learned Fuji used to deal with depression and anxiety. But it doesn't say why he was depressed. Then Devin showed me a file where Fuji revealed to Silouanus about a secret room in The Show Mayor and how it might have caused him to become a hoarder. Me and Devin wondered where in The Show Mayor could this secret room be at. We made copies of the files and got out of there. We got back to The Show Mayor and Mallory couldn't wait to hear how things went. I told her to give me the key. Mallory was furious that me and Devin didn't become friends and refused to give us the key. Devin grabbed Mallory and started making out with her. Unfortunately Mallory was still mad after they were done making out. However to my surprise and Mallory's, Devin did that in order to get the key. He unlocked The Inderpal Venanzio Indeeo and ask me could we be friends. Worried that I might get hurt and dealing with the fact that I'm not cool, I just simply walked away. Devin asked Mallory what should he do. Mallory told him that he has to prove to me that he wants to be my friend. With the day almost over, I thought going to an unlikely source could help us uncover The Mad Ffraid Brat's true identity. However, not everybody wanted to go. So, me, Alex Whitehouse and Thomas went to talk to The Hinkley Youga Shirk and to our surprise, we met boy members of The Hinkley Youga Shirk. Two guys, the first guy was named Hazon and the second guy was named Erastus. We told them that we're here to talk to Seini. Hazon and Erastus gave Alex and Thomas a tour of the house while I went to talk to Seini. I found her in her room stuffing her face with ice cream. It looked like she's been eating ice cream all day. There were bowls everywhere. "What do you want?" Seini asked me. "It's nice to see you too. Sorry to disturb you but I need your help. I was wondering do you have any videos of AJ from past performances." "Why?' Seini said. "Because I think the person behind all of this could be someone from AJ's past. Will you help me?" I asked her. Seini went in her cabinet and gave me a flash drive. She told me this should help. I asked her how many videos are on there. Seini told me about five hundred. A shocked look came on my face and I told her thanks. Before I left, I asked Seini what was wrong. I could tell she was depressed about something. "You wouldn't care." Seini told me. "Yes I would." I told her. Seini put her ice cream down and she cut the TV off and told me, "No matter how hard I try, I'm always going to be a loser. Sometimes I wonder why I was even born. I'm nothing but a disappointment and always will be. I can't even get my crush AJ Mitchell to kiss me. For years I have tried and I always fail. Maybe I'm not meant for love." Seini said. "And maybe I'm not meant to have friends." I told her, "your both wrong." Alex said as he came into the room. "Seini, you are beautiful and kind. As for you Benny, don't you ever say that again. Of course you are meant to have friends. I'm your friend and I like you for you." "You do?" I asked him, "yes bro, I really do. We're friends." Alex said. "At least you have your friends Benny, I have no one." Seini told me and Alex a story about her first crush. She said back in High School, she met a guy who she thought was a good guy and tried to get him to notice her. Unfortunately she was wrong about him. After she admitted her feelings, the guy told her to meet him under the bleachers . So she did and she waited and waited. He finally came and she thought he was about to kiss her. Turns out it was a trap. He told his buddies to dump some mud on her and whispered to her, 'I don't kiss muddy girls.' From that moment on, Seini's life at high school was a living nightmare. She was constantly bullied and had no one to turn to. Nobody wanted to be her friend. Seini told me and Alex that she gave up on love until she saw AJ. She decided that AJ would be her first kiss. "Did you tell him that?" I asked her, "for what? I give up. It doesn't matter anymore. Love is for attractive people only." Seini said. Me and Alex felt sorry for Seini. "You have us." a voice said. We all looked around and saw a girl come out of the heating vent. "Who is this?" Alex said. "Guys, I would like you too meet Hinkley Youga Shirk 17. Her real name is Exene." "It's nice to meet you all, I can't believe you Seini." "What?' "You said you have no one. You have me, Razzy, Hinkley and the rest of The Hinkley Youga Shirk. We're a family. All we have is each other and don't you ever forget that" Exene said. Seini smiled. Seini offered to make Alex and Thomas a snack while I stayed in the room. Thomas asked me was I alright and I shook my head. He also told me we are friends whether I believed it or not . We also met Hinkley, who has a shrine of Jonah Marais and cut out boards of him that she makes out with.

After that, me and Jacob went to The Delahoussaye Psych Sisters. I kept my distance from Jacob. He's an another one I don't think would become my friend. Jacob had a plan to convince me. We arrived at The Delahoussaye Psych Sisters shop and when we went inside, they were still arguing about Trevor Donovan after all this time. "Ladies please, we need your help" I said. Orangia, Orangina and Orangetta were happy to see me. "We were wondering when you were going to get here." Orangia said . "So you know why we're here?" I asked them. "Of course we do. We're psychics remember? But we can't help you. We're trying to settle an agreement about which one of us would Trevor Donovan make out with." Orangetta said. "Are you serious? Do you have any idea what me and my friends have been through. We need your help please." I told them. But they didn't pay me any attention. Then, I decided to show them a certain name from The Flame Feast guest list for tomorrow and they freaked out. I bribed them with extra tickets to Flame Feast in exchange for some information. They finally gave in and each told me something. Orangia told me that me and my friends will find out who killed Esdras Jamison. Orangetta told me and Jacob that The

Mad Ffraid Brat will place another crime on AJ tomorrow night and Orangina said the answers we seek are in that journal. "That's it?" Jacob said. The Delahoussaye Psych Sisters shook their heads and told us all will be revealed in time. Before we left, Jacob asked them do they see him becoming great friends with someone who has given up on making friends. "Yes we do, but this person has to take a leap of faith and start trusting people again. Whoever this person is feels like all hope is lost and that he'll never make any friends because of everything he's been through." "Okay, that's enough" I told them. "Actually it's not. You think Devin and the others will never become your friend, well we're here to tell you that they will. Devin and you will be the best of friends, I promise." Orangetta said. I didn't know what to believe. "I just can't imagine Devin becoming my friend and why would he? Nobody ever gives me a chance."

Jacob didn't stop until he convinced me that we are friends. Later that day, me and Devan Key and Collins Key investigated Badaidra's dressing room. It was dark so we used some flash lights and started searching for clues. I didn't think Devan or Collins would give me a chance and become my friend so I just focused on the mystery. Anyway, we discovered several creepy puppets and Ventrilgoust dummies, then Devan found six Ventrilgoust dummies. Each one had a name on it. The first one was me. The second one was Mallory, the third one was Simon, The fourth one was Doyle. The fifth one was Nasser. However the sixth one was missing. A Ventrilgoust dummy of AJ. Me and Devan wondered why his Ventrilgoust dummy is missing. Meanwhile, Collins was still searching and found embalmed heads. He told us to come over here and we couldn't believe it. There were seven embalmed heads and they were real, freaking me and The Key brothers out. "Why would she have these?" Collins said. I told him I had no idea, after that we continued to search the dressing room. Suddenly Badaidra popped up, she was hiding behind a bunch of Ventrilgoust dummies. "Okay, things just got more creepy." Devan said. "No kidding bro," Collins told him. "Well hello Benny, It's nice to see you again. What are you doing in my dressing room?" Badaidra said. "We're trying to find anything that can clear AJ's name." I told her. "You and your

friends should be careful, you have no idea who you're messing with."
Badaidra told me. "I'm not scared of The Mad Ffraid Brat." I told
her. "Really? I find that very interesting." Badaidra said. "I want to
know why you have Ventrilgoust dummies that look like me and my
friends and where is the AJ Ventrilgoust dummy?" I asked her. "That's
none of your concern." Badaidra said with a creepy smile. "Why do
you have embalmed heads?" Collins asked her. Badaidra told me and
The Key brothers to sit down, then she put on a show for us using the
Ventrilgoust dummies. This is what she said, '**Once upon a time there
was a lonely girl who got teased because she would always play with
dead things. Unfortunately her parents were ashamed to call her
their daughter and would keep her locked in, away from the outside
world. Even her siblings didn't want anything to do with her. The
young girl had nobody to turn to and felt rejected so she started
making puppets and Ventrilgoust dummies that resembled her
family and would practice tormenting them. It got so bad that the
young girl got kicked out of school and faced punishment for her
misbehavior. Then one night the girl snapped after finding out her
parents were planning to send her to a very far away asylum. The
girl, fed up with her family, decided to murder them and embalmed
there heads and made sure nobody ever found out.**'

"OMG, you murdered your family?" Collins said . "Yes, I did."
Badaidra said as she laughed. Her laugh creeped me, Devan and
Collins out. We quickly got out of there. Me and Sean investigated
Montagew's dressing room. I didn't think Sean would become my
friend so I kept my distance. We split up and started searching, I went
through Montagew's computer and didn't find anything. As for Sean,
he found vials with skulls on them. There were 50 of them. This is
poison he told me. "Why would Montagew have poison?" I asked him.
Suddenly I heard a hissing noise and so did Sean. We quickly grabbed
our flash lights and couldn't believe our eyes. We were surrounded by
snakes. "OMG." Sean said. We thought things couldn't get any worse
but they did. Montagew appeared and couldn't stop smiling. This is the
end for you Benny Breezy. Montagew said, me and Sean looked at each
other and tried to come up with an idea. While Sean looked through

The Cybernetic Falconieri Penzance Communicator, I tried talking to Montagew. "Why are you doing this?" I asked him. "I can't tell you. My only orders were to kill you." Montagew said. I looked at Montagew and realized that Montagew is being bullied, just like Edvardas. "I don't know what The Mad Ffraid Brat has on you but you can't let them bully you." I told him. "You think it's that's easy? I became part of the team for the money and gold but when I realized how far The Mad Ffraid Brat and Deveral were going and how dangerous they are, I tried to get out and was planning on telling the cops and Mr. Accerly Jamison everything but The Mad Ffraid Brat threatened to reveal a dark secret of mine that could ruin my career and put me in jail for a very long time. So I had no other choice." Montagew said. "You always have a choice." I told him. Montagew called off his snakes and told me I'm right. Then me and Sean asked him what is the poison for. Montagew looked around and whispered to us that The Mad Ffraid Brat is planning to kill someone they think will reveal a big secret to us. "What secret?" I asked him. Montagew told me and Sean that he can't tell us for his own safety knowing what The Mad Ffraid Brat would do to him if they found out that he went behind there back. But he did tell us that the next clue lies in the Jamison Family statue. Something that could make life better at The Show Mayor. Me and Sean wondered what he meant.

Before we left, Montagew decided to reveal his secret to us. I told him he didn't have to but he felt like he owed us something due to everything The Mad Ffraid Brat has put AJ through. Montagew told me and Sean that a few years ago his cousin came to visit him. Unknowing to him, his cousin was smuggling a Black Mamba, one of the most dangerous snakes in the world. Unfortunately the snake got out and bit two people, a maid and a guest. To make sure this didn't get out, Montagew and his cousin got rid of the bodies and Montagew never spoke to his cousin ever again. He also killed the snake as well. Montagew said this secret has been haunting him for years and he wished he could go back in time and save those two people. Montagew told me to be careful and to be aware of my surroundings. Before me and Sean went back to the penthouse, Sean told me when you talk to people, share what you are. Stop focusing on all of the physical features that you think people won't like about you. Stop focusing on your inabilities or lack of talent. Instead, focus on those physical features that you know people already love about you. Focus on your abilities and the talents that you do have. You have been blessed with all of the above and that makes you worth getting to know in my book. You're my friend Benny Breezy and I mean that, Sean said. Later on, me and Alex investigated Conant's dressing room. Alex is another one I didn't think would become my friend. Anyway, the only thing we found was a collage of some guy named Packard. Me and Alex wonder who Packard was. Suddenly Alex told me to duck, it was Conant. He was using his fire breath, trying to burn us. We hid behind a table and quickly came up with a plan. Me and Alex used The Cybernetic Falconieri Penzance Communicators and pressed the fire extinguisher button and sprayed Conant. After that Alex trapped Conant inside a bubble gum cocoon. Conant was furious. But me and Alex didn't care. We asked him who is Packard. With no way out, Conant decided to tell us. He told me and Alex that Packard is his brother and told us what happened to him. This is what he said, '**Me and my brother were the best fire breathers and inseparable. I did everything with my brother and depended on him. But that all changed when all the girls started falling for him. They would throw him flowers, ask for his autograph and some would even sneak in our dressing room just to meet him. The attention was getting to Packard's head and it was interfering with our act and me and Packard started to drift apart. It was like I didn't know my brother anymore. Then one day, after the show, I heard Packard talking to Grand Dunixi Jamison, but I couldn't hear what they were saying and I jumped to conclusions. I thought my brother wanted to be a solo Fire Breather so I had a major confrontation with Packard and, ended up pushing him in cooking oil. I didn't mean too. I was just so angry at him, I killed my best friend. And that's why I have a collage of my brother. I miss him and I wish I could have him back. The pain I feel and the suffering will never go away. Conant said.**

Me and Alex looked at each other and couldn't believe that Conant actually has a soul. "Why are you helping The Mad Ffraid Brat?" Alex said. "For the money. The Mad Ffraid Brat promise me a fortune and with that money I can finally get out of here and start a new life." Conant told him. "Running away won't solve your problems." I told him. "You need to fix your mistakes so you and your brother can find peace." Alex said. We left Conant's dressing room and Alex told me each friend represents a world in us. A world possibly not born until they arrive. And it is only by this meeting that a new world is born. "We're friends Benny, always." Alex told me, the next dressing room was Terentilo's. Me and Grant went investigating. Once again, I kept my distance because I knew Grant wouldn't become my friend. When we got to Terentilo's dressing room, Terentilo was in there talking to someone about a place called The Salvatore Day Ray. We eavesdroped on there conversation and wondered who Terentilo was talking to. Grant eased his head up and saw a cloak figure. He quickly got back down and told me The Mad Ffraid Brat is in there, before we had a chance to come up with a plan, Terentilo left the dressing room. Alone, we looked inside and couldn't believe it. The Mad Ffraid Brat was gone somehow. We decided to follow Terentilo. As we followed him, Grant tried to talk to me and told me you've got a friend in me. Grant told me I don't have pretend to be something I'm not and that he likes me for me. "My brother from another mother." Grant said. I was happy that we were friends. Wherever Terentilo was going was far away from the city and near water. Finally we reached our destination and discovered a warehouse. Me and Grant went on top of the roof and saw several monetary print presses and stacks and stacks of money. There were also several women who were stacking the money up. Me and Grant wondered what was going on. So Grant used a pulley and eased his way down to talk to one of the women. He met a young Chinese girl named Chun, who told him some disturbing news. Meanwhile I watched as Terentilo placed some cash in his pockets. He shouted out I love The Salvator Day Ray. Terentilo noticed that Chun was talking to someone and went to see who she was talking to. She quickly handed him some documents and told Grant to save her and the others. Grant managed to get back to the top without Terentilo noticing. I asked him what did he find out. Grant was quiet and couldn't believe it. He told me that the Salvator Day Ray is a place where Deveral is trafficking and making women make him illegal money.

We read through the documents and realized that these are the names that me and Mark saw at The Jamison Adonijah Industries. With the day almost over with, me, AJ, Mallory, Colton, Simon, Why Don't We, Lucy, Collins Key and Devan Key went to talk to Ross Lynch after AJ got a text from Ross, telling him there's something he needs to see. Unfortunately security wouldn't let us in, we found out that Ross Lynch is performing at a wedding here at The Show Mayor so Mallory came up with an idea. She disguised herself as a maid and had Why Don't We hide in a laundry cart. Meanwhile, Me, AJ, Lucy, Colton, Simon and The Key brothers used a Window washer's platform. Only my friends know this but I'm afraid of heights and I started to freak out a little. Lucy tried to calm me down. She, Colton and AJ thought singing a song would ease my mind. They sung How Far We've Come and I started to feel better. While we used the window washer's platform, Mallory and Why Don't We made it to the suite that Ross was staying in. Unfortunately he wasn't there, but that didn't stop Mallory from snooping through his stuff. She grabbed Ross's jacket and rubbed it against her face and she sniffed Ross's Cologne. Jonah and the others just stared at her. Jonah used The Cybernetic Falconieri Penzance Communicator and called me. Suddenly the window washer's platform cable sarted to break and me, AJ, Lucy, Colton, Simon, Devan and Collins tried to hang on. I asked Jonah and the others do they see anybody. Corbyn used The Cybernetic Falconieri Penzance Communicator and saw The Mad Ffraid Brat cutting the cable. "What are we going to do?" Daniel said.

Mallory had no idea how she would save us. Colton came up with an idea and told all of us to swing, so we did and we all crashed into a glass window. To our surprise we were at the wedding and everybody was staring at us, especially Ross. He helped me up and asked me was I alright. I never imagined myself meeting Ross Lynch. I didn't think I stood a chance of becoming friends with him and I just nodded my head. Ross shook my hand. With all eyes on me and the others, Colton whispered something to the DJ and started singing 'What a Feeling'. Me and the others joined him and got the couple and their guests to join in. Mallory and Why Don't We joined in as well. After the ceremony, Mallory was the one to catch the bouquet and looked at Jonah. Mallory freaked out when she met Ross. The two sung 'The Heart Never Forgets' at the wedding. After that, Me and the others talked to Ross and he took us to his tour bus and we couldn't believe our eyes. Half of the stolen gold from The Federal Reserve Bank of New York was in his tour bus. AJ was starting to get tired of The Mad Ffraid Brat. Mallory checked her Kiss Printes List and decided to cross off another name. She grabbed Devan by the shirt and made out with him. Simon, who was getting jealous of Mallory kissing so many guys took pictures of the stolen gold. With the day over with, me and Mitchell Hoog found out that Quintonette is at a retirement home called Present Avalon. Mitchell noticed how quiet I was being and tried to get me to talk. "You don't have to be shy around me. I'm your friend." Mitchell said. But I didn't believe him. We asked the nurse what room is Quintonette in. She told us room 333. We knocked on the door and Quintonette whispered softly to come in. Me and Mitchell noticed how shaking and nervous Quintonette was and asked her why was she working with Tielyr. When we mentioned that name, Quintonette started freaking out and locked her door and windows. "How do you know that?" She asked us. "We can't tell you." Mitchell said, "just please tell us. There are lives at stake." Mitchell told her. "I knew this day would come sooner or later." Quintonette said. "What day?" I asked her. "The day my life fell apart and everything changed." Quintonette said. This is what she told me and Mitchell. "My life used to be stressful and tiresome. "I would work and work everyday and never had time for my family or friends because I always thought work was my main priority but that all changed when I met Tielyr. It was love at first sight. He introduced me to Grand Dunixi Jamison, Esdras Jamison, and Bregusuid Jamison and they hired me. I felt like we were one big happy family. Tielyr opened up a candy shop called The Pythias Olyver Swirls and had the hardest time selling his candy to people. And just when he was about to give up, I created The Mccanna Bomboons and to our surprise people actually loved them. Tielyr thought he had everything. Unfortunately, life at The Show Mayor started to change when Tielyr found out that Grand Dunixi Jamison, Esdras Jamison and Bregusuid Jamison were keeping things from him. He was furious and their friendship started to fall apart. Tielyr wanted to form a partnership with Grand Dunixi Jamison and Esdras Jamison but they didn't trust him or liked his ideas. Tielyr decided to leave The Show Mayor and opened up his own business, 'The Horror Herculano', it was nothing like The Show Mayor. It was dark and scary. Tielyr became a different person and forced me to choose a side. Faced with a difficult choice and blinded by love, I secretly worked on both sides and was a spy for Tielyr. And The Jamison Family never knew.

Things took a dark turn when I found out that Esdras was working on some secret projects for The Show Mayor so I told Tielyr which was a big mistake. He was consumed with hate and wanted revenge on his former friends. He decided to steal the blue prints but we didn't expect Esdras to be there that night. Esdras refused to let Tielyr steal his ideas and threatened to call the police. Filled with anger and rage, Tielyr used a dumbbell and constantly hit Esdras until he was dead. I couldn't believe it. Tielyr hid the body and made Grand Dunixi Jamison. Believe that he killed his brother. Then Tielyr used some kind of memory erase serum and erased the memories of Esdras from everybody who ever loved him, after that I broke up with Tielyr and lost all contact with him and The Jamison Family. My life was never the same again. I spent most of my life in The Rasalas Retro of Words Worth." Quintonette said. Me and Mitchell couldn't believe it. Mitchell asked her where did Tielyr hide the body at. She told him she doesn't know and I asked her did she ever meet a guy named Silouanus and Quintonette told me yes. She said he used to creep her out. We left Present Avalon. After that, me, and Mitchell were overwhelmed and now knew who killed Esdras and why no one remembers him. Then Mitchell Hoog told me this. 'Don't walk behind me, I may not lead. Don't walk in front of me, I may not follow. Just walk beside me and be my friend.' Mitchell said with a smile. "So we were finally friends." Later that night, me, AJ, Ashley, Chris McNally, Ruel, Doyle, Mitchell Hoog and Ross went to The Storm Gorilla. Ruel unlocked the door. Then, Chris opened the door and what we found inside was terrifying. Inside the storage was some guy who was taped to a theremin. Before we had a chance to untie him, suddenly a Ventrilgoust dummy of AJ popped up and pressed a detonation. The theremin electrocuted him. "OMG," Ashley said. Chris McNally used The Cybernetic Falconieri Penzance Communicator and destroyed the theremin but it was too late. Then the Ventrilgoust dummy started shooting out pictures through his mouth. AJ fed up with this, grabbed the Ventrilgoust dummy and threw him in the air and threw ten Aigeos Juppar jawbreakers and destroyed the dummy. Ruel, Ross, Chris and Mitchell looked at the pictures and realized The Mad Ffraid Brat has been watching them more than they thought. Doyle found a picture of his brother and started crying . Me, AJ and Ashley went to comfort him. Ross heard some ticking and told all of us to run. So we did, and an explosion of confetti came out of the storage. "What are we going to do now?" Mitchell said. "We grabbed the pictures and started burning them. Then Mitchell called the police and we quickly got out of there.

CHAPTER TEN

CRASHING FLAME FEAST

The next day, Colton woke me up and told me he wanted to show me something. So I got up, ate some breakfast and then followed Colton. I had no idea where we were going until Colton told me that we're going to a place that people have forgotten about. Wherever we were going, it was somewhere in The Show Mayor. Colton smiled and told me that we're here. I looked and saw a sign that said welcome to The Meinhard Bannerjee Wonder. I asked Colton, "Where are we?" He told me this is where The Show Mayor guests used to come too years ago. Me and he looked around and saw so many attractions. These are the things that The Meinhard Bannerjee Wonder has, like A Ferris wheel, a fun house, bumper cars, games, log flume, a petting zoo, stuffed animals, a merry – go round, ring toss, house of mirrors and a roller coaster, I couldn't believe it. "What happened to this place?" I asked Colton. "That's a long story," a mysterious lady said. "Um hi, Who are you?" I said. "My name is Soft Dolly. You must be Colton's friend." Soft Dolly said. "He has told me so much about you," Soft Dolly said. After meeting Soft Dolly, me and Colton. followed her into her tent and she offered us some lemonade and blueberry muffins. Then she told us the story about what happened to The Meinhard Bannerjee Wonder. This is what she said. "Growing up was hard. I was always misunderstood because of my face. Everyday at school, the kids would always tease me and bully me. Calling me Barbie and doll. And they made jokes saying I was born in a doll house. Anyway, none of the teachers defended me, it got so bad that my parents took me out of school. I used to think

I was a freak and I wondered why was I born. I was the only one in my family that looked different. I would cry my eyes out every night, thinking that my life would always be the same. Everybody ran away from me. They called me weird and questioned whether or not I was human. So I never had any friends because nobody would give me a chance or get to know me, all I had was family until I turned sixteen. When I got older, my parents started resenting me and were ashamed to call me their daughter. So my brother, the only one left who loved me packed our things and told me we're running away to start a new life. He wanted me to have a happy life. One where I would find more people like me who would accept me and a place to call home. We searched and searched and didn't find anything. Just when we thought all was lost, we met two strangers named Dunixi Jamison and Esdras Jamison.

We became fast friends and they offered me and my brother a place where I would belong and feel welcomed. That place, my friends is The Show Mayor. I never imagined finding a place that I would fit in but I did and I met others like me. Ones who were outcast and abandoned by their families. The Show Mayor became a magical and acceptance place where you could be yourself and be surrounded by love. A judgement free zone. With Dunixi and Esdras in charge, I felt safe and knew we would always be a family. Unfortunately life at The Show Mayor took an ominous change when Mr. Accerly Jamison became in charge and made several changes. He went mad with power and took me and the other outcasts not only out of the show but away from the public as well. He banished us, here at The Meinhard Bannerjee Wonder. This place used to be an important part of The Show Mayor. Now it's just a memory. It wasn't right what Mr. Accerly Jamison did to us."

After that, me and Colton each hugged her. Then we asked her a few questions. "How come you and the others never left?" Colton said. Soft Dolly looked at us and told me and Colton that Mr. Accerly Jamison owns them, and that she and the others haven't seen the outside world in over 58 years. "We have no freedom," Soft Dolly said in a down voice. I asked her where is her brother. Soft Dolly told me that her brother died 7 years ago and that losing him was the hardest thing she's ever been through. Then I noticed several pictures of Packard and asked her was Packard a good friend of hers. Soft Dolly told us that she and Packard were secretly in love, and dating. She smiled and said Packard was her first and only true love and that they were planning to get married. Unfortunately, Packard killed himself and she thought she was the reason he took his own life, feeling alone and depressed. Soft Dolly said she was planning on commiting suicide. She didn't want to live anymore but she changed her mind after she found out that she was pregnant and had a beautiful baby girl and named her Sericea. Soft Dolly didn't feel like she was alone anymore and promised Sericea that she would never leave her. But once again, Soft Dolly lost somebody she loved. After finding out about her baby, Mr. Accerly Jamison took Sericea away and made sure Soft Dolly would never find her. Me and Colton couldn't believe that Mr. Accerly Jamison would take someone's child. Meanwhile, I kept wondering should I tell Soft Dolly what really happened to Packard. Tired of talking about her past, Soft Dolly took me and Colton on a tour of The Meinhard Bannerjee Wonder and introduced us to the other outcasts who lived in tents. Their names are Steel skin, Pig Face, Glow teeth, Bone Teeth, Web Mouth, The Troglodyte conjoined triplets, Stone Girl, Mirror Man, The Tall Freak, Razor Man and Snake Eyes. Then we met Rostya, a fortune teller. He took me and Colton inside his tent and told us to look into his crystal ball. He told me that the answers me and the others seek lie in Grandma Bregusuid's diary. After that, he left his tent, leaving me and Colton to wonder what's in that diary. Then I asked Colton did he mean what he said. Colton smiled and told me without a doubt. Unfortunately I just couldn't believe that Colton Haynes would want to be friends with me. "Why is that so hard to believe?" Colton asked me. I decided to tell him why I always assume people wouldn't want to be friends with me. I told Colton the story about Nora, somebody I wanted to become friends with. Back before I met Simon and the others., I had a hard time making friends so when I met Nora, I tried to take a leap of faith. First I started saying hi and to be honest, I didn't think she would speak. There were times where I wanted to give up. Nora never tried to get to know me and I honestly felt like I had to be something I'm not. To be her friend, how do you become friends with someone who won't give you a chance. We live in a world where people care so much about physical appearance and popularity that it consumed them, like if you aren't good looking or cool or smoke, do drugs, drink, party or have a tattoo, people don't want anything to do with you. I don't care about any of that stuff. I just want to be me and find people who like me for me. Nora wasn't who I thought she was and she wasn't the only one. After dealing with jerk after jerk, I simply gave up trying. I learned that if a person isn't willing to get to know you or even try, then they aren't worth your time. That's why I don't want to get close to Shawn, Logan, Mark, Hunter, Jonah, Daniel, Corbyn, Grant, Reed and the others. And especially you. I'm afraid of letting people in and warming up to them. People judge me before they even get to know me. It's hard making friends and you know what, I'm actually really afraid that no one would ever want to be my friend. So there you go.

Colton looked at me and told me this, "As soon as I saw you, I knew an adventure was going to happen. I like you for you. You can't let Nora and those other jerks stop you from making new friends. You're an awesome dude, anyway my next question is do you want to be my friend?" I looked at Colton and couldn't believe how incredibly kind he was. And I told him yes. So I made another friend. Then me and Colton rode on some of the rides. We got on The Bumper cars. Then we went in the fun house. After we were done, Soft Dolly gave me some key and told me That Grand Dunixi Jamison gave that to her years ago and told her this key would open something that would make life at The Show Mayor great again. She also gave me a letter that Packard wrote for his brother. He just never had the courage to tell him. Later that day, me and Peter went to The Los Angeles Union station. Peter wanted to talk to me before we went inside, so Colton told me and the others why you feel like none of us would ever want to be your friend. Peter said I'd rather not talk about it. "So let's just go inside." I said. But Peter stopped me. "This is important." he told me, "why do you even care?" I asked him. "Because I'm your friend and I just want you to know that you can always count on me." I looked at Peter and told him thanks, then we went inside and found the locker. Peter used the key and unlocked the door, inside we found a tape recorder. So we took it out and played it and what we heard made us concerned. On the tape recorder, me and Peter listened to an intense conversation between Grandma Bregusuid and Tielyr. Somehow she found out that he killed Esdras and was planning on exposing him to her husband and the police . But Tielyr threatened to kill her and her family. Me and Peter wondered if Tielyr could be The Mad Ffraid Brat. Then me and Rudy went to The Jamison Mansion and searched the statue on their front lawn. Rudy found a secret compartment and inside was a map that lead to a secret lake. So we followed the directions and made it to our destination and discovered that what we're looking for is in the lake which caused me to panic a little bit. "Are you alright?" Rudy asked me. I looked at Rudy and told him that I can't swim. Rudy told me that it's okay and that he'll go in. I was worried about him going in that lake but he wouldn't take no for an answer. Be careful I said.

So while I stayed on land, Rudy was swimming and found a sunk cabin cruiser. He went inside and uncovered a treasure chest. He quickly grabbed it and swum back to the surface. We discovered that it was locked and tried to find ways to open it. Then I thought about the key that Soft Dolly gave me and to my surprise, it worked. We opened the treasure chest up and found a top hat. At first we thought about all that we went through to get this and we thought it was all for nothing, until Rudy found a secret compartment inside the top hat and discovered some papers. He took them out and we couldn't believe what we found. Grand Dunixi Jamison's will!. We found out some important information. As we read his will, Rudy looked at me and told me, "Some friends come into your life for a reason. Others come only for a season. I'm always going to be your friend and will have your back. And that's a promise," Rudy told me. With the day over with, me and the others prepared for tonight. While we got ready, I asked Colton what am I doing. All those names that me and Mark saw on the guest list are rich and famous. I'm not part of that world, I told him. What if they judge me or make fun of me. Colton smiled and told me to just be myself and to remember that he and the others will be with me all the way. So after talking to Colton, me, AJ, Mallory, Simon, Doyle, Mark, Brandon, Nick, Sam, Hunter, Callan, Why Don't We, Jacob, Shawn, Grant, Jack

Maynard, Devan Key, Collins Key, Mitchell and Aunt Fanny arrived at The Zvezda Three Ples and there were so many people. Cameron Mathison was the host. He announced the names of each guest . Anyway, I was a little shy to meet him. Then, me and the others went inside The Zvezda Three Ples. It was more beautiful and bigger than we could ever imagine. We found Sollie and he showed us around. I was worried that I didn't see Luke, Logan and the others. So after we sat down, Cameron introduced the guests and the world to Mr. Accerly Jamison. He waved at everybody and was excited about this year's Flame Feast. He told us that this year, he has a surprise for the fans of The Black Butterfly. This is what he said. "Please put your hands together as I introduce you to the new heroes who will be starring in the upcoming two part special. First we have Pierson Fode. The Stranger Moth, powers Shadow Mimicry, Mystic Blast and Psychic Shadow. Second, Jared Gilmore, Storm Cricket, powers Storm Manipulation. Weather Soul and Storm Mimicry. Reed Horstmann, The Cataclysm Web – Spinner, powers Elemental Web Creation and Transcendent Superhuman mage physiology. Chace Craword, The Canarsie Armadillidiidae. Can curl up into a ball and roll at incredible speeds. His other powers are Stone Mimicry and Petrification. Luke Korns, Smoke Termite, powers Toxic smoke generation. Deoxy generation, Smoke Manipulation, Smoke Portal Creation and Smoke Mimicry. Case Walker, The Granville Bug., powers Floraportation, Plant Manipulation, Plant Mimicry, Memory Erasure, Memory Restoration, Plant Portal Creation and Atomic Dissociation. Amarr Wooten, Black Bee, powers Dark Energy Manipulation, Umbrageous Teleportation, Darkness Wave Emission, Dark Bolt Projection and Shadow Ball Projection. Casey Johnson, from Rise, Casey's Sting. Powers Honey Manipulation, Bubble Encapsulation, he can shoot thorns out of his mouth, Force Field Generation, Esoteric Light Generation and the power of zap. Meaning he can release elements / energy. Ajay Friese, Brain Billbug, powers Brain soup. Meaning he can turn people's brains into liquid. Electrical Telepathy, Mind Control, Astral Manipulation and Visual Mind Reading. Logan Shroyer, The Swarm of Wrath. Can disperse his body into any swarm of bugs, Genesis Blood and

Disassembly. Hayes Grier. Demonic Cockroach. Powers Antenna Protrusion, Shimmering, Demon Morphing, Wall Crawling, Fire Ball Projection, Energy Balls, Wing Manifestation, Head Liberation, Darkness Adaptation, Apportation and Appendage Adaptation. Cody Linley, Speed Buggy. Powers Speed Augmentation, Telekinetic Speed, Invisible Speed and Speed Clones. Alex Saxon. Bugged Out. Cyberlingualism, Technology Manipulation, Techno Screen – Teleportation, Cyber Mind and Computer Virus Physiology. Ty Wood, Hammer Moth. Powers Hammer Generation, Bionic Physiology and Energy Generation. Cayden Boyd, Mammoth Moth. Moth Physiology, Proboscis Protrusion and Mammalian Physiology. Jordan Doww, Mothball Trapson, powers Ballistic Scream. Explosion Inducement, Jet Propulsion and can create explosive balls. Noah Schnapp, The Monstrous Butterfly. Powers Monster Physiology, Feral Mind and Fear Inducement. Devin Hayes, The Vampire Bee. Powers Vampire Physiology, Electrolytic Blood, Daytime Walking, Blood Transformation, Dark Fire Ball Projection and Shadow Camouflage. Grant Knoche, Comet Scorpion. Powers Space Embodiment, Laser Vision, Black Hole Creation, Gravity Magic, Meteor Summoning, Galaxy Destruction, Missile Generation, Laser Beam Emission, Void Creation and Destruction. Miles Nazaire, The Silver Arrow Orka Grub. Powers Water Manipulation, Flood Creation, Water Transmutation, Water Mimicry, Aquatic Adaptation, Water Maneuverability, Merfolk Physiology and Arrow Generation. Ashley Benson, Butterfly Ruby. Powers Ruby Exoskeleton, Ruby Generation, Ruby Blast, Gum Generation, Ruby Ball Projection, Ruby Constructs and Premonition. Trevor Donovan, Death Beetle. Powers Death – Force Bomb Generation, Death – Force Ball Projection, Reanimation, Living Hive, Omnidirectional Death Waves, Beam Emission and Death Breath. Freddie Stroma, Red Cricket. Powers Elasticity, Combat Specialist, Aero Telekinesis, Rubber Blade Construction and Puppet Mastery. Austin P. Mckenzie, Echo Wasp. Powers Sonokinetic Constructs, Sound Manipulation, Musical Spell Casting, Musical Weaponry, Fearful Scream, Death Song, Musical Animation, Sound Beam Emission, Voice Thievery, Empathic Voice, Persuasion and Verbal Teleportation.

Kendrick Sampson, Electric Flea. Powers Electricity Generation, Itching Inducement, Electrokinetic Flight, Electrical Transportation and Electricity Mimicry. David Mazouz, The Amazing Mad Gastax Locust. Powers Magic Transcendence, Magic Weaponry, Spell Blades, Binding, Magic Arrows, Magic Whip Generation, Card Vortex Creation, Pestilence Manipulation, Orthoptera Physiology and uses a spell called Animazing, to cast spells and make his powers stronger. Harrison Webb, The Daumier Ezeroc Boxelder Earwig. Powers Chemical Energy Manipulation, Enhanced Hearing, Vocal Replication, Chemical Weaponry and Echolocation. Tyler Posey, The Bone Moth. Powers Idiosyncratic Manipulation, Infinite Jump, Mental Scramble, Possessive Replication, Bone Manipulation, Bone Weaponry and Bone Spike Protrusion. Douglas Smith, The Bearnas Stink. A stink bug, powers Selective Invisibility, Stink Breath, Goo Generation, Garbage Mimicry and can create stink bombs. Chris Salvatore, Night Wasp. Powers Sleep Inducement, Night Manipulation, Night Empowerment, Darkness Manipulation, Darkness Bomb Generation, Absolute Darkness, Shadow Breath and Darkness Attacks. Antoni Porowski, Red Leech. Energy Drain, Flammable Blood, Fire Generation, Blood Absorption and Leech Regeneration. Spencer List, Battle Dragon Fly. Powers Faithifery, Hypnosis, Levitation and Telekinetic Constructs. Darren Barnet, The Blue Jay Fly. Powers Anger Augmentation, Force Field Attacks, Blue Fire Manipulation, Intuitive Aptitude, Psychometry, Accelerated Probability, Wing Manifestation, Cloaking, Psionics and Athletics Empowerment. Jeremy Irvine. Disguise Tick, Powers Shapeshifting and Thermovariance. Lucy Hale, The Dove Moth, Powers Light Manipulation, Light Absorption, Light Breath, Light Mimicry and the power of healing. Colton Shires, The Dragon Worm. Powers Fire Breath, Elemental Breath, Enhanced Roar, Wormhole Creation and Dragon Morphing. Rudy Pankow, Dark Crawler. Powers Dark Vision, Darkness Aura and Shadow Generation. Matthew Daddario, The Snake Butterfly. Powers Snake Manipulation, Snake Swarming, Snake Physiology, Venomous Claws, Snake Den and Venomous Fangs. Charlie Carver, The Mad Gentleman. A Harlequin Bug, powers Insanity Inducement, Madness Manipulation, Insanity Projection and Illusion

Manipulation. Christopher Bones, The Noha Paper Bug. Powers Imagination Manifestation, Artistic Creation, Animation Picture Imprisonment, Photography Vision, Drawing Creation, Ink Manipulation, Ink Portal Creation and Reading Empowerment. Nolan Funk, The Masked Mothra. Powers Psychic Blade Construction, Absolute Strength, Empathic Electricity Manipulation, Morale Manipulation and Communing. Mitchell Hope, Green Crawler. Powers Shape Generation, Personal Environment, Psioplasmic Field Generation, Green Fire Manipulation and Multi – . Drew Fuller, The Black Shirt Scorpion. Powers Poison Breath, Miasma Emission, Celerity, Energy Whip Generation and Scorpion Physiology. Keegan Allen, The Masked State Crawler Pseudoscorpion Beast. Powers Animal Kingdom Embodiment, Animal Swarming, Fusionism Mutation, Fusionism, Animal Telepathy, Animal Morphing, Animal Empathy, Animal Manipulation, Poison Manipulation and Zoolingualism . Chris McNally, Black Wing. Powers Black Lightning Manipulation and Dark Fire Manipulation. Sean Depner, Moth Dusk. Powers Dust Generation, Granulation and Dust Aura. Gordon Winarick, Thunder Hornet. Powers Thunder Manipulation, Thunderstorm Creation, and creating thunder sonic blast. Austin Butler, The Hardinge Flying Ant. Powers Plasma Projection, Primordial Ooze Manipulation, Paint Bow Construction and Magma Blade Construction. Jax Malcolm, The Jerzy Titan Beetle. Powers Necrosis Inducement, Remote Possession and invisible skin. Harris Dickinson, The Mighty Moth Man, powers Energy Signature Manipulation, Hair Teleportation, Symbiosis, Telekinesis, Orbital Field, Synonymous Linking and Undead Plant Physiology. Ruben Beasley, The Quantum Waspman. Powers Quantum Manipulation and Quantum Energy Manipulation. Ryan Malaty, Bug Time. Powers Time Travel, Time Stopping, Accelerated Time Bolts and Chronoskimming, Felix Mallard, Professor Armed Moth. Powers Army Annihilation, Army Manipulation and Arm – Blade Proficiency. Levi Miller, Evolution's Sting. Powers Phantasm Manipulation, Energy Blast and Volatile Constructs.

"Man, that was a mouth full." Mr. Accerly Jamison said. "Now, I'm going to give you a sneak peak of the two part special with the help of

the main cast, well, except for Gerwazy. He couldn't make it tonight."
Thomas grabbed Mr. Accerly Jamison's microphone and told them to
roll the clip. This is what we all found out. In the upcoming two part
special, The Black Butterfly and his team face their biggest challenge
yet when new mutant monsters start attacking Sesto Hive City. The
Black Butterfly and the gang team up with some new heroes who are
trained by a hero named Professor Golden Ant. But when a new foe
called The Butterfly Queen kidnaps Professor Golden Ant and turn
some of the heroes evil, The Black Butterfly and the remaining heroes
try to find a way to save their friends and join forces with a mysterious
guy named Stranger Moth. Unknowing to them, The Butterfly Queen
is using Professor Golden Ant powers and a weapon called The Moth
Crystals to make a new threat. A powerful being, The Dove Moth in
part two. The Black Butterfly and the others learned that The Butterfly
Queen is pregnant and plans to release an army of new bugs called
The Carrow Voletine. More powerful than The Amisquew Ortegon
Physco and that she plans to take over the world. With earth in danger
and outnumbered, The Black Butterfly, Stranger Moth and the others
meet another hero called Comet Scorpion and they set out to stop The
Butterfly Queen and find the nest before the eggs hatch and destroy
the world and convince The Dove Moth to use her powers for good.
And that was it. Me and the others clapped our hands. Then we ate.

The waiters brought out the dishes and lifted up the tops. Me, AJ,
Shawn and the others looked at each other and couldn't wait to dig in.
We ate Roasted Rosemary Chicken with Potatoes, Pork and Cabbage
with Wild Rice and Spiced Apple, Alton's Crown Roast of Lamb, Pan
Roasted Chicken Thighs with grapes and olives, Black – Eyed Peas
Burgers, Beef Wellington, Chicken Teriyaki, Meatballs, Kabobs, Rolls
with homemade button and Crustless Caprese Quiche. For dessert
we had Warm Peanut Butter Cookie Cakes. Vietnamese Coffee and
Condensed milk, Panna Cotta, Chocolate Cheesecake and Chocolate
Mousse. While we ate, Cameron Mathison told us it was time for the
performers, The All Nizar Riddles, Ten incredible women. They came
out and started performing some amazing fire tricks, then they sung.
After that, The Ptarmigan Seissylt Clowns came out and performed,

to our surprise Seissylt and the others sung a song called it's A Flame Feast Celebration. After they were done, Sollie introduced me and the others to his father. I asked Mr. Accerly Jamison how did he get Placydo and the others out of jail. He told me that he's the most powerful man in Los Angeles and that no one says no to a Jamison. "I see why people don't like him. He's too cocky and thinks he's better than everybody else." Then he told everybody to look underneath their seats . So we did and found a bag. Inside the bag was a cell phone but these weren't no ordinary cell phones. Mr. Accerly Jamison said we are the first people to have his newest invention, The Baltasaru Iegriusol Dusk. He went down the list of what these phones can do. The Baltasaru Iegriusol Dusk can teleport a person anywhere in the world. It has a battery that can last for ten years, it's water proof, it can read people's minds, it can transform into a car, a boat, a train, an air balloon and an airplane. The Baltasaru Iegriusol Dusk has the ability to transform into a laptop and become a jet pack. Me and the others couldn't believe that The Baltasaru Iegriusol Dusk could do so much unlike other phones. Mr. Accerly Jamison couldn't wait to start selling these cell phones around the world. Anyway, I went to The Zvezda Three Ples soda bar and got a coke float. Jonah joined me and asked me was I alright. I told him I had a lot on my mind. "Are you worried about Nasser?" He asked me. I told him that's one of the things on my mind. "What about Gerwazy?" Jonah said. I told him Gerwazy means nothing to me and that I wish I never found out that he's my half brother. "I know he hurt you and he's a jerk. But I want you to always remember that there's always hope. Hope that people will change. That's what you need right now, hope." I smiled at Jonah and told him he's started to become one of my best friends.

Then Devin came over. Jonah left and told me to give him a chance. So I drunk some of my coke float and was wondering should I even try due to all of my fail attempts to make friends and people not giving me a chance. So, I took a leap of faith ince again and got to know Devin. I started by congratulating him on his new role. He told me thanks and told me that Jonah and the others told him I'm a fan of Pretty Little Liars, Once Upon A Time and other shows and movies. He wanted me to talk more about them and asked me were there any other movies or shows I forgot to tell the others about. This is what I told him. "I'm a huge fan of Sliders, it was one of the best shows they ever made, but I was sad when the actor and actress who played Quinn and Wade. left the show. The show wasn't the same without them. And what happened to Wade still gets to me. That was so sad. Ghost Whisperer is my other top favorite show. Jennifer Love Hewitt is an incredible and a kind person. Her character, Melinda went through a lot and made people lives better. She was open minded and one of a kind. One of the saddest moments on Ghost Whisperer is when Melinda lost Jim. What she went through to get him back showed how powerful love can be. I love Ghost Whisperer because it was a show about hope, faith and love. It was sad when Ghost Whisperer got cancelled. Pretty Little Liars means a lot to me. These girls went through a lot but no matter what A – threw at them, they never drifted apart. Their friendship was unbreakable. Once Upon A Time was a show that taught me about hope and belief. Henry and Emma, Regina, Zelena, Hook, Snow, Charming, Ariel, Jasmine, Graham, and Belle were my favorite characters. The Good Doctor is an another show about hope. Shaun and Claire are my favorite characters and friendship goals. Claire knows how to talk to Shaun and cares about him. Shaun is a brilliant Doctor who prove the doubters wrong. SpongeBob SquarePants is always funny. My favorite characters are SpongeBob, Squidward and Sandy. There are two shows that got cancelled that I really miss. My Babysitter is a Vampire, and Spooksville. These shows were good. I'm a Harry Potter fan. My favorite characters are Harry, Hermione and Professor Minerva McGonagall and Dobby. I always hoped Harry and Hermione would end up together. They brought out the best in each other. As for Dobby, he died a hero. Anyway, there are four movies that never got the credit that they deserve. The 5th Wave, it would've been amazing to see part two. I really enjoyed this movie. Next, Godzilla, the one made in 1998. That was one of the best Godzilla movies they ever made. X – Men : Apocalypse, now that movie was awesome. I'm just sad that Alex Summers got killed. Out of all the X – Men characters, Storm is my favorite. Halle Berry is too amazing and talented. And the last one is Cats & Dogs – The Revenge of Kitty Galore. There was nothing wrong with this movie. It was good, I told him. Devin told me no friendship is an accident and asked me could we finally become friends. I looked at Shawn and the others and told Devin I would like that, I shook his hand and couldn't believe I was actually friends with Devin Hayes.

After warming up to him, me and Corbyn searched for the vault where Mr. Accerly Jamison kept Soft Dolly and the others' contracts. While we looked, AJ sung Girls! I asked Corbyn "Are you my friend?" He smiled and said always . Then we found the vault and we had no idea how we would get inside. So we texted Sollie and he stole his father's key. The three of us went inside and found several contracts. We found the ones that we were looking for and grabbed them. Then me and Corbyn placed The Zayenthar Spyder all over The Zvezda Three Ples. Meanwhile, Matt Cornett was investigating Grandma Bregusuid's room hoping to find something and just when he was about to give up, he found an old type writer and discovered a secret compartment. Inside was Grandma Bregusuid's diary. When he opened it, he found out some shocking information. Elsewhere, Luke, Harrison Webb and Van Hansis were searching all the rooms in The Zvezda Three Ples and didn't seem to find anything until Luke used The Nymphas Onesimus Goggles and found a hidden door behind a painting of some mysterious man. So they grabbed one of the swords from the knights display and cut the painting opened and discovered documents, pictures and stories of every bad thing The Jamison Family has ever done. Every crime and scam their ancestors committed and the ones who are alive today. Then Van found a diary that belongs to Mr. Accerly Jamison. He, Harrison and Luke read it. Back in the ballroom, Shawn was performing and sung Lost In Japan, while me and the others got ready to find the treasure. Daniel got my attention and we got concerned, we saw Deveral. He was talking to a mysterious person in a cloak. Me and he wondered could that be The Mad Ffraid Brat and we hid underneath a table, eavesdropping on their conversation. Whoever it was was telling Deveral about some chip. Me and Daniel looked at each other and wondered what chip. Daniel told me that I'm a cool person and that he's glad we're friends. I told him same here. After that, it was time to dance and Lucy grabbed me and told me we're dancing, I was really nervous because Lucy is one of the greatest and kindest people in the world. And I always dreamed of becoming friends with her. Lucy told me I'm one of a kind and that we are friends.

At first I didn't believe her but she proved me wrong. I was actually having fun. Mallory grabbed Daniel and the two started dancing. So did the rest of our friends. A girl made out with Harrison. Another girl made out with Zayne on the dancing floor. And a girl name Tuptim made out with Grant. After the song was over, Mallory stopped me and Lucy from leaving and almost fainted when she saw Anthony De La Torre. He sung, Know Me. Carson Rowland sung Game! After he was done. Why Don't We sung, 8 Letters. Ross sung Preacher Man. AJ sung Unstoppable. Scott Gardner was also at Flame Feast and he sung Getting Over You. Bruce Wiegner performed Malicious. Christopher Bones performed Chasing Your Love. Charlie Puth was also at Flame Feast. Making Mallory scream. He performed Girlfriend! After they were done, Doyle. Zach, Jack, Mark and Darren went to the auction while me and the others went to find Grand Dunixi Jamison's treasure. Before I left, AJ told me that he's not coming with us and that he wants to find out who Deveral is talking to. I told him that wasn't a good idea and that I would stay with him. He told me that the others need me too and he promised me that he would be careful. I told him he better and I ran to join the others. AJ smiled and realized how much he means to me. He noticed Deveral was going upstairs and quickly followed him. However he also noticed that the mysterious person who was with Deveral was gone and wondered where did they go. Meanwhile, Chris McNally heard Mr. Accerly Jamison arguing with somebody but he couldn't tell who. Callan was helping Aunt Fanny stuff food in her bag. Mallory was back on the dance floor with Daniel, then she grabbed him and started making out with him. As for AJ, he was still following Deveral. Suddenly, someone grabbed AJ and used knock out gas on him. Me, Simon, Jonah, Shawn, Devin, Logan, Grant, Chris Salvatore, Lucy, Austin Butler, Alex Whitehouse, Chandler, Ross, Hunter, Sebastian, Sam, Jacob, Case and Antoni followed Brandon. He took out the map and told us there should be a secret door behind The Memorial Statue of Grand Dunixi Jamison. So Logan moved it and we followed him inside. I gave Corbyn the tablet and told him to keep an eye out for anything suspicious. Since we put cameras all over The Zvezda Three Ples, Corbyn told me to be careful.

Me and the others went down a tunnel that leads to an Antechamber. When we got there, we found ourselves dodging swinging pendulums, darts and more boobytraps. I almost fell in an acid river but Jonah saved me. After getting through all the boobytraps, me and the others arrived at a door and learned that the only way we could get in was by saying the password. It was voice activated. Unfortunately when Brandon checked the map, he discovered that the password is in spanish. Devin smiled and translated it for us. He said the first part, "I sought my soul", Simon said the next part, "But my soul I could not see." Logan said. "I sought my God," Grant said. "But my god eluded me." Then me, Shawn, Lucy, Jonah, Brandon, Hunter, Jacob, Chris, Alex Whitehouse, Austin Butler, Chandler, Case, Sam, Ross, Sebastian and Antoni said the final part, "I sought my brother and I found all three." After we said the last part, the door opened and we went inside. To our surprise, there weren't any diamonds or treasure or even money, just a time capsule. Meanwhile, Callan was searching Deveral's car and found a printed out profile for a Mail Order Bride. A Latin woman named Luz. Simon learned that Deveral's plans to get marry on the day of his brother's birthday. Zayne was checking the guest list and discovered that Tielyr and Silouanus Prater are somewhere in The Zvezda Three Ples and he warned me and the others. Back at the auction, Doyle and Jack and Zach were passing out The Cybernetic Falconieri Penzance Communicators to Jared and the others. Austin P. Mckenzie was Investigating Grand Dunixi Jamison's room. He got interrupted when he heard some voices. He quickly hid underneath the bed and saw Tielyr and Gewnsnay talking. Gewnsnay was telling Tielyr that me and my friends are getting closer to the truth and that we need to be stopped. "I thought you knew who was taking care of Benny Breezy and his pesty friends." Tielyr said. "The Mad Ffraid Brat was but things are getting out of hand and The Mad Ffraid Brat is worried that Benny will get in the way of their final plan, the one that will ruin AJ's career forever," Gewnsnay said in a devious voice. "Fine, I'll take matters in my own hand." Tielyr said. Austin wondered what Tielyr was planning. Sean investigated Esdras Jamison's room and found two people in his old room. "Who are you and what are you doing in here?" Sean Grandillo asked them. "I'm Rance and this is my twin sister Nance. We're Mrs. Bannerjee Jamison's assistants and we were looking for something." "Looking for what?" Sean asked them. "It was nice meeting you." Nance said, she and her brother left leaving Sean to wonder what were they doing in there.

The Delahoussaye Psych Sisters found Trevor and were trying to win his affection. Orangia got Trevor away from the crowd and started making out with him. Then Orangetta and Orangina did the same thing. Each one made out with him. Ryan Malaty found Silouanus in some secret room stealing some blue prints and hid. Silouanus smiled and got out of there. Ryan Malaty got up and discovered that Deveral isn't the first Jamison to ever build a bomb. Matt Bomer, Collins Key, Devan Key, Jack Maynard, Nick Mayorga, Ashley Tisdale, Thomas and Mitchell Hoog found one of the biggest vaults in the world and wondered what could be inside. Then Matt thought about those numbers he found in the yearbook and started typing the numbers to see if they would open the vault. To his surprise, they did. He and the others found a map that reveals a secret hiding compartment in a Memorial Statue of Esdras Jamison. Elsewhere, Corbyn couldn't believe what he was looking at and alerting me, he told me that AJ was talking to The Mad Ffraid Brat. I was shocked and wondered is something wrong with AJ. Meanwhile, Mallory was still making out with Daniel. While they continued to do that, Doyle, Zach, Darren and Jack couldn't believe how big the jewel Mr. Accerly Jamison was trying to sell. The one and only, The Emerald Brain. A jewel that has been in The Jamison Family for years. Suddenly AJ popped up and knocked Mr. Accerly Jamison unconscious and told the buyers and all the guests that this Flame Feast is over. Doyle, Zach, Darren and Jack tried to stop AJ but he had company. Sollie wondered where his father's bodyguard was. AJ and his helpers grabbed Mr. Accerly Jamison and The Emerald Brain and escaped. Corbyn told me and the others everything that just happened and we were speechless. Then we opened up the time capsule and found a bunch of pictures and other things. Matt Bomer found something really interesting, The deed to The Show Mayor. When he grabbed it, he accidentally triggered another boobytrap. Before we had a chance to react, water burst through the walls and the floors and a flood washed me, my friends and all the guests out of The Zvezda Three Ples. We couldn't believe what just happened. I kept my distance from Jared, Matthew Daddario, Ryan Malaty, Jax, Van and the others knowing that they wouldn't become my friend. Anyway. The Zvezda Three Ples was a mess. Me and the others split up after hearing police sirens. Aunt Fanny, Doyle and the others went back to The Show Mayor while me, Simon, Mallory, Chris Salvatore, Why Don't We, Jared, Van, Luke, Jax, Case, Pierson, Matthew Daddario, Darren, Lucy, Cayden, Miles, Mitchell Hoog, Austin Rhodes, Jacob and Thomas looked for AJ. We used The Cybernetic Falconieri Penzance Communicators to find him. We found him in a graveyard. He was unconscious. I ran to AJ and woke him up. AJ had no clue what happened. We told him that he kidnapped Mr. Accerly Jamison. AJ couldn't believe it. I was starting to get more and more worried about my bud. The night got even worse when Aunt Fanny called me panicking, so me and the others quickly got back to The Show Mayor. Aunt Fanny and Doyle told us that someone broke in the penthouse and stole some of Nasser's clothes. "What do you think they will do with them?" AJ asked me. "I don't know but I have a feeling it's something bad." I said with a concerned look on my face. Matt pulled me to the side and showed me Grandma Bregusuid's diary. We were both shocked. Elsewhere, At Present Avalon, Quintonette was more jumpy than usual and had a feeling something bad was about to happen. Then a male nurse gave Quintonette her medicine. Unfortunately when she took it, she felt weird and asked the male nurse what kind of medicine was that. The nurse whispered to her, "That's what you get for being a rat." The nurse said as he laughed. Quintonette fell on the floor and watched as the nurse walked away.

CHAPTER ELEVEN

THE HORROR HERCULANO

With time running out and one day left until Sollie Birthday, me and the others got up early to find anything that could finally clear AJ's name. AJ was watching the news and couldn't believe what he did last night. It was on every news channel. Suddenly, Detective Plaxido came up in the elevator with twenty cops. I told AJ to hide. Me, Simon, Mallory, Doyle and Aunt Fanny wondered what does he want now. He smiled and told us. He's here to arrest Doyle. Me and the others surrounded Doyle and asked him what are the charges. Detective Plaxido told me and the gang that Doyle is under arrest for the murder of Quintonette. "What do you mean?" I said. Detective Plaxido showed me and the others a video of Doyle posing as a nurse. He also told us that Doyle was the last person to see her alive. Last night, me and the gang tried to explain but Detective Plaxido and the others wouldn't listen and arrested Doyle. Then he asked us where is AJ and told the officers to search the whole penthouse, so when they did, they told him it was clear. Detective Plaxido was suspicious and wanted to know what happened last night at Flame Feast, but Aunt Fanny defended us and told him to get out or he'll be sorry. Detective Plaxido told me I better watch my back and left. I shouted aloud "It's clear," and AJ appeared. He used the Cybernetic Falconieri Penzance Communicator to make himself invisible. Me and he looked at each other and ran towards the elevator. "Where are y'all going?" Simon asked us. "To save our friend." Both me and AJ said. Me, AJ, Chace, Jacob, Mallory and Hayes visited Doyle in jail. He couldn't believe this was happening. Doyle was scared and worried with his brother being held captive and now he's been accused of murder. Doyle was missing Nasser more than ever. Jacob wondered who made a mask of Doyle's face. Chace tried to calm Doyle down. As for me and the others, we couldn't believe Quintonette was dead and wondered who really killed her, The Mad Ffraid Brat or Deveral. I told Doyle we will get him out of here no matter what it takes. Me and Mitchell Hoog went back to Present Avalon to find clues. At first, we didn't find anything until Mitchell moved one of the pictures which opened up a secret room. We went inside and discovered that Quintonette has a model of The Show Mayor. I checked the pills that the fake Doyle gave Quintonette last night and I found out that Quintonette was poisoned. Me and Case investigated Edvardas' room. I still couldn't believe that Edvardas is working with The Mad Ffraid Brat. As we searched his room, Case tried to get to know me. I was a little nervous. I didn't think we would become friends, but to my surprise he became an another bud of mine. Me and he found Edvardas' diary and learned why Edvardas is working for The Mad Ffraid Brat. Me and Jeremy Irvine went to Fuji's room to see if we could find any more clues and I saw what Mark and the others were talking about. Fuji was definitely a hoarder. It was disgusting. As we looked for clues, suddenly Jeremy heard some noise and quickly got me out of the room and before we could react, the room blew up. I told Jeremy "Thanks for saving my life." Me and him couldn't believe that The Mad Ffraid Brat blew up Fuji's room .

We wondered what could've been in there. Jeremy smiled and found a letter that had the address of Fuji's old house. Me and Matt Cornett drove over to Fuji's old house to check it out. I was quiet because I knew Matt wouldn't become my friend. We got out of the car. When we arrived, we discovered that Fuji used to be a farmer and we wondered what happened to the animals. We broke into the house and started searching for clues. As we tried to find anything that could help us, Matt told me that I don't have to worry. I asked him worry about what. This is what he told me, "You think I won't become your friend. And that you're not the type of person I would want to hangout with, but I do. I really want to be your friend and I just want you to know. You never have to pretend to be something you're not in order to be my friend. I like you for you and I believe in you because that's what friends do. And you are my friend and I won't stop until I convince you." I looked at Matt and couldn't believe I have made another new friend. Something I thought would never happen because of all I had been through. Then Matt found Fuji's old journal and we read it. We learned the reason why Fuji became a hoarder is because of his depression and he became emotionally attached to his possessions and that he and his wife were starting to drift apart. He felt so alone. Me and Jared Gilmore talked to Sollie and Deveral's old Nanny, Bionda, who now works at a fast food restaurant. Anyway, I was nervous because I'm a big fan of Jared Gilmore and Henry is one of my favorite characters on Once Upon A Time. I just didn't think he would want to get to know me so I just focused on the case. We walked inside a restaurant called The Nicos Burp Burgers. Me and Jared thought that was a weird name for a fast food restaurant. Anyway, we had no idea what Bionda looked like, we just knew her name from Grandma Bregusuid's diary. We walked up to the register and asked one of the cashiers about Bionda. One of the girls told us that Bionda doesn't come in until two o clock. So to pass the time, me and Jared ordered some Nicos burp burgers and fries and to our surprise, the burgers were big and actually good.

While we ate, Jared asked me do I believe in magic. I smiled and said yes, then he asked me am I a Star Wars fan. I told him I'm a mega fan and that Master Yoda, Ahsoka, Obi Wan Kenobi, Jar Jar Binks, C- 3PO and R2 - D2 are my favorite characters. Then I started talking about Star Wars Clone Wars and told him how much I miss the show. I couldn't stop talking about the unbreakable bond between Anakin Skywalker and Ahsoka. I mean seriously, these two looked out for each other and had a powerful friendship. They became attached to each other. I told Jared they simply don't make shows like that anymore where you see the characters bonding and the development of that special bond. After that, I started talking about how incredible Ahsoka was in Star Wars Clone Wars. Through out the seasons, she became a powerful and fan favorite character. How she would stop the separatists and outsmarted them and her amazing skills. One of my favorite episodes is when Ahsoka went to Mandalore and kicked butt with the help of her students. Ahsoka is always kicking butt and the one when she fights the mind – controlling Geonosian worms. But I was sad when the Jedi council accused her of murder after all the good she has ever done. Plus we never got to see Lux Bonteri and Ahsoka become a couple. Lux was one of my favorite characters. I miss him. "You are definitely a fan," Jared said. Then Jared asked me do you want to be friends. I tried not to get too excited and said that would be great. "Awesome," Jared said as he shaked my hand. After that, Bionda walked in and we ran to talk to her. "Are you Bionda?" Jared said. "Who wants to know?" "Me and my friend are here to talk to you about your former bosses, The Jamison Family." When he said that, Bionda started yelling. "Don't you ever mention that cursed family too me. They are the ones who ruined my life. So sorry I can't help you." Bionda said. "What about Grandma Bregusuid, was she cruel to you too?" I said. Bionda looked at me and Jared and told us to have a seat. She was a little nervous but she thought it was time she told somebody about how her career was destroyed because of The Jamisons. This is what she said, "My life used to be good. I was one of the best nannies in the world. I took care of the kids and I always made sure they were my main priority. But that all changed when I met The Jamison Family. I became Sollie and Deveral's nanny. Sollie was a sweet baby. Unfortunately, Deveral was the opposite. He was a devil child. Unknowing to their parents, Deveral would always try to kill his brother. He almost dropped him in a pool and he even tried to poison him. It got so bad that I had to stay by Sollie's side all the time. And when I tried to expose him to his parents, Deveral slept with me and used that to blackmail me. I was horrified, I didn't know what to do but I knew Sollie's life was in danger and decided to tell his parents no matter what happens. Little did I know Deveral had a backup plan. He made everybody believe that I was a child predator and sent that false information to everybody in Los Angeles. I couldn't believe Deveral framed me and his parents believed him. They fired me and filed a restraining order. From that moment on, my career was finished."

Me and Jared looked at each other, then we asked her how did she know Grandma Bregusuid. Bionda told us that after the death of her brother in-law, then her husband. Grandma Bregusuid mysteriously disappeared. But one night she came to my house to talk to me and told me one day the world will know the truth about Deveral and the rest of her family. She comforted me and couldn't stop apologizing for her grandson devious ways and gave me ten million dollars and that was the last time I saw her. "She was the only Jamison that showed me kindness," Bionda said. Me and Freddie. looked through Grandma Bregusuid's diary for the next clue and found out that Grandma Bregusuid hid something on top of The Show Mayor's sign, so we went on top of The Show Mayor and I was afraid. But Freddie didn't let anything happen to me. Something a friend would do. We found a secret compartment inside of one of the letters and pulled out a video camera. Freddie pressed play and we watched the video. Me and Freddie discovered a shocking secret. We learned that a guy named Great Uncle Teton formed an agenda with a young Mr. Accerly Jamison. Mr. Accerly Jamison's best friend, Cosimo Smalley and Mr. Accerly Jamison teen crush, Avis. The agenda was called The Fouxar 4. Me and Freddie found out that Fouxar 4 was an agenda that committed crimes and that Great Uncle Teton made a serum called the Cellest Clinicriptine and hid them inside statues called The Creayatuary Chalmus Jamison Statue and would sell them to criminals and that was the end of the video. Me and Freddie wondered why would Mr. Accerly Jamison join something like that back when he was a teenager. And what happened to Great Uncle Teton. Freddie pointed out to me that Tielyr has a son and that Grand Dunixi Jamison's son and Tielyr Smalley son. Somehow became best friends which is so hard to believe. Me, Rudy, Van Hansis and Ajay read the next page in Grandma Bregusuid's diary and found out about The Jamison Achives and discovered a key tape to the page and went to investigate. Rudy, knowing how shy I am, encouraged me to get to know the others. I just couldn't. I didn't think they would like me so I kept quiet, something I'm good at. Anyway, we arrived at The Jamison Archives. Rudy used the key to unlock the door and we went inside. Me, Van, Rudy and Ajay couldn't believe how big this place was. Anyway, we started searching for any clues that could help us.

Suddenly, someone popped up behind Ajay, scaring him and the rest of us, "who are you?' Van said. "Hi, I'm Burnell Wordlaw. The keeper of The Jamison Archives. It's nice to finally meet you Benny Breezy and your friends." "Um, how do you know my name?" I asked him. "Oh I know a lot of things. I have been The Jamison Archives keeper for years. I know every secret about The Jamison Family. Things that would get them in some serious trouble and ruin their family name. So how may I be of service?" Burnell said. "Well, we need any information you got about…" before I could finish, Burnell said, "Oh boy, so you know about Siothran and his wife Heleonor." "Um who?" Van said. "We're here to find out more about Great Uncle Teton." Rudy said. "Oh, pretend I didn't mention those other names." "Right." I said. He told us to follow him, so as we followed him.

We passed by several documents, pictures and records that holds secrets about The Jamison Family. Burnell Wordlaw took us to the section where Burnell keeps everything there is to know about. Great Uncle Teton,there wasn't much though. Burnell pulled out a book and started reading about Great Uncle Teton. This is what he said. "Great Uncle Teton was a Tousignant. The Tousignant are kin to the Jamison Family. Unlike The Jamison Family, The Tousignant actually helped people and used to go on a lot of adventures together. Great Uncle Teton was the son of the famous Siothran and Heleonor. He was a good guy but his life took a dark turn when he used to watch Mr. Accerly Jamison. His nephew was a devious and greedy person who wanted money and power and brainwashed his uncle into wanting the same thing. So Mr. Accerly Jamison decided to form an agenda called The Fouxar 4 with his best friend, his crush and his uncle. They became an unstoppable team and did a lot of illegal things without their families knowing. Then Great Uncle Teton Tousignant came up with a devious plan that would make them more money. He created a serum called The Cellest Clinicriptine which made The Fouxar 4. Rich. Everything was going good until Great Uncle Teton's Parents found out. They were so heartbroken and shocked that they decided to disown him and lost all contacts with him. The silence of his family really got to him and made him realize he made a huge mistake. So Great Uncle Teton tried to make things right and was planning on coming clean to the police. But Mr. Accerly Jamison wouldn't allow it and took matters into his own hands and killed his uncle. The only witnesses were Cosimo and Avis and that's the end." Burnell Wordlaw said. Me and the others couldn't believe it. "It doesn't say how Mr. Accerly Jamison killed him." Van said. "I know." Burnell said, me and the others flicked through the book and saw a glimpse of information about Siothran and Heleonor. Unfortunately, Burnell ripped the page out and told us that's a story for another time. Then, I asked him what does he know about The Saterfiel. "How do you know about them?" Burnell said with a curious look on his face. "Maybe, when this is over with, I'll tell you. Now please tell us everything you know about The Saterfiel Family." Burnell told us he can't tell us. "Why?" Ajay said. "Because there are secrets about that family and it's up to you to find them out on your own." "Do you know what me and my friends have been through?" I asked him. "Yes I do. Losing friends, finding out secrets that have been hidden for years, creepy puppets and Ventrilgoust dummies, snakes, explosions, threats and dealing with attacks from The Mad Ffraid Brat and their gang."

"How do you know about all of this?" Rudy said. "I just know things," Burnell Wordlaw said. "Uh huh. You know I'm starting to think you're the Mad Ffraid Brat." I told him. "I promise you guys, I'm not. I'm just a keeper who knows everything. But I will tell you this, even though The Jamison Family are horrible people, you have something they never had. The Value of Friendship. From what I know, you have made a lot of new friends and you know the importance of friendship. Remember this, two are better than one. If either of them falls down, one can help the other up. But pity anyone who falls and has no one to help them up . My advice is, don't be afraid to let people in. Forget about all the ones who have ever hurt you and let people who want to be part of your life in. Everybody needs friends and you can never have too many." Burnell told me to give Ajay and the others a chance. I told him what if they don't like me. "They will bro. Believe me." Rudy said as he walks up. We told Burnell Wordlaw goodbye. Then, Rudy pushed me towards the others. He told me to go ahead so I introduced myself and I told them I have been shy my whole life and that I'm afraid to talk to people due to the ones who have hurt me. Ajay walked up to me and told me this. "I want to be your friend," after he said that, Van did the same. I took a leap of faith and told them I would like that and we had a group hug. "See, I told you." Rudy said with a smile.

After that, me and Noah went to a seedy hotel called Safe Doom that's run by Deveral. After finding out about it in Grandma Bregusuid's diary, we disguised ourselves as UPS men using The Cybernetic Falconieri Penzance Communicators. Even though I have made some new friends, I had some serious doubts that Noah Schnapp would even want to become my friend. He was aware of this and had a plan. Anyway we met one of Deveral's employees, a girl named Salviana and asked her has she noticed anything unusual. Unfortunately Salviana wouldn't talk. So Noah grabbed her and started making out with Salviana. While he distracted her, I went searching through the computer and discovered that a girl named Vigee Gautreaux is the only employee who lives at this dump who doesn't even do anything and somehow she still gets paid, I found out she's staying in Suite 233. So after getting the information we needed, I gave Noah the signal and he stopped kissing Vigee. Before we went searching for the suite, Vigee grabbed him and started making out with him again. I told Vigee that me and Noah have to go. Me and him went in the elevator and made it to our destination. As we walked, I couldn't believe that Deveral would run a seedy hotel. The hallway was dirty and in bad condition. Just when we thought things couldn't get any worse, suddenly Noah heard something and we stopped. When we looked back, Me and Noah panicked and started running. There were a thousand hissing cockroaches chasing us. We ran as fast as we could and made it to the suite. There were stacks and stacks of cash everywhere. Making me and Noah more suspicious. We split up and started searching for clues. Noah found a journal inside a zipped couch cushion and I found a card taped underneath a table. A number for an Anger Management Therapist named Doctor Coolio. Me and Noah opened the journal and read through it and discovered that Vigee Gautreaux is The Mad Ffraid Brat and that she is suicidal. Each page had suicide notes. We now knew two new things about The Mad Ffraid Brat. Before we left, Noah told me to promise to stay. I promised I'll always be the friend you need. "You're afraid to let people in because you think they will leave you, just like the ones that have hurt you. But I promise I will never ever do that. You can count on me." Noah said. Later on, me and Mitchell Hope decided to pay Mr. Hildefuns a visit at his magic shop. When we walked in, Mr. Hildefuns and a young guy magically appeared and welcomed us to his magic shop. Mr. Hildefuns Introduced me and Mitchell to his son Rube. They grabbed some sparklers and put on a show for us. Then Mr. Hildefuns and his son gave us a tour. I asked Mr. Hildefuns how come he didn't tell me and the others that he has a son. He told me that he's a private person and that his son is his main priority. Then he asked me is Mitchell my friend. I told him I don't know. Mitchell smiled and told Mr. Hildefuns that it is by chance that we met. By choice that we became friends. "See you are friends." Mr. Hildefuns said, while me and Mitchell looked around, I noticed a picture and got Mitchell's attention. We both looked at each other and asked Mr. Hildefuns who is this clown in the picture with him. Mr. Hildefuns told us that was Mads Caractacus Troncoso, a unique clown who also performed magic tricks. He was one of the best performers at The Show Mayor and his best friend. Unfortunately he died in a tragic accident. Thanks to Mr. Accerly Jamison. He convinced Mads Caractacus Troncoso to join his circus, The Meinhard Bannerjee Wonder.

"Wait, I thought that part of The Show Mayor belonged to Grand Dunixi Jamison and Esdras Jamison." I asked him. "No, since his father wouldn't listen to his idea. Mr. Accerly Jamison decided to make his own circus a travelling one. The Meinhard Bannerjee Wonder was his idea. That side of The Show Mayor where all my outcast friends live at used to be part of The Show Mayor until Mr. Accerly Jamison changed that. He also put his wife name in his travelling circus. The Show Mayor used to be a wonderful place. Me and Mitchell noticed how creepy Mads Caractacus Troncoso looked and wondered how did that accident happen. Suddenly, Me and Mitchell, Mr. Hildefuns and Rube heard some noise and went to investigate. We couldn't believe it, once again the police was here at The Show Mayor. We asked Mr. Stumbo what's going on and he told us that Montagew was murdered last night. "How?" Mitchell said. "He was shot. However, from what the police said, he should've survive." Mr. Stumbo said. I picked up my cell phone and called AJ. I just couldn't believe Montagew was dead.

With two pages left in Grandma Bregusuid's diary, me, Colton and Nick Mayorga found out the whereabouts of Soft Dolly's long lost daughter who enters a hot air balloon festival every year, so we used The Simplicius Transito and turned it into a hot air balloon. However we had no idea what Sericea looks like or what her air balloon looked like. Then Colton saw something and told us we got trouble. We looked and saw The Mad Ffraid Brat in a dark and creepy air balloon who was shooting lasers at an air balloon. Unlike the others, it had a picture of AJ which made The Mad Ffraid Brat more angry. Colton pressed some buttons firing lasers, unfortunately The Mad Ffraid Brat wasn't alone. Four more hot air balloons surrounded us and were blocking our way. Nick took down the first one. Meanwhile Nick had a plan and went over the plan with me, he used The Cybernetic Falconieri Penzance Communicators and pressed a button and got into an inflation suit. Then me and Colton used The Cybernetic Falconieri Penzance Communicators and made a slingshot net. Me and Colton told Nick to be careful and launched him. He took out two of the air hot balloons and The Mad Ffraid Brat's air hot balloon and landed on top of the hot air balloon she was in and got in the basket. "Who are you, and why were those people attacking me?" Sericea said. "Everything is going to be okay now. You're safe. My name is Nick." "Hi, I'm Sericea." After the hot air balloon festival, me, Nick and Colton talked to Sericea and told her about her birth mother. At first Sericea couldn't believe it and had a hard time adjusting to the news. Me and the others decided it's time for her to meet the mother she never knew she had, and took her to The Meinhard Bannerjee Wonder. It was the reunion Soft Dolly always dreamed of. She told us thank you. With the day almost over with, me and Grant read the final page of Grandma Bregusuid's diary about a young disfigured boy who lives in suite 11K, however when we got there, the suite was different from the others. It was rusty and the door was broken. We went inside and could tell somebody has been living here. There were burger wraps and candy wraps everywhere. We searched the suite and noticed that whoever this person is, is a huge fan of Grand Dunixi Jamison and Esdras Jamison. Then Grant noticed something. A picture of Grandma Bregusuid. Before he could touch it, somebody popped up scaring us. The person ran and told me and Grant to go away. We felt bad that we frightened him and went to apologize. "Hi, I'm Benny Breezy and this is Grant. A good friend of mine. We're not here to hurt you. Just to ask you a few questions." "What's your name?" Grant said . "I'm Sefi The Show Mayor." Me and Grant looked at each other and wondered what does he mean. We asked him could he come out. Sefi told us that he's afraid that we'll judge him. Me and Grant told him we're not like that.

So after we told him that, Sefi came out. Me and Grant saw why Sefi would think we would judge him. Sefi had a disfigured face and told us his life story. This is what he said. "I'm an outcast. I always have been, People always say the world, but it's the people in the world. People can be so cruel, mean and hateful. They judge you on everything. From your face to your voice, your body and more. I never had a friend before or been in love. Even my own parents didn't want me. Do you have any idea how it feels to be rejected by people just because of your appearances. I felt alone and unwanted until I met Grand Dunixi Jamison and Esdras Jamison. They were the kindest people in the world. Especially Grandma Bregusuid. She was the mother I never had, they liked me for me and became my new family. I was the first outcast to join The Show Mayor. I was afraid though, afraid to show the world my face. But Grandma Bregusuid and the others helped me with my self esteem and I became a better and stronger person because of them. They taught me that it's. What's inside that counts and that you should never be afraid to show the world who you really are, I embraced my weirdness and became something special. After trying to come up with names for the hotel, Grand Dunixi Jamison had a brainstorm, after many sleepless nights. He decided to invent a name that no one has ever thought of and came up with The Show Mayor and named me after the hotel as well. So I became The Show Mayor, one of the biggest names in the world. I felt wanted and appreciated. Every show was different from the last and I always thought, I would be The Show Mayor. But those days are over with. I'm just simple old Sefi who doesn't have a future," me and Grant smiled and asked Sefi has he ever heard of The Hunchback of Notre Dame. He told us no. I told him The Hunchback of Notre Dame is one of my all-time favorite movies. The message and songs mean a lot to me. I told Sefi that Quasimodo is courageous, kind and enthusiastic. Grant told Sefi the message of the movie is to not judge people by their appearances . We both agreed that Esmeralda is another one of our favorite characters and how kind she was to Quasimodo. Then I told Sefi I like weird people. The black sheep, The eight balls, the left of the centers, the wallflowers, the underdog, the loners, the rejects, the outcasts, the outsiders, the odd ducks, the eccentric, the broken, the lonely, the lost and forgotten. Grant told Sefi being different isn't a bad thing. It means you're brave enough to be yourself. You two make a good team Sefi told us. I smiled and looked at Grant and told him I've got a best new friend for the rest of my life. "Always." Grant said. "I wish I had a friendship like that. Sefi said. "You do, me and Benny. We're your friends now and we like you for you." Grant said.

After that me and Pierson Fode went to talk to Jumoke. I knew Pierson wouldn't become my friend so I kept my distance. Suddenly we heard a noise and saw every animal of The Show Mayor going mad. Diot almost stomped on me until Pierson saved me. We watched as the animals prepared to attack the guests, causing me and Pierson to act fast. We used The Cybernetic Falconieri Penzance Communicators and use sleeping gas to stop them. The guests were relieved. As for Mr. Stumbo, he couldn't stop apologizing to the guests, I looked at Pierson and told him thanks for saving my life. He smiled and told me that's what friends do. "We're really friends?" I asked him. "Yes bro we are." Pierson said. Once again, I tried to hold back my excitement but I couldn't help it. I was glad that Pierson liked me for me. I was afraid that he wouldn't. Then Jumoke came running. She was upset and told us she don't know how much more of this she can take. I told Jumoke about. The Princella Khione of Aurex. and where the rest of her animals were. She was shocked and wondered why would Deveral experiment on her animals. She then got distracted when she realized who was with me. She started blushing. Unknowing to us, Jumoke has a gigantic crush on Pierson and always dreamed of kissing him. With her animals and job in danger, Jumoke decided to make a move. She grabbed Pierson and started making out with him. "You have been hanging around Mallory haven't you?" I asked her. I just watched as those two made out, a few hours later me and Jax and another person I never thought would become my friend noticed a girl at the front desk that we had never seen before, and we went over to talk to her . The girl kept panicking and was timid. Me and Jax calmed her down and introduced ourselves. The young girl told us that her name is Ebonney and that she's Stiles sister. "Why are you here?" I asked her, she told me that she's filling in for her brother because her brother loves The Show Mayor. "It's his life." Ebonney said, her brother is the bravest person she knows. unlike her who's afraid of her own shadow and a bit paranoid. She also admitted to us that she has never been kissed before and feels like she never will. I asked her how Stiles is doing. She told me Stiles is getting worse which made me worried. Then she looked at Jax. Took a chance and started making out with him . "Just what we need, another Mallory" I said. Me and Cayden Boyd, Case, Van and David Mazouz went to talk to Mr. Accerly Jamison's bodyguard Zahair. The one that couldn't be found when Mr. Accerly Jamison was kidnapped. However when me and the others arrived at The Jamison Mansion, Zahair was in a hurry and packing his things. He panicked after he saw us and tried to escape but Van stopped him. He used The Cybernetic Falconieri Penzance Communicator and wrapped Zahair in a silly string goo cocoon. Zahair called in back up so me and the others took care of them, David trapped three in bubbles and knocked out the rest. Case electrocuted five of them.

As for me and Cayden, we used inflation suits and turned ourselves into balls and took out the rest, shocking Zahair. "What do you want?" He said. "Answers." David told him, "where were you last night?" Case said. "I don't know what your talking about." Zahair told us. "Your boss got kidnapped at Flame Feast and you weren't around to save him." Cayden said. "You're his bodyguard, it's your job to protect him." Van said. "So start talking" I said. "Fine, someone paid me one million dollars just to leave Flame Feast so I did." "You abandoned your boss for money?" Cayden said. "Yep that's right." Zahair said, "you been working for The Jamison Family for twenty years and decided to turn your back on them just like that." Case said. "Have you met these people?" Zahair said as he laughed. Me and the others looked at each other. I came back to The Show Mayor and Keegan and Austin Rhodes, Ryan Malaty, Antoni, Alex Saxon, Harris Dickinson, Ashley Tisdale, Christopher Bones and Tyler Posey were waiting for me. "What's going on?" I asked them. Ashley told me That The Show Mayor is closing down forever. I couldn't believe it. Mr. Stumbo was making the announcement to the staff members and told them it has been an honor working with them. Tears started falling from his eyes and he quickly got off the stage. "Are you okay?" Austin Rhodes asked me. I told him, "No I'm not." We all had a group hug. Me And Ryan Malaty went to talk to Mr. Stumbo who also lives at The Show Mayor. I kept my distance from Ryan Malaty . I knew for a fact that Ryan Malaty would never in this lifetime become friends with a loser like me. Anyway, Mr. Stumbo was drunk. "What do you want? Can't you see that I'm busy." Mr. Stumbo said. "We need to talk to you," Ryan Malaty said. "We want to know why The Show Mayor is closing down." I asked him, "Ugh!" Mr. Stumbo said as he poured more liquor in his cup. "Where do I begin? Hmm, let's see. First we let a criminal that has been on the news a lot stay at The Show Mayor. Then The Ptarmigan Seissylt Clowns got arrested for being accomplices to another crime that AJ committed. The animals turning rogue, Stiles becoming ill. A room I have never seen before blew up. An employee got murdered and the kidnapping of Mr. Accerly Jamison. Plus someone wrote a threatening message on your aunt's door and they almost killed you in an elevator. When does it end? I mean seriously that's why The Show Mayor is closing down before something else goes wrong. Anyway! Somebody that Mr. Accerly Jamison knows is buying The Show Mayor," Mr. Stumbo said. "Who?" Ryan said. "Avis Freels." When he said that, me and Ryan Malaty looked at each other. "Are you kidding me?" I asked him. "Nope, it's all in this email." Mr. Stumbo said. He showed us the email and we couldn't believe this. "Who sent you this email?" Ryan Malaty said. "Gewnsnay," Mr. Stumbo told him. "Seriously? She could've forged that email." I told him. "Who cares?"

Mr. Stumbo said. "We care." Ryan Malaty said, "you know when I first met you, and your friends, I thought you were going to be a problem but then I got to know you and hoped you would save the day. But now I give up. There is no hope," Mr. Stumbo said. "AJ isn't The Mad Ffraid Brat, somebody else is behind all of this and me and my friends are trying our best to unmask this person. Also this person isn't working alone. Gewnsnay, Badaidra, Conant, Terentilo, Edvardas, Deveral and maybe Tielyr is working with The Mad Ffraid Brat. Montagew was working for them as well." "Uh huh, it doesn't matter anymore. The Show Mayor is dead." When he said that, I told Ryan Malaty we're leaving. Before we left, I asked Mr. Stumbo does he remember Grand Dunixi Jamison's Motto. "Yeah, how do you know about it?" He asked me. "Because I read about it in Grandma Bregusuid's diary and I think it's a good motto." I shouted out. " Have a Little Faith ". Mr. Stumbo got up, took off his hat and handed it to me. "I'm done, you're the manager now." Mr. Stumbo said. Me and Ryan Malaty left after that. While going down the hallway, Ryan Malaty stopped me and told me this, "Good friends help you find important things when you have lost them, your smile, your hope and your courage." Since Deveral is a model, me, AJ and Mallory went to The Ermioni Appius. A fashion company to talk to his manager, Klove.

Unfortunately when we got there, Klove was panicking after one of the models got seriously ill and the dress she was supposed to present got ruined. Seeing how Klove needed someone to save the show, Mallory went through her bag and told Klove she'll be his model. Without any other choice, Klove agreed and told Mallory to go get ready. Me and AJ looked at each other and got a little concerned. So the fashion show begun and the models started posing. Then, when it was Mallory's turn, she shocked me and AJ, the guests and especially Klove. Mallory showed the world the dress she made. She was so beautiful and enjoying every moment of it. Her dream to become a model came true. The crowd was going wild after the show. Me and the others congratulated her. I was so proud of her, then when AJ complimented her about how beautiful she was, Mallory grabbed AJ and started making out with him, I just smiled and went to talk to Klove. He couldn't believe how talented

Mallory was. I asked him about Deveral. At first Klove didn't want to say anything because he knows what Deveral will do to him if he found out, but since Mallory did him a favor, Klove decided to talk. He told me Deveral doesn't like competition and that he will either bribe a person or take them out permanently. Klove said Deveral always gets what he wants and he warned me that Deveral is a dangerous person. And to be careful. After that. He gave me a card, and told me. To give it to Mallory. In case she ever wants a job. Me and Klove. Watch as Mallory and AJ. Continued to make out. Nine hours later, me and Sean. Went to Leonel lab. To find more information. About, Nance and Rance. After Sean. Caught them snooping through Esdras room. We better get started, Sean. Told me. I looked at him. And told him no, and to leave. Sean asked me. Why? I told him. The Mad Ffraid Brat, has almost killed me in a elevator. I almost got burned. I was chased by hissing cockroaches. I almost got stomped on. By rogue, circus animals. One of my best friends. Has been kidnapped. And the other one, is in jail . I'm worried about my bud. AJ. Safety, and I'm afraid. That. The Mad Ffraid Brat. Will try to hurt. Shawn, Logan, Why Don't We, Reed, Grant, Hunter, Mark, Luke, Lucy, the others. And you. The Mad Ffraid Brat. Is targeting my one true weakness. You and the others, my friends. So just go. I can't bare to lose anyone else. Sean, looked at me. And told me that he's not going anywhere. Then he told me this. "The Mad Ffraid Brat might be dangerous, smart and has who knows how many people working for them. And they have done some evil things. But no matter what The Mad Ffraid Brat throws at us, me and the others will always have your back, that's what real friendship is about. We don't give up on people that we care about. Our friendship is the one thing that The Mad Ffraid Brat will never break. We are in this together. If friendship is your weakest point then you are the strongest person in the world." Sean said.

I looked at him and was speechless, then we asked Penzance Frisco and she started searching through the system and found everything there is to know about Nance and Rance. We discovered a shocking secret and learned that Nance and Rance are Shaviv's kids and that their last name is Greenwell. Me, and Sean also found out that Nance and

Rance are FBI Agents . Me and AJ. Ruben, Ryan Malaty, Christopher Bones, Colton Shires and Ashley Tisdale went to The Jamison Adonijah Industries to see what Gewnsnay is up to. When we got there, we were shocked. Gewnsnay has completely taken over The Jamison Adonijah Industries and has Mr. Accerly Jamison's employees working for her now. "What is going on?" Ruben said. "Oh no, what do you want?" Gewnsnay said as she drank a fruit smoothie out of a coconut. "We're here to talk to you," Colton said. "What have you done to The Jamison Adonijah Industries?" Ryan said. "I made it better. With Mr. Accerly Jamison gone, I'm in control of The Jamison Adonijah Industries." "Mrs. Bannerjee Jamison would never allow that." Ryan Malaty said. Gewnsnay smiled, "Well, with her husband missing. Getting him back is the only thing on her mind." Gewnsnay said. "What gives you the authority to take over The Jamison Adonijah Industries." Ashley said. "I'm glad you asked. Follow me." Gewnsnay said. She took us to the conference room and showed us a gigantic contract that is pinned to the wall but it was so hard to read . The words were tiny. She gave AJ a magnifying glass and told him to read what it said aloud. So he did and this is what it said. "If anything ever happens to me. I leave all my businesses to my trusting assistant Gewnsnay." AJ said. Me and the others couldn't believe this. "When we found Mr. Accerly Jamison, we're going to tell him the truth about you." Christopher said. "Are you now? Hah! Who's going to believe you? Especially you AJ Mitchell. I'm sorry but you have lost and it's almost time for the finale." Gewnsnay said. "That's it, I'm calling." Sollie I said. "I wouldn't do that if I were you." Deveral said as he came walking in. "Oh great, more trouble." Ruben said. "What are you doing here?" AJ said. "None of your business. However I will tell you this, if any of you, especially you Benny, tell my baby brother about any of this, I will personally take matters into my own hands and make sure you and my brother are no longer a problem." Deveral said with a devious smile. Then we met Gewnsnay's fiance Ettore, who's a software engineer and a computer whiz. He tried to shake my hand but Gewnsnay wouldn't let him. "What are y'all up to?" Ruben said, "let's just say things are about to get interesting at every single business my father runs." Deveral said. "You won't get away with this." I told them. "Who's going to stop us? You?" Deveral said. Ryan noticed Gewnsnay's car keys and took them without her noticing. Then Deveral called his guards and told them to take us away, but before they did, Ettore stopped them and told me I drop this. It was a pen.

At first, I didn't know what he was talking about. Then he gave me and the others a signal and we left. When we got outside, me and the others found a secret note inside the pen that said meet me at this address if you want to know the identity of The Mad Ffraid Brat. Me and the others looked at each other, "this could finally clear my name." AJ said. After Ryan stole Gewnsnay's car keys, me, Ryan and Colton Shires went snooping through her car. I was checking through the front seats. Ryan was checking the back seats and Colton Shires was checking the trunk and he found something interesting. He told me and Ryan to come here quick. He discovered a brief case and when he opened it, he found a manilla file folder inside. So when he opened it up, he couldn't believe what he uncovered and neither could me and Ryan. Colton found the recipe on how to make Hade Wild. We went down the list and learned that the main ingredient is Death Nettles. "What is that?" Colton said, "I don't know" I told him. "And why does Gewnsnay have the recipe on how to make Hade Wild?" Ryan said. That's a good question I told him. Me and Jordan Doww tried to find out more about Vigee Gautreaux. I kept my distance again because I didn't think he would become my friend either. We were in Leonel's lab trying to find any information on Vigee Gautreaux and we were having a hard time . While we search for answers, Jordan tried to get to know me. I was a little nervous and didn't want to get attached to anyone else because The Mad Ffraid Brat keeps attacking my friends. So I just didn't say anything, but Jordan didn't give up. He wanted to become my friend and noticed my song book, Konstanty. "May I?" Jordan said. I shook my head, so he went through my song book and found a song that he liked and started singing. As he sings, I realized that maybe I do stand a chance of becoming friends with him, and I started singing with him. After we were done, Jordan told me I have talent and told me we're friends now. Then he found something about Vigee Gautreaux and we went to investigate, what we found was a graveyard. Me and he wondered why Vigee Gautreaux would be in a graveyard. We quickly found out why. Me and Jordan discovered a tombstone that said here lies Vigee Gautreaux. A loving wife and mother. "OMG." Jordan said. Just when we thought things couldn't get any worse, we found a package with my name written on it. We used The Cybernetic Falconieri Penzance Communicators to make sure a bomb wasn't inside. The Cybernetic Falconieri Penzance Communicators said, "No threat detected." Jordan opened it up and discovered a red herring. "Was does this mean?" I asked Jordan. He told me a red herring means The Mad Ffraid Brat is trying to distract us and mislead us because we are getting closer to the truth. "Great, I'm never going to save AJ, The Daily Maglorix Newspaper, Doyle, Stiles, Raysel, Mr. Accerly Jamison and The Show Mayor." I said "Yes you will. I believe in you bro, you can't give up now." Jordan said.

After finishing Grandma Bregusuid's diary, me and Harris Dickinson wondered if there are anymore clues or secrets that me and my friends should know about. I was really nervous and shy around Harris Dickinson because I didn't think I stood a chance of becoming friends with him. Harris was aware of this and started searching Grandma Bregusuid's Diary, to find something useful. Unfortunately all he found was the same stuff we had already read. Then he discovered something inside the spine of the book. A key along with a map to The Jamison Family grave. So me and Harris went to the graveyard and boy was I scared but Harris helped me and told me we're in this together, we used the key to unlock the gate. Then we went inside. The map led us to a marble bust and we found another diary that belonged to Grandma Bregusuid . We grabbed the diary and quickly opened it and discovered new secrets including a shocking one. Me and Harris learned that Sollie and Deveral have a sister. To get more information, me, AJ, Mallory and Gordon Winarick decided to go on Deveral's talk show, The Domotor Deveral without him knowing. When he came onto the stage to introduce the show . He panicked when he learned that we were his guests. He came over to us and asked me and the others what were we doing here. "For answers. And we're going to get them, one way or another." Gordon said. "We'll see about that." Deveral said. "Welcome! Everybody back to my show. Today we have the main person who stays on the news. The thief who stole The Ape Skull from The Diamond Museum Amsterdam and he's done other things like kidnapping my father." "Enough, AJ is innocent. I'm tired of people, especially people like you accusing him of all these crimes. Somebody else is behind this. The person who's trying to frame him is a masked maniac known as The Mad Ffraid Brat." I said. "And this is Benny Breezy, a huge pain in the butt. He's an Investigative Reporter who thinks he can actually clear AJ Mitchell's name and this is his beautiful friend Mallory. I don't know why Mallory or the famous Gordon Winarick would want to be friends with him." "Because Benny is a nice and a good person unlike you." AJ said. "And Gordon isn't my friend," I said in a down voice. Deveral couldn't stop laughing. He was happy that Gordon wasn't my friend, "who would want to be friends with you anyway." Deveral said.

When he said that, Mallory stood up and shouted out. " Shut up ". Then she took over the show. "Welcome to The Domotor Mallory Styles Show." "What do you think you're doing?" Deveral said. "Taking over, now sit down." Mallory said. "It's our turn to ask the questions. Tell your fans why are you marrying a Mail Order Bride? Or we can talk about your connection to The Mad Ffraid Brat? So who is The Mad Ffraid Brat?" When Mallory said that, Deveral was starting to get mad and told the camera man to cut to a commercial. When they did, Deveral asked us how in the world did we find out about Luz. "None of your business. Now tell us who is The Mad Ffraid Brat?" AJ said. Deveral smiled and showed us a video. It was Nasser. "Where is he?" I asked him. "He's safe for now. But if you tell the world about Luz, or keep asking questions about The Mad Ffraid Brat, you'll never see your friend again." Deveral said, "so keep your mouth shut." "Fine. If we can't ask you anything, then can you at least free Chun and the others from The Salvator Day Ray." When I said that. Deveral wanted to know how I knew about that. Then he decided to make a deal with us. He told me and AJ if we beat him in a demolition derby tonight, he'll let Chun and the others go, however, if he wins, he gets me. AJ was horrified by Deveral's demands and refused, but I knew how important it was to get Chun and the others out of there and I shook Deveral's hand, much to my friends dismayed. After that, the commercial was over with. Me, AJ, Mallory and Gordon were nervous and a bit frightened. Before Mallory finished the show, she had a surprise. She gave Gordon a Zorro mask and told him to put it on. Then she went over to him and started kissing him on the lips and started a new record for the longest make out. Deveral got angry and tried to stop her, but Mallory used The Cybernetic Falconieri Penzance Communicator and shot out ten tranquilizers that put Deveral to sleep. While he slept, me and AJ drew on his face. Meanwhile Mallory continued to make out with Gordon and was enjoying every minute of it. They made out for fifteen hours and she broke another record.

That night me and Devin went to the hospital and used The Cybernetic Falconieri Penzance Communicators and disguised ourselves as candy stripers. We went down to the morgue. We were both creeped out. It was so cold. Me and Devin started searching through the files trying to find Great Uncle Teton's file. I was also trying to find Montagew's body and the bullet. Devin found Great Uncle Teton's autopsy. We opened it up and discovered shocking news. Me and Devin found out that Great Uncle Teton was drowned in antifreeze. We couldn't believe how cruel Mr. Accerly Jamison was when he was a teenager. We kept the file and looked for Montagew's body. After we found it, me and Devin were sad and wondered who killed Montagew. Then we analyzed the bullet and discovered what really killed Montagew. Me and Devin discovered that the bullet has Cellest Clinicriptine. "How is that possible?" Devin asked me, I told him I don't know. We now knew how Montagew really died and how Great Uncle Teton died. We have evidence, but before we left. Suddenly eight drawers from the morgue fridge opened up. Each one was a mask cloak figure and two got up from the morgue tables. "You're not going anywhere." One of the cloak figures said. "You and your friends have been a real problem but that all ends now." I told Devin to save himself. "I'm not leaving you," Devin said. He looked around trying to find a way to get us out of this mess. He hopped on one of the morgue tables and I did the same. "Do you trust me?" He asked me, "always bro." I said. We used the morgue tables like they were skateboards and escaped the morgue. We were glad to get out of there.

The cloak figures were furious. Me and Brandon went to the funeral home to see Quintonette's body and to find any helpful clues so we could find out who killed her. Brandon knew I didn't think he would become my friend so he set out to prove me wrong. The funeral owner told me and Brandon that Quintonette's family will be here tomorrow and took us to the room that Quintonette's body was in. After he left the room, me and Brandon just couldn't believe that the Mad Ffraid Brat has killed two people. I was getting more and more worried. Brandon thought singing would help relieve my stress. He sung I'll be your friend By Michael W. Smith. One of my favorite songs, then he told me every new friend is a new adventure, the start of more memories. "I'm your friend. I really am. You never have to pretend to be something you're not in order to be my friend." Brandon told me. I felt good that I was making friends and being myself. Then me and Brandon noticed something odd with Quintonette's body and we couldn't believe what we were looking at. Me and Brandon discovered a fake rubber prop body. "Okay, this is getting creepy." Brandon said. We found a small bottle inside the fake Quintonette's rubber prop hair and used a magnifying glass. We both read it, this is what it said. '**Wanna make a deal? Meet me tomorrow night at The Vangy Arungedan restaurant.**'

"The Mad Ffraid Brat has Quintonette's body." Brandon said. "I don't know how much more of this I can take," I told him. Suddenly we heard a ticking noise and found out there was a bomb inside the fake Quintonette's brain and one inside the body. We quickly got everybody out and watched the funeral home blow up twice. Me and Brandon looked at each other and wondered where is The Mad Ffraid Brat keeping Quintonette's body. Brandon and Lucy went to talk to Gerwazy. They found him in his swimming pool. "What do you guys want?" Gerwazy said. "Can't you see I'm busy." "You miss Flame Feast and the screening of The Black Butterfly, upcoming two part special." Brandon said. "Before or after you, my brother, and the others destroyed The Zvezda Three Ples." Gerwazy said. "We didn't mean to." Brandon said. "And that isn't any of your concern or business, you should be ashamed of how you treated Benny." Lucy said. "When are you going to change?" She asked him. "You don't understand." Gerwazy said.

"Then enlighten us because your brother needs you and you need him."
Brandon said. "Our father threatened me. Okay, I'm afraid of my own
father and thanks to him I lost my brother." Gerwazy said, "I'm tired of
pretending that my life is perfect. To the world. I'm this famous and hot
star, but behind the camera is a boy who has no one. I want to be better,
I didn't realize that until I met Benny. He taught me that life isn't about
abs, arm muscles, hair, being cool, popularity, being stuck up, shallow,
fame, wealth and pretending to be something you're not." Gerwazy
said. Lucy looked at him and told him this, "I don't care how attractive
you think you look. If you have an ugly heart you're ugly." Lucy said.
Gerwazy was shocked because no girl has ever called him ugly before.
But he realized that he has to change his ways and asked Lucy and
Brandon what can he do to make things right. You can start by coming
with me and Mallory, Ashley Tisdale. Ashley Benson, and Aunt Fanny.
"We're breaking in Tielyr's mansion." Lucy said. "So go get ready,"
Brandon told him. Back at The Show Mayor, me, AJ, Hayes, Nolan,
Peter, Sean Depner, Kendrick, Sollie, Keegan, Case, Chris Salvatore,
Colton, Colton Shires, Ty and Miles did a séance in Aunt Fanny's
penthouse with a friend of Sollie, a young medium named Pashenka
Brayboy. Me and the others got to know him. Pashenka told us that he
used to live here at The Show Mayor until Mr. Accerly Jamison took
over. After we got to know him, we got ready for the séance. Pashenka
said this, "Our beloved Grand Dunixi Jamison, we bring you gifts
from life into death. Commune with us Grand Dunixi Jamison and
move among us," at first nothing happened, but then we heard Grand
Dunixi Jamison's voice come from Pashenka Brayboy. "Is that really you
Grandpa?" Sollie said. He looked at him and smiled, "My dear boy, you
have grown so much. I have missed you." When Grand Dunixi Jamison
said that, tears started falling from Sollie's eyes and he went over to hug
him. Then me and the others introduced ourselves but he already knew
who we were and was happy that somebody finally knows the truth
about his family and how him and his brother died. AJ asked him does
he know who The Mad Ffraid Brat is. Grand Dunixi Jamison told him
yes and that the answers we seek are at Mount Jamison and that the

diary that Mr. Thersander gave me and the secrets in Mount Jamison will reveal the identity of The Mad Ffraid Brat.

Before he left, Grand Dunixi Jamison told me and AJ that we can't give up now and to unmask The Mad Ffraid Brat and save The Show Mayor so he and Esdras can finally rest in peace. He also told Sollie that he's proud of the man that he has become. After that, me and the others wondered what could be at Mount Jamison. Later that night, me, AJ, Austin P. McKenzie, Hayes, Harris, Casey, Cody Linley, Ajay, Matt, Jax, Luke, Jack Maynard, Austin Rhodes, Case, Chandler, Peter and Noah went to The Horror Herculano. We were all nervous. We sat in the grandstand and got ready for the show. Tielyr came out wearing a creepy top hat and introduced the first act. Me and the others met The Skull Zuberi. They're something like The Ptarmigan Seissylt Clowns but more creepy and dark. There names are Ezell the leader, Valo, and two girls, Coline and Terka. They started off with a ritualistic performance. Then they sung, the song was called The Horror Herculano Man. There were a lot of special effects and the performance was actually good, but then I noticed their acrobat skills and realized those are the same moves that the thieves who stole The Nation Diamond had. I told AJ and the others that The Skull Zuberi are part of this. Then Tielyr started looking for a volunteer for his disappearing box act and chose me. I tried to tell him that I didn't want to but he encouraged the crowd to make me go along with it. I was really afraid but AJ and the others promised me that they won't let anything bad happen to me. So I reluctantly went in the box. I have been very eager to meet you, Tielyr told me. He closed the box and said the magic words and when he opened it up, he showed the empty box to the audience and my friends. But when he tried to bring me back, a pile of bones fell out. The audience thought it was part of the act, however AJ and the others realized that I was in trouble and went searching for me. AJ told the others to investigate and see what secrets Tielyr was hiding while he rescued me. But Matt told him that he will rescue me. AJ told Matt that he promised that he would protect me and that I'm his friend. But Matt told AJ that I'm his friend too and that he cares about me just like AJ does. We're in this together, Matt said. So after seeing how much Matt cares about me, AJ, Luke, Jack and Jax went searching for clues. While Matt, Harris, Austin P. McKenzie, Case, Peter, Jacob and Hayes went to rescue me. Noah went in the elevator and Casey, Cody and Ajay and Austin Rhodes went their separate ways as well. Matt used The Cybernetic Falconieri Penzance Communicator to find me.

Meanwhile, Cody found Tielyr's office and used a picklock from The Cybernetic Falconieri Penzance Communicator to get inside, he used The Cybernetic Falconieri Penzance Communicator again to hack into Tielyr's computer and discovered that Tielyr had created some type of malicious virus that he plans to use against The Jamison Family. He also found out that Tielyr has placed Hade Wild inside the AJ Bobbleheads. Ajay found the security room and started searching through the footage and discovered a secret. He found footage of Tielyr and Deveral using The Devil's Breath on Seissylt. Ajay was horrified and made a copy of the tape. Elsewhere, Noah was getting out the elevator. Each floor he went to was scary than the last. While he searched for clues, he met a creepy Psychic named Madame Bybee who told him that he and the others will never see me again and started laughing. Then Noah met a creepy jester named The Skull Horror Herculano Jester who got in Noah's way and wouldn't let him leave. Noah tried to escape but The Skull Horror Herculano Jester used knocked out gas on him. He and Madame Bybee took him away. As for me, I thought I was finished, Terka took some of my blood. I don't know why though. I asked her what were they going to do with me. Terka smiled and told me Tielyr is going to hand me over to The Mad Ffraid Brat. Just when I thought all was lost, Matt, Harris, Austin P. Mckenzie and the others jumped out a heating vent and knocked out Tielyr's henchmen, Terka was furious and escaped. Matt untied me and was happy that I was safe. Harris helped me up. I couldn't stop shaking but Austin P. McKenzie and the others, especially Matt and Harris calmed me down. "We're here for you. Everything is going to be fine," Matt told me. Casey went snooping through The Skull Zuberi's dressing room and discovered a shocking secret about Ezell. "What are you doing in here?" Ezell said as he came storming in. "You're Terentilo son." Casey said in a shocking voice. "You don't know what your talking about." Ezell said. Casey showed Ezell his birth record. Ezell closed the door and told Casey that years ago, Terentilo fell in love with a fan of his and the two had a child. Unfortunately Ezell's mother died while giving birth. Terentilo didn't care about him and decided to give him over to Tielyr to raise. Ezell told him that he grew up at The Horror Herculano and wants revenge on Terentilo for abandoning him. Casey told him he's sorry that happened to him. But he also told him that revenge is never the answer. Ezell didn't care and told Casey to come with him. Knowing how dangerous Tielyr is . He used The Cybernetic Falconieri Penzance Communicator and trapped Ezell in a confetti web.

Then he grabbed Ezell's birth record and ran. Austin Rhodes was in a room filled with costumes, and started searching for clues. While he looked through the costumes, he started to feel like someone was watching him. Suddenly The Skull Horror Herculano Jester popped up and introduced himself. But Austin wasn't in the mood for introductions. However The Skull Horror Herculano Jester wasn't going to let him leave and took out a confetti cannon that shot out exploding whoopee cushions. Austin dodged each one and started running. While he did that, Luke was snooping through one of The Horror Herculano. Staff members' dressing room and discovered bugs everywhere. Then he met Vovka, an Entomophagy, which means he eats bugs. He grabbed some beetles and started eating them. "What do you want?" Vovka said. "Hi, me and my friends are here trying to find answers to clear our friend AJ Mitchell's name. So if you can tell me any helpful or using information about Tielyr, I would really appreciate it." Luke said. Vovka looked at him and told him that coming here was a big mistake. Then he called in Tielyr's henchmen and they surrounded Luke. Luke smiled and used The Cybernetic Falconieri Penzance Communicator to release a fire extinguisher on them and escaped. While he was running, he noticed that Austin was in trouble and tripped The Horror Herculano Jester. Then he and Austin beat him up and trapped him in a streamer web coccoon. Back in Tielyr's office, as Cody was printing out the information, Tielyr popped up behind him. He came out of a secret passage. Cody attempted to flee, but Tielyr used a bull whip as a lasso and tied him up. "Going somewhere?" Tielyr said . As for AJ,

Chandler, Jack and Jax, they found a secret room underneath The Horror Herculano but they had no idea what was inside. After breaking the door using The Cybernetic Falconieri Penzance Communicators, AJ and the others discovered a cryogenic pod and inside was something shocking. They opened it up and found Cosimo. Me and the others rejoined Luke. Ajay, Casey and Austin Rhodes. But AJ, Jax, Jack, Noah, Chandler and Cody were missing.

Suddenly all the doors and windows were being locked. "What's going on?" Hayes said. "The Horror Herculano is going on lockdown. You and your friends aren't going anywhere." Tielyr said as he came from the corner with Cody and Noah. "Are you guys okay?" I asked them. They told me they were fine. The others were happy to see me, "let them go." I told Tielyr. "No! You and your friends are coming with me." "We aren't going anywhere," Austin P. McKenzie said. "You killed Esdras. How could you?" Cody said. "He was your best friend," Luke said. "You stole Esdras' secret project ideas." Harris said. "And the world will find out," Matt told him. "And you probably killed Quintonette." Case said, Tielyr was shocked that we knew about him killing Esdras and stealing his secret ideas. "You know my secret and now you're my prisoners." Tielyr said. "Is this all true?" A voice said. Me and the others looked and got excited when we saw AJ, Jack and the others. However, they weren't alone. AJ and the others were happy that I was alright. "Um, who is this?" Noah said. "My son." Tielyr said in a scared voice, "what have y'all done?" Tielyr asked them. "They set me free. Do you know how long I've been in that cryogenic pod? Ten years, just because my evil father didn't approve of my friendship with Accerly." "Seriously, what kind of sick person would do that?" Jacob said. "You were best friends with my enemy son. I couldn't allow that and now nobody is leaving The Horror Herculano." "We'll see about that." Ajay said. He used The Cybernetic Falconieri Penzance Communicator and shot out fire workers to distract Tielyr. While the fire workers caused damage to The Horror Herculano, I used The Cybernetic Falconieri Penzance Communicator to hack into the system and unlock everything . Once the doors were unlocked, me and the others ran. Cosimo joined us. We quickly got away from The Horror Herculano and sworn to never go back. After that, Mallory, Aunt Fanny and Lucy, Ashley Tisdale and Ashley Benson. Gerwazy and Sean Depner and Brandon, plus a member of The Hinkley Youga Shirk were arriving to Tielyr's mansion flying in Stranger Red. While the others broke in, Hinkley Youga Shirk 100 stayed in Stranger Red and was the look out. Mallory was a little distracted. She couldn't stop thinking about that kiss between her and Gordon, but Lucy told her to focus.

So Mallory used The Cybernetic Falconieri Penzance Communicator to hack into the security system and turned it off. After that, Mallory and Lucy, Ashley Tisdale and Ashley Benson went searching for clues while Gerwazy and Brandon went on their own search. Sean went to the north wing and Aunt Fanny searched for the vault. Mallory and the others discovered a secret room that was guarded by several boobytraps. But they worked together and managed to Dodge each one. They found The Nation Diamond and wondered why Tielyr has it. Sean searched through Tielyr's bedroom and found Esdras' secret project ideas that Tielyr stole years ago. He grabbed them and quickly got out of there. Gerwazy and Brandon were searching through each room and realized that The Jamison Mansion is way better than Tielyr mansion. As they looked for clues, Gerwazy asked Brandon does he think I will ever forget him. "I don't know." Brandon told him. The two uncovered a secret passage. After picking up a picture of Tielyr's son, they went down the secret passage and couldn't believe what they found, they discovered a factory where Hade Wild is made. They watched as the machines poured Hade Wild in jars and in a thousand of AJ Bobbleheads. Gerwazy and Brandon took pictures, meanwhile Aunt Fanny was in the vault having a blast. Suddenly Hinkley Youga Shirk 100 saw somebody coming towards the mansion. It was Tielyr. She quickly alerted the others. Gerwazy, Brandon and Sean returned to the spaceship while the girls left a surprise for Tielyr. They used The Cybernetic Falconieri Penzance Communicators and shrunk The Nation Diamond and got out of there. After getting back in the spaceship, Ashley Benson drove Stranger Red back to The Show Mayor. Happy that the others were safe, especially Sean Depner, Hinkley Youga Shirk 100 took a chance. She grabbed Sean and started making out with him much to Mallory's dismay. So when they all got back to The Show Mayor, Lucy and the others went to the elevator. While in the elevator, Lucy, Ashley Benson and Ashley Tisdale and Gerwazy found out that Aunt Fanny stole about ten thousand dollars from Tielyr's mansion. Meanwhile, back in the lobby, Sean and Hinkley Youga Shirk 100 were still making out which was aggravating Mallory. So she grabbed Brandon and started making out with him. Back at Tielyr's mansion, when he walked inside, he saw the surprise that the others left for him. A gigantic Ptarmigan Escavalon Of Edsel exploded and left him and his mansion covered in dye. Tielyr was furious. Anyway, me and AJ were at Leonel's lab. He introduced us to our ride, AJ Sire. After that, me and AJ went to the demolition derby. Deveral couldn't believe how nice AJ Sire was, I was really nervous but AJ told me we're in this together and that we can do this. So the demolition derby began and boy was it rough, especially when Deveral is evolved. He decided to take out the rest of the competition with lasers and torpedoes. But me and AJ weren't giving up. Even though AJ Sire has gadgets, we decided not to use them. Deveral was happy and was trying to damage AJ Sire. Me and AJ whispered a new plan and drove away. Deveral thought he won but we surprised him and drove AJ Sire up in the air, shocking Deveral and the crowd. Then we landed on top of his vehicle, crushing it. We were the winners, me and AJ celebrated. We actually beat Deveral. A deal is a deal, I told him. Deveral was speechless and mad. He called his henchmen and they released Chun and the others. Simon, Matthew Daddario and Keegan were there to take them to a safer place. Chun and the others hugged them and couldn't stop thanking them. Simon took pictures for evidence. Me and AJ were happy and tired. We also won the grant prize. I was so happy to go to bed that night but I couldn't stop thinking about being trapped in that box. So AJ and Simon, Aunt Fanny, Austin P. McKenzie, Noah, Harris, Jack Maynard, Luke, Chandler, Jax, Cody, Matt, Hayes, Ajay, Peter, Case, Jacob and Mallory didn't leave my side.

CHAPTER TWELVE

UNMASKED AT LAST

With Sollie's birthday tomorrow, me and the others got up early and were determined to find anything that could finally put an end to this mystery. To save AJ, Doyle, Nasser, The Show Mayor and the others. We had a big day ahead of us. After eating breakfast, I was in Mr. Stumbo's old office. Today was my first day being the new manager / ringmaster of The Show Mayor and I was a bit nervous while I tried to adjust being in charge. Austin P. McKenzie came in, he showed me a page from Grandma Bregusuid's other diary and told me that Grand Dunixi Jamison and Esdras Jamison have a sister named Oceon who works at a diner called The Lime Cloud. Me and him wondered how come nobody has ever mentioned her before. Anyway, Austin wanted me to go with him. I told him I have other things to do and that he should take Mallory or Simon. But Austin wanted to be the next one to have an adventure with me and he knew I needed one after what happened at The Horror Herculano. So we left The Show Mayor and set out to The Lime Cloud. I left Aunt Fanny in charge of The Show Mayor. As we drove to The Lime Cloud, Austin noticed how quiet I was being and he knew I didn't think he would become my friend but Austin had a plan. When we got to The Lime Cloud, there were no customers so we went inside and didn't see anybody at first. Then a woman from the back came out, "hi, I'm Oceon. Welcome to The Lime Cloud. Sorry to tell you fellows this but my cook called out today and he's the only worker I have." "You own The Lime Cloud?" Austin said, "yes I do.' Oceon said. "Why do you ask?" "Because we're here to ask you about your brothers, Grand Dunixi Jamison and Esdras Jamison." When I said that, Oceon started to get mad. "I don't know who you are, but don't you ever mention that cursed name. I'm not a Jamison anymore, I'm free and I'm never going back." Oceon said. Me and Austin realized that Oceon really despised her family.

I had no idea how we would get her to talk until Austin came up with an idea. "Since your cook is out today, me and Benny would be happy to help you out. All we ask in return is information." Austin said. Without any other choice, Oceon agreed to his terms and told us to go wash our hands and get ready. I whispered to Austin I don't know how to cook, but Austin smiled and told me he'll teach me and to think of it as a adventure. So we got ready for our first customer. Me and Austin made waffles, Eggs, pancakes, sausages and toast. Then we noticed how dull The Lime Cloud was, so Austin decided to give them a performance and started singing Ain't No Mountain High Enough and convinced me to join him. I was actually having fun and our performance shocked Oceon. She was impressed. Anyway, after we were done, me and Austin went back to the kitchen and made some more pancakes. While we made them, Austin got to know me. "Tell me something that you have never told anyone before?" He said. "Can I trust you?" I asked him. "Always." Austin told me. So I told him the story about how I used to be in Special Ed. Before I met Simon and the others, I was placed in Special Ed because I was a little slow and people would always make fun of me. It was hard going to school in Iceland. I didn't have any friends and would always hate going to school. People love to judge you before they get to know you. Sometimes people bullied others for no good reason. They think it's funny to make fun of someone who has no friends and sits by himself at the lunch table, the guy who's so afraid to raise his hand in class or stand up in front of his classmates. Bullying is one of the biggest problems in the world and I wish it was outlaw. That's why I stay to myself and away from people because of all I've been through and all my failed attempts to finally make some real friends. I'd rather be myself than be something I'm not. In today's society, people prefer looks and popularity over being true to yourself and kindness. I feel like I have to pretend to be somebody else in order to be in people's lives. That's why I don't think I stand a chance of becoming friends with Dakota Lotus, Will Jay, Isaac Cole Powell,

Dane Jamieson, John Harlan Kim, Logan Allen, Benjamin Freemantle, Patrick Luwis, Taylor Zakhar Perez, Sven Johnson, George Sear, Harris Dickinson, Matt Adlard, Josh Green, Tiera Skovbye, Jordan Burtchett, Nolan Funk, Katherine McNamara, Shay Mitchell, Josh Killacky, Scott Eastwood, Logan Pepper, Kyle Selig and especially Aaron Hull. I just don't believe anymore." I told Austin. He had no idea and told me this, "In a world full of people pretending to be something they're not, don't be one of them and just be yourself." I smiled and told Austin thanks for being my friend. "Friends forever," he told me.

After The Lime Cloud closed for the day, Oceon told us thank you. Then she started talking about her family, something she really hated doing. This is what she told me and Austin. "Dunixi and Esdras were all I had. We did everything together. Unfortunately our parents were rotten and horrible people. They used to manipulate me and my brothers and I believed they hated us. Our parents never had time for us, we were raised by nannies and maids and locked away from the outside world. Me, Dunixi and Esdras fell like prisoners. All we had was each other. Unlike our parents and the rest of our family, we didn't care about the wealth or fame. We just wanted to help people. But everything changed when Dunixi met Bregusuid. He was madly in love with her, but mom and dad didn't approve of Bregusuid and threatened to cut him off financially and disown him. So Dunixi did the one thing that none of us ever had the courage to do. He left and never came back. Esdras went with him." "How come you didn't go?" Austin asked her. "Because my parents were monsters and went to extreme measures to make sure I could never leave.' "Like what?' Me and Austin said. "Some things shouldn't be mentioned." Oceon said. "Anyway, I never saw my brothers ever again, and it broke my heart when I found out that he died. As for Esdras, I don't know where he's at?" Me and Austin told her what really happened to Grand Dunixi Jamison and Esdras Jamison and Oceon couldn't believe it. She cried and shouted out why. Me, and Austin hugged her and calmed her down. Before we left, Oceon told us that if we talk to her parents, to be careful. Austin told her team Ausy got this. "What is that?" I asked him, "it's my name and yours. We're Team Ausy." I smiled and told him yes we are. After we got back to

The Show Mayor, me and the others found out that in the next page of Grandma Bregusuid's Diary, that Esdras hid his will somewhere at The Meinhard Bannerjee Wonder. So me, AJ, Matthew Daddario, Keegan, Charlie Carver, Harris, Nolan, Case, Lucy, Miles and Colton followed the directions of the map and went searching for it. However, for some reason, it was dark and Soft Dolly and the other outcasts were missing. Me and Colton wondered why.

As we searched, suddenly a bunch of bouncing balls came out of nowhere, but these weren't any ordinary bouncing balls, each one was lit. "Everybody get down." Matthew Daddario said, so we all did. "What was that?" Case said. 'Bouncing balls that explode like bombs.' Lucy said. "Who is responsible for this?" Nolan said, "I am" a mysterious voice said. Me and the others got concerned when a mysterious person in a clown costume wearing a mask appeared like magic and told us he wanted the map. "Over my dead body." I said. The person laughed and said that can be arranged. Matthew Daddario told me to get behind him. Then he told the others to split up. So we all ran. Miles and Colton hid in the bumper cars. Unfortunately that didn't last too long when the mysterious person found them. Miles and Colton tried to use the bumper cars to knock the masked person out but they wrapped Miles and Colton with handkerchiefs and tied them up. Charlie and Keegan were in a rollercoaster. However the masked person didn't let that stop him and jumped on top of the ongoing rollercoaster, scaring Keegan and Charlie and threw a rubber chicken that released a net, trapping Charlie and Keegan. Case and Harris were in the petting zoo, thinking they were safe. But once again, the masked person showed up. Case and Harris tried to escape. Unfortunately the mask person wouldn't allow it. He threw Red foam noses that released a sleeping gas. "Night, night." The person said as he laughed. AJ and Nolan were on the merry – go – round, trying to hide. At first they thought. they were safe, but the masked person used his next trick, a deck of cards and trapped them in a deck of cards twister. They couldn't see anything. Lucy was walking by several circus booths trying to find me and the others. She then noticed someone and asked the mysterious person have they seen her friends. "Yes I have my dear, don't worry though, you'll be joining them." The person said. Lucy realized who the person was and started running. The person threw linking rings and captured her, Lucy found the others and the outcasts inside a crystal clear cube. She noticed that me and Matthew Daddario were missing and asked the others have they seen us. "They're still out there." Keegan said.

Meanwhile, me and Matthew Daddario were in the fun house. We tried to reach the others using The Cybernetic Falconieri Penzance Communicators, but for some reason the signal wouldn't go through. That's when I started to panic. "It's going to be okay bro." Matthew Daddario said, he tried to calm me down. "You can stop pretending." I told him. "What are you talking about?" 'I know I don't stand a chance of becoming friends with you, so just go. You don't care about me anyway." "That's not true and don't you ever say that again. So let's be friends and I do care about you, always bro," Matthew Daddario said. He shook my hand and we became friends. Before I could get too excited, the masked person. showed up with a sledge hammer, separating us. Matthew tried to find me and I was trying to find him and I got frightened when the masked person started chasing me. I used The Cybernetic Falconieri Penzance Communicator and released some oil to slow the mysterious person down. Then I checked the map and realized Esdras' will is somewhere on a tight rope. So I used The Cybernetic Falconieri Penzance Communicator and released a grappling hook and got on the tight rope. I was really scared because I have never done this before. But while I was up there, I noticed the others and used The Cybernetic Falconieri Penzance Communicator once again and broke them out using a laser. Meanwhile, Matthew was in the hall of mirrors trying to find me, he used The Cybernetic Falconieri Penzance Communicator and scanned the hall of mirrors to make sure he was alone. Unfortunately, he wasn't. The masked person came smashing out of one of the mirrors and demanded to know where I was at. Just when Matthew was ready to fight him, he suddenly got a call from me. I told him where I was. The masked person smiled and quickly left the fun house.

Matthew knew where he was going and came up with a plan. Anyway, I was still on the tight rope trying to find the will, but for some reason I couldn't find it. Just when I thought all hope was lost, I felt something and discovered that the will was inside the rope. So I used The Cybernetic Falconieri Penzance Communicator and cut it open and found the will. Before I even had a chance to look at it, the masked person showed up again. Give me that will, the person said. "Never," I said. The mysterious person was getting angry with me and tried to make me lose my balance using a boxing glove gun. I was trying my best to dodge each attack. "You're either working with The Mad Ffraid Brat or you are The Mad Ffraid Brat." I said. "The masked person didn't answer me and continued to used the boxing glove gun. Then Matthew came to my rescue and used The Cybernetic Falconieri Penzance Communicator and shot out several hand buzzers and electrocuted whoever that was. The masked person disappeared, however, he cut the rope before he left causing me to fall, but Matthew caught me. "See, I'll always have your back." He said with a smile. After we were all safe, me and the others read Esdras' will and found out that Esdras left the Zvezda Three Ples and his fortune to some guy named Gan. Me and Charlie went to the one place I hate the most, The Mall. After we found out that Grandma Bregusuid wrote about Gan and where to find him, we wore The Aristotelis Setser Suits and found out that Gan either works at an antique store called Three Kin Or he owns it. However, when we went inside there were no customers. We met a woman who was happy to meet us. "Hi, I'm Capitola. Welcome to Three Kin. How may I be of service?" "Um, Hi, my name is Benny Breezy. I'm an Investigative Reporter who's trying to clear AJ Mitchell's name and my job at The Daily Maglorix Newspaper, my friends and The Show Mayor and this is Charlie Carver. "Is he your friend?" "Sadly no." I said. "Anyway, we're here to ask you about Gan. Do you know where he is?" I asked her. "Yes, he went out to get us something to eat. What is this about?" Capitola said. "Well, he's in Esdras Jamison's will." Charlie said. When he told her that, Capitola dropped some rare vases and couldn't believe. She was so shocked she passed out. A few minutes later she woke up and found me and Charlie standing over her. "Are you okay?" We asked her. "I'm not sure, I just had the weirdest dream about Gan being in Esdras' will." "Um, that wasn't a dream." Charlie said.

"OMG, this is really happening. After all these years." Capitola said. "I honestly can't believe. How do you know about Esdras, everybody who knew him had their memory erased." Charlie said. "What do you mean?" Capitola said. "A cruel and evil man named Tielyr murdered Esdras with a dumbbell. Hid his body and used a memory erase serum and made sure nobody ever remembered him." I told her. Tears started falling from Capitola's eyes. She told me and Charlie that she was in love with Esdras, shocking me and Charlie. Capitola tried to pull herself together and told us about how she and Esdras met and how they fell in love.

This is what she said, "My life was going nowhere until I met Esdras. It was love at first sight. We met at a poetry club. The moment we shared our first kiss is when I knew I found Mr. Right and I wanted to marry him and spend the rest of my life with him. Unfortunately, someone from his past came between us and made it their goal to keep us apart. That's why he never told his brother or sister or even his sister in-law about us. He was afraid. But one night, after hiding our relationship for a year, he finally proposed and was about to tell everyone about us. But that all changed when he went back to The Show Mayor to check up on something and never came back. That night I received a letter from him telling me that I'm not worthy of being his wife and that he never wants to see me again. That letter broke my heart and from that moment on, I gave up on love, but now I know what really happened and I wished I was there. Maybe I could've done something. It's all my fault," Capitola said. "Me and Charlie look at each other and told Capitola that none of this is her fault and that Tielyr probably would've killed her as well. "I think Esdras was trying to keep you safe." Charlie said. "Because he knew how dangerous Tielyr was," "do you still have that letter?" I asked her. Capitola told me yes and went in the back. Then she handed it to me. "Who was the threat that was trying to come between you and Esdras?" Charlie said. "A woman named Orssa." Capitola said. "She was Esdras' psycho ex girlfriend who used to stalk him.' When she said that, me and Charlie got even more concerned and asked her was Orssa handicapped. She told us no. Me and Charlie used The Cybernetic Falconieri Penzance Communicators and scanned the letter. Then we asked Penzance Fisco can she find out whose hand writing is this. So she went through the system and sent us the results. We found out that Tielyr wrote this letter. Capitola was furious and wished Esdras would've, told her about Tielyr. She was upset that she and Esdras never got married. Then Gan came walking in. Me and Charlie introduced ourselves. Gan asked his mom what is going on. "Wait, Mom?" Me and Charlie said, "this is your son?" "Yes he is, Esdras is his father. I found out that I was pregnant the night he proposed. I just never got the chance to tell him. I'm sorry I didn't tell you guys." Capitola said. We gave her the will and left Three Kin while Capitola told Gan about the father he never knew. As we left the mall, Charlie told me this, "Friendship is weird. You pick a human you've never met and you're like Yup, I like this one and you just do stuff with them." "So, what are you saying?" I asked him. "I'm saying I want to be your friend if that's okay with you" Charlie said. "It's more than okay," I told him. Before we went back to The Show Mayor, we stopped by Leonel's lab to find out more about Orssa and discovered a shocking secret. Me and Charlie found out that Orssa is Tielyr's sister. A few hours later, me and Kendrick Sampson drove to The Key Claw to talk to a mask maker after reading another page of Grandma Bregusuid's Diary.

As Kendrick drove, I was being quiet as usual. Kendrick was another one I didn't think would ever become my friend. Kendrick remembered what the others said and decided to ask me about what I like about 7th Heaven, Charmed, Hetty Feather, Supernatural and Ghost Whisperer. This is what I told him, "7th Heaven was one of the best shows, The Camden Family were good people who always helped others. Annie was one of my favorite characters. She was one of the bestest moms anybody could ever ask for. Matt was another favorite character of mine. I always got excited when he would pay his family a visit and Lucy was definitely one of my favorite characters. She was the only camden kid that actually stayed and was around unlike her brothers and sisters. Lucy was hilarious and kind. One of my favorite episodes is when Lucy, Ruthie, and Simon were spying on Kevin when he was trying to find an engagement ring that Lucy might like and the episode he proposed to her. And the day of their wedding were some of my favorite episodes. About Lucy, Eric was another favorite character of mine. He helped so many people and still made time for his family. It was sad when he found out that he needed heart – bypass surgery and it was heartbreaking when he gave up on the ministry and stopped going to church. Then in the final season, he found out he was having problems with his heart again. Anyway! 7th Heaven was a touching show. Also, Eric and Annie were the best parents in the world. Charmed was another favorite show of mine. The unbreakable bond Piper, Prue and Phoebe had was incredible. They kicked butt, but when they lost Prue, Piper took it the hardest. The acting was incredible. Paige was the one who brought the family back together. Piper and Leo were the best couple and their love was unbreakable. Charmed was and will always be one of the best shows on TV. Supernatural is another awesome show. I wished Supernatural and Charmed would've had a crossover. What I like about Supernatural is the strong and unbreakable bond Dean and Sam have, they always have each other's back and are always willing to die for each other. They're brothers forever. Ghost Whisperer was an incredible show that had a lot of heart and touching moments. Melinda was just an incredible and unique person. One of my favorite episodes is Leap Of Faith. The moment when Melinda gave up and the scene when she said, " faith " was a powerful scene. I really miss this show. As for Hetty Feather, she is too incredible. She was the only one who stood up to Matron and tried to finally get rid of her once and for all. I love Miss Smith, she was so kind. As for Vince, I can't stand him. He was such a jerk, but he and Shelia changed a little in the season 3 finale. Also, Shelia was the one that saved Hetty. Anyway, these shows mean a lot to me. "I can see." Kendrick said, after telling him that, I stopped talking. Kendrick told me this, "once you are my friend, I am responsible for you." "Does this mean we're friends?" I asked him, "Yes," he told me. After we became friends, we arrived at our destination. We walked into Key Claw and met the Mask maker who looked just like Fuji. "Um Fuji, What are you doing here?" I said. "I don't know who Fuji is, but my name is Fujimoto. What can I do for you?" "First we want to know do you have a twin brother?" Kendrick said. "No I don't," Fujimoto said. Me and Kendrick were getting suspicious. We showed him a picture of

Fuji and he couldn't believe it. "How is this possible?" Fujimoto said. "Maybe you and Fuji were separated at birth?" I told him. While he adjusted to having an identical twin brother, me and Kendrick met Fujimoto's daughter Tella, who was smitten with Kendrick.

Anyway, me and Kendrick asked Fujimoto did he make any AJ masks and a masks of Raysel. Fujimoto told us that a young guy came to Key Claw and payed him two million dollars to make a hundred masks of AJ and to make a mask of a girl named Raysel. "It took me weeks but I managed to make that many for Deveral. Was I wrong to do that?" Fujimoto said. "Yes," Kendrick told him. "How about a guy named Doyle?" I asked him. "Nope, never heard of him," Fujimoto said. "Um I actually did dad." Tella said. "For who?" Fujimoto said with a shocking look on his face. "A girl named Karitas asked me to make one. She showed me a picture of him." Tella said. Me and Kendrick were shocked and told them thanks. Just before we left, Tella told Kendrick that today is her birthday and asked if he could kiss her for her birthday, so Kendrick went over to her and was about to kiss her on the cheek but Tella surprised him and ended up kissing him on the lips and started to make out with him. As they kissed, I asked Fujimoto was it really her birthday. He told me no. "She just always dreamt of kissing Kendrick Sampson." Fujimoto said. He also asked me when can he see his twin brother. I wrote down an address and told him when this mystery is over with, then he'll finally meet Fuji. AJ, Mallory, Simon, Sollie, Tyler Posey, Ashley Benson, Freddie, Felix, Ryan Malaty, Nick Mayorga, and Grant went to talk to Mrs. Bannerjee Jamison at her family bank. That's right, Mr. Accerly Jamison and his family have their own bank called The Zandro World Artur Jamison Bank that is heavily guarded. Sollie had to scan his eye and whisper a secret password to get inside, once my friends were inside, they couldn't believe how big The Zandro World Artur Jamison Bank was. Mallory saw all the money and her eyes grew big. She and the others met Mrs. Bannerjee Jamison, who was really busy. At first Sollie and the others didn't know why, until Mrs. Bannerjee showed them a video that she got this morning. She told them that The Mad Ffraid Brat Is holding her husband hostage and is demanding all the money from The Zandro World Artur Jamison

Bank for his release. "OMG." Sollie said in a shocking voice. "What does this mean." Grant said, "if we give all the money to The Mad Ffraid Brat, we'll be broke. All our money is in this bank." Sollie told them. It's ridiculous that someone would kidnap your father. "He's a good man," Mrs. Bannerjee said. When she said that, AJ and the others looked at each other. "What is going on?" Mrs. Bannerjee said, "Sollie, is there something I should know?" She asked him. Sollie didn't know how to tell her. So Ryan Malaty handed her a file on everything we know about Mr. Accerly Jamison. When she read it, her eyes started getting watery. "I don't know my own husband." Mrs. Bannerjee said, she couldn't believe that he killed Uncle Teton. "Who did I fall in love with?" Nick gave her the file on everything that we have found out on Deveral causing her to really get upset. Tyler calmed her down and told her to think about the babies. She wanted to know how did we find out about that. Ashley showed her the love letters from the women that Mr. Accerly had affairs with. Grant asked her about Sollie and Deveral's long lost sister, shocking Sollie. Unfortunately, Mrs. Bannerjee kept her mouth shut about that secret. AJ and Simon told her about Gewnsnay. Nick Mayorga and Felix asked her about what happened to The Meinhard Bannerjee Wonder. She told them she doesn't know. Grant told her about Mr. Accerly Jamison's other son. Freddie wanted to know was she close to Grandma Bregusuid. And Tyler told her about Avis. Tired of all these questions, Mrs. Bannerjee told her employees to stop what they are doing.

"Mom, where are you going?" Sollie said. "I'm leaving, The Mad Ffraid Brat can keep your father. I'm done. I should have never married into The Jamison Family." "But." Sollie said. "But nothing. I'm done. And oh, tell Benny I'm counting on him." Mrs. Bannerjee and her workers left and they placed all the money back into the safe. Unknowing to her and my friends, The Mad Ffraid Brat was watching them and was angry that there plan failed. Meanwhile, Mallory was busy stashing cash in her purse, concerning her friends. Simon met a girl who got smitten with him and started making out with him and some more girls joined in, one was making out with Felix. Another one was making out with Nick Mayorga. One grabbed Freddie and started making out with him. One of their friends grabbed Tyler and started making out with him and her friend made out with Grant. When Mallory saw another girl kissing Simon, she was furious. She went up to Ryan and started making out with him. AJ and the others just shook their heads. Me and AJ went to the hospital after we found out that something happened to Seini. When we arrived, we discovered that she was experiencing the same symptoms that Stiles had. Unfortunately hers were more deadly. After checking up on her, me and AJ talked to her friends and asked them what happened. Razzy, a girl who always dreamt of kissing Luke Korns told us that they were just making Fan Cakes. Something they sell to make money and all of a sudden Seini started acting weird and couldn't breathe and started turning colors. We asked them do they have any fan cakes with them.

Then me and AJ used The Cybernetic Falconieri Penzance Communicators and analyzed The Fan Cakes and we discovered some shocking news. We found Hade Wild and The Princella Khione of Aurex, inside the fan cakes. "Why would someone mix both of them?" AJ said. "That's a good question." I told him. Me, AJ, Chris McNally, Miles, Levi, Shawn, Rudy, Mallory, Simon, Ty, Antoni, Tyler, Nick Mayorga, Jeremy, Case, Casey, Hayes, Callan, Luke, Jack Maynard, Reed, Chandler, Peter, Sam, Jacob, Ruben, Grant, Harrison Webb, Mitchell Hoog and Devin Hayes went to Montagew's Funeral. We were the only ones there. None of his family showed up to his funeral. Both me and AJ were sad. Me and the others still couldn't believe that The Mad Ffraid Brat killed him. Devin thought singing a song would help. He sung Going Up Yonder. Then AJ sung If you get there before I do By Collin Raye. I was actually crying, I don't know why though. I wasn't close to Montagew. I hardly knew him. But AJ and the others comforted me. Suddenly we heard a hissing noise and wondered where that noise was coming from. Chris was the one who found something. He discovered a box inside the Coffin and discovered a fake snake with a note sticking out of his mouth. He grabbed the note and read it aloud. This is what it said, "The snake will always bite back." Making Chris and the rest of us nervous. Suddenly black snake fireworks started shooting out of the coffin. After that, me, Casey, Spencer List, Grant,

Case, Jordan Doww, Chandler and Bruce wore some black clothes and skully hats and broke into Terentilo's dressing room. After Casey found out some new information about him, me and Grant wondered what else is Terentilo hiding. At first none of us found anything, suddenly Spencer discovered one of Terentilo's Dumbbells and he realized it looked familiar. When he picked it up, it opened up a secret room and we all went inside. We discovered pictures of Terentilo. To our surprise, he used to be really skinny. Casey found several pictures of Ezell's mother. Case discovered pictures of some guy.

As for me, Grant, Jordan, Chandler and Bruce, we found several dumbbells. After scanning the dumbbells, Spencer told us that this dumbbell is the same one Chandler found which was used to kill Esdras. Me and the others wondered did Terentilo give one of his dumbbells to Tielyr. That's when Terentilo came in, "you just don't know how to quit do you?" Terentilo asked me. "I should call the cops," "why?" I asked him. "Because you broke into my dressing room and you and your friends are dressed as thieves." "How about you tell us about your son. The one you abandoned." Casey said. "I have no son. I was never the father type anyway." Terentilo said, "fine, you can tell us about these dumbbells. Did you ever give one to Tielyr?" Spencer said, "no I did not, but one of my dumbbells was stolen years ago, anything else you want to know?" Terentilo said in an aggravated voice. "Okay, well who is this guy in these pictures." Case said. "My brother who I lost years ago." "How?" Chandler asked him. "He died in Mr. Accerly Jamison's show. The Meinhard Bannerjee Wonder, the fatal accident that killed so many lives. I lost my brother because Mr. Accerly Jamison wanted his own business, so he created The Meinhard Bannerjee Wonder. He thought it would be a big hit and make him a lot of money since The Show Mayor stayed in Los Angeles and never traveled anywhere." Terentilo said. "Okay, what about these other pictures?" Jordan said. "How about you and your friends get out of my dressing room." Terentilo said. "Not until you tell us." Bruce said, "Fine, before I became a strong man, I used to be really skinny and boner, I got bullied all the time. I used to hate school. The only one who was there for me was my brother. I never had any friends and I still don't. Maybe that's why I'm like this, because of the way people treated me back then, now get out of my dressing room." Terentilo said. Me and Grant looked at each other and actually felt sorry for Terentilo. As we walked back to Aunt Fanny's penthouse, Spencer showed me and the others Terentilo's diary. "Where did you get that from?" Case said, "I took it." He told us. "Why?" Chandler said. "Because I found something that Terentilo didn't tell us." Spencer told us that Terentilo had an affair with Tielyr's wife and used to work at The Horror Herculano. Unfortunately he had to leave after Tielyr found out. So Terentilo's brother got him a job at The Show Mayor. Me and the others were shocked. "Maybe that's why Tielyr stole one of Terentilo's dumbbells, to frame him for Esdras' murder." Grant said, "how come he didn't?" Case said. "Because somebody stole the dumbbell from him before he had the chance to and hid it at The Jamison Mansion," I said. "But who?" Casey said. "That's a good question," Bruce said. Spencer continued to look through the diary.

Me and Miles Nazaire found out about an abandoned school that Mr. Accerly Jamison used to run and we went to investigate. I didn't say one word to him. We went inside and started searching for clues. We didn't know what we were looking for. It was a bit creepy. Suddenly we found Edvardas, Deveral and the nut who attacked me and the others at The Meinhard Bannerjee Wonder. We listened in on their conversation. "This is getting out of hand. Benny Breezy and his friends are becoming a real problem. I thought you and your boss could handle them." The masked person in the clown costume said. "Seriously? You were beaten by Benny and his friends, that is hilarious." Deveral said. "You have to admit, Benny and his friends are impressive." Edvardas said. "I wouldn't go that far," Deveral said. Then The Mad Ffraid Brat appeared, "trust me. Benny will no longer be a problem. I have a plan in store for him," The Mad Ffraid Brat said. After that, they left. "Are you okay?" Miles asked me. "To be honest, I don't know. And I'm sure you don't care anyway." I told him. Miles told me he does care. Then he told me this. "A friend in need is a friend indeed." So that's when I realized that me and Miles are friends. After that, we tried to find out what The Mad Ffraid Brat was hiding there. First, we had to hide from several of The Mad Ffraid Brat henchmen. Then we found a room that had a lot of computers and blue prints. I went through the blue prints while Miles hacked into one of the computers. Miles found out that The Mad Ffraid Brat has made several mind control chips called The Trygg Derock.

As for me, I discovered that The Trygg Derock are really tiny. Me and Miles wondered who are the mind controlling chips for. Me and Ty Wood went to the dump and discovered an RV, we wondered who it belonged to. Ty opened the door and told me he would let me know if it's safe. But I told him we were in this together, so we both went inside and couldn't believe our eyes. We found the same tricks that mysterious person in the clown costume used on us were in the RV and more tricks that we haven't seen yet. I found out that whoever this person was had a huge grudge against Mr. Accerly Jamison, they wanted him dead. Then Ty discovered something really interesting. Ty told me that this RV belonged to Mads Caractacus Troncoso. "But that is impossible. He died years ago." I told him, "he must have survived somehow." Ty said. What we found next really got to us. Me and Ty discovered a clown rainbow mask. "OMG." I said. "What," Ty said. "Mads Caractacus Troncoso was the one who attacked Nasser in the greenhouse, that's why Deveral. Bought the mask. Him and the others are the only ones who know that Mads Caractacus Troncoso is alive." I said. "And he's the one that attacked you and the others at The Meinhard Bannerjee Wonder." Ty said. Before we could search the RV some more, all of a sudden the RV started moving. "Um what's going on?" Ty asked me. "Something bad," I told him. We found ourselves on the highway trying to dodge the traffic. Unfortunately we weren't in control. "You two just don't know how to mind your own business." A mysterious voice said, "who said that?" Ty asked me. We both looked around and noticed a stuffed clown toy that looked just like Mads Caractacus Troncoso. The toy was talking. "So you finally know my secret." Mads Caractacus Troncoso said. "Well don't worry, you'll be joining Nasser in a few minutes. I have taken control of my RV and I'm sending you and your friend over to The Mad Ffraid Brat." "That doesn't sound good." Ty told me. I told him to hang on. I noticed that Mads Caractacus Troncoso has ejecting seats and I pushed the button which made Mads Caractacus Troncoso angry. Me and Ty used The Cybernetic Falconieri Penzance

Communicators and released two parachutes. We landed safely on the ground and wondered why Mads Caractacus Troncoso is working with The Mad Ffraid Brat. After that, Me and Ty became fast friends and he promised me when we solve this mystery, Me and him will hang out. I tried my very best not to get too excited. I couldn't believe we actually became friends.

Me and Austin Butler went to The Meinhard Bannerjee Wonder to finally hear the story about the accident. Austin was another person I never thought would become my friend. So I did what I do best. I kept my distance from him and was being quiet. Anyway, Rostya told us to look into his crystal ball. To our surprise, me and Austin were seeing the past, the day of the accident. This is what Rostya said, "It was January the 22nd and The Meinhard Bannerjee Wonder was heading towards it's next destination and Mr. Accerly Jamison's performers were wore out. They had been going for six months, but Mr. Accerly Jamison didn't care. All he cared about was the money instead of the well being of his workers. Anyway, a woman named Celestial was worried about her family since she hasn't seen them in six months. It was late and the conductor wanted to pull over to rest. Unfortunately Mr. Accerly Jamison didn't believe in getting rest, so he told the Conductor to keep going, upsetting his performers. The only one who stood up to him was Mads Caractacus Troncoso. Him and Mr. Accerly Jamison used to butt heads all the time. That night, something changed in Mads Caractacus Troncoso. Tired of Mr. Accerly Jamison and his selfish ways. He punched him and gave Mr. Accerly Jamison a black eye. Mr. Accerly Jamison was furious, and locked him up in one of the boxes that are used for a disappearing act and told him his career is finished. Then at that moment, the train started going out of control and went off a cliff, and that is the story of how Mr. Accerly Jamison's circus fell apart." Rostya said. Me and Austin looked at each other. "How did Mr. Accerly Jamison escape?" Austin said. He told his father and the public that he jumped off before it crashed. Rostya told us. I noticed that Celestial was wearing a magician costume and asked Rostya about her. He told me that was Mr. Hildefuns' wife. "Her death really hit Mr. Hildefuns, and their two sons hard." Rostya said. "I thought he only had one kid?"

I said. "No he has two. The oldest one works at The Vangy Arungedan. A magic theme restaurant that Grandma Bregusuid built. She left the restaurant to Mr. Hildefuns after the death of his wife." Do you think you can show us what happened to the conductor?" I asked him. "I'll try." Rostya said. So he told me and Austin to look into his crystal ball. Once again, this time we saw what exactly caused the accident. Me, Austin and Rostya watched as someone brought the conductor something to eat. The conductor wasn't paying any attention to what he was eating because he was so tired. He was eating an albatross. But after he took the first bite, he started feeling weird and tried to call for help, but nobody heard him. He accidentally broke the throttle, causing the train to move really fast. Then he discovered that the brake was broken and died after that. Me and Austin wondered what was inside that albatross. So we finally knew what really happened. After that, me and Austin told Rostya thank you and left. We wondered how did Mr. Accerly Jamison really escape and what happened to the brake. Before we went back to Aunt Fanny's penthouse, Austin told me friends are chosen family. "So we're family now?" I asked him. "Yes we are. Brothers for life." I smiled and told him I could use some more brothers in my life. Mallory popped out of nowhere and made out with Austin.

Me and Chace went to talk to Mr. Hildefuns. "Hey fellows. What can I do for you?" Mr. Hildefuns said. "We know." Chace said. "Know what?" He asked us. "We know about your wife, is that why you keep your life private?" I asked him. Tears started falling from Mr. Hildefuns' eyes, "she was the love of my life." He said. Mr. Hildefuns played their wedding tape and started reminiscing. He told me and Chace that she was his best friend and his whole world and that losing her was the hardest thing he's ever been through. He told us that Mr. Accerly Jamison didn't even care. He acted like nothing ever happened. Mr. Accerly Jamison is a monster and always will be. "That's why you can't give up Benny. The Show Mayor and my sons are all that I have. This is our home," Chace looked at me and told me this, "Stick with the people who pull the magic out of you and not the madness. You two make a good team." Mr. Hildefuns said. "I suppose we do," I told him. Before we left, Me and Chace told Mr. Hildefuns that Mads Caractacus

Troncoso is alive and that he's working with The Mad Ffraid Brat. When we told him that, Mr. Hildefuns told me and Chace that Mads Caractacus Troncoso used to have a beautiful assistant named Primula, but nobody knows what happened to her. "Was she on the train?" Chace said. "No, she stayed behind." Mr. Hildefuns said. Wanting more information about The Meinhard Bannerjee Wonder accident, me and Keegan Allen went to The Jamison Archives. Me and Keegan were looking for Burnell. Unfortunately we couldn't find him so we started searching for answers on our own. Keegan found the section where The Jamison Family keeps everything there is to know about The Meinhard Bannerjee Wonder. Me and Keegan grabbed some boxes and tried to find anything useful. We found a video of The Meinhard Bannerjee Wonder's first show and decided to watch it. Then we discovered records on every performer of The Meinhard Bannerjee Wonder.

There were fifty performers. We kept looking for answers and still couldn't find any records on Primula. Suddenly a video started playing. Me and Keegan were shocked. In the video, we learned that Primula was secretly on the train those past six months without Mr. Accerly Jamison knowing. "Why would she do that?" Keegan asked me. "Because Mads Caractacus Troncoso had a devious plan to ruin Mr. Accerly Jamison's business and needed some help," Burnell said as he came out from the shadows. "How long have you been standing there?" I asked him. "Me and Keegan were looking for you," "I know, remember I know everything." Burnell said. "Right. Um Keegan, this is Burnell Wordlaw. The keeper of The Jamison Archives." "Nice to meet you." Keegan said, "like wise.' Burnell said. "Now please tell us what you meant?" I asked him. "Oh, well like I said, Mads Caractacus Troncoso had a deadly plan in store for Mr. Accerly Jamison. Unfortunately his plan fell through when Mr. Accerly Jamison somehow escaped. Anyway, Primula was the one who put something in the albatross. She would do anything for Mads Caractacus Troncoso." "What was in that albatross?" Keegan asked him ."The Cellest Clinicriptine," Burnell said. Me and Keegan looked at each other and felt sorry for that Conductor and the performers of The Meinhard Bannerjee Wonder. After that, we left The Jamison Archives hopefully for the last time. Keegan told me true friends don't come with conditions so that's how we finally became friends. I was so happy that he liked me for me. Me and Levi found out that Primula is alive and where to find her. We arrived somewhere in the woods and discovered that Primula lives in a circus cart. We were a little nervous. Levi knocked on the door. At first nobody answered, so he tried again and someone finally came to the door. "Are you Primula?" He asked her. "Yes I am. Who wants to know?" "We would like to ask you a few questions." Levi said. "Come in." Primula said. "So what do you want to know?" Primula asked us. "What really happened to your boss?" Levi said. "Why he faked his own death?" I said. "Where he's been all these years?" Levi said. "Why he caused that accident that took so many lives. Why you left The Show Mayor?" "Wow, you guys are really nosey. How about this. Primula mashed a button and suddenly her circus cart was being overfilled with popcorn. Me and Levi couldn't see a thing. Levi used The Cybernetic Falconieri Penzance Communicator and sucked up all the popcorn. After it was all gone me and Levi discovered that Primula got away. To my surprise, me and Levi became friends. Something I never thought would happen. Me and Sean went searching through Montagew's dressing room. Once again we wondered if Montagew had left anything for us, something that could finally reveal the Mad Ffraid Brat's identity. As we looked, I felt awful. "What's wrong?" Sean asked me. I told him I feel like Montagew's death is my fault because he told us things that he wasn't supposed to. "Stop bro. None of this is your fault, in fact, I think you brought out something in Montagew that he used to have." Sean said. "What" I asked him. "You brought out the good in him. He told you those things because he knew he made a huge mistake and wanted to help. So don't you dare blame yourself," Sean said. "Thanks." I told him, "thanks for being a friend." We continued to look and Sean found a note inside the mirror. He pulled it out and read it. We found out that Montagew wanted us to apologize to those families that the snake killed. He also revealed where we can find the bodies and he told us where we can find Esdras' remains. Shocking me and Sean. After that, me and Alex went to talk to Conant. He wasn't happy to see us. "What do you want now?" Conant said, "we just came to give you a letter."

Alex said. He gave Conant the letter and once Conant opened it up, he was shocked and asked us is this true. "Yes it is." Alex told him. Conant gave us something in return and actually told us thank you. Me and Alex read the note and discovered the password for Tielyr's bank. On the note, Conant told us that there's a video we need to see inside the vault so Mallory and Felix took care of it. They went to Tielyr's bank, The Asterope Tielyr, they learned that Tielyr's bank is heavily guardedly just like the Jamison Bank. Worried that she might not make it, she asked Felix could she kiss him. Felix told her sure and they started making out. After they were done, Mallory managed to destroy all the boobytraps. Impressing Felix.

He and Mallory used the code to get inside. Then they got to the vault and used The Cybernetic Falconieri Penzance Communicators to destroy the other boobytraps. Mallory was stealing money again. As for Felix, he found the flash drive and they played the video. Mallory and Felix found out some shocking information. They discovered footage of Tielyr using a fire poker to kill Shaviv and discovered that Mr. Accerly Jamison helped. He used a bat. "Why would Mr. Accerly Jamison do this and help his enemy?" Felix said, "I don't know." Mallory told him. Me and Case followed the directions that Montagew left and went to a dock. We were looking for a certain shipping container. I thought it would take forever but Case found the one that we were looking for. We eased our way up to it and Case opened it and we discovered something that nobody has ever found, Esdras remains. We used The Cybernetic Falconieri Penzance Communicators to scan the bones to make sure they were his. We couldn't believe this. Me and AJ and Devan and Nolan, Sollie and Mallory went to a cosmetic trade show with Mrs. Bannerjee. She couldn't wait to show her new product to the world, something called The Berthiaume Saavedra. Mallory was so excited. Unfortunately when some of the people tried her new product, several green spots were popping up on there face. Then they turned black causing everybody to freak out. "Mom, what is going on?" Sollie said. "I don't know, this shouldn't be happening." Mrs. Bannerjee said. Me and the others realized what was happening and told her that the Mad Ffraid Brat is behind this. "Why would The Mad Ffraid Brat do this?" Mrs. Bannerjee said. "Because you didn't pay the ransom." Devan told her. "Now The Mad Ffraid Brat is after you." Nolan told her. "This can't be happening," Mrs. Bannerjee said. "Welcome to our world." AJ said. "The Mad Ffraid Brat must have put something in The Berthiaume Saavedra." Mallory said. "Like what?" Mrs. Bannerjee said. Seeing how everybody was freaking out, Mallory grabbed Devan and started making out with him and a girl who was a big fan of Nolan started making out with him. So me, AJ, and Sollie were trying to calm Mrs. Bannerjee down. Me, Douglas, Christopher Bones, Grant and Tyler Posey went through Grandma Bregusuid's Diary and discovered that in The Show Mayor's basement, Mr. Accerly has a hidden stuffed toy lion. Somewhere in the basement, me and the others. wondered what's so special about a stuffed toy lion. Unknowing to us, Telmo was eavesdropping on our conversation outside of Aunt Fanny's door and went to find the stuffed toy lion.

Meanwhile, me and the others were in the basement. We discovered old props that The Show Mayor used to have. Like a gigantic gorilla hand, a ball pit and old arcade games. As we looked for the stuffed toy lion, suddenly Mads Caractacus Troncoso and The Mad Ffraid Brat appeared. "What are y'all doing here?" Douglas said. "We're here to find that stuffed animal." The Mad Ffraid Brat said. "You'll have to get through us first." Grant said. "I thought you might say that," The Mad Ffraid Brat said. The Mad Ffraid Brat revealed to us that they have Telmo. He was tied up and hanging over a dunk tank. The Mad Ffraid Brat told me I had a choice. I can find the stuffed toy lion or save Telmo. Mads Caractacus Troncoso told us that dunk tank has sulfuric acid. So me and the others came up with a plan. Me and Douglas went to save Telmo while Grant and Christopher and Tyler stopped The Mad Ffraid Brat and Mads Caractacus Troncoso. Christopher was fighting Mads Caractacus Troncoso on top of the gorilla hand. Mads Caractacus Troncoso was using his same tricks and Christopher managed to destroy each one using The Cybernetic Falconieri Penzance Communicator. Tyler and Grant were fighting The Mad Ffraid Brat. They discovered that The Mad Ffraid Brat had some impressing acrobat skills. But they didn't let that stop them. Tyler used The Cybernetic Falconieri Penzance Communicator and released some foam gum on The Mad Ffraid Brat hands. Then Grant used The Cybernetic Falconieri Penzance Communicator and wrapped The Mad Ffraid Brat in a tight rope. He and Tyler smiled, they couldn't believe that they actually had The Mad Ffraid Brat. As for Christopher, he was still fighting Mads Caractacus Troncoso. That clown couldn't believe that none of his tricks were working on Christopher. So he came up with a new idea. Christopher didn't like the look on Mads Caractacus Troncoso face. Mads Caractacus Troncoso threw a sticker at Christopher that landed on his arm. At first Christopher thought it was funny. But Mads Caractacus Troncoso didn't. He pressed a button on his bow tie and suddenly Christopher was being controlled by Mads Caractacus Troncoso. "Now that you're under my control, I want you to attack your friends while I free The Mad Ffraid Brat. Do you understand?" "Yes Master." Christopher said. He quickly ran over there and started fighting Grant while Mads Caractacus Troncoso dealt with Tyler. "I'm not letting The Mad Ffraid Brat get away," Tyler said. "Yes you are. Glaze into my bow tie," Mads Caractacus Troncoso said. So when Tyler did, he was hypnotized. Mads Caractacus Troncoso freed The Mad Ffraid Brat. Then he used several Bone Neck Crackers and trapped Tyler in a force field. "Um guys, I could use some help." Grant told us. Mads Caractacus Troncoso told Christopher to go find that stuffed toy lion while he took care of Grant. Me and Douglas were trying to save Telmo. However The Mad Ffraid Brat made things more difficult when they released all the balls from the ball pit. With the others in trouble, we tried to hurry up. Douglas took care of The Mad Ffraid Brat and I used The Cybernetic Falconieri Penzance Communicator and shot out a grappling hook just in time and saved Telmo. Douglas used The Cybernetic Falconieri Penzance Communicator and tried to see who was behind the mask, but The Mad Ffraid Brat escaped before he had the chance. Douglas went searching for Christopher while me and Telmo helped Grant. Mads Caractacus Troncoso was furious that The Mad Ffraid Brat ditched him. Mads Caractacus Troncoso threw several Fortune Teller Miracle Fishes at us that exploded, meanwhile Christopher found the stuffed toy lion inside an old arcade game and was about to take it to Mads Caractacus Troncoso. But Douglas stopped him. He used The Cybernetic Falconieri Penzance Communicator and tried to get the stuffed toy lion. But Christopher wouldn't let him and managed to get away.

Me and the others couldn't believe what we were seeing. Christopher was about to give the toy to Mads Caractacus Troncoso. I couldn't bare to lose another friend and wondered how Mads Caractacus Troncoso was controlling him. Tyler shouted out it's the bow tie. So I used The Cybernetic Falconieri Penzance Communicator and shot a laser at the bow tie while Douglas and the others freed Tyler. Mads Caractacus Troncoso's bow tie was destroyed and on fire. He took the stuffed toy lion out of Christopher's hands and vanished. Me and the others were happy that was over with but we couldn't believe that The Mad Ffraid Brat had the stuffed toy lion. We still don't know why they would want that. "Thanks for saving me," Christopher told me. "Anything for a friend." I told him. "What were you doing down here?" Douglas asked Telmo. "You could've gotten yourself hurt or killed." Grant said. "I just wanted to help. With Stiles being in the hospital and The Show Mayor in danger. I just wanted to prove that I'm not useless." Telmo said. "We understand and you're not useless." I told him. "We could use all the help we can get." Tyler said. "You just have to be careful. There is too much at stake." Christopher told him. "So are you with us?" Grant said. "Yes I am, so what's the plan now?" Telmo asked us. "To find out what The Mad Ffraid Brat and Mads Caractacus Troncoso stole." I told them. I was in Mr. Stumbo's office trying to adjust to my first day of being the new boss of The Show Mayor. I was wearing Mr. Stumbo's top hat and learned that being the manager / ring master is not easy. While trying to get some work done, I had some unexpected visitors. I met one of The Hinkley Youga Shirk members. A girl named Erewhon who was confessing her feelings for Thomas Kuc. I asked her didn't she kiss him at the convention. Erewhon told me no and that one of her friends was making out with him which really broke her heart. Then another girl popped in who wanted to kiss Jonah Marais, a girl named Ciendauos. But she didn't think she stood a chance. After that, a few more girls came to talk to me. Drucy who wanted to kiss Logan

Shroyer. Nkromma who wanted to kiss Callan. A girl who's in love with Amarr, her name was Yanixia. A girl named Daggi who was in love with Mark Thomas. A girl named Razzy who wanted to kiss Luke Korns. Then Tripta came in telling me that she had a secret crush on Seissylt. Hinkley who wanted to kiss Devin and the last girl was Roopa who wanted to kiss Timothee Chalamet. They were all talking at the same time which was getting on my nerves. "Quiet now, I will see what I can do." I looked at all of them, especially Erewhon and told them that love is worth fighting for and to never give up. As for Roopa, I told her if me and the others ever meet Timothee Chalamet, I will let Mallory set them up together. "How come you can't do it?" She asked me. "Because Timothee would never be friends with me. Now everybody please get out, I have some work to do." I told them before Erewhon left. I told her when you like someone, you should let them know how you feel. "What if he doesn't like me?" Erewhon asked me. "You'll never know if you don't try." I told her.

After that, I went back to work. Suddenly someone knocked on the door and I thought it was more members of The Hinkley Youga Shirk or Tripta again. So I hid underneath the table. "Bro, are you here?" I popped my head up. It was Shawn. "Oh hey bro," I said. "What are you doing Bro?" He asked me. "I was hiding," "why?" He said. "Because some of The Hinkley Youga Shirk showed up, and Tripta. Because they want to kiss their future crushes but they don't think they stand a chance." "Oh I'm sorry to hear that bro. Anyway! I came to check up on you to see how you were doing. I know what happened last night at The Horror Herculano." Shawn said. "Oh I'm fine." I told him. "Bro this is me you're talking to, so please tell me the truth." Shawn said. "Okay I lied, I'm not fine. Ever since Tielyr and his henchmen tried to kidnap me. I have been afraid, being trapped in that box did something to me. Every time I go to sleep, I'm afraid I'll end up back in that box. These last few days have been crazy," I told him. Shawn looked at me and could tell how scared I was and told me I'm not going to let anything happen to my bro. "I promise I'm here for you," Shawn told me. Then he noticed a key to Mr. Accerly Jamison's office and suggested that we should check it out. After I took care of everything, we went to investigate. I wondered how come none of us thought about checking out Mr. Accerly Jamison's office before. Shawn told me. Mr. Accerly Jamison barely comes to The Show Mayor, only if it's necessary. So we went inside and started searching for answers. At first we didn't really find anything, then Shawn found out what was so special about that stuffed toy lion. After finding a hidden file inside one of Mr. Accerly Jamison's pictures, he couldn't believe it. He showed me the file and told me that a flash drive is inside that stuffed toy lion that has a password to unlock Argider X Enterprise, Mr. Accerly Jamison's lab that holds some of his biggest secrets and a certain one that could be really dangerous to the world if it falls into the wrong hands, Shawn said. Me and Gordon went to Argider X Enterprise and disguised ourselves as grass. We were waiting for The Mad Ffraid Brat to arrive while we waited. Gordon asked me so you think we're not friends. "Yep." I told him, "well that's not true. I honestly can't believe you would think that." Gordon, said. "It's fine, I'm used to it." I told him. Gordon told me new friends are like new adventures. "You never know what life lessons they will teach you. So stop thinking we're not friends because we are bro, okay?" Gordon said. I shook his hand and said okay. After we finally became friends, someone popped up but it wasn't the Mad Ffraid Brat, it was someone far worse. It was Deveral Jamison. He was alone and went up to the gate. He typed in the password and the gate opened up. He managed to disable the alarms and boobytraps plus the cameras and started searching for what he came for. Me and Gordon used The Fuchsia Bax Piarres, a remote control spy helicopter. Another gadget that Leonel made. We were watching his every move on the screen. Deveral found what he was looking for and walked up to something called Thirdy Born Starr, an interface computer system who wasn't happy to see Deveral. And he tried to escape and alerted the authorities, but Deveral uploaded a malicious virus that took over Thirdy Born Starr, shocking me and Gordon. Deveral told Thirdy Born Starr to download all his father secrets onto a flash drive. Then Deveral downloaded Thirdy Born Starr and left Argider X Enterprise.

Me and Gordon told Leonel to find out everything that he could about Thirdy Born Starr. So Leonel hacked into Argider X Enterprise and went through the database to find files on Thirdy Born Starr. He told us that he held sensitive information that Mr. Accerly Jamison didn't want anyone to know, plus he has the passwords to get into some of Mr. Accerly Jamison's most heavily guarded organizations and banks where he held some of his most prize possessions and secrets and he could control Mr. Accerly Jamison's satellites. Leonel said. When he said that, me and Gordon wondered could Deveral be targeting his father's satellites, and why. Me and Colton Shires went to talk to Ettore who wanted to meet in The Jamison Mausoleum Crypts. It was creepy though, we took our time. We couldn't believe how big The Jamison Mausoleum Crypts was. We couldn't wait to finally learn the identity of The Mad Ffraid Brat, especially me. Ettore was shaking like crazy. "Are you okay?" Colton asked him. "No I'm not. I feel like Gewnsnay and her friends have been watching me, I don't want to end up like Montagew." Ettore said. "And you won't, once you tell us who The Mad Ffraid Brat is, we can save AJ, The Show Mayor and the others." I said. "So please tell us," Colton said. "Okay, The Mad Ffraid Brat is…" but before Ettore could finish, Colton noticed some bouncing balls and asked us what was going on. "Oh no." I said, before we could react, the bouncing balls released a sleeping gas knocking all of us out. A few minutes later, when we woke up, Ettore was gone. "No! We were so close." I said. Then Colton discovered that one of the coffins were different from the others. So he slowly opened it and couldn't believe it, neither could I. It was Quintonette's corpse . Me and Colton looked at each other. Colton found a note and read it aloud. This is what it said. **'Nice Try, I can't wait for tomorrow night.'**

Me and Colton couldn't believe this. After that, me and Reed were going over all the clues in Aunt Fanny's penthouse trying to find out who is The Mad Ffraid Brat. I was slamming things and Reed had to calm me down. "What's wrong?" He asked me, I told him I was upset. I just couldn't believe this. "We almost found out who The Mad Ffraid Brat is and as usual The Mad Ffraid Brat foiled our plan." I asked Reed how did The Mad Ffraid Brat know anyway. He told me that he doesn't know and that we can't give up now. Then he went over to the table where me and the others had placed every clue we had found so far.

He asked me, "Whose phone is this?" I told him that's Edvardas's cell phone. I told him that's how me and the others found out he's working for The Mad Ffraid Brat. "Did y'all check any of the videos or photos?" Reed Said. I told him no, so Reed hooked the cell phone to the laptop and we started searching for clues and couldn't believe what we found. Me and Reed discovered pictures of Andi the physical actor, who works here at The Show Mayor. The same girl who kissed Hunter and the same girl Mallory threw a custard pie at. Then we found pictures of Andi with some girl. So we asked Penzance Frisco to see who she was and we discovered that's Karitas and that her and Andi were sisters. "Andi is definitely a suspect." Reed told me. At that moment Mallory came in. Before we had a chance to tell her what we found, she grabbed Reed and started making out with him. After that I quickly called Levi. Me and Levi went to talk to Panini while Miles searched Paini & Andi's dressing room. "Be careful," I told him. "Same to you bro." He said with a smile. Me and Levi found Paini in The Show Mayor dance room. He was practicing for the upcoming show. He stopped when he saw us. "What are you guys doing here?" He asked us. "We need to ask you a few questions about your partner Andi." Levi said. Meanwhile Miles used the key I gave him and started searching.

As for me and Levi, we sat down with Paini and asked him did he trust Andi. He told us yes and that Andi is his best friend. He wanted to know why we were asking him questions about Andi. We showed him the photos and his smile went away. "Who is that?" Paini said. "That's Andi's sister who's helping The Mad Ffraid Brat and we believe that Andi is working for The Mad Ffraid Brat as well," Levi said. "So she never told you about her sister?" I asked him, Paini told me that Andi told him she doesn't have any sisters or brothers. "She lied to you." I told him. "Are you working for The Mad Ffraid Brat too?" Levi said. "No I'm not. I love being a Physical Actor and living at this magical place. I would never jeopardize my job. You have to believe me." Paini said. Me and Levi looked at each other. Elsewhere in The Show Mayor, Miles was still searching. Suddenly Andi came in the dressing room asking him what was he doing. To stop her from asking questions and getting suspicious, he started kissing her. As they kissed

Miles notice that one of the floor boards was different from the others and used The Cybernetic Falconieri Penzance Communicator to open it up and found a box with vials that had poison in them. The same ones that Montagew had. However he found out one of the vials was missing and he stopped making out with Andi. He secretly grabbed the box and used The Cybernetic Falconieri Penzance Communicator to release several doves, giving him the chance to escape. There were so many doves that Andi opened the window. When she did, all the birds went out. After they were gone, Andi realized Miles was gone. Miles showed me, Levi and Panini the vials, "the one that's missing must have been used to kill Quintonette." Levi said. Me and Matt Bomer found out where Ettore lived and broke into his apartment, we were determined to find something. Matt found Ettore's laptop and used The Cybernetic Falconieri Penzance Communicator to hack into the laptop. Once we got in, we discovered that Ettore had notes on Karitas, Mads Caractacus Troncoso, Deveral and The Mad Ffraid Brat. So we read the notes about Karitas. Me and Matt found out that Karitas is wanted in ten States. She's a master of disguise and that she has a talent for growing Borrachero Trees. After we read that part, I thought about Seissylt. We also found out that Karitas and Andi's last name is Memmott. Then we read the notes that Ettore had on Deveral. Me and Matt discovered that Deveral's mail order bride is staying in Deveral's suite at The Show Mayor. We didn't care about the notes that Ettore had on Mads Caractacus Troncoso and the others. We just wanted to know the identity of The Mad Ffraid Brat. I was so excited. Unfortunately everything that could go wrong did, as we opened up the file that Ettore had on The Mad Ffraid Brat, suddenly Thirdy Born Starr popped up and started deleting all the files, including the one that had the identity of The Mad Ffraid Brat. I honestly couldn't believe this. Matt tried to stop Thirdy Born Starr but it was too late. Thirdy Born Starr overheated the laptop, Matt dropped the laptop. Then he told me to take cover. After the laptop exploded, the explosion caused the smoke alarm to go off and Matt told me we had to go, I couldn't move though. I couldn't believe what just happen . Matt grabbed me and we got out of there. Before the cops and the fire department showed up. Matt thought getting some ice cream would cheer me up, but I couldn't eat anything. I was too upset. "I know The Mad Ffraid Brat stopped us once again. But we will save AJ and the others and The Show Mayor." I promise, Matt told me. I told him I don't even know if we can defeat The Mad Ffraid Brat and there minions. "It sounds like you're giving up. What are you trying to prove?" Matt asked me. "That I can do this and that I belong. This is the biggest case I've ever had and a lot of people are counting on me and my friends. I just feel like this is it." "You are stronger than you know bro, and of course you belong. I want you to remember this. You are never alone. You got me, Shawn, Jonah, Corbyn, Daniel, Zach, Jack, Logan, Lucy, Mark, Hunter and the others and we're not going anywhere." Matt, said. "So does that mean we're friends" I asked him. "You better believe it, now eat some ice cream." Matt told me.

So we both ate some ice cream and I started to feel better. Later that day, after finding out that Detective Plaxido is taking Doyle's lawyer on a date to the movies, me and Ryan Malaty went to spy on them. While Mallory and Levi snooped through Detective Plaxido's apartment, me and Ryan Malaty tried to stay out of plain sight. We decided to hide in the projection room . The perfect hiding spot. We kept our eyes on Detective Plaxido. Ryan used binoculars, as for me, I was trying to find any information on Doyle's lawyer and discovered her name is Rhapsody Angers and that she's one of the best lawyers in LA. Ryan Malaty asked me who was paying her. I told him my aunt is. He couldn't believe it and neither could I. Ryan got to know me and asked me what's my favorite holiday. I told him Christmas is my favorite holiday and I gave him a list of all my favorite Christmas movies. I also told him my birthday is on Christmas. I still couldn't believe I was talking to him. I just never thought Ryan would be my friend . Ryan told me there are friends, there is family and then there are friends that become family. I smiled and told Ryan I guess we're family now, meanwhile Mallory and Levi were breaking into Detective Plaxido's apartment. They started searching for clues. Mallory was searching the bedroom and Levi was checking the front room checking all the furnitures . Mallory found a door behind a secret door bookcase and discovered a cloak figure costume along with files on me. She, Simon,

Doyle and Nasser. She grabbed the files and placed them in her purse. She also took pictures of the cloak figure costume. As for Levi, he was checking Detective Plaxido's books and discovered one of the books was hollow and found an AJ mask along with prototypes of Doom Fault. Suddenly Levi and Mallory heard someone and quickly got out of there. When they found out it was the security guard, Mallory came up with a plan. She grabbed Levi and started making out with him, making the security guard believe they were a couple. The security guard didn't pay them any attention and kept going the other way. After that, Mallory and Levi got in the elevator and started making out again. Back at the movie theater, Me and Ryan were still spying on Detective Plaxido and Rhapsody Angers. Ryan got my attention and told me that Detective Plaxido was putting on some chapstick.

After that, Detective Plaxido started making out with Rhapsody. Me and Ryan noticed something unusual. As Rhapsody kissed Detective Plaxido, she started feeling bad and suddenly she collapsed, scaring the rest of the audience. One of the ushers went to see if she was alright and told everybody that she was dead, causing everybody to panic. Detective Plaxido escaped, me and Ryan couldn't believe this. We knew something had to be done about The Mad Ffraid Brat and the others. Me and Sean went to the morgue at the hospital and disguised ourselves as Candy Stripers. After what me and Devin went through at the other hospital, I made sure there were no surprises at this morgue. Me and Sean went inside the heating vent. We kept going until we reached our destination. We made sure the coast was clear and climbed out. Then we started searching the morgue fridge, checking each drawer. When we found Rhapsody's body, we still couldn't believe she was dead. Sean went to find Rhapsody's autopsy. I told him don't leave me alone with a corpse. He went through the files and told me it doesn't say how she died, making us suspicious. Sean used The Cybernetic Falconieri Penzance Communicator and started analyzing Rhapsody's corpse, hoping to find out what really killed her. After he got the results, Sean looked at me and told me that The Cellest Clinicriptine killed Rhapsody. He wondered how it got in her body. I told Sean to scan her lips and when he did, he learned that her lips were covered with The

Cellest Clinicriptine. I told Sean that I remember Detective Plaxido was putting on some chap stick before he kissed Rhapsody. "He must have put The Cellest Clinicriptine in his chap stick." Sean told me. Elsewhere, at the prison, Doyle was doing something he has never done before, read a book. Suddenly all the guards were acting strange and surrounded Doyle's jail cell. "Um what's going on?" He asked them. "Sorry champ, they only listen to me."

When Doyle saw who was coming towards his cell, he tried to call for help, but nobody heard him. The person started laughing and opened the cell. " Dr. Silouanus ", Doyle said. "What do you want?" "You." He said. Dr. Silouanus used his hypnosis powers on Doyle. After Doyle was under his control, Dr. Silouanus told Doyle to follow him. A few minutes later, me, Ashley Benson, Cameron Mathison and David came to talk to Doyle and let him know that his lawyer was murdered. Unfortunately when we got there, Detective Plaxido told us that Doyle was missing, and accused me of breaking Doyle out. But Ashley and the others defended me. Before we left, Detective Plaxido told me if he finds out that I'm responsible for Doyle's escaping, he'll arrest me. Outside of the prison, I thanked Ashley and the others for defending me. Ashley told me that's what friends do. Cameron told me not to let Detective Plaxido get to me. As for David, he could tell how worried I was about Doyle and told me we will find him and reminded me I'm not alone. Elsewhere, Doyle found himself in a room with Nasser, Mr. Accerly Jamison, Raysel and a few others. Doyle ran over to his brother and wouldn't stop hugging him. Nasser was doing the same, they were happy to be reunited. He asked his brother where are they. Nasser told him he didn't know. Doyle wondered why he was there. That's when The Mad Ffraid Brat showed up. "Oh, I have plans for you." The Mad Ffraid Brat said as they laughed. Back at The Show Mayor, me, Simon, AJ, Jeremy, Lucy, David, Chace and Thomas went to my temporary office after Aunt Fanny told me that someone who knows Mr. Accerly Jamison wanted to meet me. When we got there, we met a young guy named Cullinan Gurule, "So who are you?" David said. "Hi, I'm Cullinan. The guy who made Thirdy Born Starr." "Wait, you made him? We thought Mr. Accerly Jamison did?" Jeremy said, "No I made

Thirdy Born Starr." Cullinan said. "Why?" I asked him, "because Mr. Accerly Jamison has several enemies and always feared that they would steal his ideas. So he hired me to build him something. Something to keep all of his secrets and sensitive information in." After making Thirdy Born Starr, I downloaded all of the information into his system. Mr. Accerly Jamison would always tell me if this information ever fell into the wrong hands, it would be the end of The Jamison name." Cullinan said. "Can you tell us more about Thirdy Born Starr?" David asked him, "yeah I can." Cullinan told him. He showed us his laptop and told me and the others that Thirdy Born Starr is more powerful and smarter than any of us could ever imagine. "What all can he do?" Chace said. "He can shut down vehicles, airplanes, boats, any technology, take control of them as well and more." "What is his power source?" Lucy asked him. "That's classified information." Cullinan told her. "Anything else?" Thomas said. "Well, he can create weapons." Cullinan told him. "Is Thirdy Born Starr the only interface computer system or are there more?" Jeremy asked him. "Um, that's classified information." Cullinan said. "Well does Thirdy Born Starr have any information on any of the other Jamison members?" AJ asked him. "More than you know," Cullinan said. "Well is there any way we can save Thirdy Born Starr?" AJ asked him. "Yes but I have to find him first. Unfortunately I can't seem to find him anywhere." Cullinan told me and the others. "Have any of the satellites of Mr. Accerly Jamison been effected?" I ask him. Cullinan checked and told me yes, all of them. He couldn't believe this. "This is not good news," Simon told me. "What are we going to do?" David said.

Meanwhile Mallory and Devin were in Aunt Fanny's penthouse. Suddenly, Mallory got an unknown call from someone and answered it. She put it on speaker so that Devin could listen too. Mallory and Devin couldn't believe who it was, Tielyr's wife. A woman named Amalgunde. She was freaking out. She told them that she's being held captive by Tielyr and needs their help. Without even thinking, Mallory promise that they would rescue her. Amalgunde told Mallory that she's being held captive at The Horror Herculano. After that, the call was ended. "Okay let's go." Mallory told Devin. "Wait, shouldn't we tell

Benny and the others?" Devin asked her. "No, we got this. Trust me." Mallory said, "have you forgotten what happened to Benny and what he went through. The Horror Herculano is dangerous," Devin told her. "We'll be alright. Now come on," Mallory said. She checked her hair before they left. While she did that, Devin quickly wrote me a note to let me know where they were going. A few minutes later, me, AJ, Chris McNally, Simon and Aunt Fanny were coming in the penthouse. We were about to eat something, AJ found the note and told me and the others that Mallory and Devin are going to The Horror Herculano to rescue Tielyr's wife, Amalgunde. I couldn't believe this, I tried to reach them using The Cybernetic Falconieri Penzance Communicator but for some reason I couldn't get through to them. "This is not good," Chris said. "What are we going to do?" AJ asked me. I told him I'm going to The Horror Herculano. As I walked towards the elevator, AJ stopped me. "Have you lost your mind bro, you were trapped in a box and almost kidnapped. I am not going to let Tielyr and his henchmen hurt you again. I'll go," AJ told me. "I appreciate you trying to protect me bro. But The Mad Ffraid Brat could be lurking around The Horror Herculano. I already lost Nasser and now Doyle, I can't lose you too bro." I told him, "then I'll go with you." Simon said. "Are you kidding me?" "Since we've been here, I feel like we aren't even close anymore or best friends." I told him. "What? But we are best friends and brothers." Simon said. "I'm having a hard time believing that these days, I'm better off on my own." Before I could get in the elevator, Chris stopped me. "Then I'll go with you, and I'm not taking no for an answer." Chris said. I looked at him and told him okay. "Be careful bro." AJ told me. "I will bro," I said. After that, me and Chris left. Aunt Fanny was worried about me. So was AJ. And Simon wondered why am I so upset with him. Meanwhile, Mallory and Devin were arriving at The Horror Herculano, they disguised themselves as Tielyr henchmen and went inside. As they walked, they wondered where were all the guards. They met a creepy ventriloquism named Mad Kran Drucker who was talking to Ventriloquist dummies that look like Mallory and Devin. "Um hi, why do those Ventriloquist dummies look exactly like us?" Devin said. "Oh, because these two are not minding there own business and are in for a surprise. Isn't that right my little friends," Mad Kran Drucker said to the dummies. "Yes indeed." The one that looked like Devin said, as he laughed. "There is no escape." The one that looked like Mallory said, she kept repeating that over and over again, causing Mallory and Devin to run. "I think we should leave," Devin told Mallory. He tried to call me using The Cybernetic Falconieri Penzance Communicator, unfortunately there was no signal. So he tried calling me on his cellphone and that didn't work either. "Something is wrong." Devin said.

Suddenly, Mallory and Devin heard Amalgunde's voice and Mallory ran to go find her. However Devin had a bad feeling about this. They kept running until they found out where she was at. Mallory and Devin went inside, but when they did, the lights came on and they discovered a recorder. "What? 'Mallory said. The doors slammed shut and Devin told Mallory that it was a trap. Elsewhere, me and Chris were arriving at The Horror Herculano. Unfortunately I couldn't go in. I was too afraid to go inside. "Are you okay?" Chris asked me. "I can't do this. It's up to you, I'm sorry." I said. Chris could tell how frightened I was and reminded me of all the things I had done so far and he told me that there's nothing wrong with being afraid. Then he told me this. "A true friend knows your weaknesses but shows you your strength. Feels your fears but fortifies your faith. Sees your anxieties but frees your spirit. Recognizes your disabilities but emphasizes your possibilities." I told Chris thank you. Then we both eased our way inside. Chris told me I can do this with Chris by my side. I wasn't so afraid. We tried to use The Cybernetic Falconieri Penzance Communicators to find Mallory and Devin. Unfortunately they weren't working which was not good news. We hid when we heard somebody coming. Me and Chris had no idea how we would find them. Then we heard some of Tielyr's henchmen talking about The Horror Herculano Escape Room and we went to go find it. After we found it, we started running towards The Escape Room. Unfortunately as we ran, suddenly me and Chris both slipped on some banana peels and landed on the floor. "Who did this?" Chris said as he helped me up. "I did" a mysterious voice said. When we realized who it was, we started to get a little nervous. It was

Mads Caractacus Troncoso and he wasn't alone. He introduced us to his minions and Mad Kran Drucker. "We thought you might show up." Mads Caractacus Troncoso said. He laughed and told us that in a few minutes, The Escape Room will fly off. "Where is it going?" I asked him, he told me straight to The Mad Ffraid Brat. Mads Caractacus Troncoso started blowing up some balloons, then he made some animal balloons and started throwing them at us. Chris thought it was funny. But then the animal balloons exploded, scaring me and Chris. I told Chris to go save the others. Chris didn't want to leave me but I told him I'll be alright, he ran while I dealt with Mads Caractacus Troncoso and the others.

I was outnumbered and wondered if The Cybernetic Falconieri Penzance Communicator will ever work again. Mads Caractacus Troncoso told his minions to take me out. So they all came running towards me. Without The Cybernetic Falconieri Penzance Communicator, I was on my own. I took out his first minion using a backflip, surprising Mads Caractacus Troncoso. I tried to take out the others but they kept coming back. Things got worse when Mad Kran Drucker and his army of Ventrilgoust dummies robots got involved. Just when I thought that Mads Caractacus Troncoso was going to win, suddenly AJ came smashing through the glass roof, shocking me and the others. "What are you doing here?" I asked him. "To save my best friend. I'll always have your back," AJ told me. I smiled at him and we started taking out Mads Caractacus Troncoso's minions together. AJ showed me some strange device and told me this is why The Cybernetic Falconieri Penzance Communicators aren't working, I asked him how did he know. AJ told me that he and the others tried to reach me, he asked Leonel to hack into the security cameras to check on me and the others. So that's how they found out about the device. AJ broke it, when he did, The Cybernetic Falconieri Penzance Communicators started working again. Meanwhile as Chris got to The Escape Room, he found himself being surrounded by several of Tielyr's henchmen. I shouted out to him that The Cybernetic Falconieri Penzance Communicators were working. He was so happy and pressed a button that gave him multiple boxing gloves arms, and he started taking out the henchmen. As for

Mallory, she thought this was it. She and Devin noticed a timer and wondered what is going to happen when the timer runs out. Thinking that The Mad Ffraid Brat had finally won, Mallory grabbed Devin and started making out with him. Once again, Me and AJ finished off Mads Caractacus Troncoso minions and were about to start with him next. But Mad Kran Drucker and his army tried to stop us. "Are you related to Badaidra?" AJ asked him. "No I'm not," Mad Kran Drucker said. Just when me and AJ were about to attack him, all of The Ventrilgoust dummies robots were destroyed by a ray. "What was that?" Mad Kran Drucker said, me and AJ looked and couldn't believe who was there to help . It was Shawn who had a big ray gun. "What are you doing here?" I asked him. "I heard my brother / best friend was in trouble, so I came to help." Shawn said. I told him I was happy to see him. Shawn told me and AJ that he got this and he started fighting Mad Kran Drucker while me and AJ fought Mads Caractacus Troncoso. He was getting tired of us, he used some new tricks on us. First he threw some sponge balls at us that exploded. Then he threw some spinning plates that were like boomerangs. Me and AJ had a hard time dodging all of them. After that he threw propeller hats that shot out darts. He even shot out flames from his white gloves. But me and AJ didn't give up, we kept fighting. Mads Caractacus Troncoso started throwing decks of cards that exploded. AJ, tired of Mads Caractacus Troncoso, punched him in the face. Then I kicked him. We were tired of Mads Caractacus Troncoso's tricks. AJ noticed that Chris was still fighting the henchmen and realized time was running out and told Chris to catch. He threw an Aigeos Juppar jawbreaker. Chris grabbed it and threw it straight at The Escape Room making a hole and stopping the count down. The explosion knocked out the henchmen. Me, AJ, Shawn and Chris watch as Mallory and Devin made out. They stopped after they realized they were free. Mallory was happy to see us and so was Devin, Shawn knocked out Mad Kran Drucker and Mallory dropped kick Mads Caractacus Troncoso causing him to escape once again. Then Tielyr showed up. He wanted to know what was going on. Devin took care of this one and used The Cybernetic Falconieri Penzance Communicator and trapped him in a foam marshmallow cocoon. After taking care of that, I asked Mallory had she lost her mind. Mallory told me she thought Amalgunde was really in trouble. She had no idea it would be a trap, I told her what she did was dangerous. I stormed off because I was so angry with her. Shawn made sure I was alright. AJ was disappointed in Mallory. Mallory didn't know how she would make it up to me. She was curious about what happened to the real Amalgunde. Chris told them that it's time to go. With the day almost over with, Mallory decided to spend some time at The Show Mayor radio station. Ty Wood tagged along to keep her out of trouble. They met DJ Beast who asked Mallory would she like to sing a song for the listeners. Mallory didn't hesitate and she knew exactly which song she would sing. She sung What About Us. Impressing Ty and DJ Beast. After she was done singing, Mallory took over the show and answered a few callers much to DJ dismayed. One caller asked her had she ever thought about becoming a singer. Then another one asked her who is her celebrity crush. Mallory shouted out Noah Urrea. She told the viewers that's her future husband, then she said this, "Noah if you are listening to this, someday our lips will touch and I'll finally get that kiss that I always dreamed about." She started to whisper her phone number, causing Ty and DJ to end the broadcast, but Mallory turned it back on. She wanted to answer one more question from a viewer but the next viewer was somebody that she knew, it was Nasser. He told her that he's been held captive on Deveral jet and needs her help. That's when Ty called me using The Cybernetic Falconieri Penzance Communicator. So Leonel checked too see if it was really Nasser and to his surprise it was. But I still had a bad feeling about this. Unfortunately, Mallory decided to check it out regardless. So she and Ty went to The Jamison airbase and found the jet. They eased their way inside and found Nasser strapped to a chair. Mallory quickly ran towards him and started to untie him. She was happy that he was safe and asked him where was Doyle. Ty noticed something strange about Nasser and told Mallory that they should go.

Suddenly, the doors slammed shut and Nasser started laughing. He smiled and said this is getting too easy. Scaring Ty and Mallory. "How could you?" Mallory said to Nasser. He mashed a button and Mallory and Ty found themselves in the air. "Where are we going?" Ty asked Nasser. "Oh you'll see." He said. He opened the door, put on a parachute. Then he grabbed the rest of the parachutes and jumped off the plane. Mallory couldn't believe it. Neither could me and the others. Without Nasser knowing, Ty was using The Cybernetic Falconieri Penzance Communicator showing us everything that was happening. Ty and Mallory went to see who was flying the private jet and discovered that there was no pilot. Things got a lot worse when they learned that Thirdy Born Starr was controlling the plane, causing Ty and Mallory to panic. "Where are they going?" AJ said. Leonel quickly checked the computer and discovered that Mallory and Ty were heading to a peninsula. "Can you stop it?" Simon asked him. "I don't know." Leonel told him. "We need to do something, and fast." I told them. Leonel tried to take control of the private jet but Thirdy Born Starr wouldn't let him. So Ty came up with an idea. Then he found another parachute and told Mallory to hold on. After that, they jumped out and Ty pulled the parachute. Mallory told me and the others that they were safe. While in the air, Mallory grabbed Ty and started making out with him. It was her first time kissing a guy in the sky and she was enjoying every moment of it. Me and Hayes went to investigate Deveral's yacht. I knew. Hayes wouldn't become my friend, plus I had a lot on my mind. So I decided to be quiet. However Hayes didn't like that and he was determined to prove to me that he wanted to be my friend. As we searched the yacht, we didn't find anything unsunsal at first. Suddenly we heard some noise and went to investigate, the door had a lock on it. So we used The Cybernetic Falconieri Penzance Communicators and broke it. What we found inside the room was shocking. Me and Hayes met a young girl who looked familiar. "You're Prideaux aren't you? What are you doing here?" I asked her. She told me and Hayes that she's being held captive by Deveral just like the others. "What others?" Hayes asked her. "The ones that Deveral also got pregnant. Some have already had their babies and the rest of us haven't. But he has each one of us under surveillance because he's afraid we'll expose him to the world." Prideaux said. Before she could say anything else she started crying. "What's wrong?" Hayes said, Prideaux told him that she's having contractions pain. "How long have you been on this Yacht?" I asked her. Prideaux told me and

Hayes that she's been on there for months and that Deveral checks on her everyday. We couldn't believe that Deveral would go this far. Me and Hayes tried to help her up but her water broke. "Uh oh." Prideaux said. "What's going on?" Hayes asked her. She told us that the baby is coming, concerning me and Hayes.

Just when we thought things couldn't possibly get any worse, they did. Deveral arrived and he wasn't alone. "What are we going to do?" Hayes asked me. I told him we're going to deliver a baby. Hayes was nervous and so was I. So we called Leonel and he walked us through. Prideaux was in so much pain and we tried to keep her calm, however, Deveral heard her shouting and wanted to know what was going on. Him and his guards were coming our way, much to our dismay. I used The Cybernetic Falconieri Penzance Communicator and released a knock out gas, hoping it would keep them out for a while. Me and Hayes looked at each other and we couldn't believe we were delivering a baby. Both me and Hayes told her to push, a few minutes later, Prideaux gave birth to a baby boy. She was so happy, however, me and Hayes realized she wasn't done. "What's going on?" Prideaux asked us. Me and Hayes looked at each other and told her she's carrying octuplets. Prideaux was shocked and told me and Hayes that she doesn't think she can go through that again, me and Hayes realized that she was scared and I started singing a song to ease her mind, Hayes grabbed her hand and told her to push. We kept going until we got all the babies out. After we got the last baby out, the newborn wasn't moving, concerning me and Hayes and especially Prideaux. I told Leonel we need to get Prideaux and her baby to the hospital and fast. Leonel quickly started up the machine and teleported all of us out of there. We made it to the hospital and the doctors checked on the last baby. Me and Hayes were in the waiting room. Suddenly we heard a baby cry and jumped for joy. The doctor told us that the baby and his siblings and his mother will be just fine. Me and Hayes were so happy. We watched the newborns from the window. Hayes told me we did good. Then he told me, "Be willing to take a chance, because you never know how perfect something can turn out to be. I know you have been hurt in the past, but you should always give new people a chance. I want to be your friend, so will you give me a chance?" Hayes asked me. I looked at Hayes and told him sure. I also told him we're Team Bayes. After that, we got a chance to hold the babies. Prideaux couldn't stop thanking us. But she was worried about her safety and her kids. Me and Hayes told her that we're not going to let Deveral hurt her or her babies. Me and Hayes placed several Zayenthar Spyders in Prideaux room to keep an eye on her. Then Mallory showed up. She was happy that we were all safe. To express her happiness, she grabbed Hayes and started making out with him. Knowing how long this will take, I decided to get a snack from the vending machine. Me, AJ, Simon, Spencer List, Ajay, Ashley Tisdale, Sean Depner, Jared, Miles, Jeremy, Hayes, Douglas, Ruben, Casey, Matthew Daddario, Levi, Case, Mitchell Hope, Chace, Nick Mayorga, Cayden, Alex Saxon, Jordan Doww, Harrison Webb, Charlie, Christopher Bones, Grant, Antoni, Colton Shires, Darren and Thomas went to investigate Raysel's house. We hid behind some hedges and saw two big guys come out of Raysel's house. Simon took a picture of them. We wondered who they were.

After they left, we took turns crossing the street. Then Darren used The Cybernetic Falconieri Penzance Communicator to get inside and led the others inside. Me and AJ were the last ones, we wanted to make sure everybody got across. Meanwhile Mallory and Cody Linley were at The Zvezda Three Ples to see if they could find anything else that could help solve this mystery, something we might have missed. Back at Raysel's house, me and the others split up and went to find out what happened to Raysel and her family. Ajay, Simon and Miles investigated Raysel's parents room. Ashley Tisdale, Jared, Ruben and Case checked out the attic. Sean, Chace, Tyler, Cayden, Mitchell, Darren, Grant and Colton Shires checked out the basement. Casey and Christopher Bones investigated the garage. None of them found anything. As for me, AJ, Thomas, Matthew, Nick Mayorga, Antoni, Levi, Spencer, Jordan Doww, Alex, Hayes, Jeremy and Charlie, we Investigated Raysel's room. We couldn't find anything either and just when we were about to give up, me and Levi noticed the mural in Raysel's room and wondered if the mural could be a clue. We used The Cybernetic Falconieri Penzance Communicators and discovered something shocking, "What do y'all see?" AJ asked us. Levi told him that there's a Morse code written in invisible ink. Me and Levi translated the whole thing and found out that it's a map of Raysel's secret hiding places. So we told the others where to look. Thomas discovered a note book inside the mattress. He opened the note book and found out that Raysel has been spying on The Jamison Family for months, Matthew discovered several flash drives inside a hollow lamp and played them.

He learned that Raysel has been spying on Tielyr as well. Douglas discovered tapes inside a globe and listened to them. He told me and the others that Raysel knew about Deveral's trafficking. Spencer and Jeremy discovered a secret passage behind a book shelf and we all went inside. Me and the others found out that Raysel was a news reporter who was planning on exposing The Jamisons, especially Deveral to the world. Jordan Doww played the surveillance cameras and found out that Raysel caught footage of The Mad Ffraid Brat talking to Deveral and was trying to find out who The Mad Ffraid Brat was. Alex, Spencer and Antoni found a secret room that had pictures of The Mad Ffraid Brat, Tielyr, Deveral and Mr. Accerly Jamison. "She was spying on all of them." Jeremy said. Me and AJ found even more notes. "Raysel was obsessed with The Mad Ffraid Brat." AJ told me, then me and Charlie discovered a picture of Raysel with some guy. "Who is that?" Charlie asked me, I couldn't believe it and told the others to come over here. We also alerted the others and they came inside the secret room. Me, AJ, Nick Mayorga, Hayes and Ashley told Charlie and the others that's the guy who was killed in Storm Gorilla. Me and the others found out his name was Treveze Teems and he was Raysel's camera man. We still don't know what happened to Raysel's mother and father. "And her older brother" Austin Butler said. I told him I think The Mad Ffraid Brat kidnapped Raysel's family as well and that they need our help. Elsewhere at The Zvezda Three Ples, Mallory and Cody were searching for clues. They had to be careful though, after what happened at Flame Feast. There were a lot of holes and damage. Mallory and Cody went upstairs. As they went up the stairs, Mallory stepped on one and almost fell through, but Cody saved her. Mallory thanked him and they kept moving. As they searched and searched, Mallory was starting to believe that there were no more secrets At The Zvezda Three Ples. Suddenly Cody was checking the fire place and discovered a secret passage. He grabbed Mallory's hand and they went inside. Mallory and Cody found Grandma Bregusuid's study and they found a video recorder. They played the footage and discovered why Fuji is the way he is and they uncovered the mystery about what happened to Tielyr's wife.

After watching the video, Mallory and Cody got out of there. Before they left, Mallory grabbed Cody and started making out with him. Me and Antoni went to talk to Raysel and Treveze's Boss, he closed his office door and told me and Antoni that Raysel has been missing for months. "How come you didn't call the police?" Antoni asked him. "Because someone threatened me and told me I would be next." Raysel's boss told us. He showed us the emails and letters plus he told me and Antoni that someone tried to cut the brakes on his car. I looked at Antoni and then I asked Raysel's boss why was Raysel investigating The Jamisons. He told me that Raysel wanted a good story and she always suspected that something was going on with The Jamisons. So she started with Deveral. "She would always tell me that this would be the story of a lifetime." Raysel's boss said. "I think the story is why she is missing" Antoni told him. After that me and Antoni went to the last place Raysel and Treveze were seen, a camp called The Hideki Deveral. Me and Antoni couldn't believe it, a summer camp run by Deveral. However we learned that Hideki Deveral was closed down. So Antoni went online using The Cybernetic Falconieri Penzance Communicator to find out why. He told me that Camp Hideki Deveral was closed down because Deveral noticed someone lurking in the woods. Me and Antoni investigated the camp and wondered why Deveral really closed the camp down. As we checked each cabin, Antoni used this opportunity to get to know me. He wanted to become my friend too. He asked me was I worried about graduation next year. I looked at him and told him I'm terrified. I told Antoni that deciding between going to college or getting a job is scary. Then I told him something I have never told my friends. I told him I'm not college material. I thought he would make fun of me, but instead he was acting like a real friend and asked me what was I passionate about. Music I said. "Becoming a singer is my dream," Antoni told me I should go for it and that he believes in me. He also told me I won't promise to be your friend forever, because I won't live that long, but let me be your friend as long as I live. I told him we're Team Antoy. After we finally became friends, me and Antoni discovered something unsunsal. After moving several branches, we found a news van. To our surprise, everything still worked. We found a tape and played it. Me and Antoni learned that Raysel and Treveze's cover was blown.

In the video Raysel was shaking with fear. She couldn't believe how dangerous things were getting. She started crying and said all she wanted was a story. Suddenly someone broke into the van and threw a smoke grenade and kidnapped Raysel and Treveze. The video ended after that. Me and Antoni were more worried about Raysel than ever before. Me and Van Hansis discovered that Shaviv had a storage at Storm Gorilla, so we went to investigate. I didn't think Van would be my friend and I kept my distance from him. We found the storage and used The Cybernetic Falconieri Penzance Communicators to get inside, all we found was a bowling ball which was weird. Then Van discovered a secret compartment and found a flash drive. He placed it in his Cybernetic Falconieri Penzance Communicator and we discovered footage of Shaviv spying on Tielyr and Mr. Accerly Jamison. We also learned that Shaviv found out about Doom Fault, I guess Raysel wasn't the only one spying on them, Van told me. Then we discovered that Shaviv was an Agent for a witness protection program called The Sarolta Gide Borboleta. That's why he was pretending to be a Butler. Van told me we also found out that Shaviv had a partner. Me and Van tried to find out who she was. We went to the public library to see if we could find out more about The Sarolta Gide Borboleta. Unfortunately we couldn't find anything. Meanwhile Van was checking the flash drive to see if he could find any information on Agent Shaviv's partner. While he checked, he tried to get to know me. He asked me do I miss my family. I looked at him and told him more than you know. I told him that before I met Simon and the others, my family was all that I had. He asked me how come I left Iceland and started attending Glass Art, a school so far away from home. I told him that's a story for another time. Anyway, after searching through Agent Shaviv's files, he found something and told me it's something I need to see. So he played the video and I couldn't believe it. Orssa was working with Agent Shaviv. She was undercover as a security guard, Shocking me and Van. Then I remembered the note that Sean found wrapped around the fire poker. "What's wrong?" Van asked me. I told him what if Orssa betrayed Agent Shaviv and told her brother and Mr. Accerly Jamison about who he really was.

After that, we left the library. As we walked, Van told me we don't meet people by accident, they are meant to cross our path for a reason. "So can we be friends?" He asked me. I shook his hand and told him we're Team Venny. So I finally became friends with Van. To my surprise, I didn't think he would like me for me. Me and Alex Saxon went to The Rasalas Retro of Words Worth after finding out that Fuji drew a picture of the secret room. We were determined to find it by any means necessary. Me and Alex went through the heating vent and we kept crawling until we reached our destination. I had no idea where that drawing could be. So we searched Fuji's whole room. I wondered if it could be in Silouanus' Office. Then Alex found something underneath a floorboard. Just when we were about to open up the drawing, Silouanus appeared. He wrapped me and Alex in some tight streamers and took the drawing from us. "You know you're really becoming a problem," he told me. "How did you know we were here?" Alex asked him. Silouanus smiled and told us that The Mad Ffraid Brat has bugged this whole room. Me and Alex looked at each other, "what are you going to do with us?" Alex said. "Well first, I'm going to burn this drawing." He took out a lighter and burnt the drawing right in front of us, " no ". I shouted out. "Did you really think you stood a chance? I always wondered where Fuji hid that drawing, and thanks to you, it's finally destroyed." Silouanus said. "Now I'm going to do what the others couldn't do. Hand you over to The Mad Ffraid Brat, and if you give me any trouble, I'll just use hypnosis on you like I did to your friends, Doyle and Nasser." Silouanus said. "You're the one who kidnapped Doyle.' I asked him. "Yeah I am. And I used hypnosis on Nasser to set a trap for Mallory." Silouanus said. "Well aren't we confessing a lot." I told him. "We're not going anywhere," Alex said. He spit out some gum on Silouanus, suddenly Silouanus found himself being frozen in a block of ice.

Then I used The Cybernetic Falconieri Penzance Communicator cutting the streamers. I ask him what was in that gum. He told me it's something Leonel invented. I told him cool. Then we got out of there. As we walked back to The Show Mayor, Alex noticed how down I was and asked me what was wrong. I told him once again The Mad Ffraid Brat foiled our plan. Alex told me that somehow we will find out who The Mad Ffraid Brat is and solve this mystery. Then he told me a real friend is like having one more person in your family. I told him we're Team Balex. So I made another friend. Later on, Bruce wanted me to help him Investigate Tielyr' secret bunker. I told him he should ask Mallory but Bruce told me that he wanted to have an adventure with me, so he showed me the page he read from Grandma Bregusuid's Diary and we went to a Hayfield area. At first, all we saw was hayfields, then Bruce discovered something unsunsal about one of the hayfields and found a secret passage. Me and Bruce went inside and found ourselves inside the bunker. There really wasn't anything but computers and surveillance cameras. Then Bruce found a gun and discovered that one of the bullets was missing. "I think this is the gun that killed Montagew." Bruce told me. I found the bat that Mr. Accerly Jamison used to kill Shaviv years ago and I found a knife. We put all the weapons inside a bag and got out of there. Just when I thought there wouldn't be any attacks from The Mad Ffraid Brat and there minions, suddenly Mads Caractacus Troncoso appeared. He wanted the bag that was in my hand. Bruce took it out of my hand and told Mads Caractacus Troncoso come get it. Mads Caractacus Troncoso took out a confetti cannon and started shooting out nets. Bruce dodged each one. He told me to run. So I did, however Mads Caractacus Troncoso made sure I didn't escape the hayfields. I hid inside one of the hay stacks. I was starting to get scared of this crazy clown. Mads Caractacus Troncoso started searching each hay stack . He got closer and closer causing me to get nervous. I noticed Mads Caractacus Troncoso's clown shoes and used The Cybernetic Falconieri Penzance Communicator and shot out a fart bomb, giving me the chance to escape. Then Bruce popped up and used The Cybernetic Falconieri Penzance Communicator and shot out several confetti bombs. We ran after that. Before we got back to The Show Mayor, Bruce told me friendship is a game where the rule is simple, watch the other's player's back. He also told me friends are the part of our family that we never knew we had. I smiled at him and was happy that he actually liked me for me. Then some random girl ruined our bonding moment. She grabbed Bruce and started making out with him. Me and David became fast friends and we went to investigate the Anger Management program that Deveral used to attend and met an Anger Management Therapist named Coolio. We asked him did he know Deveral. He told us yes. We read that people who attended anger management write in something called a angry journal. "Does Deveral have one?" David said. "Um I'm going to have to ask you guys to leave now." Coolio said. Me and David looked at each other and used The Cybernetic Falconieri Penzance Communicators to release a knock out gas on Coolio. After he fell unconscious, me and David searched a room where Coolio keeps all the anger journals. David found Deveral's journal and read it, he told me that Deveral really hates his father and dreams of killing him. Then he found a section filled of angry journals that belonged to Deveral. As for me, I found angry diaries and I couldn't believe who wrote them. I told David that these diaries belonged to The Mad Ffraid Brat. Me and David found out that The Mad Ffraid Brat really had a grudge against AJ. However some of the diaries were different, surprising me and David. Later on, I was in Aunt Fanny's penthouse by myself until Thomas showed up. "What are you doing?" He asked me. I showed him the files that Mallory and Levi found in Detective Plaxido's apartment. "Seriously, how did he find out all this information about you, Mallory. Simon and The Stickle brothers,"Thomas asked me. "I don't know. He even has information on our families." I told him. "This is getting out of hand." He told me, "you can say that again" I said.

Thomas grabbed Grandma Bregusuid's diary and started searching for the next clue. He discovered a map, so me and Thomas went to investigate. We discovered a wall mirror in the hallway. Unknowing to the guests, there's a secret doorway. We went inside and discovered a bunker that belonged to Grandma Bregusuid . The only thing that was inside was a safe. However it had a finger print scanner. Thomas used his Cybernetic Falconieri Penzance Communicator to get inside. We discovered a manuscript that Grandma Bregusuid wrote. We learned in her unpublished manuscript that she was planning on telling the world the truth about her family and about Tielyr. "Maybe that's why she disappeared, because she knew too much." Thomas told me. Me and Callan went inside an underground tunnel after finding out that Grandma Bregusuid knew where Shaviv was murdered at. It was creepy walking in a tunnel but Callan had my back. We had no idea what we were looking for but we felt sorry for Shaviv. I showed Callan the video that Mallory and Cody found. Callan asked me "is Orssa still alive?" I told him, "I don't even know." Then Callan noticed something and we went to investigate. Me and Callan were shocked, we discovered Shaviv's remains and wondered what will his kids say. Me and Harrison Webb went searching for Grandma Bregusuid's sister, Cerria. However where we found her was a disgusting place. Me and Harrison found her in an alley. She was sleeping in a cardboard box. "Um hi. My name is Benny Breezy and this is Harrison Webb." "What do you want?" Cerria said. "We want to know do you know what happened to your sister and why she disappeared?" Harrison said, "hmm for a price." Cerria said. Me and Harrison looked at each other. "What do you want?" I asked her." Something to eat would be nice." Cerria said. So me and Harrison took her to Nicos Burp Burgers. Cerria was starving and eating like there was no tomorrow. After she was done eating, Cerria told us that she hasn't seen or talked to her sister in years ever since the fall out between their parents. "What do you mean?" Harrison asked her. She told us that when Bregusuid introduce Dunixi to their parents, they gave her a choice, The family or Dunixi, so when she chose him, our parents disowned her and never spoke to her again and they took their anger out on me causing me to leave. Without my sister or family in my life, I spent my time partying and drinking. That's why I'm living in the alley. All I have is my cardboard box. Me and Harrison felt sorry for her.

Before we left, Cerria shouted out that her sister abandoned her and that she doesn't care whether her sister is alive or not. Me and

Trevor went to Mount Jamison after reading the last page in Grandma Bregusuid's second diary. She wrote that Mount Jamison holds secrets. We discovered a door, however, it needed a password. Me and Trevor tried to guess the password. Unfortunately, nothing worked. Then Trevor thought about something and pressed some numbers in, unlocking the door. I asked him how did he figure it out. He told me the password is the date of Grandma Bregusuid's and Grand Dunixi Jamison's anniversary. After that, we went inside and discovered documents, files, surveillance cameras, computers, pictures and more. We started searching and discovered that all of this stuff had nothing to do with the mystery but it might lead to new mysteries about The Jamison Family. Anyway, Trevor found an old photo album and went through it. As he went through the pictures, Trevor discovered a big revelation. He looked at me and told me that The Mad Ffraid Brat is related to The Jamison Family. Also, The Mad Ffraid Brat might be more than just one person. He showed me some pictures. We discovered pictures of two sets of twins. I couldn't believe this. Unfortunately there weren't any names. "This is crazy." I told Trevor. He told me for now on we can say we're dealing with The Mad Ffraid Brats. I quickly sent this information out to the others, especially AJ. While searching for more clues, Trevor was becoming not only a friend to me but a father figure as well. Me and Pierson went to talk to Mrs. Teems, Treveze's wife. We had no idea how she would react to the news about her husband. Pierson knocked on the door and we waited for her to come to the door. "How may I help you?" "Um hi, my name is Pierson and this is my friend Benny. We're here to talk to you about your husband." When Pierson said that, Mrs. Teems told us to come inside. "I have been so worried about him. Is he alright?" She asked us. Me and Pierson didn't know how to tell her which made her worried. "Please, one of you, just tell me. Is Treveze safe. I haven't seen or heard from him in months. So if you have any information, it would relieve my stress." Mrs. Teems said. "Your husband is dead." I told her. "He was electrocuted by a theremin." Pierson said. When we told her that, Mrs. Teems fell apart. She couldn't stop crying. Me and Pierson comforted her. An hour later after she calmed down, she told us that Treveze was a devoted friend to Raysel and that he was so excited about getting that story about The Jamison. "It's all he could ever talk about. However Mrs. Teems notice her husband was acting strange before he disappeared." She said. "He would freak out and felt like someone was watching him." Then on the last day she saw him, Treveze whisper to her that he and Raysel were on the verge of something big. A story that could cost their lives. Me and Pierson left after that. As we drove back to The Show Mayor, Pierson told me when all of this is over with, we should hang out. "Does that mean we're friends?" I asked him. "No." Pierson said. "Oh," I said in a sad voice. "It means we're friends for life and I mean that." Pierson said with a smile. So I made another friend. Anyway, that night me, AJ, Sollie, Darren and Kendrick went to talk to Grand Dunixi Jamison and Esdras Jamison's parents who live on a peninsula. We rode in Stranger Red. AJ still couldn't believe that there are now four Mad Ffraid Brats. Kendrick wondered who they can be. Sollie was angry because he's related to these psychos. Me and Darren were worried about meeting the world's worst parents. Sollie knocked on the door and we met an elderly Butler named Quindlen. He told us to come in and got Sollie's grandparents. "What do you want, you sorry excuse for a human being." Sollie's grandma said. "You have visitors." Quindlen said as he grind his teeth. "Who in the world would visit us?" Sollie's great grandpa said. "Your great grandson." Sollie told them. When he said that, his great grandparents both fainted. A few minutes later, Quindlen tried to wake them up. "Mrs. Anstass and Mr. Sulayman." Quindlen said. Unfortunately they still wouldn't wake up. So Quindlen went to the kitchen and came back with a bucket of fish heads and rotten eggs and then he threw on them shocking me and the others. "Have you lost your mind?" Mrs. Anstass said, "this one is going to cost you." Mr. Sulayman said. "I don't care you prune poops." Quindlen told them. "We'll deal with you later." Mrs. Anstass said. "So you are our great grandson, wow we sure haven't missed anything, she said. "What a disappointment," Mr. Sulayman said. "Hey that's your great grandson. You shouldn't be talking about him like that. Sollie is the only good Jamison in your family and he's a really good person." I said, "Well what do we have here, this is my friend Benny Breezy. He's an Investigative Reporter,"

Sollie said. "Oh we heard of you. The boy that thinks he can save AJ Mitchell's career. Hmm we were hoping for somebody interesting, all I see is a boy who has no future, no friends and no life. You are nothing and you always will be." Mrs. Anstass said. "Tell me AJ, do you really believe that this loser can actually save your career?" Mr. Sulayman asked him. "First of all Benny is one of my buds and I care about him. He's not a loser, and second of all I do believe in him. He has come a long way." "Isn't that nice," Mr. Sulayman said. "Instead of insulting our friend, why don't you tell us why you were so awful to Grand Dunixi Jamison and Jamison?" Kendrick said. "What are you talking about, we were fantastic parents." "You can stop that lying. You and Mrs. Anstass used to treat those kids like they were nothing to you. The things y'all did to them are unforgivable." Quindlen said. "It's time for you and your wife to tell the truth." Darren said.

"Fine, maybe we were rough on our children, but guess what, so were our parents. Dunixi and Esdras and Oceon didn't deserve to be treated any better." Mrs. Anstass said. "Me and my wife kept a roof over their head. Food on the table and clothes on their back, and how did they repay us? One fell in love with a woman who had no chance of ever becoming a Jamison, Bregusuid wasn't worthy. As for Esdras, he always stood by his brother's side no matter what, we threw at them or how many times we tried to tear them apart, they always had each other's back. And last is Oceon, the biggest mistake that we ever had. Oh she gave us trouble. Especially when her brothers left. We thought she would take over the Jamison business but Oceon found a way to escape and we never saw her again. After that we disowned our children and grand children, the only thing we care about is money and power. Family means nothing to us." "How can you be so cruel?" Darren said. "Ha if you think that's cruel, listen to this. Did you know after your grandpa lost Esdras and Bregusuid, he was lost. He was filled with rage and wasn't the same. He decided to give your father to us to raise. We kept Accerly until he was a teenager." "That can't be true." Sollie said as his eyes got watery. "But it is. Sorry to burst your bubble," Mrs. Anstass said. "You see Dunixi didn't think he could raise Accerly on his own and abandoned his own child. Isn't that hilarious?" "You two have no souls."

AJ said. "Thank you. We'd rather be feared than love." "I'm surprised nobody has reported y'all." Kendrick said. "If they tried, they would never be seen again." Mrs. Anstass said. "What can you tell us about two sets of twins in your family." I asked them. After I said that, they both got nervous. "I think it's time for y'all to leave." "Why?" AJ said. "Because you're asking for trouble, sticking your nose where it doesn't belong." Mr. Sulayman said. "Now leave. Quindlen show them out," "Why don't you show them out yourself you prune poops. For years y'all have pushed me around and mistreated me. Well not anymore, I quit." He grabbed his things and went out the door. Me and the others followed him. Sollie was the last one out. He looked back and told them you're dead to me and closed the door.

After that, me and the others went back to The Show Mayor to get ready to go out to The Vangy Arungedan. I convinced Sollie to ask Vigdess out on a date and Mallory told Mitchell to ask out Kimbriella. So they did. Kimbriella thought she would have a heart attack when Mitchell asked her out. She was so happy. As for Vigdess, she thought Sollie was joking and didn't believe him. So Sollie put on a performance to prove her wrong. He sung You are beautiful, surprising her. She had no idea that Sollie could sing and agreed to go out with him. Meanwhile, Mallory had her own plan. She asked me, AJ, Simon, Felix, David, Cayden, Case, Miles, Cody, Casey, Jonah, Freddie, Jeremy, Chris McNally, Hayes, Luke, Van, Harrison, Mark, Miles, Grant, Mitchell Hoog and Levi to come to the lobby. She was standing by something big. "Drum roll please." Mallory said. She took the sheet off showing us a big spinning wheel that had pictures of her all crushes. Some of the names on the spinning wheel were Marcus Dobre, Kaden Dayton, Levi and more. She said whoever the arrow lands on will be her date for tonight. She started spinning the wheel and we all waited anxiously. After it was done spinning, it landed on AJ, surprising all of us. Mallory was excited. "Seriously Mallory?" I asked her. Mallory told me and the others that tonight might be the end of her Kiss Printes List. So She grabbed Grant and started making out with him, then a few fans of hers appeared. One made out with Jonah. The other one made out with Jeremy. Another one made out with Miles and the rest made out with Case, Casey, Cody, Mark, Cayden, David, Chris McNally, Hayes, Levi, Luke, Freddie, Harrison and Felix. Me and the others went back to Aunt Fanny's penthouse. A few hours later, Vigdess and Kimbriella came running to Mallory, panicking because they didn't have anything to wear tonight. Mallory smiled and told them to leave it to Fairy Mallory. Me, AJ, Simon, Leonel, Devin, Mitchell Hoog, Sollie, Rudy, Luke, Grant, Van Hansis, Austin P. McKenzie, Matthew Daddario, Shawn, Colton Haynes, David, Levi, Logan Shroyer, Brandon, Kendrick, Felix, Reed, Why Don't We, Chris Salvatore, Nolan, Noah, Hayes and Thomas were waiting downstairs for them. Lucy came down first. She looked so beautiful. She told the others to come on down. Kimbriella and Vigdess both looked beautiful, especially Mallory. Before we all left, Chef Xathieur showed up. He wanted to meet Mitchell. Unfortunately worried that he would make fun of her, Kimbriella quickly got out of Aunt Fanny's penthouse hurting her father's feelings. "I guess she's embarrassed by me." Chef Xathieur said. Me and the others tried to comfort him. We all rode in The Simplicius Transito while Simon, Amarr, Ashley Benson, Rudy, Matt and Keegan tried to find out what's on that CD that Amarr found in Leonel's lab. Me and the others arrived at The Vangy Arungedan and it was bigger and more magical than we could have ever imagined. We went inside and met Wray. "You must be Benny. My father has told me all about you. It's nice to finally meet you." I told him I'm sorry about what happened to his mom. He told me thanks and took us to our table and whispered some magic words. When he did, several decks of magic cards appeared and turned into menus. He told us that The Vangy Arungedan is all about magic and said. all we have to do is say Arabesquea Bamboo. So AJ was the first to try, and suddenly several doves flew out of AJ sleeves.

Then Wray performed a song and was putting on an amazing performance. Me and the others were having fun saying Arabesquea Bamboo. Then Wray asked me to perform a song but I was too nervous. AJ and Shawn gave me the push that I needed and the three of us went on the stage together. I felt like I was going to puke. "You can do this bro." AJ told me. "We believe in you, come on bro we got your back." Shawn told me. I looked at them and told them okay. I took my time and the three of us sung Brother by Gavin Degraw and boy were we having fun. I couldn't believe it. I was singing in front of people who cared about me and liked me for me. Then I sung I Got you by Leona Lewis, with Austin P. McKenzie. I even sung a song with my buddies. Why Don't We, Jonah and the others were so proud of me. After that, Mallory sung Voices Within. Mitchell Hoog and Kimbriella took some pictures together in a photo booth. Then they danced. As they danced, Kimbriella dreams finally came true after Mitchell leaned in to kiss her and the two started making out. Mallory was about to kiss AJ's lips but she thought about Simon and wonder could Simon be her one true love. Meanwhile back at Leonel's lab, the others found out that on the CD, Amarr found blue prints of the places The Mad Ffraid Brats planned to destroy using Doom Fault. "What are we going to do?" Amarr said. Simon couldn't believe this. Ashley wrote down all the places. Rudy made copies of the blue prints. Matt realized that each bomb is timed differently. Back at The Vangy Arungedan, while the others danced, me and AJ and, the rest of the gang were looking at the time and wondered where are The Mad Ffraid Brats. Meanwhile, outside of The Vangy Arungedan, Leonel was on The Simplicius Transito. Still trying to get into that laptop. Suddenly, after so many unsuccessful tries, he finally got in and discovered who The Mad Ffraid Brats are. He couldn't believe this. He also discovered that two of The Mad Ffraid Brats are people me and the others know. Before he had a chance to alert me and the others, Penzance Frisco told him that he was being attacked. Leonel told her to put The Simplicius Transito on lockdown, but it was too late. Penzance Frisco got shut down and the doors swung open, scaring Leonel. Back inside The Vangy Arungedan, Sollie and Vigdess were finally about to share their first kiss, unfortunately it got interrupted by Deveral. "Well what do we have here?" "Oh no." Corbyn said, "what are you doing here?" I asked him. "To make a deal of course," Deveral said. "We're supposed to be making a deal with The Mad Ffraid Brats, not you." Lucy said. "I know, but since y'all found out that there are more Mad Ffraid Brats, they sent me instead." Deveral told us. "I'd rather deal with them or Mads Caractacus Troncoso." Vigdess said. "Hold on Benny. I'll deal with you in a minute, first I have to deal with the maid.

So this is Vigdess, wow, well I'll admit. She's pretty, but she will never be a Jamison. I mean look at her, do you really think mom and dad would approve of her. Haha, I can see the headlines now. Youngest Jamison kid falls in love with a maid. Just think about what it would do to this family. She will never fit in our world. The media would eat her up." Deveral said. "Why do you always act like you're better than everybody else?" I asked him. "Because in my world, I am, you know since I met you, you're the only person I know that has ever stood up to me. Well guess what, that ends tonight," "what are you going to do about it?" I asked him. "You'll see." He said. He took out a remote control device and pressed a button. Then he told AJ to teach me a lesson.

At first AJ didn't know what Deveral was talking about, suddenly AJ's eyes turned blue and he threw me. I landed on a table, shocking me and the others. I tried to get up but AJ kicked me, sending me straight through a wall. Shawn, Hayes and Grant helped me up. It was like AJ was in some kind of attack mode and I was his target. But I refused to fight him, much to Deveral dismayed. Lucy and the others tried to get the controller. I couldn't believe my bud was beating me up and there was nothing I could do. Just when I thought this was it, Deveral stepped in and said this is what happens to heroes. "I have to admit it has been fun. Attacking you and your friends but this ends now, did you really think you stood a chance? Haha you're more pathetic than I thought. You are nothing but a loser who has no future and no friends. I find it amusing that you thought you were friends with AJ, Shawn, Devin, Hayes, Grant, Levi, Reed, Jack Maynard, Colton Haynes, Hunter, Lucy and the others. It was all a lie. They don't care about you. In fact, they don't even like you. And you are a fool to believe that they actually did. Nobody cares about you and who would want to be friends with you anyway? You were right to believe that Parker Queenan, Trevor Stines, Kaden Dayton, Drew Ray Tanner and especially Noah Urrea will never like you, you don't belong here. I hope I made my point." Deveral said. As he walked away, AJ was back to his normal self and he couldn't believe what he did to me.

He tried to see if I was alright. I told him to leave me alone, then I got up and asked Deveral can we make a real deal. "What do you want?" Deveral asked me, "do you have an antidote for Hade Wild and The Khione Princella Khione of Aurex?" He smirked and said yes. "But what do you have to offer?" Deveral said. I looked at the others and told Deveral I'll leave Los Angeles in exchange for the antidote, shocking AJ and the gang. "Hmm, you have yourself a deal." He told me. Before he left, he told Mitchell Hoog about Kimbriella and Chef Xathieur and went out the door laughing. Me and the others left after that. Kimbriella was so embarrassed and thought Mitchell wouldn't like her anymore and she ran back to The Show Mayor, crying. Sollie thought about what his brother said and told Vigdess that they can't be together. Vigdess was so heart broken and left. AJ, Shawn and the others tried talking to me but I just ignored them. Jonah got in my way and tried to convince me that we are friends. Unfortunately I didn't care anymore. Things turned from bad to worse when we found out that Leonel was missing and the laptop was gone. Levi turned Penzance Frisco back on. We asked her what happened. She told us The Mad Ffraid Brats and Mads Caractacus Troncoso kidnapped Leonel after he found out the identities of The Mad Ffraid Brats. "Too bad," Deveral said as he drove away on a motorcycle. AJ told me and the others to get inside, he got in the driver seat and started following Deveral. Deveral speed up and so did AJ. However, things got even worse when the police started chasing us. We found ourselves in a high speed chase. To slow Deveral down, Grant and the others started pressing buttons, throwing everything that The Simplicius Transito had. Deveral used a laser on a truck carrier, breaking the chains, causing several vehicles to fall off. AJ was trying his best to dodge them all. Then a helicopter appeared. It was those same two guys that me and the others saw at Raysel's house. Sollie told us that's Ture and Creedence, two brothers that worked for Deveral, they picked Deveral up and got out of there. Leaving me and the others to deal with the police. Mallory pressed the orange button. After she did, we found ourselves flying. The Simplicius Transito was in the air, AJ tried to fly The Simplicius Transito back to The Show Mayor. Unknowing to us, The Mad Ffraid Brats and Mads Caractacus Troncoso were near by and fired a missile. Penzance Frisco tried to get us away from the missile but it was too late. It destroyed the engines causing The

Simplicius Transito to crash. Thankfully we were alright, but the cops showed up and surrounded us. Mallory panicked and started running, and so that's how we ended up at the police station. "Well it's quite a story. Thank you" Detective Plaxido told me. Then he closed his office door to talk to me and the others privately. "So you know I'm involved. How interesting," Detective Plaxido said. "Why are you doing this?" Felix said. "Because he's Deveral buddy." Jack Avery said. "You're the buddy we saw in that video." Zach told me and the others. "See y'all are too smart for your own good," Detective Plaxido said. "What are you going to do with us?" Devin said, but before Detective Plaxido could answer him, Aunt Fanny and Porfirio showed up, she was happy to see that me and the others were alright. She told Porfirio to take us back to The Show Mayor while she talked to Detective Plaxido. "Do you have a problem?" Detective Plaxido asked her.

Aunt Fanny swung her purse and knocked him out, "I don't care if you come after me because I'll give you a fight you'll never forget. But nobody messess with my nephew." She flipped him over a table and left, scaring Detective Plaxido. Before we left the police station, I told Porfirio I'll catch up. "Where are you going?" AJ asked me. I didn't answer him and I kept walking. Matthew Daddario joined me. "Can you please talk to me?" He asked me. I was too hurt and I kept my distance. Me and him broke into Detective Plaxido's car and found Nasser's clothes along with vials of my blood, Mallory's blood. Simon's and Doyle's. "How did Detective Plaxido get this?" Matthew said, I thought about what happened at The Horror Herculano. When The Skull Zuberi kidnapped me and I told Matthew, "but that doesn't explain how he got the others' blood." Matthew said. I thought about the day Mallory and the others went to The Jamison Mansion. Him and the others must have took blood from the others when they were unconscious. I told him. "But why?" Matthew asked me. "The Mad Ffraid Brats stole Nasser's clothes and are going to use our blood to make everybody believe that me and the others murdered Nasser." "But he's not dead." Matthew told me. "Not yet" I said with a concerned look on my face. We took the clothes and vials. After that, me and the others got back to The Show Mayor. Trevor and all the friends that we have made plus the entire staff of The Show Mayor except for Andi. Edvardas. Terentilo. and Conant were waiting for us in the lobby. "What are y'all doing here?" I asked them. "To talk to you bro." Colton Shires told me. "Well I'm not in a talking mood, it's been a long day and I'm tired. So goodnight everybody." I said. Before I got towards the elevator, Shawn stopped me. "Please bro. You know me and the others would never do that to you." Shawn said. "Our friendship is real bro." AJ told me. "It doesn't matter anymore, I was stupid to think that any of you were really my friend. I'm done. Nolan you never called me your friend. Neither did Harris. So Mallory, from this moment out, you're in charge, it's up to you to unmask The Mad Ffraid Brats. As for you Simon, you really want to know why I have been so mad at you, it's because you and the others haven't talked about what's going to happen to us next year." "Everything is going to be fine." Simon told me. "Stop lying, after we graduate, we'll all be going our separate ways." I told him. I looked at AJ and told him I'm sorry for letting him down. Then I told Sollie that he had to make things right with Vigdess and start making his own decisions instead of acting like his family. I also told him when he and Vigdess do become a couple, to not let the media split them apart like they do to other couples, I told him the media and social media is toxic. Corbyn and the others tried to stop me. So did Lucy. Before I left, I told Simon and the others I'm leaving first thing in the morning to join my family in New York and that I won't be attending Glass Art with them next year. I'm going back to my old school in Iceland. I didn't even give Simon or Mallory a chance to react and left. Mallory and the others split up to find me.

As for AJ, Simon, Jack Maynard, Ryan Malaty, Noah, Grant, Brandon, Lucy, Devin, Shawn, Logan, Chris Salvatore, David, Matthew Daddario, Harris, Thomas, Luke, Van, Charlie, Miles, Mitchell Hoog, Hunter, Mark, Callan, Ruel, Levi, Nick Mayorga, Keegan, Kendrick, Why Don't We, Austin P. McKenzie, Jordan Doww, Case and Hayes, they couldn't believe this was happening and they tried to come up with a plan to prove to me that my friendship with each one of them is real. As Simon searched for me, suddenly a random maid came up to Simon. She grabbed him and started making out with him, shocking

Mallory. When the maid saw Mallory, she walked away. Unknowing to them, that was Karitas. Simon tried to explain to Mallory but she was so upset and stormed away. She ran into AJ. He asked her has she found me, but when he saw her crying, AJ asked her what was wrong. Angry with Simon, Mallory grabbed AJ and started making out with him, before Karitas left The Show Mayor, she bumped into Harris and started making out with him to keep her cover. After that she ran into Andi and told her everything is going according to plan. Then she quickly got out of there. When Levi showed up, he asked Andi had she seen me. She told him no she hasn't. Before he left, he asked her how come she wasn't in the lobby with the others. Thinking that Levi could be on to her, she distracted Levi by making out with him.

Meanwhile, I was saying goodbye to Sefi. He was sad that I was leaving but I told him I'll stay in touch. I gave him his very first cell phone and we said our final goodbyes. Elsewhere, AJ was in Aunt Fanny's penthouse. He was really upset, Aunt Fanny tried to calm him down. Suddenly Gerwazy showed up in the elevator. "What are you doing here?" AJ asked him. "Lucy sent me a text message. Is it true? My brother is leaving?" Gerwazy said. "I'm afraid so," Aunt Fanny said. Gerwazy couldn't believe I was leaving. At two in the morning, I snuck inside Aunt Fanny's penthouse to get my stuff. To my surprise, none of my friends were around. I wondered where they could all be at. Before I could step in the elevator, Aunt Fanny popped up. "Leaving without saying goodbye? I think it's time we have a talk Benji." "Aunt Fanny, it's been a really long day and I just want to go home," "park it Mr." Aunt Fanny said. "First I would like to say how very disappointed I am. You're giving up and leaving just when you're so close to figuring out who The Mad Ffraid Brats are. Your friends need you more than ever now and you need them to...." "What friends? I have no friends, it was nothing but an illusion. How could I be so stupid to believe that AJ is my friend. None of it was real." "Yes it was, AJ and the others are worried sick about you. They're out there right now searching for you." "At this time of night?" I asked her. "Yes Benji, everybody except for Mallory, we don't know where she is at." Aunt Fanny told me. I used The Cybernetic Falconieri Penzance Communicator to find Mallory and found her making out with AJ Mitchell. "Yeah some friends." I told Aunt Fanny as I grabbed my things and started walking towards the elevator. "You have to believe me, they all care about you." "Aunt Fanny, it's nothing but a lie. AJ doesn't care about me. Neither does Logan, Corbyn, Jonah, Hayes or Chris Salvatore, especially Shawn, Alex Whitehouse and Nolan. I was stupid to think I could save the day and be a hero. I failed and everything Deveral said about me was right. I was stupid enough to think that Noah Urrea, Nicholas Hoult, Michael Johnston, Jordy Searcy, Chaz Cardigan, Andrew Gray, Nathan Kehn and Antonio Marziale would become my friend. None of them would ever hangout with me. They only hangout with cool and popular people which I'm not. Noah and the others will never accept me or like me. Especially! Noah. I doubt he would become my friend. I'll always be a loser, why do you care?" I asked her. "What's that supposed too mean?" Aunt Fanny said. "It means you were never around when I was growing up and I want to know why" "Because of my feud with your grandma, Aunt and uncle. I abandoned our family for show biz and wealth. I thought I was better on my own. I let my pride consume me and for that, I'm really sorry Benji." "You missed several family gatherings, holidays, birthdays and you forgot the meaning of family. I'm just done. Goodbye Aunt Fanny." "Wait Benji, please, isn't there a way I can make it up to you?" "Yeah, call your sisters and brother and end this feud." I said. After that I got in the elevator and left. Aunt Fanny grabbed her phone and dialed a number, after that she heard a voice she hasn't heard in years. "Hey sis, It's been a long time." Aunt Fanny said.

Meanwhile at the hospital, I went to check on Stiles and to tell him goodbye. However when I walked in Stiles' room, Shawn was there. I tried to get out of there but Shawn used The Cybernetic Falconieri Penzance Communicator to close the door. "Seriously bro? You're running away from me now?" Shawn said. But I didn't answer him. I gave him the silent treatment. "Fine, you won't talk, then I'll do the talking." Shawn said. This is what he told me. "How could you ever think that I would hurt you. You know me better than that. You're my brother, you're my friend. Deveral is evil, manipulative and a horrible person. But I am not going to let that jerk tear us apart. I wasn't pretending to be your friend. Our friendship was real and to prove it, I'm going to sing a song and I hope the lyrics remind you of all the adventures we have shared. I call this song The Benawn Brothers," so Shawn started singing, and as he sung, I started thinking about all we had been through and how he's been there for me. As he performed, he wanted me to sing along. At first I hesitated, but Stiles woke up and convinced me. So after that, me and Shawn were singing The Benawn Brothers and boy was I having fun. After we were done, Shawn told me that Deveral was lying and that he would never do that to me. I looked at Shawn and could tell he really was my best friend and liked me for me. I told him I was sorry. I asked him how did he come up with that amazing song. He told me after what happened at The Vangy Arungedan, he decided to make a song about our friendship. He smiled and told me we're Team Benawn. Elsewhere, Kimbriella was crying while Vigdess ate cookie dough and ice cream, Kimbriella couldn't stop thinking about making out with Mitchell. Their lips finally touched and she was crushed that she and Mitchell may never be a couple since he knows the truth now. Kimbriella was also sad that she hurt her father, "at least you and Mitchell shared your first kiss. I was stupid to fall in love with a Jamison. Once a Jamison, always a Jamison." Vigdess said in a down voice. The next morning, me and Shawn left the hospital and he took me to the train station.

To my surprise, there were no people around. Anyway, I hugged Shawn goodbye and got on the train, as it moved, I waved at him and watched as the train moved slowly out of Los Angeles. Unknowing to me, Deveral was lurking around and told The Mad Ffraid Brats I'm no longer a problem and to drop off the antidote at Aunt Fanny penthouse. He hung up and walked away laughing. Meanwhile, back on the train, I couldn't believe I was really leaving. As I looked out the window, a friendly dining car service attendant asked me am I okay. I told her no and that I have a lot on my mind. But before I could go on, I couldn't believe who it was. "You're Queen Latifah." I said. "Yes I am. It's nice to meet you," I tried not to get to excited but I couldn't help it. "What are you doing here?" I asked her. "Well, your friend Mallory tweeted me several times and told me what happened at The Vangy

Arungedan. She thought I could help. My advice to you is sometimes beautiful things come into our lives out of nowhere. We can't always understand them, but we have to trust in them. I know you want to question everything, but sometimes it pays to just have a little faith. I'm your friend and I always will be." One of the passengers on the train said "Um, do I know you?" I asked him. "Yes you do bro." I couldn't believe it, it was Jonah. He was wearing an Aristotelis Setser Suit and so were the rest of Why Don't We. Not only were they on the train, so was Logan, Chris Salvatore, Grant, Hunter, Lucy, Luke, Van Hansis and the others. They were all wearing The Aristotelis Setser Suits disguising themselves as passengers. I couldn't believe it, then I met Alex Aiono. We became fast friends. He was disguised as the conductor and told me this. "Courage doesn't always roar. Sometimes courage is the quiet voice at the end of the day saying I will try again tomorrow, you have to believe us. None of us would ever do anything to hurt you." Daniel said, "We need you bro." Van told me "Today is the big day and we have to stick together." Lucy told me, "We're a team, and I will always have your back." "Our friendship is real. You know I care about you bro. You have to believe me." AJ told me. Devin asked me, "Are we still bros?" "So are you staying or leaving bro?" Shawn said. "I thought you left." I asked him . "Never." Shawn said. Chris told me that this isn't a train and that we're all on The Simplicius Transito. Back at The Show Mayor, Deveral was getting ready to marry Luz. He couldn't believe that after today, he'll be starting a new life away from his family. Before Luz and Deveral could say I do, me, AJ, Sollie, Sean Depner, Case, Ruben, Chris McNally, Mitchell Hope, Peter, Grant, Pierson, Alex Aiono, Antoni and Austin Rhodes showed up, shocking Deveral. "What are you, doing here? I thought you left." Deveral asked me. "I decided to stay," I told him. Austin Rhodes walked up to Luz and handed her a file. So Luz opened it and found out the truth about Deveral. She went up to him and slapped him in the face and told him goodbye. Before she left, she told me and the others thank you. "What just happened?" Deveral said. "You just lost your mail order bride." Sean said as he smiled. "It's over," Alex told him. "It's not over and you will pay for this Benny." He snapped his fingers.

Suddenly me and the others found ourselves surrounded by Deveral's henchmen, "y'all take care of them and I'll care of my brother." Sollie said. Austin, Antoni, Pierson, Mitchell, Chris McNally, Grant, Case, Peter, Ruben and Alex took care of the henchmen while me, AJ and Sean fought Ture and Creedence and Sollie was preparing to fight his older brother. Deveral was attempting to escape but Sollie made sure he didn't get away. "I waited my whole life for this. To put you in your place baby brother and now I'm finally going to end you," but before Deveral even had a chance to swing the first punch, Sollie surprised him and used some martial arts on him, sending him flying into the wall. Shocking me and the others. Deveral who was hurting and a bit out of it, tried to call The Mad Ffraid Brats, however, Sean used The Cybernetic Falconieri Penzance Communicator to destroy Deveral's phone. "How did this happen. I'm the good looking one and powerful one. I was supposed to be the last Jamison. My dreams and plans are ruined and when did you learn Martial arts?" Deveral said. "Goodbye and good riddance bro." Sollie said. "What are y'all going to do to me?" Deveral asked us. "You'll see," Austin said. Before we left, Luz sisters made out with Pierson, Peter, Ruben, Chris and Sean. A few hours later, me, AJ, Mallory, Antoni, Grant, Pierson, Alex Aiono, Chris McNally, Ajay, Cody, Casey, Cayden, Mitchell, Harrison Webb, Jacob, Ty, Jeremy, Chace, Case, Peter, Cayden, Darren, Alex Saxon, Jax, Carson and Lucy were in Aunt Fanny's penthouse going over all the clues. We were trying to figure out who The Mad Ffraid Brats are. Suddenly Edvardas showed up in the elevator. We all aimed our Cybernetic Falconieri Penzance Communicators at Edvardas just in case he was planning on attacking us. But it turned out he wanted to apologise for getting involved with The Mad Ffraid Brats and Deveral. To make things up to us, he told me and the others to follow him. So we did. When we arrived at our destination, there was nothing but a dead end. Or so we thought. Edvardas took out a deck of cards and said Arabesquea Bamboo. When he said that, the deck of cards turned into a door. Me and the others couldn't believe it, Edvardas turned the knob and told us to come inside. Me and Alex Saxon looked at each other. "This is the secret room isn't it?" we asked him. "Yes." Edvardas said. Inside the secret room were cameras, sound equipment, computers, pictures of Grand Dunixi Jamison, Esdras Jamison and Grandma Bregusuid. Also, we found the Severed Head presented as Henri Landru's and the rest of the gold bullions from The Federal Reserve Bank of New York. And Carson Rowland found the blue prints that Deveral stole from The Zvezda Three Ples. We learned that a Jamison named Roko built a powerful bomb called Storm Fault.

Then Chace found out what The Mad Ffraid Brats final plan for AJ is. Edvardas told us that tonight when everybody sings Sollie's happy birthday, The Mad Ffraid Brats will use The Trygg Derock to make him press a detonate that will eliminate anyone who has a Baltasaru Iegriusol Dusk and will make sure AJ takes the fall to finish his career once and for all. "OMG." Mallory said. "What's inside The Baltasaru Iegriusol Dusk?" Ty said. "Dooms Fault." Edvardas told him. "Each one has a powerful Doom Fault and there are over a billion people who have one," Edvardas said. "So that's why I haven't been acting myself because of The Trygg Derock." "Yes, The night you and the others attended Flame Feast," Edvardas said. "We have to get it off you immediately." Edvardas told AJ. Then Edvardas told us that The Ape Skull the cops have is fake. "Where is The real Ape Skull?" I asked him. He told me that it's in a room that used to belong to an Escaplogoist name Gaidar. I told him I didn't know that The Show Mayor had an Escaplogoist. "Where is Storm Fault?" Harrison asked him, "under The Jamison Mansion. There are about a thousand of them and there's one behind the wall. Deveral has been working on it for years, he calls it Doom Storm." Edvardas told us. Ajay looked behind the wall and saw it. "What are we going to do?" He asked me. An hour later, me and Felix tried to find out where the Trygg Derock is. On AJ, we used our Cybernetic Falconieri Penzance Communicators and scanned AJ. We found out that The Trygg Derock is on AJ's neck, Felix grabbed a magnifying glass and couldn't believe how a tiny device could control someone. He asked me how are we going to destroy it. At first I had no idea because I didn't want to hurt AJ. Then an idea came to me. I told Felix to hand me a ketchup bottle. So when he did, I asked him to point out where The Trygg Derock is on AJ's neck. After Felix did that, I squirted some ketchup, causing The Trygg Derock to malfunction and it fell off AJ's neck. AJ stomped on it and was happy that The Mad Ffraid Brats could no longer control him. Me and Felix were also happy after destroying The Trygg Derock. Me and the others gathered in The Big Top Show Mayor, including the staff of The Show Mayor. Everybody was talking among themselves and not paying me any attention. AJ could tell how nervous I was and told everybody to pay attention. Then he said this. "This guy right here needs our help and so do I and The Show Mayor, bro you keep thinking that me and the others aren't your friends and that you aren't cut out for this. But that's not true. You are stronger than you know and we need you. I mean look at all the good you and your friends have done since you have been here. You have done things you never thought you could do. Do you know how Incredible that is. You brought all of us together and even though The Mad Ffraid Brats tried many times to tear us all apart, you didn't give up. Whether you believe it or not, you're one of a kind bro and I'm happy to call you my friend and my brother.

"You got this." AJ said, I honestly couldn't believe it, I was best friends with AJ Mitchell. It took me a minute to take that in. After that, I started with my speech. This is what I told them. "All my life, I have hid my face, afraid that no one would care what I have to say. I have been bullied and I always felt like no would ever want to be my friend. People can be so mean and cruel. I just never had the courage to meet new people. I was too afraid of getting hurt again, after all I have been through and my failed attempts to make friends, I gave up. I didn't think there were any good people left in this world until I met AJ, Shawn, Why Don't We, Lucy, Chris Salvatore, Ryan Malaty, Hunter, Austin P. McKenzie, Reed and the others. I never imagined becoming such great friends with them. They taught me how to believe again and restored my hope and we need your help. The Mad Ffraid Brats has a devious plan that could cost a million lives and we need all the help that we can get for a final confrontation against The Mad Ffraid Brats. Who's with us?" I asked the staff. Mr. Hildefuns was the first volunteer. Then the others joined in. After that, thinking that this might be her only opportunity to kiss Jonah, Ciendauos went up to him and started making out with him. Daggi did the same thing with Mark and Nkromma made out with Callan. Mallory of course joined in and made out with Felix. Before we could move on with the second phase of our plan, Jumoke told me and the others that Tullio is missing. So me and Darren went searching for him. We became fast friends and used The Cybernetic Falconieri Penzance Communicators to find him. To our surprise, he was in his dressing room. Unfortunately when we arrived at his dressing room, Tullio was being held hostage by several of Mads Caractacus Troncoso's minions. With so little time, me and him kicked some clown butt and managed to defeat all of them. After that, we untied Tullio who was happy to see us. Knowing that he can't talk, he decided to use a notepad to communicate with us and we found out that Tullio caught Mads Caractacus Troncoso's Minions walking out of Deveral's suite, carrying bombs . Me and Darren alerted the others and we tried to figure out what The Mad Ffraid Brats are up to now. Me and Harris went to find Deveral's suite and we found out that he stayed in the second penthouse. I was scared to go in there. I had no idea what we might find but Harris told me we're in this together and that he has my back. At that moment, I realized we were becoming friends. I couldn't believe it. Anyway, me and Harris used The Cybernetic Falconieri Penzance Communicators to get inside and started searching for clues. Harris used The Cybernetic Falconieri Penzance Communicator to hack into Deveral's laptop while I searched the rest of the penthouse. At first I didn't find anything, but then I found Deveral's vault and I discovered a secret. This wasn't any ordinary vault. After I got inside, I found a secret door that lead to a secret passage. I couldn't believe what was down there. That's when Harris called me using The Cybernetic Falconieri Penzance Communicator, he told me he found something. We discovered that Deveral went to a boarding school called The Cees Cliamain. However, this was no ordinary school. The Cees Cliamain is for rich kids who have mental problems. It's more like an Asylum, Harris told me that's all he found. I showed him what I discovered. Me and Harris looked through some files that Deveral was trying to hide. Now I know why these files were from The Cees Cliamain.

The first one was about Deveral. Harris read one about a guy named Actaviano Fishburn, Deveral's best friend, who went to The Cees Cliamain as well. Harris couldn't believe what he was reading about Actaviano. Then we read a file that frightened us. Me and Harris looked at each other, suddenly Hayes, Jared and Cody came into the Deveral's suite. They noticed how scared we were and asked us what's going on. Harris showed them the file and told them that Deveral went to an Asylum and that he was working on a project called The Pacificus Meriadoc Aide. "What is that?" Cody said, "a device that could destroy the world." Harris said in a concerned voice. Hayes read a file about a girl named Eloquence Manuelito and told us that Eloquence also went to The Cees Cliamain and she was Deveral's first girlfriend who might be more evil than him. Jared discovered a file about a woman named Netaniella Papadopoulos who's Mr. Accerly Jamison long lost sister who works at The Cees Cliamain. Me and the others couldn't believe this. Before we could look through the rest of the files, Cody reminded us about the mission and told us that this is a mystery for another day. I told him he's right and we took the files and left Deveral's suite. After that, me and the others went to The Jamison Mansion and set up the traps. Then we went to Leonel's lab and geared up for tonight. Penzance Frisco unlocked everything and told us to help ourselves to any of Leonel's gadgets. Then she downloaded herself into a robot. Meanwhile, I was looking through the diary that Mr. Thersander gave us and it was still blank. While I looked through it, an idea came to me. I used The Cybernetic Falconieri Penzance Communicator and used a black light. When I did, I discovered that The Mad Ffraid Brats wrote in Invisible ink and I discovered who The Mad Ffraid Brats are. Reed asked me what did I find out. I told him. "I know who dunnit," I showed Reed the diary and he couldn't believe it. We told the others and AJ was excited that we now knew who's behind this. Colton Shires, Antoni, Case, Ty and Devin took the antidote to Seini, Stiles and the others.

Ty and the others told me that they are happy that I didn't leave and told me that we are friends. A few minutes later, Penzance Frisco told me and AJ that the cashier that me and Hunter met at Iron Brave is at the Airport trying to leave Los Angeles, but me and Lucy stopped her before she could get on the plane much to her dismayed. Lucy found fifteen thousand dollars in her bags. After that, me and Hayes went to Grand Dunixi Jamison and Grandma Bregusuid's old suite to investigate. Sollie told us that nobody has been in their suite since the death of his grandpa and the disappearence of his grandma and Sollie was right. The moment me and Hayes walked in there, all we could see was dust and spider webs. At first, we didn't find anything until Hayes found a book, he picked up the book and told me that someone named Maxi Sasueda, an Author and apparently a big fan of The Show Mayor wrote a tell all book about The Show Mayor. Me and Hayes read the book and discovered that one of the chapters talks about a woman named Celesley, a Giantess. Me and Hayes wondered what happened to her and why nobody at The Show Mayor talks about her. Hayes used his Cybernetic Falconieri Penzance Communicator to find Maxi. He wanted to know what else this guy knows and so did I. Then we found a secret bunker that lead to a secret room. Me and Hayes found blue prints and discovered that Grandma Bregusuid wanted to build a magic School but never had the chance to. Before we left, Hayes told me our friendship means a lot to him and that he would never hurt me. I looked at him and told him he's one of my best friends and that I'm thankful to have him in my life. After that, me, AJ, Reed, Felix, Antoni, Charlie, Carson, Pierson, Jeremy, Case, Logan and Lucy went to Maxi's house to ask him some questions. Unfortunately, when we got there, a new mystery was born. AJ knocked on the door but no one answered. Felix looked through the window and told us that we have to get inside now. AJ broke the door down and we all went inside and discovered that someone ransacked Maxi's house. Me and the others started searching for him. Felix and Reed found out that Maxi is a huge comic book fan and that he has every comic book that has ever been made. Jeremy Investigated the basement. Logan and Lucy searched the attic. Pierson and Carson checked out the garage. As for me, AJ, Case, Antoni and Charlie, we were searching for clues in Maxi's room. Whoever ransacked Maxi's house was looking for something. Pierson told us. "I wonder what happened to Maxi." AJ said. "I think we might know." Reed said. He and Felix showed me and the others Maxi's cell phone. "Where did y'all find this?" Lucy asked them. "We found his phone in a hollow comic book," Reed said. Felix told me there's a video on here that I need to see. So we all gathered around and watched the video. It was a message from Maxi and this is what he said. "I'm sorry I can't be there in person to meet you. But there are eyes everywhere. I know you're an Investigative Reporter and I need your help. The Jamison Family mystery is bigger than you think. There are more secrets that you and your friends have yet to discover but in time you will. I'm afraid that someone is after me and will do whatever it takes to make sure I don't reveal what I know so I'm on the run fighting for my life. I'll be in touch, be careful Benny."

After the video ended, me and the others looked at each other. "It looks like we had another mystery for another day on our hands." AJ told me. Case started searching through Maxi's computer trying to find more clues. Antoni was looking through the book that me and Reed found at Grand Dunixi Jamison and Grandma Bregusuid's old suite. Antoni used The Cybernetic Falconieri Penzance Communicator and discovered a map that lead to a secret hideout. I told him good job. Jeremy didn't find anything in the basement. Later on, me and Shawn went back to The Jamison Mansion to free the animals, especially Brio, Burly and Caisi. While we were freeing the animals, Shawn could tell something was bothering me and asked me what's wrong. I told him about Maxi and how I was worried about him. Shawn told me after this mystery is over with, we'll find a way to help Maxi and solve the mystery that surrounds The Jamison Family together. I told Shawn I'm very blessed to have a friend like him. Shawn told me he's proud of me and that he believes in me, "brothers forever." he said with a smile. After that, me and AJ went searching for the secret hideout and discovered an abandoned Mausoleum Crypts. We went inside and found a lair that has been abandoned for years. At first, all we found were pictures of Grandma Bregusuid and Mr. Accerly Jamison. But then we uncovered two new secrets. I found out that Tielyr has a twin brother named Tierson, me and AJ wondered why Tielyr hasn't mentioned anything about him. As for AJ, he told me that someone else has been searching for Grandma Bregusuid as well, a threat known as The Heart's Brat. Someone who could be more dangerous than The Mad Ffraid Brats. "I think we're going to have to make a file about these other mysteries." AJ told me. As me and the others got ready for the party, me, AJ, Ryan Malaty, Grant, Thomas, Van Hansis, David, Logan, Ty, Antoni, Alex Saxon, Jax, Levi and Reed went to talk to Burnell Wordlaw who tried to lock the doors. But Ryan Malaty stopped him. "Why are you trying to keep us out?" Van said. "Oh, no reason. What brings you back to The Jamison Archives?" Burnell said. "We need to ask you a few questions." AJ said. "Mr. Mitchell, it's nice to finally meet you and the others but I must be going. What can you tell us about a guy named Maxi." Grant said. "No comment." Burnell told him. "How about Celesley?" Reed asked him. "Or what about Tielyr's twin brother?" Thomas asked him. "How about you tell us who The Heart's Brat is?" When I said that, Burnell started to get mad and told us this. "You and your friends are way over your head. You're following the same path that got Celesley and Maxi into some serious trouble. When it comes to The Jamison Family, it's best you look the other way or you'll end up like Celesley and Maxi, stay out of this and don't ask anymore questions because you might not like what you'll find out. I will tell you this, The Heart's Brat will be one of your biggest challenges yet."

After that Burnell, left. While getting ready for tonight, me and Alex Saxon received a video chat from Mr. Thersander. However we couldn't see his face. All he told us was that Deveral has a house in Beverly hills and sent us the address. So me and Alex went to investigate. Unfortunately getting in wasn't going to be easy. There were guards everywhere. Me and Alex used The Cybernetic Falconieri Penzance Communicators and took out all the guards. Then we went inside Deveral's house. We had no idea what we were looking for. While we searched Deveral's house, me and Alex found out that Deveral has a room mate named Konstancji. While searching Deveral's room, Alex found notes that belonged to a Doctor named Potnmeroy and he couldn't believe what he was reading. Meanwhile, I discovered a secret room that was filled with meth cookies and if that wasn't bad enough, I found a list of all the people Deveral has sold cookies to and I learned that Deveral is running a drug trafficking business.

Then Alex came running into the room to show me what he found and I was shocked. Alex told me that Celesley was a patient at a place called The Rasine Mourngen Swarm. A mental hospital and that it was run by Tielyr, scaring me and Alex. Alex also told me that he cares about me and that our friendship is real. After finding a picture of a dog in Deveral's house, I asked Sollie did he and his brother ever had a dog and he told me yes. A St. Bernard named Demetrien, who Deveral got rid of. Me and Jack Maynard went to The Jamison Mansion to search Demetrien's dog house to find clues. At first we didn't find anything until Jack moved the dog house. When he did, me and Jack found an Atlas Survival Shelter. I was actually afraid to go down there but Jack helped me. After we climbed inside, we couldn't believe what we found. There were two corpses along with some letters. Jack read some of the letters and told me that Deveral has a prison pen pal who might know the identity of The Heart's Brat. Then me and Jack used The Cybernetic Falconieri Penzance Communicators to identify the corpses and found out that one of the bodies is Celesley. The other one is a guy named Naisbit. A Rola Bola who used to perform at The Show Mayor . Me and Jack wondered what happened to them and why they are down here. Before we left, Jack told me that our friendship means a lot to him and that he couldn't believe that I ever doubted our friendship. A few hours later, me and Alex Whitehouse went to investigate The Rasine Mourngen Swarm that has been abandoned for years. Alex was trying to prove to me that we are friends but after the Deveral thing, I still had my doubts. I just didn't believe that Alex was my friend and I wondered why would he want to be friends with me. Anyway, I'm just a loser. As we searched The Rasine Mourngen Swarm, me and Alex found out that The Rasine Mourngen Swarm used to belong to Doctor Emmonual. A plague doctor who treated victims of the bubonic plague way back in the 19th century. "This place is really old." Alex said. We found several bird – like beak masks . Gloves, wooden canes, boots and ankle length overcoat and a wide brimmed hat. Then we discovered autopsies of every patient they ever had, plus the patients Tielyr had after he reopened The Rasine Mourngen Swarm. Alex checked the computer and was surprised it still works. As for me, I was checking the other rooms and I found out where Tielyr kept his files. Unfortunately,

Celesley's file was missing. I tried to find out which room she was in. Meanwhile, Alex uncovered some shocking information but before he could tell me, someone wearing a plague doctor costume attacked him. I found the room and I wondered why Celesley was in here in the first place.

While searching for clues, I realized that one of the floorboard was loose and I found a diary inside. I grabbed my flash light and read the diary and I couldn't believe what I was reading. I went to show Alex what I found but he wasn't there. That's when I got concerned and I tried to find him. Elsewhere in The Rasine Mourngen Swarm, Alex woke up and found himself strapped. "You're finally awake," the mysterious person who was wearing the plague doctor costume said. "Who are you?" Alex said, "I'm The Heart's Brat." When they said that, Alex started freaking out, "what do you want?" He asked them. "For you and your friend Benny to stay out of my way. Benny has no idea who he's dealing with. There are things that don't concern him. If you care about his safety, I suggest you keep him away from The Jamison Family or he could get hurt."

"You stay away from him." Alex said. The Heart's Brat started laughing. Suddenly, The Heart's Brat got hit by a bowling ball. Alex was happy to see me. I hurried up and freed him. The Heart's Brat was furious and told us we have been warned. I told The Heart's Brat when me and my friends solve this mystery, I will find out who they are and that's a promise. Alex smiled and we watched The Heart's Brat vanish. Alex told me what he found and I was horrified. Alex said that Tielyr turned The Rasine Mourngen Swarm into a Kidney trafficking center and that he used to torture patients. Especially Celesley. Me and Alex never imagined that Tielyr could be that twisted. I told him I found Celesley's diary and I learned that Celesley had a baby by Doctor Potnmeroy. Alex couldn't believe it. He asked me what happened to the baby. I told Alex it doesn't say. The rest of the diary talks about a woman named Heartly who might know something. Before we left, Alex told me thanks for saving him and that he really is my friend and likes me for me. So that's when I learned that we are true friends and I wouldn't change it for anything in the world. Pierson went with me to talk to Heartly but before we left, we found Mallory and the others in the lobby. "What are y'all doing?" I asked AJ. He told me that Mallory dared some of her fans on her web show to beat her record for the longest make out. "She has a web show?" Pierson said. "Unfortunately she does." I told them. There were a bunch of fans. One started making out with Miles. The others made out with Peter, Ryan Malaty, Jax, Jack Maynard, Jonah, Luke, Jeremy, David, Noah, Alex Whitehouse, Logan Shroyer, Nick Mayorga, Ruel, Kendrick, Felix, Cody, Reed, Freddie, Brandon, Rudy, Levi, Grant, Sebastian, Ruben, Devin and Jacob. Me, AJ and Pierson were about to leave. Mallory was worried about me especially with The Heart's Brat lurking somewhere in Los Angeles. With so much going on, Mallory did something really crazy. She grabbed me and started kissing me. Then she grabbed Pierson and started making out with him. After she was done, she introduced us to some of her fans. One of them set out to break Mallory's record by making out with Brandon. The other one did the same with Nick Mayorga. After that, Mallory did the same with Peter. "I thought I was the last one, right Benny?" AJ asked me. Unfortunately I couldn't answer. I was still in shock. So Pierson carried me out because I couldn't move.

A few hours later, Me, AJ and Pierson arrived at Heartly's place, she was a little shaky and timid and kept looking out her window and told us that there are eyes everywhere. Anyway she told us that she's a Death Doula and that Celesley was her sister. Pierson asked her did she know anything about Tielyr. Unfortunately, she wouldn't answer. I asked her how did Celesley die and why she was in The Rasine Mourngen Swarm. Heartly still wouldn't answer. Then Pierson asked her about the baby and that's when Heartly started talking. She told us realizing that she was dying. Celesley asked Heartly to help her write her will. She also gave Heartly custody of her child. She showed us pictures of the baby and told us his name is Nazaret. Then Heartly told us that her sister gave her a letter and told her to make sure Grand Dunixi gets it. "Why?" AJ asked her. "I don't know. She just told me it was urgent." "Is that it?" I asked her. "Well, there is one more thing my sister told me." Heartly said. "Well, what is it?" Pierson said. Before she took her last breath, she told me that Quintonette had a baby by Tielyr. When she said that, me, AJ and Pierson couldn't believe it, before we could ask her more about the baby,we heard a noise and found several Motion Sensor Bombs. With so little time, Pierson grabbed me and AJ. We jumped through a glass window before the explosion hit us. "Are you guys okay?" He asked us. We told him were fine but Heartly didn't make it and her house was destroyed. There were flames everywhere. Pierson noticed someone in the dark and got our attention. It was The Heart's Brat. They waved at us and got away, scaring me, AJ and Pierson. Me and Ajay decided to check out The Show Mayor Fortune Teller Machine. At first we thought it was just an ordinary Fortune Teller Machine until we asked it a question. We read the card and it said the answers we seek are behind me.

At first, me and Ajay had no idea what the Fortune Teller machine meant, then Ajay found a secret passage behind the machine. So we went inside and discovered a secret room. The only thing we found was a journal that belonged to Naisbit. That revealed Celesley didn't get pregnant by Doctor Potnmeroy, instead she had a surrogate mother. Ajay asked me how come Celesley lied in her diary. I told him I think someone stole the real diary and placed it with a fake one. As we searched for more clues, I stopped and told Ajay I guess we'll never become friends. Ajay realized how down I was and told me this, "Are you kidding me? I believe destiny brought us together for a reason. You're my friend and our friendship means a lot to me no matter what The Mad Ffraid Brats do. They will never tear us apart. Our friendship is real. It's a shield that will protect us from whatever The Mad Ffraid Brats throw our way." Me and Cayden found out that The Show Mayor has a secret underground vault. After we got inside, me and Cayden discovered records of forgotten performers of The Show Mayor. I didn't say much to him because he's one of the few that I feel like will never become my friend. Anyway, we went through the records and learned that Syntyche a Strong Woman, Rowlando, Priam and Stiabhan, Who were Tumblers. A Hula Hoop Artist named Murielia and a Pantomime Clown named Zelmo mysteriously disappeared. Me and Cayden wonder what happened to them. Me and Sebastian investigated Naisbit's old dressing room. I didn't say one word to him knowing that he wouldn't become my friend anyway. I found out that Naisbit is Jumoke's brother. Me and Sebastian wondered why she didn't tell us about her brother. As for Sebastian, he found out that Naisbit was being stalked by The Show Mayor Sword Swallower. After one of the employees told me that Luz was still here, me and Cameron Mathison went to talk to her, she was so upset. She told us she was stupid to take a chance at love and feels like she's destined to be alone. Me and Cameron looked at each other and told her this. I told her to believe in Love and Cameron told her don't give up on love because there is always someone who loves you even if it's not the person you were hoping or wishing for. After listening to our advice, Luz realized that maybe there is somebody out there for her.

Suddenly, Jeremy Irvine and Peter showed up without any hesitation. Luz went up to Jeremy and started making out with him. Then her best friend showed up and made out with Peter. Then Alex Whitehouse popped up. He told me I texted him. I told him I didn't. Suddenly Mallory popped up. She grabbed Alex Whitehouse and started making out with him. After that, I went back to Mount Jamison. This time with Carson Rowland. I couldn't believe I was actually searching for clues with him and to my surprise. we became fast friends. Carson found something interesting about Mrs. Bannerjee. Me and him went to talk to her. "What do you want this time?" She asked me. I told her I'll let Carson tell her. Carson smiled and told her that we know she had an affair with Tielyr. When he said that, she acted like she didn't know what we were talking about until Carson showed her some pictures . Me and Peter decided to check out all the information that Mr. Accerly Jamison had on his employees from The Jamison Adonijah Industries. There was only one that became a new suspect. A guy named Rainart. So we decided to find out more about him. I found out that Rainart was a secretary who used to work for Mr. Accerly Jamison. Peter discovered that Rainart was secretly working with The Heart's Brat and he told me that Rainart knew every secret The Jamison Family had including the ones we haven't discovered yet. Tyler Posey found out where Rainart used to live. So me and him went to investigate his house while we searched for clues. Tyler asked me could we be friends.

At first I had my doubts but then I took a leap of faith once again and I told him sure. So we became friends, something I never thought would happen. Tyler found eyes ball inside a snow globe, creeping him and me out. He smashed the snow globe opened and discovered something unusual about these eyes balls. We found tiny cameras inside them and wondered what's on them. So we went through the footage and discovered a dark secret about Rainart.

We learned that Rainart is a Cannibalism and that he places tiny cameras into his victims retina and uses them to steal top secret information from The Show Mayor. We read some of the files he had about some of his victims and me and Tyler were shocked to find out that Celesley was one of his victims. With the day almost over with, Everybody was getting ready for tonight. Everybody except for me and Pierson. We were going over all the new clues. Some that will start a new mystery. Suddenly, we got a text message from Mr. Thersander who told us there's something in Tielyr's bank that we needed to see. So without any hesitation, me and Pierson went to Tielyr's bank. We used grappling hooks from The Cybernetic Falconieri Penzance Communicators to get on top of the bank. After dodging all the boobytraps, I almost dropped in coins. But Pierson saved me. We used The Cybernetic Falconieri Penzance Communicators to get inside the vault. We had no idea what could be inside besides money. Suddenly Pierson found something we couldn't believe what was in Tielyr bank. Pierson used his Cybernetic Falconieri Penzance Communicator to scan it. After getting the results, I asked him is that really who I think it is. He told me yes and that we have found Amalgunde's remains. Me and Charles were in Aunt Fanny's penthouse and learned that The Show Mayor has a panic room. So we decided to go investigate. But before we left, Mallory set up a kissing booth and wouldn't let us leave until Charles agreed to give her a kiss. With time running out, Charles decided to kiss her and the two ended up making out. After that, me and Charles went to the panic room. To my surprise, me and Charles became fast friends. We searched the panic room and at first we didn't find anything until Charles found a hole behind the wall. Inside the hole was a music box. He opened the box up and found a flash drive. He placed it inside his Cybernetic Falconieri

Penzance Communicator and found a video. Me and Charles watched the video and we couldn't believe what we were watching. In the video, a guy named Kiefert who was a Human Fire Cracker died and it was all Mr. Accerly's fault. Me and Charles wondered why did Mr. Accerly kill this guy. Me and AJ Mitchell were reading Grandma Bregusuid's manuscript, I didn't say one word to AJ. He noticed how I was acting and attempted to get me to talk. He asked me are there any shows that I wish never got cancelled.

At first I didn't say anything but I could tell he was trying to prove to me that we are friends. So I told him that the Librarians is a show I really missed. I couldn't stop talking about the characters and their amazing friendship. Then AJ noticed some tiny numbers written on the back of the manuscript. He used a magnifying glass using The Cybernetic Falconieri Penzance Communicator and discovered a phone number. So we called the number and listened together to see who picks up and we couldn't believe who answered. "Hello?" This is Tielyr. Me and AJ looked at each other. A few minutes later, me and AJ discussed what just happened. "So what does this mean?" AJ asked me. "It means that this whole time Tierson has been pretending to be his twin brother." I told him. "But why though?" AJ said. "I don't know bro," I told him. Me and Devan went to The Horror Herculano. I couldn't believe that I was going back to this creepy place but Devan told me that I'm not alone. With Devan by my side, I didn't feel so scared. He asked me what were we looking for. I told him we're looking for the deed to The Horror Herculano. It was really quiet, too quiet. We wondered where is everyone. I had no idea where Tierson could be keeping his brother deed. Suddenly, Devan found a secret door behind a mirror. So we went inside and discovered a Sentry Safe. I used The Cybernetic Falconieri Penzance Communicator to get inside. While I tried to get inside the safe, something knocked me out. Devan ran over to see if I was alright and he helped me up. We found out we were not alone. There was a strange woman with long hair. A guy with a hat and a girl who kept laughing. "Who are you guys?" Devan said. "I'm Tinuviel, a hair hanger. This is Mauridsje, a Carnival Barker and this is Aggi a Target girl." Me and Devan looked at each other. 'Well, it was nice getting to know y'all but we have to be going now." I said. "Not with that deed you aren't." Tinuviel said. "We work for Tielyr," Mauridsje told us. "For years, nobody knew Tierson was pretending to be his brother until you and your friends showed up. We have been watching you." Tinuviel told me. Realizing that me and Devan are in danger, I quickly got the deed out of the safe. I gave it to Devan and I told him to run. Devan didn't want to leave me but I told him I don't care what happens to me but I do care about him. I used my Cybernetic Falconieri Penzance Communicator to create a distraction giving Devan the chance to escape. Mauridsje went after him while Tinuviel took care of me. Unknowing to me, she knew karate and kicked my butt. Then she used her hair to knock me out unconscious.

I woke up and found myself tied up and dangling over a Pool filled with circus fleas "Any last words?" Tinuviel asked me. I told her no. Suddenly, Mauridsje got electrocuted by Devan. He was using his Cybernetic Falconieri Penzance Communicator. Then he trapped Tinuviel inside a magic 8 ball. After that he made out with Aggi. Then he used some knock out gas on her. With Tielyr's henchmen defeated, Devan got me down. "I thought you left?" I asked him, "nope." He said. "Why did you come back?" I asked him. Devan smiled and said to save my friend. I hugged him and told him thanks. Me and Alex Aiono learned that The Show Mayor has an escape room. Before we went inside, Alex told me that he knows what I have been through and told me we are friends. I shook his hand and said alright. After we got inside, we found Tinuviel searching for something. I was in no mood to deal with her. I guess she felt the same way. She quickly got out of there. Before we had a chance to ask her what she was looking for, Alex find a chest behind a mirror. He opened the chest up and found a elfa vintage organizer. He went through the pages and discovered new secrets. He told me that Grand Dunixi Jamison and Esdras have a half brother named Ynocente who runs a circus school. We also learned that Tinuviel was the surrogate mother and if that wasn't crazy enough, Alex told me that this journal belongs to Kiefert, the Human Fire Cracker who was a Private Investigator hired by Ynocente after he received a letter from someone revealing that he has half siblings. Me and Alex couldn't believe this. After reading a page in Kiefert's journal, me and Chandler discovered that The Show Mayor has an abandoned wax museum. So we went to investigate. Knowing I don't stand a chance of becoming friends with him, I just kept my distance. Me and Chandler wondered why this place has been abandoned for so many years. We found a vast of wax. However what we found inside creeped us out. We found several remains and used The Cybernetic Falconieri Penzance Communicators and identified all the remains and we learned that they belonged to Syntyche, Rowlando, Priam, Stiabhan, Murielia and Doctor Potnmeroy. Me and Nick Mayorga found Rainart's cell phone number in Kiefert's journal. So instead of calling his number, I decided to track his phone using The Cybernetic Falconieri Penzance Communicator. To my surprise, Rainart was somewhere in The Show Mayor. I figured I would do this on my own but Nick stopped me. "Where are you going?" He asked me. Knowing that we weren't friends, I simply ignored him. Before I had the chance to get into the elevator, Nick shouted out I want to be your friend. I slowly turned around, "What did you say?" I asked him. "I said I want to be your friend if you'll let me." Nick said. At that moment I finally became friends with Nick. Unfortunately, Mallory just had to be in the spotlight. She was so happy that me and Nick became friends, she grabbed Nick and started making out with him. After they were done making out, me and Nick discovered that Rainart was somewhere in The Show Mayor Furnace. We wondered why he would be down there. Nick called the number and we heard it ringing. I found the phone but Rainart was nowhere in sight. Suddenly, Nick saw a hand sticking out from a pile of trash. We ran over to see if he was still alive but we were too late.

Me and Nick found out that Rainart was murdered but the question was who killed him and why. Me and Sam went to Tielyr's family Mausoleum after we found a page that was ripped out of Kiefert's diary. As we went down the Mausoleum, I kept my distance from Sam and I didn't say one word to him. I figured he wouldn't give me a chance. As we searched for clues, Sam told me he can't wait for our next mystery. I told him me too. "If we survive this one, we will. You have to believe that we're gonna unmask The Mad Ffraid Brats and clear AJ's name."

"How do you know?" I asked him. "Because I believe in you my friend!" "We're friends?" "Yes we are." Sam told me. Me and Sam discovered one of the caskets were different from the others, so we opened it up and found a diary inside a corpse, we read the diary and we learned why Tierson had been keeping Tielyr's secret all these years. Me and Mallory went to talk to Vigdess who felt stupid for falling in love with a Jamison. We asked her was she coming to Sollie's birthday party tonight. She told us that maybe it's time for her to leave The Show Mayor and say goodbye to Sollie. I felt sorry for Vigdess, I could tell she had given up on love. But Mallory wouldn't let her. Mallory told her obstacles are put in our way to see if what we want is worth fighting for. "Listen to me, a Styles knows that Love is worth fighting for. Come on I'll help you get ready." Mallory said. Before they left, Mallory told me she wants to kiss Josh Beauchamp and I told her I want to be friends with Chase Stokes, Noah Urrea, Sean Giambrone, Parker Queenan, Dane DeHaan, Katherine McNamara and Jeremy Hutchins. "Unfortunately! I know they won't give me a chance." Me and Hunter went to talk to Kimbriella who was crying her eyes out. She wanted to be left alone but me and Hunter were determined to make her feel better. Kimbriella kept telling us that maybe she doesn't deserve to be loved. I told Kimbriella "Take a chance, you never know what might happen." And Hunter told her, "I know you're scared, but you have to open your heart to let love in." After that me and Hunter hugged her. As we walked back to Aunt Fanny's penthouse to get ready, I told Hunter he's my best friend and that I'm happy. That he likes me for me.

As we got out of the elevator, Mallory scared us and told Hunter if she dies tonight, that she's not dying without knowing how it feels to kiss his lips. She went up to Hunter and started making out with him. Then me. Hunter and Brandon. went to the company where Baltasaru Iegriusol Dusk are made. We used a password that Sollie gave us and went inside. As we made our way to the control room, suddenly a huge gorilla came smacking through the window. He had some weird symbol on his chest. I quickly handed Hunter a flashdrive. "What is this?" He asked me. I told him and Brandon that I made something that will help us stop The Baltasaru Iegriusol Dusk from exploding but they have to upload it to the supercomputer. "What about you?" Brandon asked me. "Right now, uploading that flashdrive is more important. Now run!" I told them. After they left, the gorilla starting chasing me. As Hunter and his brother ran, Hunter stopped knowing that I needed help. Hunter gave the flashdrive to Brandon and told him it's up to him. He went back to help me. As I was running for my life, I had no idea how I would stop this gorilla. Suddenly! The gorilla grabbed me. I tried to get away but he was holding me tight. Just when I thought this was the end, Hunter came. He used his Cybernetic Falconieri Penzance Communicator and released some knock out gas on the gorilla, saving my life. "I thought I told you to run." Hunter smiled at me and told me he couldn't leave a friend behind. As Brandon made his way to the supercomputer, someone stopped him, a Female Foot Archer. Instead of attacking him, she simply grabbed him and starting making out with him. Unfortunately it didn't last too long after me and Hunter showed up. Realizing who I am, the Foot Archer fired some arrows. Then she made out with Brandon one more time and jumped through a glass window to escape. "Who was that?" Hunter said. "I have no idea bro." Brandon said. He quickly uploaded the flashdrive and told me it's done. Me, Brandon and Hunter wondered who was that Foot Archer and better yet, who was she working for. After getting ready for the party, Chandler checked up on me. He asked me am I nervous about tonight. I told him I was terrified. Chandler told me, "Friends fight for you. Respect you, include you, encourage you, need you, deserve you, stand by you. You are not alone bro. Me and the others are here for you and we won't let anything happen to you and I am your friend no matter how many times I have to prove it." I smiled and told Chandler okay. I went to The Show Mayor sound studio to write a song and Devin helped me. He could tell how nervous I was and he told me that I can do this and that he believed in me.

Me and Luke went to Nicos Burp Burgers to talk to someone without the gang. Knowing Luke told me that we are friends and that he can't believe I doubted our friendship, he also told me we're Team Luny. I could tell that he really did care about me. Anyway, me and Luke were talking to someone who kept their face hidden from the public. The person asked us are we sure about tonight. Me and Luke told him yes. While the rest of us were getting ready, Peter decided to pay Mr. Stumbo a visit. "What do you want?" Mr. Stumbo asked him. "I came to talk some sense into you. Benny is right and you know it. It's time you get your act together, your hotel needs you and so does your staff. For years you have been taking care of The Show Mayor doing an excellent job but now you have lost your touch. All because of The Mad Ffraid Brats. You can't let them win. Benny is going to save The Show Mayor and AJ. You'll see. That's all I have to say," Peter said. Before he left, Mr. Stumbo asked him how come he has so much faith in me. Peter smiled and told him because Benny is my friend and I believed in him. Elsewhere, Cody called me after finding something on Rainart's phone. We were in Aunt Fanny's penthouse and discovered that the last person Rainart talked to was Tielyr. Scaring both me and Cody. I never thought me and Cody would become friends but we did. As we searched the phone, me and Cody found out that Rainart has information on Mr. Accerly's first assistant. Meanwhile, Mallory and Alex Whitehouse were also in the penthouse. Worried about the party and unmasking The Mad Ffraid Brats, Mallory grabbed Alex Whitehouse and started making out with him. Me and Cody continued to look through Rainart's phone. While those two made out, me and AJ went to find The Ape Skull. As we got to the room, suddenly something wrapped around me and pulled me into a heating vent. I yelled AJ's name. "Benny?" AJ said. He wondered where I went. Then the room we were planning on going into opened up by itself. AJ slowly went inside and called my name. After he cut the lights on, he found me gagged and in a straitjacket hanging over a water tank. AJ was horrified and was about to save me until someone stopped him, a Cowboy. "Who are you?" He said. "My name is Welliver." "Well, it's nice to meet you but I need to save my friend, so if you would excuse me." AJ said. "I'm afraid I can't do that partner, you see The Mad Ffraid Brats are paying me big bucks to protect this beautiful skull." Welliver said as he showed AJ The Ape Skull. "Give me that," AJ said. Then AJ noticed the pictures in the room and found several of Gaidar with a little boy dressed as a cowboy. "OMG! You're Gaidar's son aren't you?" AJ asked him. "Yes I am." "Why are you working with The Mad Ffraid Brats?" AJ asked him. "Working for them? Please, I was just paid to do a job, that's it. I have my own vengeance against The Jamison Family." Welliver said. "What are you talking about?" AJ asked him. "Grand Dunixi Jamison let my father die and now your friend will die." Welliver said.

He cut the rope and AJ watched as I fell into the water tank. He started running towards the water tank but Welliver got in his way. "You ain't going anywhere." Welliver said. AJ realized I was in trouble, he popped out a cowboy hat from his Cybernetic Falconieri Penzance Communicator. Than he started fighting Welliver. When I started to close my eyes, AJ knew I was running out of time and used The Cybernetic Falconieri Penzance Communicator to taser Welliver. He grabbed The Ape Skull from Welliver. Then he quickly searched his Cybernetic Falconieri Penzance Communicator to see if there was anything useful to free me. He found a bomb and fired it at the water tank. Unfortunately It didn't go off. He contacted Penzance Frisco and asked her how come it didn't go off. She told him it had to be activated by blowing raspberries. So AJ sticked out his tongue. He took a deep breath and started blowing raspberries until the bomb was fully activated. Then it went off, shattering the glass. AJ ran over to me and popped out a towel out of his Cybernetic Falconieri Penzance Communicator and put it on me and ungagged me. He asked me, "Are you alright? "I smile and told him I'm just happy to see you and told him thanks for saving me. AJ was so happy that I was alive. As he helped me up, we noticed that Welliver got away. Before we left, a video projector started playing. Me and AJ learned that Gaidar was good friends with Grand Dunixi Jamison until something horrible happened. We learn that at Gaidar show, Grand Dunixi Jamison had him wear a straitjacket doing a burning rope trick hanging over a bed of nails. Me and AJ watched as he fell and landed on the bed of nails and died. "What just happened?" AJ asked me. "Another mystery." I told him. Realizing that The Show Mayor sign had a clue, I wondered could The Horror Herculano Sign have a clue as well. So me and Spencer went to see. Spencer noticed how quiet I was and asked me was I alright. I told him I almost drowned, plus dealing with the fact that Welliver is out there somewhere.

Spencer could tell how scared I was and knew there was only one thing that could cheer me up. He asked me were there anymore movies that I forgot to mention who never got the credit they deserved. I told him Pirates of the Caribbean Dead Men Tell No Tales is one of my all-time favorite Pirates of the Caribbean movies. Henry, Carina and Captain Armando Salazar are my favorite characters. This movie is epic. Invaders from Mars definitely deserves credit and an award including The Mortal Engines. It was epic. I want a part two. So bad. Valerian and the City of a Thousand Planets was too epic. It would be amazing if they made another one. Also, Men In Black International, X:Men Dark Phoenix, The Darkest Minds, Born to be Wild, Pitch Perfect 3 and Jurassic World Fallen Kingdom deserve a lot of credit. I also told him about a few TV shows that should had never been cancelled. In a Heartbeat, starring Shawn Ashmore. Eerie Indiana, Carol's Second Act and FreakyLinks. I also told Spencer I'm a huge Monk fan and that Natalie is the best thing that ever happened to Monk. Those two were an unbreakable team and their chemistry was amazing. I told him that Natalie was a true friend. Also Randy is one of my favorite characters. Spencer smiled, then we arrived to The Horror Herculano. This time I wasn't going in. Me and Spencer used grappling hooks and made our way up to the top of the building. We started searching each letter. I found a small box inside the H and Spencer found a journal inside the O. Spencer read the journal and told me that Tielyr and Tierson's mother was a Jocasta Complex. As for me I showed Spencer what I found. "What is that?" he asked me. I told him it's a Microdot.

After that, it was time for the Birthday Party of the year. Our mission is to unmask The Mad Ffraid Brats, save AJ's career, The Show Mayor, The Daily Maglorix Newspaper and rescue Doyle and the others. Giving up is not an option. Cameron and Queen Latifah were hosting. The party started off with a song. Colton sung the first part, then me, AJ, Why Don't We, Shawn, Case, Mallory, Lucy and the others. The song was called It's a Show Top Birthday. We were all performing on trampolines. Then Sollie made a grand entrance doing an acrobatic performance. After that, the party began, me and the others were wearing circus masquerade costumes. The party was inside a circus tent. Behind The Jamison Mansion. The decorations were amazing. There were games and everything. It felt like a real circus. Mallory made out with Rudy once again. Meanwhile, Why Don't We performed 8 Letters. After they were done, me and Gerwazy talked even though I didn't want to but Jonah gave me the push I needed. This is what he said. "I know I hurt you and you probably hate me. I just want you to know I will forever be sorry for the way I treated you and I hope you can forgive me because I need you in my life bro. You're all I have." Gerwazy started to walk away but I stopped him. "I forgive you." I told him. Gerwazy hugged me and we were brothers again. Hunter Hayes was the next performer. He sung One Shot. Sollie used this opportunity to talk to Vigdess who was still mad at him. Sollie couldn't stop apologizing. He felt stupid for what he said. Unfortunately Vigdess still wasn't convinced so he did the one thing nobody in his family has ever done. He made out with a maid. Vigdess couldn't believe it. She was making out with a Jamison. Jesse McCartney performed Better With You. Mitchell went to talk to Kimbriella who tried to run. When she saw him coming, Mitchell told her he likes her for her and doesn't care that she's a waitress. He just wants to be with her. He also told her he thinks it's cool that her father is the chef of The Show Mayor. Kimbriella was so happy, she ran up to Mitchell and the two started making out. Will Jay sung Homesick. Alex Aiono performed Young Love, Charlie Puth sung The Way I Am. Ruel sung Painkiller. Mark performed Side Chick. Harry Hudson sung Whenimma, AJ Mitchell performed Used To Be. Sean sung Fairy tale books, Devin performed Best Mistake, Austin P. McKenzie sung Crazy Beautiful!. Christopher performed Stone Cold.

As for The Ptarmigan Seissylt Clowns, they performed one of their new songs. Meanwhile Cayden was trying to talk to me. He told me we're friends and that I have to stop doubting and start believing. So after that, me and Cayden became friends. Then he noticed Tierson. I told him to keep an eye on him and to make sure Tierson doesn't leave this party. Shawn performed In My Blood. While he performed, me and Nolan went to rescue Nasser and the others. After Edvardas told us that The Mad Ffraid Brats are keeping them trapped inside of Mads Caractacus Troncoso top hat, so me and Nolan went inside The Jamison Mansion and found Mads Caractacus Troncoso's top hat down a hallway. At first we thought it would be easy, but when I started walking down the hallway, the knights The Jamison Family have, started shooting out arrows and darts. They were coming at me so fast, Nolan used his Cybernetic Falconieri Penzance Communicator and created a force field. "You saved me." I told him, "of course I did. We're friends bro." Nolan told me. I couldn't believe we were actually friends. Me and Nolan started walking down the hallway together, this time there were even more boobytraps and surprises but we managed to get through them all and finally got to the top hat. We looked inside and didn't see anything . I shouted out Nasser and Doyle's names and they responded back. They were happy that we found them. Nolan asked me how were we supposed to get them out. I whispered something to him and we both said Arabesquea Bamboo, when we did, Doyle, Nasser, Docherty, Raysel, Raysel Family, Leonel, Mr. Accerly Jamison and Ettore came flying out of Mads Caractacus Troncoso top hat. "We did it." Nolan said. Doyle, Leonel and Nasser were happy to see me. We went back to the birthday party and rejoined the others.

When The Mad Ffraid Brats saw Nasser and the others, especially Mr. Accerly Jamison freed from the top hat, they were furious and decided to change the plan. However when they tried to get AJ, to press the detonater, to their surprise, the controller wasn't working. Making The Mad Ffraid Brats more angry, they appeared next to AJ and told him this isn't over. To our surprise, there were only three Mad Ffraid Brats. AJ and the others wondered where is the fourth one. The Mad Ffraid Brats really got ticked off when they saw me. "It's time for plan Mad Z." One of The Mad Ffraid Brats said, they took out a walkie talkie and told Thirdy Born Starr to activate Mad Z using Mr. Accerly Jamison's satellites scaring me and the others. Suddenly every Baltasaru Iegriusol Dusk in the world was about to explode. "What are we going to do?" AJ asked me. With time running out, I came up with a song, I started off with the first lyrics. Then AJ came up with the next lyrics. And the others joined in. After that, we got everybody to join in including everybody around the world. As we all sang, every single Baltasaru Iegriusol Dusk malfunctioned, stopping the explosion. We all celebrated. The Mad Ffraid Brats couldn't believe this and vanished, suddenly the lights went off and the tent got foggy. Luke used The Nymphas Onesimus Goggles and told AJ to look out but it was too late. The Mad Ffraid Brats kidnapped AJ. However AJ used his Cybernetic Falconieri Penzance Communicator to separate The Mad Ffraid Brats from each other. The first one got away and took AJ. Luke told me that they are on top of the tent. So me, Why Don't We and Edvardas went to rescue him. While the rest of the gang fought the others. Trevor fought Silouanus. Queen Latifah fought Badaidra. Razzy and her friends decided to fight Andi. Rudy was fighting Terentilo. Mr. Hildefuns and Mads Caractacus Troncoso were having a magic show down. Jacob was fighting Vovka. Pierson was fighting Mad Kran Drucker and the others were fighting The Mad Ffraid Brats' minions. Meanwhile, Mallory and Lucy took care of the second Mad Ffraid Brat and made sure they didn't get away. Simon and Devin took care of the third Mad Ffraid Brat.

Elsewhere, me and the others were trying to get to AJ and found out that The Mad Ffraid Brat was getting away on a blimp. We used The Cybernetic Falconieri Penzance Communicators and shot out grappling hooks to get on top of the blimp, surprising The Mad Ffraid Brat. "Leaving so soon?" I asked them. "I have had enough of you." The Mad Ffraid Brat said. "As for you Edvardas, you know what side you belong on. Don't make me hurt you too," The Mad Ffraid Brat told him. Edvardas looked at me and the others and told us he hopes we can forget him and went over to The Mad Ffraid Brat and AJ. Just when The Mad Ffraid Brat thought they won, Edvardas smiled and suddenly he surprised The Mad Ffraid Brat and the others. Edvardas placed his hands over his face and started peeling his face off and it turns out it was me in disguise and Edvardas was disguised as me, "What is going on?" The Mad Ffraid Brat said. I gave AJ the signal and he took out several Aigeos Juppar jawbreakers and threw them in the air, when he did, The Aigeos Juppar jawbreakers landed on the blimp causing damage. The

Mad Ffraid Brat snapped their fingers and The Skull Zuberi appeared along with The Horror Herculano Jester. Why Don't We fought The Skull Zuberi while me and AJ and Edvardas dealt with The Mad Ffraid Brat and The Horror Herculano Jester. That's when Shawn showed up. He was riding Leonel's other invention, The Zeru Track Erast, a hover board. He blasted The Horror Herculano Jester off the blimp and he fell right into one of our traps. Why Don't We won the battle against The Skull Zuberi. The Mad Ffraid Brat couldn't believe that this was happening. "I'm not giving up yet." The Mad Ffraid Brat told me and AJ. "We'll see about that," AJ said. He gave me the signal and I used The Cybernetic Falconieri Penzance Communicator to call Darren and Grant. I told them to light up the sky and they started with the fire works. One by one the sky was full of fire works. Then AJ threw one very big Aigeos Juppar jawbreaker causing the blimp to explode. Me and Why Don't We escaped on our own, Zeru Tracked Erast. AJ escaped in a robot suite called The Gable Averroes. One of Leonel's greatest inventions yet, The Mad Ffraid Brat jumped off the blimp. As it blew up and landed in one our traps, a pool filled with orange slime.

When we rejoined the others, we were happy to see that they defeated the other Mad Ffraid Brats and their minions. However Karitas tried to get away but Mallory stopped her much to Karitas' dismay. After that, the police showed up and a lot of reporters. Me and AJ helped The Mad Ffraid Brat up and reveal to the world the real criminals. Me and AJ unmasked the first Mad Ffraid Brat and everybody couldn't believe that this is the person we have been afraid of. "This is Shekilla Saterfiel. The leader of The Mad Ffraid Brats." I told the reporters. Then Mallory and Lucy unmasked the second Mad Ffraid Brat, "and this is Gewnsnay." Mallory said. Mr. Accerly Jamison couldn't believe it. Raysel was happy that the truth was out. Simon and Jacob unmasked the third Mad Ffraid Brat. "This is Greco." Simon told them. I let Nasser tell the world why The Saterfiel Family did this. He read from Shekilla's diary and this is what he said. "Years ago, Shekilla was a loner. She had no friends. She was bullied and she was suicidal. Just when she thought her life would always be like that, she found out that AJ was auditing for back up dancers. She was a huge fan of his and thought this could be her chance to be famous and finally make some friends. So she went to audition and was determined to prove to him and the world that she belonged. Unfortunately she didn't make the cut, hurt and angry, Shekilla secretly took out one of the back up dancers by poisoning them and crashed one of AJ shows. But her dancing caused a stage accident that took out the rest of the performers. She was a laughing stock after that. She became a different person and her anger consumed her, turning her into a psycho path, she wanted revenge against AJ Mitchell and didn't care how long it took." Nasser said "That's right," Shekilla said. "I hated AJ and I had no idea how I would make him pay. I plotted and plotted, then one day I met Deveral at an anger management group and I decided we have so much in common. In fact I was surprised how we connected. Deveral was shocked to meet someone who was like him and told me only a Jamison would act like that. So we took a blood test and found out we were related. Not only that, I discovered that I have brothers and a sister I never knew I had. Me and Deveral managed to track them down and came up with a devious plan to end AJ's career. We formed a group and called ourselves The Mad Ffraid Brats. We also met others who wanted in. Some were after the money and others wanted revenge against The Show Mayor. We had everything sorted out. But the one thing we didn't count on was you Benny Breezy. You became a major problem and kept getting in the way. No matter what we threw at you, you kept searching for answers. Even when me and the others kidnapped your friends. I want to know why you didn't give up." Shekilla asked me.

I looked at AJ, Shawn. Jonah and the others and told Shekilla that friends don't quit on each other. "No matter what, I risk my life because I care about them." I played the video that Seini gave me after finding out which one I needed from Shekilla's diary and I showed the world how bad of a dancer Shekilla was. "I still don't know what I have to do with all of this?" Mr. Accerly said. "Are you kidding me? You ruined our lives. Me and my sister and brothers had a happy life until one night everything changed. My father caught you having a affair and you were so worried he would tell Bannerjee, so you cut the brakes on his car and killed him. Then you shot our mother. You didn't think about what that would do to us or cared to know our names. Anyway you sent me and the others to the one place in the world where evil rules. Mrs. Anstass and Mr. Sulayman. You let them decide what happened to us and you know what they did? They separated us and only kept Greco. I was furious but a few years later I became your new assistant after I killed the old one. I made sure I became the best assistant in the world. I gained your trust and was secretly working against you trying to find out your weakness and secrets. It was awful working for you. The way you treated me. But Shekilla promised me that you would suffer. I regret nothing. I hate you," Gewnsnay said. Greco told us that growing up at Mrs. Anstass and Mr. Sulayman was terrifying and that they did things to him. He looked at the cameras and told Mrs. Anstass and Mr. Sulayman that someday they will pay. Then I told everybody including Fuji who was at Sollie's Birthday Party that the reason why his mind is so messed up is because years ago, he witnessed Tielyr killing his wife in the secret room at The Show Mayor. I showed them the knife and footage. I also told Fuji that Tielyr used The Cellest Clinicriptine, Hade Wild and The Princella Khione of Aurex to make a drug and that's why his mind is the way it is. Shekilla asked us where is Deveral. I gave Grant the signal and he took out a jar and showed her and the others a tiny Deveral and a tiny Ture and Creedence. He used The Olutosin Noak and unshrunk them. Shekilla told him it's time for plan B, Deveral smiled and took out a remote detonater. Chris used The Onesimo Purves and told the monkeys to grab it. When they did, Chris smashed it. Unfortunately, to our surprise, Deveral had a second remote detonater and mashed it. Me, and AJ started laughing. "What's so funny?" Shekilla said. I told my friends to show her. Matt Bomer showed them footage of The Asterope Tielyr blowing up. Hayes showed footage of Tielyr's Mansion being blown up, Lucy told them that the abandoned school that has The Trygg Derock is destroyed. Miles said the same thing about The Salvator Day Ray. Thomas told Deveral he can say goodbye to his yacht and Chandler told them that all of The Princella Khione of Aurex, Hade Wild and The Cellest Clinicriptine has been placed inside

The Horror Herculano and we all watched as The Horror Herculano and all of the serums were destroyed. "How did this happen?" Shekilla said. "We found out where all the bombs were and decided to get rid of them." I told them, "by blowing up our hideouts?" Shekilla said. "And my yacht," Deveral said. "And my circus and my bank." Tierson said. "You got that right." Mallory told them. Matt Bomer showed Tierson the deed to the Horror Herculano, "well I have one more surprise." Shekilla told us. She took out a detonater and told me and the others to look up. So when we did, we all saw a pinata. "Seriously? What's so scary about that?" I asked her. She laughed and said The pinata is filled with doom fault. She pressed the button scaring everybody at Sollie's Birthday Party. AJ quickly used The Gable Averroes again and flew to the top. He grabbed the pinata and went outside and threw it as hard as he could up in the air, saving, all of us. "Well I give up." Shekilla said. Suddenly Primula appeared along with Mads Caractacus Troncoso's minions but Penzance Frisco took care of her. While Devin, Thomas, Reed, Austin P. McKenzie, Luke, Van, Darren, Chandler, Nick Mayorga, Peter, Sebastian, Grant, Matthew Daddario, Keegan, Case, Noah, Harris and Sam took care of the minions, Deveral tried to get away. But Hayes stopped him. Colton fought Ture and Kendrick took care of Creedence. Ryan Malaty fought Tierson. Detective Plaxido tried to get away as well and was aiming for his gun. Conant used his fire breathing and melted the gun. Then Matt Bomer started beating Detective Plaxido up. Aunt Fanny helped him. Doyle told the reporters that Detective Plaxido was involved with The Mad Ffraid Brats. Tierson refused to go to jail until Cosimo showed up. He was grown up thanks to one of Leonel's gadgets. He exposed his uncle . Mr. Accerly Jamison couldn't believe it was his old pal. Me and the others exposed Mr. Accerly Jamison to the world. Aunt Fanny decided to expose The Jamison Family.

With their plan ruined and facing jail, Gewnsnay and Karitas decided to kiss their crushes. Gewnsnay went up to Nolan Funk and started making out with him, Karitas made out with Sebastian. As for Andi, She was so upset she decided to make out with Ajay. Me and the others told the reporters everything The Mad Ffraid Brats did to us and who they killed and who there minions killed, and just when Shekilla was about to reveal who the fourth Mad Ffraid Brat was, I told

Chris it's time for the shock dust. He put on the gloves and electrocuted Shekilla and her gang. After that they were arrested. We all cheered. The reporters asked us is there anything else we would like to say. I told them dreams do come true and I said hello to my family. AJ told them that he never doubted me for a second. He also thank everybody who helped including his fans. Mrs. Bannerjee told the world that she's getting a divorce and to never ever call her Mrs. Jamison ever again. She was happy to finally be free from The Jamison Family, making, Mr. Accerly Jamison. Furious. He promised he would make her pay and reminded all of us that he's the most powerful man in the world. Chris used some shock dust on him and Mr. Accerly Jamison was arrested, me and the others celebrated. We finally unmasked The Mad Ffraid Brats and saved the day. Before they took him away, Conant apologize to Soft Dolly. Pashenka told Sollie that Grand Dunixi Jamison and Esdras want to cross over but they are worried about him and Bregusuid. Especially with Tielyr still out there somewhere. Sollie promise them that he will find Tielyr no matter what and he promised to find Ynocente. After that, they crossovered. Pashenka waved at them. He smiled and told Sollie that Grand Dunixi Jamison and Esdras have finally found peace. Gerwazy told the reporters this, "I used to think that life was about being famous, having a six pack, my hair, being shirtless like most jerks, acting cool, popularity, only hanging out with attractive people, my jawline and wealth but I don't care about any of that anymore because of this guy. Benny Breezy is my half brother and I love him. He's the only family I got. And, if any of you have a problem with that you'll have to deal with me. Life is about family. It's not about being attractive, fame and wealth. Also dad, if you're watching this, I'm moving out." Gerwazy said. Me and my brother hugged after that. I was so proud of him. Me and AJ both held The Ape Skull showing the world. Meanwhile, back in Seattle, Mr. Zed and Ms. Sheatara were watching. Suddenly, Drew Fuller showed up and handed Mr. Zed a flash drive that has the story on it and he gave him the reward money. Mr. Zed couldn't believe that me and the others actually did it and started working. Drew and Ms. Sheatara started making out. Elsewhere in New York, my family were celebrating. Grandma Maroochy asked my mother when is she going to tell me. She told her when I come to New York.

Back in Los Angeles, at Sollie's Birthday Party, Kimbriella was making up with her dad and introduced him to Mitchell. Sollie was introducing Vigdess to his mother. I was outside looking at the stars until Shawn showed up. "Can I join you?" He asked me. "Sure," I said. I asked him what was he doing out there anyway. "Well, I came out here to check up on my best friend and bud. Why aren't you happy, you and the others did it. You should be happy bro." Shawn told me. I decided not to tell him why I was so down, but to my surprise, he already knew why, "you think me and the others are going to forget about you and go on with our lives like you were nothing to us, but you're wrong bro. I would never forget about you and our friendship means a lot to me. True friends are never separated by time or distance." Shawn said. "He's right bro," AJ said. "How can I forget about you bro after all we have been through. When your world falls apart, I'll be right there to put it back together." Lucy told me we're Team Bucy and Harris told me that we are friends and that he's proud of me. We all went inside and sung happy birthday to Sollie. After he blew out the candles on his gigantic Birthday cake, me and Luke told him we have a surprise for him. He couldn't believe it, neither could the others. It was Grandma Bregusuid. She hugged Sollie and tears were falling from their eyes. Me and Luke told the others about that flash drive we found inside that Safe lettuce storage and how we discovered that Grandma Bregusuid was in the Witness Protection program hiding from Tielyr. We also introduced them to Major Lazer. The head of Sarolta Gide Borboleta, Porfirio, finally proposed to Anima and she happily accepted. Anima and Porfirio kissed. After that romance was in the air. Drucy made out with Logan, Hinkley made out with Devin, Razzy made out with Luke, Ciendaous made out with Jonah, Daggi made out with Nick Mayorga, Yanixia made out with Amarr. And the rest of The Hinkley Youga Shirk joined in. One of them made out with Rudy, another one made out with Harrison, a girl named Poppy made out with Sebastian, Jumoke made out with Pierson, Lysistra made out with Grant, one of The Hinkley Youga Shirk made out with Jack Maynard and a friend of hers made out with Kendrick. Hinkley Youga Shirk 101 made out with Alex Whitehouse.

Then Sollie and Vigdess made out, So did Mitchell and Kimbriella. Also Gerwazy made out with Mohogony. Seissylt made out with Tripta. Severeano did the same with Raysel, and a girl named Ursa made out with Darren Barnet. One of them grabbed Harris and started making out with him and the rest made out with Noah, Jacob and Austin Butler. Thomas was looking for Erewhon and I told him she's on The balcony at The Jamison Mansion. He ran and told Erewhon how he feels and the two started making out. Mr. Hildefuns released some fire works and watched as six Hinkley Youga Shirk members made out with Bruce, Hayes, Peter, Ajay, Tyler and Cody Linley. As for Simon and Mallory, they finally admitted their feelings for each other and made out. Chiquite appeared after I told Penzance Frisco to teleport her here and she made out with Alex Aiono. After that, AJ performed Without You Now. He was so happy to be back on stage. Then I performed my new song. A song I made a few days ago, I called it We Are The Show Mayor Friends. My friends joined me and I couldn't believe I was facing my fear. AJ, Why Don't We and Ross performed Slow 8 Man. Which is Slow Dance by AJ Mitchell, 8 Letters by Why Don't We and Preacher Man by Ross Lynch. Three songs combined together.

Then we all performed My Life Would Suck Without You by Kelly Clarkson. The next day, me and Rudy told Soft Dolly and Sollie that Grand Dunixi Jamison left The Show Mayor to the both of them. With Mr. Accerly Jamison's reign of terror over with, The Show Mayor became a more happier place than ever before. To celebrate, The Show Mayor did something it has never done before, have a parade and we were all in it. Soft Dolly and Sollie brought the world of The Show Mayor and the world of The Meinhard Bannerjee Wonder together. They made sure the outcasts were back in the show. The Ape Skull and The Katana were returned to The Diamond Museum Amsterdam. AJ received a public apology from them. Grandma Bregusuid adopted Sefi and became the mother he never had. Zuly got her job back, a big raise and an apology from Mr. Accerly Jamison. Mrs. Bannerjee helped Chun and the others and decided to start an organization that stops trafficking. She also gave me and the others each a thousand dollars plus she got Doyle reinstated back in Glass Art. Cullinan destroyed the virus and fixed Thirdy Born Starr. Jumoke's animals were better and back in the show. Fuji was reunited with Fujimoto and the two had an emotional reunion. The Zvezda Three Ples were repaired and Capitola and Gan moved in. Ettore was happy to finally be free of Gewnsnay. Me and Sean told Nance and Rance about what happened to their father and gave them his remains. Jax told Raysel what happened to Treveze. She was devastated but she told Jax that Treveze was a true hero and that she'll always remember him. After that, me and the others packed our things and went down the elevator one last time. When we arrived at the lobby, all our friends were there to say goodbye, everybody except for AJ. Just when I thought he wasn't coming, AJ showed up wearing The Zorro costume again. I told him I was worried he wouldn't make it. "Are you kidding me? I wouldn't miss this for the world." AJ said.

Suddenly Seini appeared. She was cured and feeling better again. AJ apologized for hurting her feelings. Then he started kissing her and the two made out. Stiles was also in the lobby and couldn't stop thanking us. Darren showed me today's paper. Me and him couldn't stop laughing about what happened to Shekilla and the others. I was so happy to see our story in the paper. Me and him also learned that Mrs. Anstass and Mr. Sulayman were arrested, Avis as well and Orssa. At that moment I got a phone call from Mr. Zed, all he said was good job and hung up. Telmo asked me who was the fourth Mad Ffraid Brat. AJ and the others wanted to know too. Me and Case looked at each other and told everybody that Edvardas is the other Mad Ffraid Brat. Before they could react, we told them that Edvardas is innocent and that he's the one that gave us the laptop. Edvardas joined the conversation and apologized for lying to us and told me and the others that he didn't want any part of his sisters and brother plan but Shekilla and Deveral threatened his life. Thinking that nobody wants him around now, Edvardas decided to quit but Soft Dolly and Sollie stopped him, and gave him a second chance. They gave him a promotion. Edvardas became the assistant manager of The Show Mayor. Sollie told me and Hayes that Prideaux and her children are safe and that his mother found out where Deveral's other girlfriends are and that they are safe now. Me and Hayes were happy to hear that. Reed wanted to know why Seissylt was drugged and Ajay told him and the rest of us what happened. Ajay told us that Seissylt was following Deveral and Edvardas. Unfortunately The Mad Ffraid Brats were watching him. They were furious when Seissylt found the secret room and made sure he didn't tell anyone. After that, it was time to say goodbye. Mallory apologized to Ashley Tisdale and the two became friends. After I said goodbye to the others, AJ, Shawn, Aunt Fanny and Gerwazy were the next ones . AJ was the first, saying goodbye to him was the hardest. I tried to hold back my tears but it wasn't working. He told me friendship multiplies the good of life and divides the evil. We will always be brothers and I will always remember you. That's a promise. We hugged each other goodbye and I told him thanks for believing in me and for being my friend. Shawn told me, "1 universe, 9 planets, 204 countries, 809 islands, 7 seas and I had the privilege of meeting you." We had a hard time saying goodbye to each other as well. Aunt Fanny apologized for not being there for me when I was growing up and told me she called her sisters and brother and that they finally made up. She also told me she had a blast with me and my friends and told me she loved me. As for Gerwazy, he started crying and told me because I have a brother, I always have a friend. "I'm really going to miss you." Gerwazy said. I asked him if he would like to come with me to New York. Gerwazy shouted yes. He was so excited. After that I had an emotional goodbye with Why Don't We. Then it was time for me, Mallory, Simon, Doyle and Nasser to say goodbye to each other. But before we did, I asked Mallory what is she going to do with her Kiss Printes List. Mallory told me she's going to rip it up. However, when I asked her about the copies, Mallory was shocked that I knew about them. But she knew she didn't need them anymore and used The Cybernetic Falconieri Penzance Communicator to burn each one. Unknowing to her, Doyle grabbed one of the copies and told us that David and Cayden were the next ones on her list. "Too bad," Simon said. Mallory smiled and told us she got this. She introduced me and the others to some of her biggest fans. One of them made out with David and the other one made out with Cayden.

After that, Mallory told me she wanted to spend her summer with me and the others and that she doesn't care about Paris anymore . Simon told me that we are brothers from another mother and that no matter what happens next year, we'll always be best friends and brothers. He also wanted to spend his summer with me. Doyle and Nasser said the same thing. Suddenly Klazinaveen. appeared and he gave us a letter and told us he's proud of us and disappeared. Me and the others read the letter and learned that this isn't over. Mr. Thersander gave us a warning about the future, then Burnell showed up. He told me and the others well done and told us that our journey is just beginning and that it will test our friendship. Before he left, he told me something else about the future. He told me that me and Noah Urrea will become great friends. I told him I seriously doubt Noah would become friends with me. Burnell smiled and told me yes he will. Burnell gave me a file and left The Show Mayor. "What is all that stuff?" Mallory asked me. I told her I don't know. Anyway we walked over to the front desk where we found Mr. Stumbo. "You're back," I said. "Yes I am, thanks to Aunt Fanny. She used some tough love on me and told me how important I am to The Show Mayor. So I apologized for the way I acted and I hope you can forgive me and thank you for taking care of The Show Mayor in my absence." Mr. Stumbo said. He also told me and the others that he got a raise and some vacation time. Then Telmo told me that he's talking to his father again. After that, me and the others asked Mr. Stumbo about our flight to New York, however, he told us our flight left at three O ' clock. "Wait, what? Isn't is one O ' clock." I asked him. "No, it's four thirty," Mr. Stumbo said. "That's impossible," Simon told him. We all checked our phones and each one had the same time. "What is going on?" Nasser said. That's when Mallory started whistling. "What did you do?" I asked her. She told me and the others that she used Thirdy Born Starr to change the times on our phones. "Why?" I asked her, "Because we belong here. Think of all the adventures we'll have." We all looked at her and I started to panic. Colton and the others tried to calm me down. "Isn't there a train?" Colton asked Mr. Stumbo. "Um no. Any trains that are going to New York have been cancelled due to bad weather." Mr. Stumbo said. "Okay, what about The Simplicius Transito?" Carson said. "Sorry guys, after that crash, it needs repairs." Leonel said. "What about the teleporting machine?" Matthew Daddario said. "After Benny teleporting Chiquite here, the machine blew up." Leonel said. "It looks like.." "don't say it." I told Mr. Stumbo. "We're stuck here." I shouted out. I fainted after that. AJ and the others tried to wake me up. Will I ever reunite with my family? What's next for me and my friends and what is this threat that Mr. Thersander and Burnell are so afraid of. I guess we'll find out.

The End.